Anita Notaro is a TV producer, journalist and director and worked for RTE, Ireland's national broadcasting organization, for eighteen years. She has directed the Eurovision Song Contest and the Irish General Election, as well as programmes for the BBC and Channel 4. *Back After the Break* is her first novel.

www.**books**at**transworld**.co.uk

BACK AFTER
THE BREAK

Anita Notaro

BANTAM BOOKS

LONDON · NEW YORK · TORONTO · SYDNEY · AUCKLAND

BACK AFTER THE BREAK
A BANTAM BOOK : 0 553 81477 X

First publication in Great Britain

PRINTING HISTORY
Bantam edition published 2003

1 3 5 7 9 10 8 6 4 2

Set in 11.5/12.5pt Garamond by
Phoenix Typesetting, Burley-in-Wharfedale, West Yorkshire.

Bantam Books are published by Transworld Publishers,
61–63 Uxbridge Road, London W5 5SA,
a division of The Random House Group Ltd,
in Australia by Random House Australia (Pty) Ltd,
20 Alfred Street, Milsons Point, Sydney, NSW 2061, Australia,
in New Zealand by Random House New Zealand Ltd,
18 Poland Road, Glenfield, Auckland 10, New Zealand
and in South Africa by Random House (Pty) Ltd,
Endulini, 5a Jubilee Road, Parktown 2193, South Africa.

Printed and bound in Great Britain by
Cox & Wyman Ltd, Reading, Berkshire.

For Gerry McGuinness.
I don't know how I ever got so lucky.

As this is my first novel, the temptation is to thank everyone I know and bore everyone else to death – so I won't. But I do need to mention the following:

Patricia Scanlan is an angel. I met her by accident on Millennium Eve and since then she has encouraged and supported me and this book would not be here without her. Best of all, we're now friends.

My family are very special to me – my mother Teresa knows how much I love her. My sisters Madeleine, Lorraine and Jean have provided me with enough material over the years for several books, but I've had to promise not to tell!! Then there's Jill, Marc, Emma, Jack, Jenny, Joshua, Caroline and Andrew.

I'm lucky enough to have a few very good friends and Dearbhla Walsh, Ursula Courtney, Caroline Henry and Deirdre McCourt have shared my ups and downs. So has Dave Fanning.

Special thanks to my editor, Francesca Liversidge, for making all my dreams come true. Everyone at Bantam has been professional and very kind, especially Sadie Mayne. Thanks also to Declan Heeney and Gill Hess.

My agent is Marianne Gunn O'Connor and she's a spiritual and calm person – just what a writer needs.

RTE Television has played an important part in my life and I send best wishes to all my friends and colleagues there – especially everyone in *Fair City*. Be assured that *none* of you feature in this story.

Lastly, all love and a million thanks to Gerry – the most talented person I know.

I hope enjoy reading the book, it's very special to me.

Chapter One

It had been a night tormented by ghosts and memories and too much alcohol. The awkward positioning of her body revealed the turmoil she'd experienced during the hours that should have brought relief. She lay diagonally across the huge old sleigh bed in the normally tidy Victorian bedroom, in the midst of chaos. Most of the bedclothes were on the floor, even her treasured antique cream eiderdown had surrendered to the trashing and now clung to the bedpost. Her long tanned legs seemed contorted and her normally glossy mane of dark brown hair was dull and twisted from the excesses of the worst night Lindsay Davidson had ever known.

Sometimes, the mind can play cruel tricks and it didn't spare the thirty-four-year-old woman who lay enjoying the last blissful moments of unconsciousness. She opened her eyes and for a few delicious seconds life was exactly as it had been for the past two years since she'd met and fallen head over heels in love with Paul. She fought the reality.

She turned her head, stretching, trying to remember what had happened and in a flash it came flooding back. It was as though a knife had ripped through her insides and she felt a pain so sharp that she almost fainted. She yanked her body into a sitting position. Reality won. The man she'd loved more than she'd ever believed possible had been lying and cheating to her for over a year. Outside a car horn tooted and a dog yapped in the distance as the city sprung into life.

This isn't happening to me, she thought desperately. Oh please God, no, I'm getting married in two months' time.

Wrong, a quiet, menacing voice whispered, he's going to marry someone else.

Lindsay tried to scream but the sound evaporated before it brought any relief. She was reminded of the day her father died. She'd been uncontrollable when they'd told her, a doctor had to be called to sedate her and when she'd woken after fourteen hours the pain had been excruciating as the realization flooded in.

This was much worse, she thought wildly because Paul was alive and well and in love with someone else and this was Dublin and everyone would know.

She knew she had to get to the bathroom fast. As she struggled into her towelling robe the telephone rang and she changed course automatically, dashing towards the hall as the answering machine clicked into action.

Please God, let it be him. Maybe it was a joke, perhaps he was drunk, or insane. Please I'll do anything, just don't let it be true. She waited, convinced and therefore calmer, for the gorgeous liquidy voice that always reminded her of a big fat glass of Baileys and ice to give the usual 'Hi Darling, it's me'.

Instead a sharp, impatient female voice, clearly exasperated, delivered an ultimatum. 'This is a message for Lindsay Davidson. It's Hilda Cullen from Personnel in Channel 6 here and we have not received confirmation that you'll be attending for interview at eleven-thirty today as per our letter of the sixteenth. Please call me immediately . . .'

Here was the chance she'd been waiting for, the first step towards the job of her dreams. And it had to come today. She oozed onto the floor in the corner of the sunshine-yellow hall and cried at the unfairness of it all.

Two hours and two litres of water later Lindsay knew she looked half decent, although she felt like one of those strange robotic characters her young nephews played with. Buzz Lightyear, that was one of them. She had to bite her lip as she drove the short distance to Channel 6, remembering the time she'd gone to New York to do her Christmas shopping with Paul and they'd spent hours looking for that particular toy for four-year-old Jake, who could talk of nothing else. Her sister Anne was in a complete panic because there wasn't one to be found anywhere in Dublin and she'd phoned Lindsay, begging her to find one. How they'd laughed because they hadn't a clue what they were looking for and felt ridiculous asking in every shop for Buzz Lightyear in a fake New York accent and then falling about laughing, high on life and love and champagne. 'To infinity and beyond' – that famous catchphrase summed up exactly how she felt today.

She checked herself in the car mirror one last time, thinking that if she could pull this off then nothing was impossible. Her skin looked like well-used putty. No amount of her favourite Clinique Moisture Surge could erase the havoc the night had played on her complexion, although she'd carefully applied concealer and foundation followed by bronzing powder and blusher and anything else she could find in her make-up bag. Her blue-grey eyes looked listless and her long thick lashes merely emphasized the dark shadows. At least the rich-chocolate lipstick added some colour, she conceded, although she hadn't time to notice that it only highlighted the deathly pallor of her complexion.

She was unaware of the striking picture she made as she walked from the car, a tall, voluptuous girl in a long black pencil skirt and fitted wool jacket, blood-red camisole peeping out. Her dark hair was pulled severely back off her face because she couldn't do anything else with it, having stood under an ice-cold shower for twenty minutes to try to get some feeling back into her heavy, sweaty, numb body. She looked confident and gorgeous yet somehow sad and forlorn, thought Chris Keating, one of the station's newest stars, as he drove past the security barrier and caught sight of her purposeful stride in his wing mirror, before abandoning the car and all thought of the intriguing girl in a desperate effort to get to the studio to record a piece for his lunchtime programme.

Lindsay was hesitant as she stepped into the Television Centre, gave her name and sat down to wait. She knew for the first time exactly how Alice must have felt in Wonderland. The scene was utterly enchanting to an outsider as the outrageous world of show business spread itself at her feet, almost smothering her with its intoxicating mix of colour and vitality and unreality and sheer unadulterated glamour.

She saw that gorgeous radio presenter with the big dark eyes looking even cuter than in his photos, watched in awe as top newscaster Maria Devlin strode past reading some lines aloud, oblivious to everyone around her. She smiled and said hello to the actress from a well-known soap, then blushed furiously because of course she only knew her from TV, sat captivated by the small tubby man and tall skinny woman in the middle of a heated argument about a script for the main news bulletin and tried to stifle a giggle at the child who was kicking her mother because she couldn't meet two of the station's most famous puppets. The long-suffering woman tried to explain to the receptionist that they had travelled from the west of Ireland and it was the child's sixth birthday. And the child obviously gets what she wants every time, Lindsay thought. She marvelled at the patience of the girl behind the desk who cheerfully explained to the screaming brat that the stars always had a nap before their afternoon show.

The interview itself was a nightmare. Three men and two women grilled her for over an hour, jumping from English to Irish – she'd forgotten that the native language was a requirement for anyone working on one of the main TV channels in Ireland. The questions came hard and fast like little silver rockets in a pinball machine, switching with lightning speed from politics to religion, from sport to music. They even produced prints from famous Irish artists, asking her to identify the period and the painter.

Jesus, she thought wildly, don't they realize I can barely focus on the damn things, let alone name the artist. She couldn't for a second imagine why an assistant producer, which was the job she'd applied for, would need to know these things. She later learned that they were testing her general knowledge in order to assess her flexibility for a wide range of programming.

They quizzed her at length about her career in interior design and why she wanted to change direction at this stage, but Lindsay was prepared for this one. She explained that she felt she had reached her full potential, working for a large company, and had decided against setting up her own business.

'Why? Are you afraid of the stress and hard work involved?' One of the men was in like a shot.

'Not at all, I thrive on hard work. But I work better as part of a team and that's one of the reasons this job interests me. Also, I feel now is the right time for me to change direction and my skills should prove beneficial here, especially in areas such as design and lighting.'

'Would you say you're a creative person?'

'Wouldn't a move to TV mean a serious pay cut?'

'Are you worried about working late nights and weekends?'

It went on and on, while her heart beat faster, her mouth got drier and her tongue felt furry.

Finally, just when she hoped they might be finished because her spine felt about as flexible as a telephone pole, the tired thin woman with the shrivelled lips looked at her and asked, 'Who is your favourite poet?'

'Yeats,' she replied automatically, her brain tuning in, without prompting on her part, to the poet she had loved for years, ever since her father had read some lines to her as a small child.

'Perhaps you would recite some of your favourite lines,' thin lips asked, faking a smile, hoping to catch her out.

Lindsay's brain, to her amazement, functioned automatically, which she knew sometimes happens in moments of complete panic. Although she could usually recite any one of twenty poems, today only one title came to mind – 'Never Give all the Heart'.

Pity she hadn't taken that advice herself. Her voice sounded thin and slightly hysterical as she struggled to get the words out without crying. As soon as she'd finished, she wondered whether she would even make it to the door before her legs buckled. Please God, she implored, let this be over soon.

As if sensing something, the guy with the kind eyes from Personnel looked at the others quickly. 'I think that's about it.' He smiled at her. 'I'm sure you're exhausted. We'll be in touch in about a week. I should tell you that we've had several hundred applications. Unfortunately, we only have eight positions to offer to successful candidates and those jobs would be subject to the completion of a three-month training course.'

Nothing registered but she stood automatically and somehow made it to the door with a smile plastered to her face, then bolted to her car where she was unrecognizable as the confident, gorgeous woman Chris Keating had been admiring less than two hours earlier.

Chapter Two

Two muffled, hesitant, broken phone calls. Two confused, angry, incredulous friends who immediately enveloped her in a cocoon of candyfloss. They talked endlessly, drank wine and anything else they could find in the house, plotted and argued and tried to reason, but mostly they listened.

She ranted and raved, her eyes like shiny black coals, felt momentarily elated, then deeply depressed. They laughed and cried, humoured and cajoled and considered what she should do, but more important than anything else, they sympathized as only girl friends can.

'He's a bastard.'

'I know.'

'How could he do this to me?'

'I don't know, you don't deserve it.'

'I love him so much.'

'Don't worry, it'll be OK.'

'I can't live without him.'

'Yes, you can, we'll help.'

'I never want to see him again.'

'Just wait, he'll be back.'

On and on it went, over and over, round and round like a particularly lurid ride at a funfair and yet she wanted to talk some more. It seemed that talking about him made him still part of her life, which he clearly no longer was. They never yawned once and neither Debbie's soft velvety brown eyes nor Tara's sparkly blue ones ever glazed over, even as she discussed for the millionth time whether she should ring him.

'That's it, I have to talk to him.'

'Are you sure?'

'I know, I'll e-mail him.'

'OK, let's work out what to say.'

'No, I'll leave a message on his mobile.'

'Right, we'll have a rehearsal.'

They were fiercely protective of her and yet each of them would have handled the situation differently, given any encouragement.

Debbie, straight as a poker, soft as a marshmallow, long, gangly, wild, beautiful, wanted to go straight to him and bust his lip, while Tara with her big sexy mouth, mass of blond hair and tiny doll-like body would have had her revenge in an entirely different way. They were quite a combination, these three strong, fragile women. Between them they'd had enough experience of men to fill the entire 'self-help' section of Waterstone's and now they called it all into play.

'Ring him and tell him exactly what you think of him and then tell him that it's his loss and hang up.'

'Let's find out where he's going to be on Saturday

18

night and then you can turn up with a gorgeous hunk.' It never occurred to any of them that they barely knew a gorgeous hunk between them.

'What about getting a male voice on your answering machine so that when he does ring he'll go mad?' Was it not obvious at this stage that he wasn't going to ring?

'I know, Tara and I'll go round to his house and let the air out of his tyres in the middle of the night, just so we all feel a bit better' – completely ignoring the fact that he was in England!

They stayed with her all hours, day and night, and when they did go home to shower and change she rang and bawled. They appeared again with muffins and chocolates and more alcohol and sat down as if they'd never heard her latest plan to win him back. Charlie, her beloved golden retriever, yawned as soon as he saw them as he knew his chances of a run on the beach were non-existent. He settled on the rug in front of the Aga, shifting himself only to push up against Lindsay now and then and lick every bit of whatever bare skin happened to be exposed. He had no idea what was wrong but he sure knew the salty taste of a wet face and he methodically licked it dry every time. Lindsay loved him to bits and Debbie liked to think that Charlie was stretched out hatching a plan to take a big juicy chunk out of whatever asshole had caused his beloved owner to turn into a slithery mass of particularly runny jelly.

Lindsay looked a complete fright and they were constantly trying to distract her.

'I know, what about a girlie night in: face packs,

hot oil conditioner, a long soak with one of those heavenly bath bombs and a large glass of chilled Sancerre? You go first.'

'I've got it, now is the perfect time to do that evening class in carpentry, and we're sure to meet a few men. OK, forget the last bit' (as Lindsay started to sniffle and Tara threw a withering glance). Even Charlie knew a bad idea when he heard one!

'We're going into town and buying you that amazing black dress in Platform, our treat.'

Nothing worked, nothing could because all Lindsay could feel was a big black hole sucking her in and swirling her round and the thought of shopping or laughing or even surviving the day was hideous. When they eventually left in the small hours of the morning, she fell into bed, fully dressed, only to wake a few hours later when the alcohol had worn off. She paced the floor, dialled his number, hung up, cursed, dialled and hung up again, kissed his picture, kicked his presents and keeled over crying until both she and Charlie fell asleep on the sofa with one of them hoping for a walk in the morning and one praying that it wouldn't come.

Debbie and Tara had a routine all worked out. Tara was a solicitor and was up early every morning, so she phoned Lindsay immediately she'd had a shower and a smoothie. Better to wake her up, she thought, so she doesn't have any time to think. She'd been in a similar situation herself, although the circumstances were very different. Even now, years later, she shuddered at the thought of what her friend was going through. God, she was going to get revenge somehow, she thought, as she mixed the fruit and yoghurt concoction, added wheatgerm and ginseng and blended it to within an inch of its life. She took a sip and grimaced, sure this was good for her but not at all sure it was worth it. She certainly needed something with vitamins these mornings, though, to counteract the self-inflicted liver damage.

Oh well, she thought, as she downed two Solpadeine to try and cure a particularly nasty headache, there'll be time enough for a real health kick later. Just as soon as they got through this. Meanwhile, if Lindsay wanted to get sloshed every day for a year, then she and Debs were going to be right there with her every step of the way. She picked up the cordless phone and speed-dialled and didn't even realize that Lindsay only pretended she had just woken because she knew her friend was a real worrier.

Chapter Three

As soon as she'd finished listening to every new thought and scheme that Lindsay had had since two a.m., Tara hung up and dialled Debbie.

'Debs, no change, can you cover this morning? I think today she's just broken-hearted.'

Debbie, in her little two-bedroomed semi on the South Circular Road, felt her insides knot. 'Sure, I'm off today.'

'Actually, I'm due a couple of hours off myself, so if you shop for goodies I'll collect you later,' Tara suddenly decided. After a few words they hung up. They had little to say these days, it was all the short-hand of people who know each other very well and don't need to waste time on trivialities.

Debbie, who didn't have to pretend that she'd been fast asleep when Tara rang, leapt out of bed and threw herself into the shower. She had long since decided that she was allergic to mornings so this was the only option, otherwise she'd be back asleep in ten seconds. God, she didn't look too healthy but compared to her best friend she knew she looked like Liz Hurley. She had a cute face, people always told her, with a mass of red brown curls and eyes like good coffee, rich and velvety. She was just a little bit too curvy for her own liking – child-bearing hips her mother often said. Well fed was her Uncle Mike's favourite phrase. Blobby was her sister's word for it.

She worked as a member of the cabin crew with Aer Lingus and she loved it, mainly because she was a people person and enjoyed solving problems. She always meant to start the day with a smoothie but as usual she pulled on sweatpants and a T-shirt and headed to the Bretzel for bagels and croissants. She vowed to have just one with cream cheese and bring the rest over to Lindsay's house after she'd made some effort to tidy the bomb-site she was living in.

She also picked up everything she could think of to try and tempt her friend. Fresh OJ, strawberries, organic yoghurt, Rice Krispies, all the favourites, even though she knew that Charlie was bursting with goodies and Lindsay was looking more gaunt each day. It was now almost a week and Debbie felt as if time had stood still for the three of them, wrapped as they were in their very own isolation ward in the Intensive Care Unit marked 'Coronary Care – broken hearts – silence please – no visitors'. She couldn't understand how anyone would knowingly hurt her friend and she didn't even begin to imagine what she'd say if she ever came face to face with the bastard.

*　　*　　*

As soon as she opened her eyes on the Friday morning, Lindsay knew she had to do something. It was exactly a week since her world had fallen apart and although she almost wished she had the courage to do something drastic she knew she never would, so she had to make some effort, however small, to try to get on with her life. She owed it to her friends, if nothing else. All this crying and not eating and drinking herself to death wasn't working, besides the girls must be sick of her by now.

Struggling out of bed, she splashed her face with cold water and brushed her teeth. Someone had painted two halogen hobs on her face for a joke, she thought, as she caught sight of her swollen cheeks.

Her face was grey and dingy and she hoped that the old wives' tale about not washing your hair being good for it was true because she now had enough natural oil to cook chips for a month. She knew she had to think the whole thing through once more and then make a rational decision. She'd talked her way into the *Guinness Book of Records* this past week and it still felt hopeless. However hard it was going to be she knew she couldn't go on as she was and maybe, just maybe that was the first step.

Dressing quickly in jeans and a big sloppy denim shirt she pulled her listless, greasy hair into a ponytail and went downstairs. She took a bottle of mineral water out of the fridge, ignoring the week-old tomatoes with their matching white, fluffy, angora sweaters. Charlie couldn't believe his luck when she picked up his lead and practically gave himself a hernia as he tore out of the door in case she changed her mind.

She didn't let herself think until she was on the beach and then she decided to let it all sweep over her, closing her eyes as the memories flooded in with a force that almost knocked her over and left her with a salty, sick taste in her mouth. Stretching her heavy limbs on the deserted sand she walked slowly – Charlie barking at her now and then as if to guide her way – and remembered how she'd felt when it happened.

How could she have been so stupid, she berated herself for the hundredth time. She wasn't naïve or easily taken in. She knew others never felt sorry for her – saw her as well sussed and streetwise. She was one of those lucky females you sometimes spotted at parties, and envied without really knowing why – one who just seemed to have it all, or at least something no one else in the room had. Now she felt small and worthless and very, very stupid. Worst of all, at that moment, alone on the gusty, deserted beach, she felt that without him it was all sort of pointless.

How had she ended up like this? She of all people who constantly warned her friends against letting anyone else be responsible for their happiness. What a laugh that was. She supposed that somewhere deep inside she'd always wanted to be rescued and he'd been her white knight. How pathetic does that sound, she chided herself.

Life had been perfect since she'd met him.

Gorgeous, funny, laughing Paul, with the huge Malteser eyes and shiny black hair, with flecks of grey he pretended he'd had put in specially so he'd look more like George Clooney. Thirty-seven years old, a talented and successful architect, Lindsay still couldn't believe that she'd ever been lucky enough to find him. Or unlucky enough to lose him.

They'd met when she'd almost finished an advanced course in interior design, which she'd been taking two evenings a week and which hopefully would make her the most senior designer in her company and the only one with a recognized international qualification, a major factor when dealing with their American clients. Paul came to talk to them, as a favour to his sister Rosie, who was their tutor.

Afterwards, they all went for a drink and she knew he had to be married – they always were, these ones who'd walked straight off the set of *ER* and caught the first plane to Dublin, just to tease all the silly, unsuspecting Irish girls. She remembered how startled she'd felt the first time she'd seen him laugh, how spellbound she'd been the first time he kissed her and how completely captivated she was the first time she saw him sleeping.

And perfect got even better. When he asked her to marry him she wanted to do a Julie Andrews on him. She knew she would never forget that feeling that comes so rarely in a life – utter and total happiness.

'The things we do come back to us, as if they know the way,' her granny had quoted to her once and that night, as she hugged herself with joy, she'd thought stupidly that maybe all her childish good deeds were being repaid.

Debbie and Tara christened her 'Ronald McDonald', because she walked around like a clown with a permanent grin, for months. Everyone, at least those who liked her, said she deserved it.

So what happened? What had she ever done to upset God so much that he had picked her out to sample this particular version of hell on earth? How could he let her feel what it was like to have it all and then drop her through that big fat roll of hospital cotton wool to this place she now found herself, in one of those big American-style fridge-freezers where things looked healthy and normal, no tell-tale icicles to warn you that everything inside was frozen solid?

Did she have any idea it would end like this? Not in a million years.

Liar, be honest, a little voice taunted. There were a few things – tiny, minuscule little shreds that the office assistant in her brain filed away in the pending folder, for future consideration. Like the way he sometimes didn't listen to his telephone messages if she was in his house, or forgot to give her the name of his hotel when he went away on business. 'Get me on the mobile, hon, I'm never here anyway.'

But he had asked her to marry him, it was all arranged, she reasoned. When was he going to tell her that he had met someone else? Would he have gone ahead with it? She felt sick, scalded by the red-hot kettle of thought that rushed through her mind. She sat down quickly on the damp sand where Charlie came to keep her warm, because she was shivering and sweating and snivelling in an effort not to cry.

She couldn't bear to think about the night it had ended – when she rang him at his London apartment and a girl with a snooty accent had told her that he'd gone to collect some food and could he call her tomorrow morning because, well, they were having an early night. Lindsay could almost hear her smiling. What a coincidence, she'd thought uneasily. She must have dialled a wrong number and got through to a house where there was another Paul. Ridiculous. Just as she was about to say so, she heard him, in the background, as clearly as if he was standing beside her. 'I'm back, have you opened the wine? Who's on the phone?'

Just when she was sure her heart was going to explode, she had heard his voice. 'Hi?' She couldn't speak, even if she'd wanted to. He knew.

'Can I call you back?' casually, as if he'd been half expecting her to ring.

She'd dropped the receiver and sunk to the floor where she stayed, huddled up, cold and frightened.

Five minutes later the phone rang. She desperately wanted not to answer it but she was afraid of what would happen to her if she didn't find out. The not knowing was the worst bit. Maybe there was a simple explanation, it was all a joke, it wasn't him . . .

'Lindsay, I'm sorry, I should have told you, I didn't really know how to explain . . . I've met someone else in London, we're, er, hoping to get married . . .'

And she knew, with absolute certainty, that this was the worst thing that could ever happen to her.

She remembered staying where she was, without moving or making a sound, until long after the room was rendered pitch-black.

He never called back.

Even now, a week later, the enormity of that night was still fresh in her mind but somewhere, deep down, she knew that she would never feel quite as bad as she had then. All she had to do now was survive.

When the girls called at her house later that morning, with the usual supplies, all ready for another session, they found her wearing a Hallowe'en mask, in September. Quite a good likeness, mind you, except when you looked at the eyes.

She was dressed and washed, even wearing make-up, but gaunt and grey and utterly unlike the girl they knew and loved.

And as they stood in the hallway, all false smiles and brown bags, not asking, not quite knowing what to say, the phone rang.

She'd got the job.

Chapter Four

It took Lindsay half an hour to calm them down.

'It's not strictly speaking a job yet, it's subject to successfully completing the training course and a medical and an audio-visual test and a million other stipulations . . .'

They couldn't hear her over the noise of champagne corks and, besides, Debbie was laughing hysterically and Tara was dancing Charlie around the kitchen. A couple of glasses of bubbly later and Tara was on the phone to her sister-in-law in Rome, while Debbie ran up her mobile bill checking flight availability to the Italian capital the following weekend.

'I've no money, none of my summer clothes fit me, there's no one to mind Charlie' all fell on deaf ears and even the real reason 'he might ring' was met with 'it'll do him good' – Debbie, stonily – and 'he'll leave a message' – Tara, sadly.

Their 'brainwave' – which she was convinced had already been plotted before they'd arrived at the house – worked, mainly because she knew she had to kick-start the survival plan somehow and also because Debbie had tactfully pointed out that she looked 'grotty and blotchy and pasty and unfit for the glamorous world of TV'. Hard to resist that one!

Lindsay was lucky in that her company agreed to let her go more or less straightaway. She had masses of leave due to her anyway and once she'd explained her personal situation to Joe Egan, the C.E.O. and a good friend, he agreed to her immediate release, which was just as well as the TV station wanted to start the training course pretty quickly.

So it was that Lindsay found herself panicking as she began a much-needed but unwanted break in the sun, still afraid of life without Paul and desperately hoping he'd somehow find out that she'd gone away and miss her and want her back.

The rain was pelting down when they returned to Dublin.

'What a surprise,' Debbie grumbled. It was eleven o'clock on a chilly autumn night and after a last drink at the airport the girls shared a taxi, dropping Lindsay off first.

'We'll miss you,' they shouted as she bundled herself and her bags out of the taxi.

'Call you in the morning.'

She felt lonely leaving them. She knew they'd be wondering. As she was.

'Do you suppose there'll be a message?'

'No, I think he's too much of a coward.'

'She'll still be devastated, even though she knows, deep down, that he won't call now.'

'Bastard, I really hope I meet him first.'

'That makes me almost feel sorry for him, having to face you sometime.' Tara smiled at her friend. 'Almost.' They were quiet for the rest of the journey, each lost in the same thoughts as the taxi sped through the dark, wet, deserted, late-night Dublin streets.

Lindsay let herself in quickly, shivering in the cold, damp atmosphere. Her heart began to thump as she saw the little red light winking furiously, teasing and torturing. I'm not going to let this bloody machine rule my life – she was angry with herself – I'll check it later, as soon as I've got myself organized. Two seconds later she pressed the play button.

First up, her sister Anne, wondering if she'd like to join them for lunch next Sunday and shouts from the boys in the background, telling her they'd missed her.

Next, the same sharp voice she remembered from Channel 6, reminding her to report to the Training Centre at nine-thirty a.m. on Monday.

'Hi, it's only me,' a male voice caused her heart to explode, even though it took only a second to recognize it as that of her neighbour John, calling to say he'd taken delivery of a package that wouldn't fit through her letter box.

Then her mother wondering what time she'd be collecting Charlie. A pause, a lifetime, before the machine clicked off. She cursed herself silently, dreading the now familiar rush of loneliness. She realized that she'd survived the break partly because she'd convinced herself that there would be several frantic messages begging her forgiveness when she got home. She hated herself for still missing him so much. Deflated, she brushed her teeth, slapped some cream on her now healthy, lightly tanned face and fell into a troubled, demon-filled sleep.

She woke to the familiar church bells, jumped out of bed immediately and fell over her suitcase.

God, this place is a tip. She looked around the normally pretty cottage. There were dead flowers, over-flowing waste bins and enough empty wine bottles for them to name a bottle bank after her. She made some black coffee, the only option as the milk looked more like cottage cheese, pulled on sweatpants and a T-shirt and got to work, having first called her sister to thank her for the offer of lunch and begged her mother to drop Charlie home to save her time.

The house had a faintly warm, unwashed human smell and she threw open every window that wasn't permanently closed thanks to a hundred years of paint. She filled two large plastic sacks with unrecognizable furry objects as well as the usual debris. Tara rang. She didn't ask, didn't have to as soon as she heard the flat voice. Her garden was still full of late summer flowers, she mentioned in passing, and she'd be offloading them later.

Lindsay vacuumed and polished and changed

the bed, she cleaned the bathroom and kitchen and washed and dried everything she could lay her hands on. She threw out anything of Paul's that she found without pausing for a second. It worked until she found his aftershave. Even though she didn't open it she could suddenly feel him all around her. The doorbell rang. Saved. Tara stood on the doorstep surrounded by glorious sweet peas and delicately scented phlox and the last of the tall creamy gladioli and small, exquisite, fat, cabbage roses. Lindsay could have kissed her, for her timing as much as for the well-chosen present.

'Wow, I think I'm in the wrong house.' Tara was delighted that Lindsay was cleaning, a very good sign indeed.

'I just decided I can't come home to this every night, especially if the training course is going to be as frantic as I think.' Lindsay's smile looked a little jaded.

They had a quick coffee and Debbie rang from the airport. She was working today, on her way to Geneva, just calling to check in.

'I'm cleaning, and Tara's just arrived with enough flowers to turn this place into Kew Gardens,' Lindsay told her. Good sign, thought Debbie, and promised to stop by the following night.

When Tara left, Lindsay showered and changed and went to the supermarket, still slightly nervous in case she met him, which was ridiculous, because even if he happened to be in Dublin he certainly wouldn't be in Tesco. He hates shopping, Lindsay thought and stopped herself. I can't keep doing this to myself, so just for today I'm going to pretend I'm OK and who knows, maybe someday I will be. She doubted it as she filled her trolley with far too much healthy food. Fruit, salads, organic vegetables, chicken, fresh juices, pasta, litres of water, brown bread and anything else she fancied that didn't contain sugar or chocolate or alcohol.

When she got back, Charlie was there, ecstatic to be home. He nearly knocked her over and she hugged him to death. He licked her face and ran up and down the stairs and threw himself at her until she had to bribe him with a treat from her shopping bag to calm him down. She'd even washed his beanbag and he rolled on it furiously, determined to get rid of that horrible fresh smell as quickly as possible.

Her mother had let herself in, as Lindsay knew she would, but couldn't wait, late, as always, for one of her many appointments. She'd left a quick note, wondering how the holiday had gone and Lindsay was glad not to have to explain in detail just yet. She'd told her family that the wedding was off but still felt too humiliated to tell the full story, even to those she knew were on her side. Later that evening she questioned her reasons for not being more open with her mother. It was always the same, always came back to the fact that nothing she did was ever quite good enough. The vague disapproval was very subtle and she sometimes wondered if she was imagining it. It didn't help that Lindsay had been especially close to her dad, therefore hadn't relied on the mother–daughter relationship as much as her sister Anne. Over the years the other two had become closer and Lindsay now felt a bit excluded, although she knew she could always rely on her sister. If only her mother wasn't so preoccupied, so distant at times, yet so quick to notice the failures. As far back as Lindsay could remember she'd always felt that she didn't quite make the grade. And it still hurt.

Charlie had settled in for the evening. The Aga had been turned on and that was his favourite place in the whole world, so Lindsay knew he was totally happy. I wish it was that easy, she sighed, as she tickled his stomach.

Over the next few days Lindsay did everything she could to boost her confidence for the new job – facial, eyebrows, nails, the lot – even a new haircut. Next problem was what to wear. A visit to Grafton Street soon sorted that one.

'You are becoming such a high-maintenance babe,' Debbie teased as they met for lunch after her shopping spree. 'How on earth will you survive on a lower salary?' All three girls had discussed the fact that salaries in television generally were quite low, but Lindsay knew she'd work there for nothing. It was simply what she'd always wanted to do.

'I know, I know, don't remind me. I'm going to have to start budgeting really seriously,' Lindsay grumbled. 'I suppose I've been spoilt because of the money Dad left. It means I only have a small mortgage and I've got very used to having a healthy bank account, which has become a tad sick lately I'd say, judging by the amount I've been withdrawing. Also, I suppose I don't have to worry because I know there's money put away for both Anne and myself for the future. Makes me feel guilty sometimes.'

'Don't be ridiculous, you deserve it.' The last thing Debbie wanted was for her friend to feel upset. 'Now I want to see all the purchases immediately and I think we deserve a glass of something nice and chilled.' The gorgeous black trouser suit was declared an instant success 'although I think you have at least a dozen already'.

'Yes, but this one is softer and lighter and definitely more tailored and it sort of says I mean business. Anyway, look, I've bought a couple of sexy little tops to wear underneath, which should work against the severe cut of the suit. Also, I fell in love with some gorgeous silver jewellery, which will make it look a bit funky. And, have a peep at these beauties.' They were indeed the cutest, deep burgundy, leather ankle boots – gloves for the feet, according to Debbie, who wanted a pair immediately – so they demolished the wine and headed for the shops again.

Suddenly it was the night before the big day and by ten-thirty Lindsay was tucked up in her comfy bed with its sundried sheets, determined to get an early night with no alcohol. She watched a bit of TV, read, turned off and on the light twice and finally gave up at midnight and slipped out of bed for a hot chocolate laced with a liberal dash of smoky, black rum. She read for a while then lay in the dark thinking about the week ahead, tired but not sleepy. She listened to the lingering weekend sounds outside her window and it was almost one-thirty when she gave up on the day and fell into a fitful but thankfully dreamless sleep.

Chapter Five

Lindsay felt like a nervous five-year-old starting school as she walked into the Television Training Centre at nine twenty-five the next morning. She'd been up since six o'clock.

She was directed towards a large classroom and felt very uneasy as she opened the door. The feeling was justified. Everyone seemed to know each other and most turned expectantly as the door opened, then turned back to their conversations almost immediately. They looked relaxed and happy and casual. Lindsay realized she was completely overdressed. She felt very schoolmarmish, all neat and tidy and scrubbed. They were all so arty and cosmopolitan, clearly at ease with their surroundings. Thankfully she noticed her name printed at one of the desks and slithered across the room, wishing she could go out and come in again, without her jacket and not clutching the soft leather briefcase quite so tightly.

The door opened and a tall auburn-haired girl dressed in black layers strode in, smiling.

39

She stopped, unsure, and Lindsay immediately smiled at her.

'Hi,' she looked as if she'd found her long-lost sister as she made a beeline for Lindsay. 'Carrie Moore,' she held out her hand and seemed delighted. 'Hey, that's me right beside you.' She looked as if she was going to kiss Lindsay full on the mouth. 'Jesus, was that seriously intimidating or am I just paranoid?' she whispered as she slipped into the seat next to Lindsay. 'By the way, please, please tell me I'm not overdressed or I really will have to take a tablet.' She spoke with her lips tightly closed and grinned foolishly and Lindsay knew they'd both be OK.

'I felt exactly the same two minutes ago,' Lindsay told her, admiring her soft black knitted coat with the flimsy, wispy layers underneath.

'I feel as though my watch says midnight and theirs all say five a.m.,' said Carrie cheerfully and Lindsay sensed that this girl was confident enough not to care too much.

'I'm Lindsay and I swear I'm not the tutor and I wasn't ever a schoolteacher, even though I'm dressed like one.' They grinned stupidly at each other, feeling vaguely apprehensive, wondering what to expect. The room fell silent and people took their places as a tall, dark-haired man with glasses and a serious smile entered. He had a kind face.

'Good morning, I'm Michael Russell, and I'm the Course Director and you're all very welcome. Let's start by introducing ourselves and then we can run through the schedule before we break for coffee and, let me apologize in advance because you're all going to be extremely busy over the next few weeks. OK, who'll start?'

'James Hewson, I'm a solicitor and over the past few years I've . . .'

'I'm Hilary Owens, I'm an actress and a broadcaster . . .'

'Hello, my name is Paul Nesbitt, I've been working as an Energy Broker . . .'

Christ, Lindsay thought, why do all these high-powered individuals want to give up much more lucrative careers for a less well-paid job in TV? But she knew that jobs in the media always attracted even well-established people and later over coffee she learned that many of her new acquaintances saw this job merely as a stepping stone to becoming a producer or director or reporter. It was seen as a really good place to start.

On and on it went and Lindsay could feel herself sliding further down in her seat, hoping they'd skip over her somehow. Carrie slipped her a note. 'I'm Carrie and I'm a prostitute and what's worse I think I feel a cold sore coming on,' she read and tried to stop herself giggling hysterically. No such thing. Carrie, it turned out, was an artist and Lindsay saw several pairs of eyes become immediately interested.

She tried to frantically rehearse her piece. Lindsay Davidson, complete idiot, barely made it through the interview and don't know how in hell they gave me a job, engaged until recently and boyfriend wanted to get away so fast he didn't even stop to say goodbye. Will probably not get through a day without bursting into tears so if any of you are qualified doctors or nurses I strongly recommend you have a few tranquillizers ready.

Instead, she mumbled something about interior design and always wanting to work in television and sat down quickly with a face you could warm your hands off.

The schedule was so intense they needed the strong coffee afterwards to revive them.

'Christ, there goes my life for the next few months,' Carrie said in a soft Cork accent. 'How about you?'

'Oh, I'm not worried, I don't have a life,' Lindsay joked.

Carrie wondered what the story was but decided not to ask. Yet.

They then had to have photographs taken and were issued with coded passes, which were needed to gain access to any of the buildings. Security was tight, especially anywhere near the TV and radio buildings. Over lunch, Lindsay got to know some of the group and realized they were mostly very friendly, with one or two possible exceptions. She wasn't sure about Hilary Owens, who smiled often, but her eyes were cold and inquisitive. John Shields was witty but a bit too sharp tongued. 'Gay,' Carrie had declared early on. And then there was Brenda Turner, already showing signs of being very, very competitive. Lindsay knew the coming weeks would tell a story about each of them.

In the afternoon, several 'real' A.P.s came to talk

to them about the job. It all sounded terribly exciting. Basically, an assistant producer helped make programmes and also worked in studio helping to record programmes or go live on air with them. This was the bit that everyone seemed to love and half the class imagined themselves shouting 'action' or 'ten seconds to air' or something equally unlikely and Lindsay couldn't wait to see it all happen, let alone be part of it. It seemed so glamorous, so terrifying, so sexy and so unreal that she found herself wondering if they hadn't made a big mistake in choosing her. She would have been somewhat reassured if she'd known that everyone felt the same, even those who already worked in the organization and knew the job.

At seven o'clock Michael Russell jokingly told them they could have a half-day. 'Trust me, the days are going to be considerably longer once we really get going.' He ignored their groans. 'However, you all look suitably shell-shocked so I won't give you any projects to work on tonight. Go home and get some rest and we start in earnest tomorrow at nine.'

'I'm going to the pub. They have a social club on the campus and the bar opened an hour ago,' John Shields decided.

'Point me in the direction and order me a very large gin,' Carrie told no one in particular. 'Coming, Lindsay?'

There goes my health kick again, Lindsay thought, knowing she was too agitated and excited and insecure to go home and take Charlie for a walk. 'I can smell the chilled white wine from here,' she smiled at her new friend.

Over drinks she got to know a bit more about Carrie, although the other girl claimed there wasn't a lot to tell. 'Studied art at college, worked as a curator in a local museum, gave it up to paint full time. Struggled like mad for a couple of years, lived in a grotty bedsit, finally decided to try something new, so here I am. No one was more surprised than me when they offered me a place on the course and I suspect I'm the only one who didn't take a massive cut in salary to be here.' She grinned foolishly. 'The money they're offering is like winning the lottery. I haven't had a regular income in yonks.'

Lindsay smiled back and didn't doubt for a minute that she had lots to offer, she was sharp as a razor.

When she got home at nine-thirty there were three messages and Lindsay felt the familiar sensation in her stomach, even though she knew there'd be three female voices on the machine. Spot on, you fool, she thought as she heard Debs, Tara and her sister Anne ask three different versions of the same question.

'How did it go, babe?'

'Any interesting men?'

'When will we see you on the News?'

Lindsay peeled off her clothes, made some coffee and returned the calls, ignoring her sister's advice to 'call Mum, she's dying to know all the gossip'. She threw the ball for Charlie for about ninety seconds, cleaned her face and her teeth and fell into bed, a bit deflated and annoyed with herself cause even after all that had happened she still wanted to ring Paul and tell him all about it.

The first week was flying by. She hadn't expected it to be quite so intense and Lindsay really had to struggle to keep up. She felt that everyone else knew more about the business than she did. They all seemed to understand the technical stuff. Lindsay worried, made millions of notes and tried not to ask too many questions. Each night she fell into bed exhausted and dreamt of crisis situations where programmes didn't get on air and the entire country was left staring at blank screens and people all seemed to be screaming at her. Or laughing. And all the laughing faces had the same dark brown eyes and gorgeous mouth.

The homework was horrendous. And then there were reports to write, following visits to various programmes. On the Thursday evening, Lindsay was told to sit in on the Nine O'clock News. She had to report to the editor at seven, give a hand if possible but mostly keep out of the way and simply observe.

Walking in to programme areas was always the most difficult bit. Mostly people ignored you. Or looked through you. Or stared. The newsroom was no different. It was a vast open-plan area which even at seven in the evening was home to at least fifty people, all of whom seemed to be talking too loudly, or whispering, or hitting keyboards too hard, or gesturing furiously. Everyone seemed to be running, or at least power walking. There was

45

a buzz, as if people were expecting something to happen at any moment. TV screens blared, shouting out news from around the world. Telephones rang constantly. The noise level was deafening.

She walked the length of the endless room, tugging at her slim-fitting black dress, which she thought was almost calf length when she'd started off but now seemed to be somewhere up around her bum. She saw one or two people glance absently at her and she tried very hard to appear nonchalant. It didn't work. She gave in and asked in a croaky voice for Martin Sheehan, the editor on duty. 'Over there,' a very haughty reporter whose face had always seemed so friendly on screen dismissed her with a vague wave.

She followed the long, pointed, red fingernail in the direction of a group of at least ten people, who all seemed to be in the middle of an argument but who were in fact having a programme meeting. She almost kept going.

'Hi, are you OK?' Lindsay nearly hugged the calm older woman who looked very normal. 'Are you the new A.P., by any chance?'

'Yes', her voice sounded croaky. Try again, Lindsay. 'Hi, I'm Lindsay Davidson, anything I can do?'

'Grab a chair, I'm Alison, the news A.P. in studio tonight, we're just about to put a running order on the programme. It's not too busy, I'll have plenty of time to talk to you later.'

Not busy, it was absolute bedlam; everyone seemed to be talking in shorthand. Lindsay tried but couldn't even follow half of the bloody thing.

'Is Blair edited?'

'Anyone seen the Minister for Health?'

'What time do we get VT?'

'Are the V.O.s in autocue yet?'

The responses came fast and furious.

'Yes.'

'On his way.'

'Seven-thirty.'

'Just going now.' Alison seemed to be the only one who knew anything and she was so cool. She thrust a sheaf of papers towards Lindsay. 'Could you get those into autocue in Studio Three? We're dead late, thanks.'

Lindsay scarpered. She was just beginning to panic when she found it. She pushed open the soundproof door and too late realized she'd come onto the studio floor instead of going into the control room. The door screeched to a close.

'Sorry.' Her face was purple as she realized she'd interrupted something. Her heels clicked, louder than a Ricky Martin video.

'Jesus Christ.' A pair of startled, ice-blue, furious eyes ate her up and spat her out.

'What the fuck . . . ? Hell, we were almost finished.' He jumped up and yanked off his headphones and Lindsay realized they'd been in the middle of a recording of some sort. She was absolutely mortified and wanted to charge back through the door but her legs were superglued to the floor. She recognized the face but couldn't put a name to it, perhaps because the features were completely distorted with rage.

'Haven't you ever been told not to enter a studio when the red light is on?' He looked as if he wanted to slap her.

'It's OK, Chris, we can pick it up easily enough,' a soothing voice explained from the corner. She saw a pair of kind grey eyes. 'Are you looking for the news crew?'

'Yes, I thought this was the control room. I didn't see the red light, I'm really sorry.' Lindsay couldn't ever remember feeling so small.

'It's an easy mistake to make, the signs on the wall are confusing,' the man explained. 'I'll show you where to go.'

'Fucking hell, I don't believe this. I need a coffee, give me five, Dan.'

The outraged presenter passed Lindsay with a swish of icy cold air and a smell of leather and after-shave and sweat. Half afraid to look but unable to resist, she saw a tall, unshaven man with tired eyes, tanned skin and thick dark hair that was too long and too fingered. As she followed him through the studio door she saw that he was much taller than he appeared on TV. He wore black jeans and a black V-neck T-shirt and a long black leather jacket so soft and crumpled it could have been a chamois. A very expensive one. He moved so fast that he was almost at the far end of the building within seconds and she saw him running his hands through his hair, head down, in obvious frustration.

'I can't believe I did that. It was the first thing they told us on the course – never break a red light. They'll probably throw me out when they hear.'

Lindsay looked horrified as she was directed towards the control room.

'Well, I don't intend telling anyone and I don't think you should either and don't worry about Chris, he won't even remember it once he's had a strong coffee,' Dan said with only slight exaggeration. 'He's having a bad day. He just got back this evening from Afghanistan and the Director of News wants a voice-over for a promo tomorrow. He's been travelling for twenty-four hours and was on his way home to bed when he got the call. He's a cool guy, you'll be fine, and', he winked, 'you won't ever make that mistake again.'

Lindsay smiled weakly.

Dan Pearson had noticed how attractive she was and introduced himself. 'I'm a floor manager, by the way, so no doubt we'll get to work together sometime soon.'

'If I survive the training, that is.' Lindsay was very glad she'd met Dan. 'Thanks.'

'No problem, I hope he's brought me back a coffee. See you later.' Dan hurried away just as Mary from autocue arrived and snatched the links from Lindsay.

'I hate working on News,' she apologized, 'everything's always last minute and you spend the entire bulletin terrified in case you make a mistake.'

The next two hours seemed to pass in minutes. It also seemed to happen in slow motion. It was like watching a behind-the-scenes TV documentary, Lindsay thought, fascinated. It looked like complete chaos yet everybody appeared to know what to do. She helped Alison as much as she could, ran with tapes, photocopied, distributed running orders and kept asking if anyone wanted coffee, which they all did, every ten minutes. She was nervous as she sat in studio beside Alison.

'One minute to air,' the older woman announced calmly.

'What's the first story?' came a voice over talk-back.

'Don't know yet, stand by with the Blair–Ahern tape and also the Bush story,' the director said quickly. 'Meanwhile, let's check our sources.'

On camera, Lindsay could see the two presenters gathering papers, making last-minute notes as make-up added their final touches.

Suddenly, the door burst open and the duty editor ran in. 'We're going with the Peace Process first, we've a statement from the IRA.'

'Ten seconds to air, stand by opening animation.' Alison never flinched as chaos reigned and people cursed silently and sighed loudly at yet another change of plan.

'We're on.'

'Good evening and welcome. First tonight to some breaking news . . .'

Lindsay's heart was thumping for the entire bulletin, convinced they were heading for a disaster and dreading the outcome. Scripts changed, stories were dropped, a tape went missing and yet viewers at home knew nothing. It seemed like only ten seconds later that she heard the familiar 'That's it for now from the Newsroom, a very good evening to you.'

'Well done, everyone, that was a bit hairy.' The director let out a sigh of relief and the studio cleared within seconds, the crew heading for coffee and a smoke before doing it all again at eleven.

Lindsay helped Alison gather tapes and clear up.

'It's great, I'm not on late tonight. Usually the A.P. for the nine has to do the late news as well.' Alison smiled. 'Thanks, you were a real help. Come back any time and good luck with the rest of the course.'

The girls left the TV building together and went their separate ways. It was a chilly, wet evening and Lindsay was completely exhausted. She made herself a large hot whiskey with cloves and lemon as soon as she got in, convinced she was coming down with something and still shivering after her earlier encounter. She tucked herself up on the couch, with Charlie keeping her warm.

She'd never met anyone quite like Chris Keating before. Mind you, tonight could hardly be called a meeting. There was something about him, something raw and sexy and slightly scary. No, definitely very scary, dangerous even. She'd never seen anyone so furious before, certainly not fury directed at her. He didn't hold back, that was for sure. Still, she probably wouldn't come into contact with him again, which disappointed her slightly, although she didn't know why. And, thanking God for the Dan Pearsons of the world, she cursed her stupidity for the tenth time.

She sighed and headed for bed, much to Charlie's disgust, as he was only beginning to get comfortable.

No way was she writing a report tonight, even if she had to get up at six tomorrow morning. She was declaring this day officially over.

Chapter Six

Next morning, Lindsay woke from a murky, grey sleep. It was seven-thirty and she was late and tired. Days like this rarely got much better, she knew from experience. She was grumpy and even Charlie, who loved mornings and bounded around the kitchen enthusiastically, was ignored as she quickly scribbled her notes, showered and dressed, grabbed a coffee and headed for work to type up her report which had to be in before lunch.

At elevenses Michael Russell smiled at her sympathetically.

'I believe last night's bulletin was rough, did you cope OK and was everything I heard true?' He stared at her questioningly. She completely misread the look.

Oh God, he knows. Lindsay felt sick. 'I just got confused and didn't see the red light,' she blurted out before she had time to think.

His eyes narrowed. 'You'd better come into the office and explain.' He didn't wait for a reply.

It turned out, of course, that he wasn't referring

to the famous incident; had merely heard that it was a particularly hairy bulletin and that Lindsay had coped very well. He made a point of asking for feedback when one of the trainees helped out on a high-profile programme and he'd been particularly interested to see how Lindsay had fared, because she was so new to the game. The report had been very good, but of course now she had to explain about the near disaster. He was furious.

God, I'm certainly making a habit of annoying influential men in television, she thought grimly, unable to believe that she'd actually brought this upon herself.

'Breaking a red light unless you're directly involved and know exactly what's going on is a mortal sin in this business and forcing them to stop a recording is even worse. We absolutely depend on our colleagues allowing trainees access to real programmes, otherwise you'd never get any worthwhile hands-on experience. An incident like this reflects badly on everyone in Training.' For the second time in less than twenty-four hours, Lindsay was mortified. Whatever shred of confidence she had left evaporated. She was sure her face resembled a two-bar electric fire. She wanted to crawl away and die.

'I know, it was stupid, I'm really sorry. It won't happen again.'

'You're dead right. I'm not letting you near a live studio for the foreseeable future. From now on all your attachments will be on pre-recorded programmes and if you make a mistake like this again you're out.' He knew he was being hard on her but if anyone had reported this he'd have his ass kicked at the next editorial. Luckily, he knew Chris Keating wouldn't give it another thought and Dan Pearson was probably the best F.M. in the business, so he'd say nothing.

Lindsay felt sick for the rest of the day. Not only had she done something incredibly stupid last night but she'd also put her new job in jeopardy in the first week. Please let this day, this week be over soon, she begged God.

She couldn't even face joining the others for a drink after work and they didn't understand why.

'Come on,' Carrie pleaded, 'we owe ourselves a celebration, we've survived and the first week is always the worst.'

'I nearly didn't.' Lindsay told her new friend what had happened earlier.

'For God's sake, it could have happened to any of us, I think he went completely over the top.'

'No, he was right. It could have been a complicated TV programme with special effects and everything and I clattered in right in the middle of it. I was lucky it was only a sound recording, although I don't think Chris what'shisname will be asking to work with me again.' She attempted a smile.

'He doesn't have any say in who he works with and he sounds like a right bollocks anyway. Come on, just the one.'

'No, honestly, I'm going to curl up on the couch and lick my wounds, I'll see you on Monday.' Lindsay felt very vulnerable as she got into her car and drove the short distance home. She'd been right about the day not getting any better.

When she got in the phone was ringing and for the first time in weeks she didn't even wonder if it might be him.

'Oh, great, you're home. I just left a message on your mobile. Get your glad rags on. Debs and I are taking you to dinner – new little Italian in Baggot Street, very trendy, supposed to be fantastic.'

'Tara, I couldn't bear it tonight. Would you mind if I passed?'

'Yes, I would and so would Debbie who is at this moment breaking her neck to get from the airport to your house to pick you up so you don't have to drive. They only have one table free at eight and I practically had to sleep with the manager to get it. Come on, babe, it'll do you good; we haven't really talked since Rome. We'll relax and have some nice food, a couple of glasses of wine, a good gossip and you'll be home by midnight.'

Lindsay didn't have the strength to argue. She pulled on her comfiest stretch black trousers and bright red Lainey Keogh sweater and added her black suede ankle boots which Debbie said made her legs look longer than Elle Macpherson's. She hadn't the energy to do anything more than touch up her make-up, adding some strong red lipstick and leaving her hair loose. She sighed. She'd have had a burning knitting needle inserted into her eye sooner than go out tonight, but she knew she had no choice.

Thirty minutes later they arrived at the restaurant and it was indeed the in place to be, if the noise level was anything to go by.

Behaviour determines mood, Lindsay remembered from one of her many self-help books, so she smiled grimly and stuck her chest out and followed the waiter down through the middle of the restaurant and almost fainted as she came face to face with Paul, sitting in a dimly lit booth on the right. He wasn't alone. A bottle of champagne was chilling beside the table. She knew she should just keep going but someone had driven a stake through her left foot and she came to a sudden and complete stop directly in front of him.

'Lindsay, hi . . .' He sounded very uncomfortable. She looked around for the girls, desperately needing support, but Tara had stopped when she'd spotted a guy from her office, someone she suspected Debbie fancied, and they'd both noticed that Lindsay was chatting to someone but couldn't see who it was.

'Hi.'

'How are you?'

How do you think I am? 'Fine, you?'

'OK, yeah . . . erm, this is Kate. Kate, Lindsay.'

'Hello.' Lindsay plastered a smile on her face and tried to take in everything about the other woman at once. Late twenties, blonde, big eyes – even bigger boobs, good looking in a very obvious way, she thought nastily. Too much make-up. Sexy. Small. Tiny waist.

Get a grip, you couldn't possibly see her waist from where you were, she could imagine Debbie saying, practical even in a crisis.

Cool, no cold. Frosty smile. Provocative, revealing dress. No knickers, she'd bet her life on it.

Definitely a man's woman. More a Rhonda or a Sharon than a Kate really.

'Oh, hi.' She didn't look that interested. Lindsay hated her for not at least being curious.

'I was going to ring you . . .'

Yeah, right.

'Paul, hadn't we better order . . . ?' The cool voice trailed off.

'Sorry, we have a lot of catching up to do.' Lindsay was as capable as anyone of being cool. And just now she felt very cold and very calm, which was a bad sign.

'Well, I think it's all history now and Paul and I have a very different relationship, so perhaps it's better we all try to move on.'

Lindsay couldn't believe her ears. You bitch, she thought, you stupid, fucking, insensitive bitch.

Without even realizing what she was doing, Lindsay slipped into the seat opposite and stared at the confident, cold face.

'Really, just how different is your relationship, I wonder? Does he not cuddle you till you fall asleep at night? Kiss you awake when he knows you're tired? Cut your toenails? Bring you home champagne and chips, or chocolate and tampons? Feed you ice cream in bed? Stick notes in your suitcase when you go away? Text you to ask if you're wearing stockings? Burst your pimples? Jump into the bath beside you with his clothes on because he can't wait? Kiss your nose when you have a cold? Swear he'll still fancy you when you're ninety? . . .' She could have gone on for ever but she suddenly ran out of steam.

She looked straight at the face she thought she knew so well but couldn't see his gorgeous brown eyes because he wasn't able to look at her.

'He did with me. In fact,' she tore herself away from his eyes and looked at the now flushed face of the woman sitting beside him, 'the only bad thing about him was his goodbye. There wasn't one.'

Lindsay stood up just as Tara and Debbie hurled themselves at the table, having just realized who she was talking to. Tara looked worried and Debbie was clearly furious. For what seemed an eternity all five of them stared at each other and Lindsay knew she had to get out. Fast.

'See you around. Next time you're asked to appear on TV, maybe.' She remembered he'd been on a programme about design once and he'd adored the buzz. 'I'm working at Channel 6 now – Assistant Producer.' She had no idea where that came from, just knew she couldn't resist it. Perhaps there was hope for her after all.

She turned and headed for the door at an incredible pace, with Tara in front and Debbie's hand on her back as a single, big fat tear rolled down her face. It was over. And there was absolutely no good in goodbye.

Chapter Seven

As she struggled to clear her fur-coated brain next
morning, Lindsay wondered for a split second
where she was. A warm, late autumn sun had
somehow found its target and hurt her eyes. She
shook her head to escape the probing rays and
almost immediately came face to face with a pair
of equally bewildered eyes. Tara groaned. 'Oh
God, I feel awful. What's that revolting smell?'

'Leftover pizza that didn't smell great last night,
come to think of it,' a muffled voice murmured
from under the duvet.

'Someone shovelled gravel down my throat in
the middle of the night, which one of you is the
culprit?'

To call what emerged from halfway down the
bed dishevelled was an act of pure kindness.
Debbie's hair was matted, her face had been white-
washed, her eyes were swollen and she had two
coal-black streaks under her lower lashes.

'The Gothic look really suits you,' was the
best Lindsay could come up with, knowing she

probably looked exactly the same, or worse.

Debbie's eyes pleaded for help. 'I need water and the bathroom, fast.' A bare bottom clambered over the other two and disappeared as life came sharply into focus for Lindsay. She pulled herself into a sitting position and looked around.

The room had been bombed. Clothes, coats, shoes, bags, make-up remover, tissues, glasses, bottles, screw tops, and several enormous boxes of half-eaten pizza that smelt vile and looked even worse were all that Lindsay could see. She sank back down, unable to face it all.

'You OK?' Tara knew what she was thinking.

'Yeah, I just remembered why you're here.'

Debbie reappeared, wearing a ridiculous jumper and no knickers, carrying a carton of juice. She passed it silently, climbed back into bed and shuddered.

'Ugh, I hope that bastard rots in hell.' She didn't need to elaborate. They stayed there for a while, each lost in thought as Lindsay came to grips with what had happened. She felt hollow. It was over, she knew that for definite now.

She made a quick decision.

'OK, come on, tea and toast.' She couldn't go any further down that particular cul-de-sac just yet. She jumped up, startling the other two who were clearly ready for a doze.

'Breakfast, showers and then a walk.' They decided not to argue.

Charlie was without doubt the liveliest one in the kitchen as they silently drank gallons of tea and coffee and, despite their earlier protests, got through a huge mound of hot, crisp, buttery toast. One by one they trooped into the shower and emerged looking no different, not having made even the slightest attempt to do anything other than make themselves feel a bit more human.

'Imagine, I should be working today, except I swapped.' Debbie felt as if she'd been run over by a train. 'Thank you, God.'

Debbie and Tara were throwing on some of Lindsay's clothes – big, baggy sweatshirts and hoodies on top and anything that fitted on the bottom. Lindsay grabbed Charlie's lead and they all piled into the car and headed for Howth, a small fishing village in North County Dublin, where they climbed the cliffs and sucked in every last bit of fresh, clean air and turned their faces towards the almost translucent sun. They looked an unlikely threesome, Lindsay striding fiercely forward, head distorted in concentration, with two grey faces and weary bodies behind, struggling to keep pace. Charlie was the only one getting any real pleasure from the outing and seemed to be egging them on, constantly running ahead and turning expectantly towards them with a big, wet, laughing face and feather-duster tail. They returned home exhausted, stopping at the supermarket, at Tara's insistence, in spite of the other two gagging at the thought of food.

'We need a Mammy's dinner,' she insisted.

'We need a curer,' Debbie pleaded.

They arrived home just as the tired sun gave up on the day and each went about their tasks without speaking, in a well-practised drill. Tara lit the fire,

Lindsay stuck a fat chicken smeared with butter and stuffed with garlic, lemon and black pepper-corns in the oven and Debbie immediately headed for the bottle she'd persuaded them to buy. By the time the fire had caught, with just a little help from a full packet of firelighters, Debbie had made three big fat tumblers of hot port with lemon and cloves and Lindsay had peeled some potatoes for roasties. They sat around the blazing black hole, grateful for the warmth and the instant sedation of the soothing liquid, despite their earlier insistence that they'd never drink again.

'I'm so glad we were able to get out of that res-taurant as fast as we did, even if it meant forfeiting our dinner,' Debbie laughed half-heartedly, 'although my insisting on ordering those awful pizzas as soon as we got home wasn't so clever.'

'It helped soak up some of the alcohol and by the time we got round to remembering to eat we'd had so much to drink that they tasted gorgeous.' Tara made a face. 'How many bottles of wine did we get through, anyway?'

'I'd say five, at least, and I don't really want to be reminded.' Lindsay managed a cynical smile. 'God, I'll bet his ears were burning all night.'

'You haven't really talked about it today,' Debbie prompted. Lindsay said nothing for a few seconds, just stared at the flames, trying to think how she really felt.

'I've just realized that it probably isn't as bad as I thought it was going to be when I first saw them together. Yeah, I got a terrible shock. It sort of made it all seem real and not just a sick joke but

I suppose I knew it was over and God knows I'd imagined them together often enough, so that when it actually came to it, well, it was never going to be as bad as the scenario I'd played out in my mind a million times. Do you know what I mean?'

They did.

'At least . . . it WAS awful . . . at first I thought I was going to faint, or throw up, or cry, or beg him to come back, but now it all seems like a dream. You know, this time yesterday if you'd asked me how I would cope if I ever met them together, I'd have said I would have handled it very differently, but when it came to it, I just went completely numb and my mind kept thinking, this is it, no reason to doubt it any more, he's not yours any longer. It felt very odd but I don't feel as bad today because I've known, deep down, that he wasn't coming back and my mind must have been dealing with it subconsciously.'

'You poor baby, come 'ere.' Debbie was her usual affectionate self.

'I guess I've no more excuses for not getting on with it.' Lindsay looked pathetic.

'I think this may be the start of you seeing him for what he is, not what you thought he was.' Tara, gentle as ever, not wanting to push too far too quickly.

'Yeah. It still hurts, but the pain has sort of dulled over the weeks, my stomach doesn't feel like a big open wound that I keep forgetting about and pouring salt on, which is how it used to be. And somewhere in the middle of all that turmoil in the restaurant last night, I realized he wasn't as big or as strong as I'd thought. So, I guess I must be getting over it a bit.'

They kissed and hugged and decided that while they didn't have any reason to celebrate they could just about manage one glass of wine with dinner, which they ate on their laps in front of the fire – crispy, garlicky chicken with crunchy roasties and a tangy green salad. By eight o'clock they were all knackered and they left her, each feeling they'd crossed yet another major hurdle and grateful to have at least survived the trauma. Lindsay took a bath and thought once again how lucky she was to have the two of them in her life. She smiled when she remembered the three of them tucked up in her bed the previous night, eating and drinking their heads off and just letting her rant. They'd refused to leave her on her own and abandoned all their plans for the weekend in order to stay as long as was necessary.

She felt OK as she climbed into bed at nine o'clock on a Saturday night, with only the TV for company. I can handle this, she thought, a bit subdued and a good bit wiser.

The next day Lindsay slept late, which surprised and pleased her, and she spent the day clearing up the bomb-site, washing clothes and generally getting ready for the week ahead. She felt quiet and sad all day, like someone recovering from a bereavement – the initial awful pain gone but the sense of loss and loneliness remaining. She was very glad to have her new job and potential new career to keep her busy and she knew she needed to work twice as hard to complete the training course to the best of her ability, because her job was about the only thing keeping her sane.

And so the weeks flew by. Autumn turned to winter but no one noticed because the weather stayed so mild, until you realized that the trees were almost naked and bird sounds were no longer a feature of mornings. It was getting harder to prise Charlie away from the Aga when she left each day and Lindsay felt sorry for him because she was working incredibly long days and most of her evenings were taken up reading or catching up on notes. She was lucky that she had a decent-sized garden and an elderly neighbour who let himself in the back gate and took Charlie for a walk each afternoon. Lindsay was so thrilled that she bought a lead and left it hanging in the garden shed for him and was always leaving packets of Werther's Original and other sweets beside it, which she suspected Charlie shared. And this Christmas Charlie was going to buy Mr Nichols a very large bottle of brandy.

Lindsay seemed to do nothing except work and sleep, try to eat healthily and not think too much about her life. And it almost worked. She no longer thought about him every ten seconds and had slowly cleared away the happy photos and reminders of a love that she'd lost. The girls were busy as well. Tara seemed to be in court all the time and Debbie kept ringing them both reminding them to make Christmas lists and give her a note of things they wanted her to get while she was in Milan or some other exotic shopper's paradise.

Both ignored her messages, Tara because she was already quite well organized and knew Debbie never managed to get exactly what you'd asked for and Lindsay because as far as she was concerned, Christmas was just not happening this year.

Suddenly it was the end of November and the course was coming to an end. Everyone was stressed out, worrying about their final project, where they had to produce and direct a thirty-minute pilot programme on any topic they wanted. Lindsay and Carrie discussed this for hours over the odd glass of wine – but mostly coffee cause they needed to stay awake. Some of the others had brilliant ideas for programmes: a documentary on transsexuals, a love story between two women, a fast-paced movie quiz and several reality TV shows. After much discussion, Carrie had decided to take a look at the gay scene in Ireland. Lindsay had a rough idea for an alternative chat show, very late-night, a bit seedy, with a studio set based on one of the new hot spots in Dublin – a show where the audience were involved and got to ask the guests questions, competitions and cookery demos were banned and new music was a feature. Every possible topic was up for discussion and the format was to be really snappy with subjects ranging from grunge to Gucci, IT girls to designer babies, masturbation to lap dancing. It was aimed at an audience aged between twenty and thirty-nine and Lindsay worked on her proposal for hours, wanting to shock yet satisfy, tease but still tantalize.

It was difficult because the audience she was trying to capture were notoriously fickle and switched channels relentlessly and although the pilots would never be transmitted, the Course Director had told them that each programme would be watched by a group of representative people in the industry who would comment and criticize and assess them as they would a real programme. It was therefore essential to treat this project as if it were for broadcast and they each spent hours throwing out ideas and looking for help. They had a small budget and four hours' recording time in studio with a real crew so the programmes would all be professionally made. This was the work on which they would ultimately be judged, although they'd been assured that their contribution and performance for the entire course would be taken into account when deciding their fate. There were twelve people on the course and only eight jobs so one in three would not make the grade, which made Lindsay very determined. She'd had enough disappointment this year to last a lifetime, so one of those jobs had her name on it.

On the Monday morning, their two weeks' preparation began and Lindsay was up at six, working on her laptop, making notes and preparing the running order for the show. They didn't have to formally report to the Training Centre during this time, except to meet with the Course Executives for half an hour at the end of the first week to report progress.

Lindsay spent a couple of hours at home and then went in to make calls and meet team leaders. It was amazing having a real crew – cameramen who knew how to frame shots, lighting directors who used their initiative. Up until now, they had crewed for each other with varying degrees of success, so having professionals really made it all come alive. Each person had access to a designer for one day and as they couldn't build a set, because of cost, they had to design their shows from stock pieces. Lindsay realized how lucky she was as soon as she was introduced to her designer. Jonathan had bleached blond hair and was as camp as anyone she'd met but he was full of ideas and enthusiasm. She had given him a brief which explained how she wanted the show to look and they spent a morning trawling through a huge warehouse where all sets, past and present, were stored. Her look was to be steel and scaffolding, with as many levels as possible, and Jonathan had found amazing stuff. He'd also begged and borrowed some really stylish seating, all aluminium and leather, and had even found rolls of muslin to form a backdrop, which could be transformed with lighting. Lindsay started to feel really excited about her project.

As guests she had found a sex therapist (whom Tara's sister had attended), a young guy who was thrown out of a boy band for being gay (chatted up by Debbie on one of her flights) and a movie executive to talk about the rise of young Irish actors in Hollywood (captain of her mother's golf club). Lindsay had phoned a couple of the radio DJs and got a list of up-and-coming bands and two of them were delighted to perform for free, so

Lindsay spent a great night in some very seedy venues in town watching them perform. The audience, all under thirty-five, comprised friends of friends so Lindsay knew they would applaud with gusto and look interested.

Halfway through the second week's preparation Lindsay panicked and decided the whole idea was shite and rang Carrie in desperation. To her amazement her friend was having exactly the same thoughts so they immediately arranged to meet for a pint and a final talk through of ideas. Lindsay thought Carrie's idea was fab. She was following three different homosexual men around for a day (supposedly) – all to be shot in four hours. The idea was to try and see the world through their eyes and look at the pluses and minuses of being a gay man in Ireland in the new millennium.

Carrie made Lindsay explain her entire format for the show and asked one or two pertinent questions that Lindsay hadn't thought of, which proved invaluable.

Even more importantly, they gave each other much-needed reassurance and with it came a surge of confidence. After two hours' talking shop they settled down for a gossip and a well-earned drink.

'You know the thing I love most about this is that it feels like a real challenge and you put everything into it because it's so exciting,' Carrie enthused between mouthfuls of crisps and beer. 'I've also met a few hunks, which really helps my dedication,' she grinned.

'Only you could find a hunk on a programme about gays,' Lindsay laughed at her.

'Well, I've had to go through a lot of straight men to get to their gay friends.'

'Well, that's something I've no interest in, which is just as well considering I haven't had time to even wash my hair for four days. God, I'll be really glad when this part is over, it's doing my head in.'

Lindsay marvelled at Carrie's calm, easy-going manner. They had a great couple of hours and Lindsay went to bed that night excited and exhilarated for the first time in ages.

Chapter Eight

The day of Lindsay's final project came at last and she felt physically sick with nerves. She'd tossed and turned all night, convinced she'd make a complete mess of it and lose her precious new job. When she did sleep she dreamt that Paul turned up in the audience and each time the camera focused on him he was kissing a different woman. She woke at six, having set three different alarms in case she overslept. Some chance. She forced herself to have tea and toast and squeezed some red grapefruit to make a rather lurid-looking juice, showered quickly and put on her favourite Ghost black dress. It was long, fitted and simple, and with a white T-shirt underneath and her huge black Lainey Keogh cardigan and boots she looked kind of funky and relaxed. She'd forced herself to make time to have her hair cut the day before, so she left it loose to reveal her new, shiny, conker-brown mop.

She went straight to the studio at eight-thirty, to check on progress, even though recording wasn't till two. The set took her by complete surprise. Jonathan, true to his word, had made it look just like a nightclub and Lindsay smiled as she watched him scurrying around yelling instructions at the staging crew.

When she tried to help he whispered, 'Want to cause a strike, darling?'

'Sorry, it's just I'm so used to doing everything myself. On the training course we have no help.'

'Welcome to the real world, although I'm not sure it's any better.' He smiled knowingly but failed to put her off even slightly. This was where she wanted to be more than anywhere else on the planet.

'For fuck's sake, be careful with that, you're ruining my perfect floor,' Jonathan tore into one of the sound crew who was dragging mike stands across the flawless white, shiny floor. Tempers flared for a minute or two and she was surprised to find that no one took any notice.

'It's drama everyday here, worse than a soap opera', the floor manager, Steve, winked at her. Lindsay watched as everyone went about their business, marvelling that this was all for her. Several of the senior crew members came to talk to her, urging her to ask them anything she didn't understand. She couldn't believe how willing they all were, despite the fact that this was a simple training programme. Everyone seemed to want her to do well and she basked in the warmth of the goodwill around her. Peter Jenkins, a shy, smiling cameraman came to introduce himself and wish her luck.

'I hope we get to work together for real some day,' he grinned and she was scared to realize how very much she wanted this job.

Lindsay's heart was in her mouth as she walked into the control room later to begin rehearsals. She was in charge, this was it and her future career might be decided in the next couple of hours. She couldn't ever remember feeling so nervous, even at the famous interview.

She was met by one of the technical people, who explained that they had a problem getting pictures from one of the cameras. Her heart sank but she forced herself to stay calm.

'Tell me the problem exactly and how long you think it will take.' He explained in detail, some of which she didn't fully understand.

'It could take ten minutes but then again it could take half an hour.'

'I have to be finished at six, no matter what,' she explained calmly. The agreement was that every person had exactly four hours' studio time and had to finish regardless.

'We're doing our best, honestly,' the older man smiled kindly, 'and I'm sorry but you can't rehearse until we have pictures.'

'OK.' Lindsay took a deep breath and put on her headset so that she could talk to everyone. Briefly and as clearly as she could she explained the problem while wondering frantically what she could do to use the time. 'As we can't rehearse I'd like to have a meeting of all crew on the studio floor to talk through the running order,' she decided, thinking quickly.

It proved to be a very good move as it was the first time all the crew were together and only the seniors knew anything about her programme. She quickly went through the plan and the script and asked for questions. There were lots, some of which brought up some difficulties she hadn't anticipated but to her surprise everyone tried to row in. Sound had a problem getting a mike to some of the audience and the senior cameraman came to her rescue. 'We can move camera one during the music number to let sound in for the next discussion.'

'But will it affect my shots on camera one for the interview?' she enquired nervously.

'No, we should be able to get the tight shots from a different position, I can show you as soon as we have pictures.'

On and on it went and suddenly one of the techies turned up to let her know that the problem was solved. Lindsay sprang into action and it all started to come together and before she knew where she was the final credits were rolling. It had all gone reasonably well.

The sex therapist was a huge hit and lots of the audience asked questions, some serious, some downright kinky, but the guest, a calm, middle-aged woman, had heard it all before and turned the tables on one or two of the audience themselves, much to everyone's delight. The gay man sparked an interesting debate with a couple of people whom Lindsay had 'planted' in the audience. Tempers flared when they appeared to be biased against gays in general and wanted them all thrown out of Ireland. It was a very lively fifteen minutes. The music was fab and some of the audience spontaneously started dancing, which added to the whole 'live' feel. When she saw the final credit 'Produced and Directed by Lindsay Davidson', she felt like bursting into tears. Of course it would never be transmitted but she'd done it, put together a half-hour programme and carried it through to fruition, from her first scribbled notes to a completed tape for posterity. It was a good feeling and she desperately wanted the chance to do it for real. The bug had bitten.

As soon as the music died she thanked everyone and invited them for a glass of wine in the hospitality room to celebrate her first programme. There was no budget, but she had decided to buy a couple of bottles of red and white wine, some beer and nibbles out of her own money, in order to say thanks to the crew. Debbie and Tara had been offered the very glamorous, two-euro-an-hour jobs as hostesses and when they all trooped into the room, she was amazed for the hundredth time that day. Debbie had cornered Jonathan and persuaded him to find a few balloons and candles and bits 'n' bobs, so that the room looked super. Everyone clapped as she came in and she almost burst with pride. She felt elated. Michael Russell, the Course Director, came in to shake hands and offer his congratulations.

'Thanks, I nearly didn't get going at all, we had a technical problem,' she burst out, absolutely brim full of the whole thing.

'I know; I arranged it.' He grinned.

'What?' She couldn't believe her ears and stared at him stupidly. Why would he, of all people, cause her a problem?

'We wanted to see how you coped with a technical problem first thing,' he laughed at the look on her face, 'and I must say you handled it exceptionally well.'

'You bastard.' It was out before she could stop herself. She burst out laughing. 'There was I thinking I was just the most unlucky person in the world and you tell me it was deliberate.'

'Afraid so, but well done again and this', he indicated the room 'was a very nice touch and should have the crew loving you forever. People in this business, especially programme makers, expect a lot and some of them don't know how to say thank you. Although I don't know how you managed it on your budget.' Lindsay said nothing, just smiled at him innocently but somehow she knew he knew. There wasn't a hope in hell of providing hospitality on the meagre amount they'd been given – she could barely afford to pay people – but as far as he was concerned she'd delivered the programme within budget and that was all that mattered.

Tara appeared as if by magic. She had no idea who Michael was but guessed he was important and came to offer him a glass of wine and some food. Lindsay left them deep in conversation and devoured a couple of sandwiches and some sausage rolls, followed by a large glass of chilled white wine. Heaven. She positively glowed and smiled at everyone. It had all been worth it. Now all she had to do was wait for the end-of-course assessment, to see if her best had been good enough.

After an hour or two people began to drift off and everyone wished her luck as they left. Lindsay was absolutely dead on her feet. Her funky, chunky boots were pinching, her bra suddenly felt too tight and she ached to be in her fleecy pyjamas. The girls, however, had other ideas.

'Come on, into town for a few drinks, maybe on to a club.' Debbie had been chatting to one particular cameraman for an hour or two and was in great form. Lindsay hadn't the energy to resist so they all piled into a taxi and headed for one of the coolest bars in town. Over a bottle of champagne, they caught up.

Tara thought Michael was really nice and seemed to have found out his life story in half an hour. Apparently, he'd recently separated from his wife and the training course had been brilliant because he'd had no time to think. Tara thought he was very cute, which surprised the other two because he definitely wasn't her normal type.

They slagged Debbie about the cameraman but apparently he was getting married shortly so that ruled him out.

'You know, being in there with you made me realize how exciting this whole thing is.' Tara was thrilled for her friend. 'And it couldn't have happened at a better time.'

'I haven't got the job yet.' Lindsay felt her insides lurch.

'OK, tell us exactly what happens now.' Tara,

practical as ever, her legal brain needing to file it all away.

'Well, as soon as everyone has done their project, a group of media people get together and assess them for content, quality, ideas, etc. Then the three main course leaders give their reports on our performances throughout the period, Michael consults with the Head of Programming and they decide how many will be offered jobs and where they will be assigned.'

'Pretty nerve-wracking. When will you know?' Debbie just wanted this next messy bit out of the way and then they could really celebrate, hopefully.

'Should be end of next week. I'm on clear-up duty from now, putting through paperwork, returning tapes, writing thank-you letters, etc. Officially the course ends next Friday so everyone says that's the day we find out. I really don't know what I'll do if they don't offer me a job. Over the last few weeks, and especially today, I realized that this is something I really want to do. It's like a different world, interesting, exciting, challenging and terrifying. I desperately want to be part of it.'

'Don't even go there, girl,' Debbie warned. 'I will not entertain any negative thoughts on this one. You are going to get that job. I can feel it.'

'You know, after the interview, if I hadn't heard from them, I'd have accepted it, especially given the state I was in. But now, they've let me in for a sneak preview, to see the rehearsals, and I really want to play the leading role. But, of course I'd settle for a place in the chorus. Hell, I'd even sweep the stage floor.' Lindsay grinned and they thought they hadn't seen her looking this animated for ages.

'You shall go to the ball, darling.' Debbie jumped up. 'Meanwhile, back in the real world, let's go work off some of this energy on the dance floor.'

'What energy?' the other two shouted but she was gone, leaving them no choice but to keep her out of trouble.

They danced themselves silly, laughed till they ached and drank far too much expensive cheap wine. No one came near them; they looked far too formidable, far too confident for most of the Irish men who watched them that night.

'That's it, my gym membership starts tomorrow,' Lindsay giggled as she got out of the taxi at three-thirty a.m.

'Tomorrow, definitely, absolutely – see you there at seven,' they laughed back and sped off into the pitch-black winter night.

Chapter Nine

The plumpest, juiciest snail in Lindsay's garden moved a hell of a lot faster than time over the next few days, although she did everything possible, including clearing the leaves from her garden with gusto and disturbing the slimy creatures, to make it pass more quickly.

She tried to work, tried not to worry, struggled with her gym visits, had no struggle with her weight because she was too uptight to eat and generally waited for the call.

Everyone else was exactly the same. The initial elation had worn off and they all felt that their own final projects were rubbish, especially when they heard some of the other ideas and the clever ways they had been executed. They moped around the Training Centre trying to look busy. They scanned the faces of the course leaders endlessly, looking for a sign and reporting each nuance to the others, over long coffee breaks in the TV canteen, the only place where they could pretend to be part of the circus. They watched jealously as programme teams had irate meetings, smiled at everyone just in case they were important and prayed to be part of all the madness someday. Even the ones on the course who had started off so cool were now reduced to a state of acute paranoia.

By Thursday lunchtime, Lindsay couldn't stand it any more.

'That's it, I'm going to the gym to do a hundred press-ups,' she told a deflated Carrie, who had only ever managed fifteen and that was after she'd been going for six months. 'Then, I'm bringing Charlie for a five-mile walk, having a bath and even if I have to munch a handful of sleeping tablets I'm going to bed at ten. Otherwise I won't survive until tomorrow. Quite honestly I'll simply expire.'

She'd just finished her toughest gym session yet and was pulling in to the car park on the beach with Charlie, about to walk for Ireland, when her mobile rang.

'Lindsay, are you on the campus, by any chance?' Michael Russell's calm voice asked, giving no clue.

'No.' Lindsay couldn't lie because the violent sea was crashing angrily in the background and Charlie was licking the phone – and her ear – to death. God knows what Michael would think she was up to. She pushed Charlie off her lap with all the force she could muster and tried to get out of the car, whereupon he climbed all over her, knocked the phone out of her hand and growled furiously at it, nearly giving Lindsay a hernia trying to rescue it and sit on him at the same time.

'Hello?' Michael's voice sounded puzzled.

'Sorry, no I'm not on the campus at the moment,'

Lindsay sounded winded, 'but I could be there in half an hour.' She flung her jacket on top of Charlie to try and muffle his excited yelps.

'Where are you?' Michael laughed. 'You sound like you're trying to put an animal into a washing machine. Very worrying.' He'll wish he was anywhere else, even in a washing machine, by the time I'm finished with him. Lindsay made a final lurch at Charlie, who barked delightedly. Honesty was the only way out.

'Actually, I needed to clear my head and I've just finished my post production, so I nipped out for a walk on the beach with my pet gorilla who masquerades as a dog.'

Oh God, ten points gone, Lindsay thought, cringing, glad that the videophone wasn't a realistic option yet.

'Very sensible,' Michael stated matter-of-factly. 'No problem, I've lots to get through. Could we meet in my office at, say, nine-thirty in the morning?'

Lindsay quickly agreed and hung up, furious with herself for not considering that he might want to see her today. She might even know her fate by now, if she'd stayed around. Damn.

She jumped out of the car and Charlie, in his haste to escape, head butted her in the behind, sending her flying. She recovered quickly, partly because of the group of school kids who were laughing hysterically at her with her bum in the air, and stormed off at a furious pace, not caring whether Charlie was following. She'd deal with him later. The walk was a dream of travel and adventure and romance and excitement. Oh, the possibilities created by one phone call!

Two hours later, just as she arrived home with a filthy, happy dog, her phone rang again.

'I'm in, I'm in, I've got a job.' Carrie's screams could be heard in Liverpool.

'Oh my God, tell me everything.' Lindsay didn't care that Charlie was streaking up and down the carpet. 'Where are you going? What did he say?' Lindsay was just as loud as she pulled off her wet jacket and boots.

'Sports,' Carrie laughed hysterically, 'and I don't care a bit, I'm just so glad I made it. Although, they must be mad, I don't know the difference between soccer and squash, but at least I should get to meet a few real men on this one.'

'Oh, that is such good news, congratulations, you really deserve it.' Lindsay knew how hard her friend had worked. 'I was the first in, so I've no other news to report. By the way, we're all going out tomorrow night for champagne and chips in that new bar off Grafton Street. It's really cool, so get your glad rags ready, girl. Now, I'm off to phone my mum, who's been doing a daily Novena for months.'

Lindsay's heart was beating furiously. It was getting closer. Please God, let it be OK, she prayed as she filled a piping-hot bath and added some calming essential oils, having promised to ring Carrie immediately she'd heard. She watched TV but didn't see a thing and fell asleep thinking about the incident with Chris Keating and hoping it wouldn't go against her.

At exactly nine-thirty next morning Lindsay took a deep breath, said a quick Hail Mary and entered the Course Director's office. She looked down just to reassure herself that her heart was definitely not visible through her thin white cotton shirt, because it was banging on her chest so hard that she feared it might just suddenly pop out. She wore black, fitted, pinstripe trousers and had pulled her hair back severely in an effort to look businesslike, adding only a sheer, creamy foundation, terracotta blusher, lashings of mascara and a translucent lip potion. She smiled brightly at the man behind the desk, knowing she wasn't fooling anyone.

'Sit down, please.' He gestured to a soft leather chair. 'I'll get straight to the point and put you out of your misery. We took a chance including you on this course, in fact you were probably the least experienced participant overall and we did worry that your lack of understanding of the television medium would prove to be too much of a disadvantage. In the early stages there were one or two incidents that almost convinced me we were right to be concerned, so I have watched your progress very carefully indeed. I was particularly interested to hear the report of the other tutors and get a reaction to your final project.'

Lindsay now feared her heart had given up the ghost altogether. She suddenly felt very cold.

'I must tell you that you can feel very proud of

yourself because the feedback has been almost entirely positive and your programme was in the top three most-promising ideas. Congratulations, we'd like to offer you a contract.'

The coldness disappeared and she was on fire. She knew she had tears in her eyes and couldn't do anything except bite her lip and try not to sniffle.

He went on to give her detailed feedback but Lindsay didn't hear a word. She struggled to hold it together.

'We've thought about your assignment carefully and we'd like you to work on *Live from Dublin*.' She stared at him stupidly.

'How would you feel about that?' He paused. She nodded even more stupidly.

'I realize we're taking a chance putting someone so inexperienced straight in at the deep end on our top-rated entertainment show, but I've spoken to the executive producer and he really liked your project and feels they need some fresh ideas, especially ones aimed at a younger audience. They were quite taken with your handling of the sex therapist item and are keen to have you on board. It's a very prestigious assignment, so I hope you're happy.'

He talked a little longer about how he would keep in touch and also about a review of her performance in six months but she could barely hear him. She'd gone through every scenario in the last twenty-four hours, from outright rejection to scraping through to getting an OK reaction but never, ever, in her wildest dreams did she imagine that she would pass with flying colours and be sent to work on the best TV show in the country.

She stood up quickly as she realized Michael was standing over her with his hand outstretched. 'Congratulations, you did very well, we're all delighted.'

He had to usher her out because she was suddenly incapable of any movement.

She remembered walking slowly to her car, calmly getting in and then suddenly screaming.

'Yes, yes, yes. Yeeeeeees.' She burst out laughing, thumped the steeringwheel, banged her feet and tried to do a little dance – sitting down, on her own, in broad daylight. She had to tell somebody.

Debbie. Voice mail.

Carrie. 'The Vodaphone customer you are calling may be out of—'

Tara. In a meeting.

Her mum. No reply.

She panicked and rang Tara's secretary back. 'Please can you disturb her? It's urgent.'

'Lindsay, are you OK. What's up?' Tara, at last, sounding concerned.

'I got it, I got it. Can you believe it? They thought I did brilliantly and they want me.'

Tara screamed, oblivious to the stares of her poker-faced colleagues. 'Oh my God, that is so cool.'

'Sorry, I just had to tell somebody.' Lindsay couldn't stop laughing.

'I'll call you the minute I get out of this, but well done, babe, that is just the best news.'

For an hour Lindsay sat in her car until she got everyone. Debbie couldn't really hear her but screamed anyway, picking up the vibe, and her mum sounded a bit teary, which was most unusual. Carrie couldn't believe her assignment. Her sister Anne said she never doubted it. Lindsay had a slight moment of regret that she didn't have Paul to share it with but she pushed the thought firmly away. This was her moment, only hers, and nothing was going to get in the way of this feeling. It was a once-in-a-lifetime achievement, against all the odds of the past few months and she intended to savour it, revel in it, indulge herself like never before. Best of all were the emotions it brought back that she thought had been lost forever – confidence, the feeling of being wanted, even of being worthwhile. It was a blissful moment and it gave her an incredible high.

She raced to reward herself, facial, eyebrow trim, nails, even deciding to have the famous St Tropez, a fake tan treatment beloved of Posh Spice and Kylie Minogue and a myriad other celebrities, if you believed the hype. Then she pulled her hair out of the rather severe knot and had it blow-dried so that it cascaded like crumpled silk around her. Next stop Grafton Street, where she bought an amazing outfit – coffee-coloured, silk, laced bodice with a sheer, long, plum-brown, chiffon almost-see-through skirt and a soft, oversized, unstructured, velvet jacket that had no buttons and wrapped itself around her. A truck load of new make-up from Mac, Eve Lom cleanser and the sexiest flesh-coloured underwear completed her purchases. She refused to feel even slightly guilty over the amount she'd spent in a couple of hours and sent up another prayer of thanks to her father for leaving her so well provided for. She felt simply amazing. She was heading for the car park when Tara called back.

'Where are you, can we meet?'

'I've just bought the most fantastic clothes, make-up and underwear and I'm looking for somebody to have a glass of champagne with, although this high cannot possibly be improved upon.' She laughed for the hundredth time that day.

'Oh and by the way I'm not telling you my assignment until you have a drink in your hand.'

'See you in the Shelbourne in fifteen minutes,' Tara giggled like a two-year-old and Lindsay spent the next hour with one of her two best friends, eating silky smooth pâté with hot buttery toast and drinking ice-cold champagne. Debbie rang from Luton airport in the middle of it and her screams could be heard throughout the entire Horseshoe bar. People stared and they both collapsed with laughter as a crystal-clear picture of Debbie dancing a jig somewhere in London crossed their minds.

This day simply could not get any better.

Chapter Ten

At eight-thirty that evening Lindsay hopped out of a taxi at the ultra-cool Cleo's Bar and ran inside to meet her friends. It was a cold, wet and windy December evening but she didn't notice. She glowed as she joined the gang. Nobody really knew the other assignments, although each had told the one or two people they had become closest to on the course. Lindsay was a bit apprehensive, wondering who hadn't got a job and thinking how they might be feeling tonight. As it turned out, the four people who hadn't been offered jobs were put on a panel for future contracts, partly because the station had already invested heavily in them. Two of them were quite happy as they were still studying, one full time and one part time. Angie, the third person, worked as a pharmacist in her parents' chemist and would stay on there until called, which sort of suited her as her parents were elderly but Tom, a quiet, deep-thinking, intelligent but very serious guy, was devastated and was the only one not to join them.

Lindsay hadn't got to know him very well but knew he was quite nervous, which probably didn't suit the temperament required to work in TV. Nevertheless, she felt very lucky to be one of the ones celebrating tonight.

To her amazement, everyone seemed delighted to hear her assignment and wished her well and said she deserved it. It was so weird, because they'd all been so competitive. She was dying to hear all the other news. Two people were sent to Current Affairs, one was delirious and one was suicidal, which made them all laugh and Serena, a tall, willowy, sexy, blonde who'd blown them all away by doing a cookery programme as her final project, had been sent to develop a new food series for children. She was delighted, which amazed them even further. Lindsay couldn't get enough of the banter. For the first time she felt she had a right to talk about it all because she was suddenly part of it.

Cleo's specialized in serving 'plain' food with a twist, such as fish and chips (plump, juicy tiger prawns grilled with garlic and chilli, served with fat, crunchy, home-made wedges) and bangers and mash (thick, herby, pork sausages made on the premises with red onion jus and fluffy, buttery potatoes), all superbly cooked using only the best ingredients. The food was served with stunning wines, all sold by the glass, as well as champagne and the trendiest beers. Everything cost a fortune and attracted the movers and shakers, the top notch amongst Dublin's wealthiest, coolest people. It was Lindsay's first time there and it felt fantastic. She revelled in the atmosphere, soaking it up like a sponge and determined to get the most out of every minute. This was her moment and she'd waited a long time for it, fearing it might never come again.

They decided to go for broke, on the strength of their new salaries – the details of which Lindsay had completely forgotten to ask – and agreed to drink only champagne for the evening, refusing even to think about the fact that most of them would be earning less money and should be cutting back.

Lindsay, however, for the first time in ages, didn't need anything to keep her on a high, although she polished off the first glass of bubbly fairly smartly and wandered around, laughing and smiling and having a ball. She felt fantastic in her new clothes but was clever enough to realize that her real feelings of well-being came from within herself. She was so thankful that she'd survived the past few months and somehow come out the other end with a spanking new career. It also helped that she knew she was looking as good as she possibly could, which she hadn't done in ages. Someone had cleverly booked one long table and they all kept changing seats as they tucked in to gorgeous food and drank gallons of cool froth. The noise level was deafening and the mood was bordering on manic.

About ten o'clock, as she wandered to the loo, Lindsay heard a voice call her name. She turned to find Dan Pearson, the floor manager who'd saved her life on that fateful night in the Newsroom, smiling at her.

'Wow, you look much less terrified than the last time I saw you.' He smiled at her warmly, taking in the sparkling eyes, shining hair and soft, sexy clothes. She hugged him spontaneously.

'Guess what, in spite of it all I passed,' she laughed up at him. 'Can you believe it? They actually offered me a job.'

'I never doubted it, I know talent the minute I see it,' he teased. 'So, you're celebrating?'

'Yep, I'm having an absolutely brilliant day, the best.' She grinned foolishly, which made her look young and innocent, like a child in a sweetshop.

'What about you? What are you doing here?' she asked shyly, conscious that she didn't really know him at all and she'd just given him a bear-hug.

'Chris and I have just finished an interview with the Taoiseach.' He nodded at the man who'd just joined them. 'We called in here for a bite to eat and a glass of wine. Very trendy, I must say, although Chris tells me it's not always quite so full of the beautiful people.'

Lindsay turned, in spite of herself, and found herself staring into the face of the man she'd hoped never to have to look at again, except perhaps on television and even then only on a bad night's viewing.

'Hi.' It came out as a squeak.

'Hello, Chris Keating,' he smiled as he held out his hand, obviously not realizing they'd met before, which made it even worse, if that were possible. He was taller than she remembered and he was formally dressed, presumably because of his interview with the Prime Minister. He wore a dark grey suit that was wool but looked expensive enough to be silk and with it a snow-white shirt and understated tie. His look screamed effortless, partly because his hair was unfashionably long for his clean-cut image and his too-blue eyes and tanned skin meant he obviously spent a lot of time not wearing a suit. The combination was quite something. Dan had clearly decided that the only thing to do in this situation was to jump in straightaway.

'You two have met before, but obviously neither of you made much of an impression on the other, or at least not the kind you want to remember. Not tonight, anyway,' he grinned at Lindsay, ignoring her strangled half laugh.

Chris Keating looked at her intently.

Please let him not recognize me, Lindsay prayed, at least until I can make my excuses and scarper. At that precise moment Carrie joined them to talk to Dan, whom she'd also met on her attachment and discovered was from her neighbouring parish at home in the country. They hugged like long-lost friends and started chatting furiously, leaving Lindsay staring stupidly and Chris looking puzzled.

'Do you work at the station?' he asked. 'Dan knows everyone, so it's great to come out with him, otherwise I end up on my own in a corner.' She didn't believe him for a second but continued to stare at him like an imbecile, afraid to speak in case he recognized her voice, which she knew was ridiculous.

'Yes, just started,' she croaked after what seemed like five minutes. 'I'm going to work on *Live from*

Dublin on Tuesday.' She couldn't for the life of her think of anything else to say.

'As what?'

'Assistant Producer.'

'Oh, you must have been on the course . . .' His voice trailed off and she knew he knew. He kept looking at her face. 'In fact, I've just remembered you're probably the only person in the world to whom I should grovel and then apologize profusely.' He stared at her intently, as if making sure she was the one. 'I was extremely rude to you one night in the News studio and I should have dropped you a note to say sorry.' He sort of grinned at her and looked a bit unsure at the same time and she was amazed at how different he seemed, hardly recognizable yet so well known to her, as he was to most of the nation.

'I had just come back from a really long trip and badly needed my sleep, which makes me grumpy at the best of times, when I got a call to go into work to record a promo. Unfortunately, you snatched my duvet from me just when it was within my grasp and I reacted badly. I'm really sorry, I'm not usually so rude.'

Lindsay, who wasn't normally lost for words, was speechless. She'd built him up in her head as a monster, partly because she thought he had the power to destroy her longed-for career before it had even started. She'd been prepared for anything if she ever came face to face with him again, but not for this.

'Well, you were pretty hard on me but what I did

was incredibly stupid and you taught me a lesson I'll never forget. I thought I hated you but I guess it's OK.' She shrugged, amazed again at the way this day was going. 'In fact, it's definitely OK because I'm having the best day ever and nothing is going to spoil it.'

Carrie had dragged Dan off to meet some of the gang and Lindsay waited for Chris to make his excuses and go off to join any one of a dozen groups of people he probably knew, but to her surprise he called a waiter and asked if he could buy her a drink.

'No, it's fine, I'm with everyone over there.' She felt a bit foolish, not sure why he was doing this when he was probably dying to get away.

'I insist, what are you having?'

'Only champagne tonight, I'm afraid. I'm celebrating,' she apologized.

'Fine and I'll have a glass of anything white and cold and dry,' he smiled at the waiter. 'Thanks.'

'So, when did the course finish and how did you get assigned to the number-one programme?' he asked and to her amazement, actually looked interested. She thought celebrities were only interested in talking about themselves. Half an hour later they were deep in conversation when Dan returned with Carrie and announced that they were off for 'some real food'. Lindsay looked at her friend and saw that her eyes were shining.

She laughed and gave her a hug. 'Talk to you on Tuesday.' Lindsay was delighted to see Carrie looking so happy. Come to think of it, Dan didn't look too unhappy either. To Lindsay's surprise, Chris didn't make any attempt to use the opportunity to leave, just continued talking to her. She felt vaguely uncomfortable. He was famous, for God's sake. He'd made enough small talk to be able to acquit himself decently and he'd paid a fortune for a glass of bubbly. He just kept asking her questions, which she found quite disconcerting.

They chatted on for ages and somewhere during the banter the atmosphere changed between them and Lindsay started thinking about sex.

With him.

About kissing him. Touching him. Holding him. Having him do the same to her.

Oh my God, what are you like, she berated herself. Women must think like this every night of the week. He's probably married, or at the very least must have a girlfriend.

But somehow, she didn't think so and she didn't know why or how she knew. Maybe it was something to do with the way he was looking at her. On second thoughts that could be the hazy glow created by the bubbles.

She wondered what he'd say if he knew what she was thinking. Suddenly she wanted mad, passionate, brilliant sex. With no complications. No being in love and wondering if he felt the same. Worrying about whether he'd go off you like your mother always said men do. Convinced he wouldn't call you. Dithering over whether to let him know how you felt. Afraid it might frighten him away. Unable to be yourself. Lindsay suddenly realized she'd never had that kind of relationship. A no-strings-attached, good-looking, intelligent, funny, great fling. She wasn't that type of girl. Men didn't fantasize about her. No one had ever said they wanted to tear off her clothes and have dirty, filthy, raw sex with her. Yes of course she'd had lots of great sex, but it had never come out of the blue. And never on a first date.

Hell, this wasn't even remotely a date. Barely a meeting, really.

For Lindsay, the pattern had always been the same. Meet man. Fancy man. Get asked out. Or not. Wait for him to call. Go out to dinner, kiss good night. Wait for him to call. Get to know him slowly. After a while have (sometimes great) sex. Sometimes not so great. Fall in love. Or think you are in love. Or pretend to be in love. Have a great time. Get your heart broken. Or break one or two yourself.

Suddenly the whole man-woman situation seemed ludicrous and she had a mad desire to rewrite the rulebook. For a start she'd settle for great sex and to hell with being in love. Or even getting to know him. At that moment, standing there beside him in the middle of a crowded bar, she didn't care, she just knew she didn't want him to go.

This crazy, ingenious idea of hers had one major point in its favour. It would be the final nail in Paul's coffin. There'd be nothing left to remind her once she'd had sex with someone else. And what a someone else to have sex with.

'Hi, Lindsay. Bet you're glad the course is over.'

She suddenly realized they'd been joined by a

couple of people from the Newsroom, including some of the nine o'clock team whom she'd worked with on the famous 'red light' night. Everyone seemed to be talking at once, laughing, ordering drinks, teasing. To her surprise, Chris made no attempt to move away from her and included her in his conversation. She knew she should make herself scarce and she edged towards the ladies, about to make her getaway.

'Look, do you fancy getting out of here and going somewhere less noisy? It's just a bit too poser-ish for me,' Chris whispered and grinned apologetically as he waited for her response. Again she thought he looked a bit unsure of himself although she knew it must be her imagination. She looked away quickly, as if she already knew what she was going to say and mentally made a last-ditch, futile attempt to dump the crazy notion before it was too late.

She didn't know how it got out of her mouth but somehow it escaped and though she immediately tried to rescue it, it hung in the air between them for an eternity. No amount of the sparkly stuff could be blamed on this one. It was the most outrageous thing she had ever said to a stranger.

'What I'd really like to do is go somewhere quiet. And talk. And touch you. And have you touch me.' Her voice was barely audible. She didn't look at him. Not yet. He had bent down to ask his question and she saw that he was still in the same position, his head close to hers. She could smell him. She didn't move. He stayed where he was.

Lindsay couldn't believe what she'd just said.

Hell, she wasn't even sure she fancied him really. No, that was a lie. She definitely fancied him.

He stared at her for ages. She could feel him staring and she knew she couldn't keep looking everywhere but at him.

She nearly missed his reply.

'Me too.'

Chapter Eleven

Lindsay grabbed her bag and they left quickly, not saying anything further. She was convinced she was dreaming.

'Would you like to come back to my place?'

'No.'

'OK then, any ideas?'

'I think it should be somewhere that's not familiar to either of us.'

No memories, was what she really wanted to say.

If he thought she was absolutely barking then he was a very good actor.

'Right then, let's think about this. It doesn't leave us with a lot of options. Even if I had my car, I'm definitely familiar with it. And there aren't too many public places where you can touch and be touched without them calling the police.' She could feel him smiling at her. Just for an instant she wondered if she was, in fact, crazy. He seemed to sense something.

'I could ring my friend Maurice, who's the manager of the Shrewsbury Hotel and see if he has a room? And we don't have to stay all night unless we want to. Let's just go there, have a drink and talk, OK?'

'Fine.' Lindsay tried to look nonchalant as they strolled through the cold, wet Dublin streets. 'At least it's stopped raining, we won't get wet,' she said sensibly, which was ludicrous, given their not very sensible plans.

Chris took out his phone and dialled what she thought was a mobile number. After a short conversation he turned to her.

'OK, he says it's not a problem. Do you mind walking?'

'No, that's fine.' She looked away quickly, not wanting him to see that she was suddenly scared.

To her surprise he continued their conversation as if it was a completely normal thing to be walking to a hotel with a total stranger. She took her cue from him and decided to pretend – at least until they arrived at the hotel, which turned out to be one of Dublin's most exclusive.

The receptionist didn't seem remotely surprised to see them and greeted them both warmly, ignoring the lack of luggage. No, not even a tooth-brush, Lindsay wished she had the courage to say it.

'Mr Dowling asked me to look after your food and drink order,' the porter explained, as if all this was quite commonplace.

'Maurice,' Chris explained as they were shown to their room, which turned out to be a magnificent suite on the top floor, bigger than the whole of Lindsay's house.

'Would you like some food?' Chris asked as the porter hovered. She shook her head, suddenly feeling nervous and a bit sick.

'We'll have a bottle of champagne and . . . erm . . . some er . . . strawberries.'

'Thank you, sir. I'll have them sent right up and if you need anything else there will be someone on duty at the porter's desk all night.'

'Strawberries?' Lindsay couldn't help asking as the porter made a discreet exit.

Chris grinned at her and again, he looked slightly vulnerable. She liked it.

'Yeah, it's the only thing I remember from that godawful movie with your woman with the teeth, when Richard Gere brought her back to his suite . . . you know, the . . . er—'

'Prostitute.' Lindsay didn't know whether to be insulted at that, or take it as a compliment that he wanted to impress her.

'God, every woman I knew, including my mother, dragged me along to see that one. By the way, I wasn't implying anything about you, you know . . .'

'Sure.'

He grinned at her. 'I've been waiting for an opportunity to try it out to see if it would impress, though. I can see it was wasted on you. And these kind of situations don't happen to me often, as you can probably tell, given that it must be ten years since I've seen the movie. Sad, eh? Come to think of it, you do look a bit like Julia Roberts.' It was the nicest comparison she'd ever had, even if it was a downright lie. And she didn't believe for one second that he hadn't had a million chances to try it out on someone before now, but she liked him for saying it.

'Well, thankfully, you look nothing like Richard Gere, or all the Dom P in the world wouldn't have dragged me up here. I'm more a Johnny Depp girl.'

'So why did you come?' She'd walked into that one. A discreet knock saved her. Chris opened the door to the waiter who left a giant silver tray on the nearest table. It was dominated by a huge cut-glass bowl of strawberries so perfect they looked waxy. Some had been dipped in thick, velvety chocolate and it added to the surreal appearance of the platter. A bottle of champagne nestled in a huge ice bucket almost overflowing with cubes. Two delicate, long-stemmed glasses and snow-white napkins stood to attention and the tray held a collection of tiny creamy porcelain dishes of nibbles – toasty, salty nuts, lurid green olives and even a little bowl of fluffy pink marshmallows, complete with a long toasting fork.

'What on earth are you supposed to do with this?' Lindsay was intrigued. 'You need a fire to be able to toast marshmallows.'

'Will this do?' Chris had left the hallway to explore and had opened the double doors to a sitting room. A big, squashy couch with about a hundred soft, fat cushions dominated the room, which also housed a large Georgian fireplace with a huge metal basket in the grate, where a sub-stantial log fire was crackling away merrily.

'How on earth did they get that going in the

twenty minutes since we rang?' Lindsay couldn't believe it.

'All part of the service, ma'am.' Chris was clearly delighted. 'God, I'll be doing favours for Maurice for years to make up for this.'

It was a beautiful room, with a line of creamy candles burning on the wide mantelpiece that was dominated by an intricately carved gilt mirror. The floor was covered in several old gold rugs. A drinks cabinet and a huge TV and video were evident yet discreet and there seemed to be flowers everywhere, masses of white lilies in balloon-like vases and scented hyacinths, seasonal at this time of year, in baskets. The overall effect was opulent yet charming, expensive but homely, something rarely achieved in modern hotel rooms, at least not the ones Lindsay was used to.

Chris appeared suddenly with the tray. 'OK, let's see if champagne really does taste better with strawberries.' He smiled, setting the tray down on the floor in front of the fire and pulling a big cushion down beside it. 'You look freezing, sure you wouldn't rather have a hot whiskey?'

'No, I told you, champagne only tonight.' She plonked herself down on the cushion before she fell down with nervous tension. Suddenly she needed something to pep her up because for all her bravado earlier she now felt terrified. They both tried a strawberry and as she bit into the soft watery red flesh and sipped the chilled wine she tried to think sanely. She could make some excuse, pretend she'd been a bit drunk earlier and leg it.

'Well,' Chris sat on the sofa and looked at her

with amusement. 'You have juice all over your chin. Is it worth it?'

She hadn't even tasted the strawberry, so intent was she on getting to the bubbles to give her Dutch courage. 'I'll have to try at least one more before I decide.' She was waffling as she popped one of the chocolate ones into her mouth, swallowed it whole and had to drink most of the champagne to avoid choking.

'What are you like.' He slid down beside her and patted her back, then took a napkin and wiped her mouth. She was mortified and before she had time to recover he leaned over and kissed her, softly at first and then more urgently, but still slowly as if they had all the time in the world. Just as she realized what was happening he stopped.

'Bite, chew and sip,' he grinned, handing her another one and refilling her glass. He sipped his and watched her. She tried to remain cool as she bit and then forgot to chew, swallowing half a strawberry, which immediately stuck in her throat. She decided to leave it there and keep drinking, anything to avoid looking at him. Unfortunately, it didn't stop her feeling him near. He was very close and in that moment, with the warmth of the fire and soft light of the candles, it suddenly felt OK. Mad, insane, incredible, ridiculous but OK.

She felt a hand under her chin, forcing her to look up. 'Tell me a secret,' he smiled at her.

'A secret?' She didn't quite understand.

'Yes, you know what a secret is.' He wouldn't let her off the hook.

'OK, a secret is that I haven't a clue what I'm

doing here and I can't believe I said what I did to you in the bar. I'm sure it happens to you all the time but I've never done it before. And now it's very scary. And very exciting. Now, you tell me one.'

'I fancied you the minute I saw you tonight and I was wondering if you'd agree to come out with me when you said what you did. This is much more than I'd hoped for.'

Suddenly she wanted desperately to kiss him properly and he must have had the same idea because they met somewhere in the middle and it was as if they couldn't get close enough to each other. They kissed for what seemed like an hour and she was surprised to find that she made the next move. She couldn't seem to stop herself tugging at his jacket and slipping her hands in under his shirt. He felt cool and lean and hard. She had to see him, so she took off his jacket and he loosened his tie and she unbuttoned his shirt and he felt gorgeous. She kissed his stomach and his neck and his ears and he let her. He ran his fingers through her hair and traced a line down her neck and around her throat and looked at her strangely with the bluest eyes.

'You're beautiful.' He smiled at her and she wanted desperately for him to touch her but he just continued to look.

'I want you to touch me.'

'Where?' He kept his eyes on her face.

'Everywhere.'

She slipped off her soft velvet jacket to reveal her tanned shoulders and long bare arms. Her bustier made her boobs look bigger and her shoulders broader and with her long dark hair cascading down her back she felt sexy and powerful as she led him back onto the sofa and straddled him, playing with the ribbon front of her top, making to undo it but leaving it for him. She wanted to feel her bare skin next to his. He kissed the top of her shoulders and every bit of exposed skin before he very gently tugged at the ribbon and undid each hook, revealing her shape a little at a time and kissing each bit he saw.

'I want to look at you,' he told her, standing up and pulling her with him as the bustier gave way, revealing her soft, warm, rounded breasts.

They were facing the huge picture window and the moonlight flooded in, silhouetting her voluptuous shape, with the contours of her bottom and legs only half hidden under the chiffon skirt. He knelt in front of her and moved his hands slowly up her legs, feeling the satiny smoothness of her tights and breathing harder when he came to the thick lace top that told him they were, in fact, stockings.

He unhooked her skirt and let it fall and she stood before him all legs and breasts with only the flimsiest bits of nylon and lace protecting her and she felt beautiful.

'My God,' he grinned at her, 'you are one incredible woman.'

He stood and pulled her to him and she could feel him through his trousers and she wanted to touch him more than anything so she moved away slightly and never took her eyes off his face as she plunged her hands inside his trousers, desperate to feel if he wanted her as much as she wanted him. He groaned and threw his head back and she got down on her knees and kissed him everywhere, exposing him, eager to see him naked for the first time. He did the same and suddenly they were glued together feeling skin on skin, revelling in each other's nakedness and beauty.

You are one gorgeous man, Lindsay thought, staring at him unashamedly.

'Tell me another secret.' He was watching her closely. She held his gaze.

'I'm wondering what it will be like to feel you inside me.'

His eyes darkened. She pulled away and took a sip of champagne. 'Tell me one.'

'I'm hoping I don't disappoint you.' She laughed, delighted that he was able to admit it.

'Somehow, I don't think disappointment is on the menu tonight. Anyway, I'm more scared than you so let's take it slowly, otherwise I might run away.'

He moved the tray and took her hand. They lay in front of the fire and kissed and touched and explored for ages before she surprised him by climbing on top of him in such a way that he seemed to shoot inside her. They both gasped at the sensation and he pushed her back to look at her, each of them afraid to move, knowing they couldn't hold on much longer yet wanting to savour the moment. She thought he had the longest legs and the sexiest stomach as he lay underneath her with his piercing blue eyes and strong beautiful face and then he laid her down and kissed her everywhere from her little toe to her ear lobes until she was laughing and crying and sweating and writhing and begging him to stop and pleading with him not to.

It was four a.m. when they finally got enough of each other and they snogged and drank some more champagne and finally got to toast the marshmallows on the still smouldering fire. Then they cleaned their teeth with their fingers and Lindsay tried out the complimentary cleanser and moisturizer and anything else she could find before pulling on the softest white towelling robe and jumping into the huge old bed beside him. Lindsay sank into the feather pillows, he pulled the eiderdown up around them and they said very little. She fell asleep thinking what an incredible night it had been.

Chapter Twelve

'Oh my God, Charlie.' Lindsay didn't realize she'd said it aloud until a sleepy voice asked, 'Who the hell is Charlie?'

Oh my God, Chris, was Lindsay's second, silent thought. She didn't know which was more worrying but she definitely knew which was the most important right now. She leapt out of bed, pushing back her tangled hair and glanced at the clock as she tried to dial a number and nonchalantly shrug on her robe at the same time, hoping he hadn't seen her undignified exit.

'Tara, it's me. I need a favour. Could you go over to my house and rescue Charlie?'

'Who's Charlie, for God's sake?' Chris was sitting up now.

'Who's that, for God's sake?' Tara was all ears.

'Can you do it?' was all that mattered right at this minute.

'Yes, but where are you? How did the night go? This must mean you didn't make it home. What happened? I insist you tell me everything.'

'I'll talk to you later,' Lindsay sounded sheepish. 'Are you sure you can get him now?'

'On my way, you just caught me going out the door. I presume you want me to feed him and let him out for a run. Will I take him back to my place just in case?' Tara was teasing.

'Yes,' Lindsay just wanted to get off the phone, conscious that Chris was looking on with some amusement and she knew she must look wrecked. Besides she needed water and coffee badly. 'Thanks, I'll ring you later.' Lindsay hung up.

'My dog, I left him in the kitchen all night and it's twelve o'clock and he'll be chewing the leg off the table to get out for a pee.' Lindsay bolted for the bathroom herself, where she managed to splash some water on her face and clean her teeth with her finger again, drinking a gallon of tap water whether it was safe to do so or not.

She emerged looking only slightly more together, running her hands through her tangled mop.

Chris was on the phone, ordering breakfast. 'I just ordered everything they had,' he grinned at her and patted the side of the bed next to him.

What the hell am I doing here, looking like something the cat dragged in, with Chris Keating of all people? Lindsay moved slowly towards him and sat down, surprised in a way that he'd bothered to order food, convinced he'd want to make his escape and mutter something about calling her.

'How are you feeling?'

'A little bit seedy and a good bit shell-shocked.'

'OK, breakfast and then a walk, that'll sort you out.'

'I've no clothes.' Lindsay couldn't believe her ears. 'How the hell can I go for a walk in stilettos and a see-through skirt and bustier?'

'Point taken.' He looked at her solemnly. She felt like bursting into tears, for no reason.

'I know, Maurice keeps a room here, he's bound to have some clothes. Otherwise I'll go out and buy you some. At least my suit isn't transparent.'

Of all the stupid things I've done, this has to rate in the top three, she thought, suddenly feeling very awkward with him.

'Back in a sec.' He headed towards the bathroom, sensing she needed time to herself.

Lindsay crawled back under the covers and propped herself up, glad that the room was still dark with the heavy drapes drawn.

'OK, let's talk.' Chris yanked back the curtains, letting the pale grey December light invade her safe corner.

A knock on the door meant breakfast, interrupting their potential heart to heart. Chris carried the giant tray over to the bed and got in beside her. She took one look and burst out laughing.

'What? Well, I didn't know what you liked so I ordered the lot.' He wasn't lying. A pitcher of freshly squeezed juice and a bowl of the most exotic fresh fruit, everything from lychees to mangos, apricots to figs sat next to a mound of golden toast wrapped in a napkin and a basket filled with croissants, pancakes, muffins and scones.

She lifted a lid to reveal fat sausages, runny eggs,

bright red tomatoes and crispy bacon. A huge silver pot of tea and a jug of frothy coffee sat beside dishes of creamy butter and sweet-smelling jams, honey and even maple syrup. She suddenly realized she was ravenous.

'Mind if I check the news heads?' he asked.

She shook her head with a mouth full of pancake. She just couldn't resist. It all smelt so delicious, sort of home-made, with vanilla and sugar wafting up from the still-warm pastries and breads. A bit of mental space was exactly what she needed and the sharp juice and soothing tea helped clear her head. They ate in silence, watching the news stories of the morning and tucking in to the feast.

'It feels like a picnic.' Lindsay felt more relaxed now. She cast a surreptitious glance at him. How come men always look the same, whereas women looked wrecked in the morning, she wondered.

'What's up?' he asked without looking at her.

'What on earth are we doing here, in bed at midday on Saturday in one of the most expensive hotels in Dublin?'

'Eating breakfast and watching Sky News. Seems OK to me. What would you be doing otherwise?'

'Oh, something equally exotic like putting out the bins or picking up dog pooh,' she laughed, realizing how ridiculous the whole thing was. 'How about you?'

'Working or sleeping or reading the papers. So, it's not that different. I presume you don't have to work today?'

'No, not till Tuesday morning. How about you?'

'Not officially, but I need to check in with the office, just in case. My mobile's been off, but it doesn't look as if there's much happening.' He jumped out of bed and switched on the phone, quickly checking his messages.

'Great, nothing. So, let's make a plan.'

'Isn't this where we get dressed and part and make a big deal about exchanging phone numbers?' Suddenly she wanted to get it over with.

'I don't really know because this is not my usual morning-after-the-first-date scenario. Why don't we go for a walk and take it as it comes?'

'I'd like that, with some warm clothes, but don't we have to be out of here?'

'First things first.' He dialled a number quickly.

'Maurice, how's it going? OK. Listen, thanks for the room, it's really great. Do you need us out, or could we stay tonight if we wanted to?' He wasn't looking at her again.

'Sure. By the way, do you have a couple of pairs of jeans and shirts we could borrow? Oh and a pair of shoes that aren't stilettos? Size five I'd say.' He glanced at her.

'Seven.'

'Or maybe a bit bigger.' He laughed. 'Of course I mean yours, I'm not asking you to go shopping. Where are you at the moment?' Chris turned to Lindsay. 'He's here.'

'I don't want to meet him,' she said quickly, afraid he was going to suggest Maurice come to the room.

'Give me fifteen minutes to have a shower and I'll meet you at your room. What number? . . . OK, great, see you then.' Lindsay looked up at him.

'Don't worry, I wasn't going to embarrass you. I'll hop into the shower and go and see what he has, then we can decide. Would that be all right?'

She nodded.

'Oh and by the way, it's fine if we want to stay here again tonight, although I'm not taking anything for granted, OK?'

Was he crazy, Lindsay wondered. It was one thing putting last night down to alcohol or passion or madness or a combination of all three, but now they were sober and they'd had sex and he'd seen her without her make-up, for Christ's sake. Surely this wasn't the logical next step?

Ten minutes later he'd showered and dressed and he looked exactly what he was, confident and vibrant and successful.

'Back in ten minutes,' he announced. 'You OK?'

'Fine.' Lindsay was up and halfway to the bathroom as she spoke, having made an instant decision to go with the flow.

She showered until her skin hurt, with her hair piled up to avoid having to wash and dry it, then rooted in her bag for her emergency supplies – foundation, blusher, mascara and lip gloss – which she applied with vigour, wishing she had half a ton of concealer to hide the bags under her eyes.

Suddenly there was a knock on the bathroom door. She hadn't heard him come back.

He was grinning although he gave her a funny look when he saw her.

'You look like a little girl, caught stealing her mother's make-up.'

The big white robe made her look smaller and she always felt like she was play-acting when she piled her hair on top of her head, so she knew what he meant.

'I'll take that as a compliment, especially as I feel about ninety, too much alcohol and too little sleep.'

'Still, all that exercise would have helped your figure.' She felt her face going red.

He looked as if was going to kiss her but then he suddenly became all businesslike.

'He doesn't have much, most of the stuff he keeps here are suits and shirts and ties, for meetings and business dinners, but I got you these jeans and a belt to keep them up, plus a big denim shirt and a warm outdoor jacket. Oh, and these trainers and thick socks. Me, I'm going to have to wear my suit although I did get a loan of a clean shirt that I can wear without a tie so that I won't look a complete prat, out for a walk on Saturday in a suit and tie.'

Lindsay couldn't help laughing at the ridiculousness of it all as she got dressed. She had no underwear, no toothbrush and was wearing a complete stranger's clothes. A man's clothes at that.

'Ready.'

She was still laughing as she emerged and used his tie to hold back her hair.

They headed out of the hotel, giggling in case anyone noticed them, or worse recognized him. Although they were only minutes from the centre of Dublin there was a magnificent park nearby and they walked for an hour in the almost deserted space, enjoying the crisp, bright afternoon. Anyone they did meet seemed to be related, families with small kids or older couples walking dogs, or grandparents with children and grandchildren. It made their relationship, or lack of it, seem strange.

'You know, I've spent the last sixteen or so hours with you and I know absolutely nothing about you,' Chris said suddenly, as if the thought had just occurred to him.

'I don't even know where you live, or if you have family, or even how old you are.'

So they walked and talked and she told him about her little Victorian cottage in Ranelagh, about her mother and her sister Anne and her two much-loved nephews. He laughed when she described Charlie and his antics and he asked about Tara, whom he'd heard her on the phone to, so she was quite happy to fill him in on Debbie as well, sharing some of their more tame adventures.

For his part, he told her he was from Galway, in the West of Ireland, where his mother and father still lived. His father was a surgeon and his mother a lecturer and he had no brothers and one younger and one older sister.

'Oh God, an Irish Mammy's only son, what a nightmare,' she teased him and he admitted that yes, she was probably slightly protective of him but he'd been away from home since college so she was now happy to let him lead his own life.

'Are you close?' she wanted to know, thinking of her own tightly knit yet slightly dysfunctional family.

'We're not on the phone every day but I see quite a bit of my parents. My sister Lisa lives in Australia at the moment so it's e-mail and the occasional phone call and Judy is here in Dublin so she cadges a meal off me every now and then when she's broke or has no guy in tow.'

'She's the younger one?' Lindsay wanted to know.

'Yeah, she's twenty-seven but still the baby, eight years younger than me and thinks all my friends are ancient. Lisa is still single as well and she's a year older than me. Luckily, my parents aren't worried that none of us are showing signs of wanting to settle down. I think they're both too busy with their own lives.'

They strolled and chatted and looked like any normal couple, Lindsay thought. He seemed relaxed and very ordinary. She kept waiting for the ego to appear, given his celebrity status, but it never showed up. She saw one or two people looking at him as they passed but he didn't seem to notice. For her part she was just very glad to have her Prada sunglasses. It made talking to him easier.

'Can't hide behind them forever,' he grinned as if reading her thoughts.

Chapter Thirteen

It was almost dark when they decided to head back to the hotel.

'What do you think about staying again tonight?' he asked her.

'OK,' she said simply, not looking at him. 'I just need to ring Tara and make sure she can keep Charlie, or at least give him to my mother, although that would raise too many questions, on second thoughts. My family are not as civilized as yours, I'm afraid, they all butt in whether you want them to or not.'

Suddenly, the pale, winter white sky turned to ashes and it started to rain so they kept under trees as much as possible on the way back, but still managed to get soaked as they ran the last quarter of a mile 'home'.

They were still laughing as they entered the room, wondering what on earth people had made of them as they ran through reception, Chris in his Armani suit and Lindsay with wet hair and wearing men's clothes. The room had been transformed again, with the heavy drapes pulled against the rain and increasing winds, fire burning brightly and lamps lit.

'Hot whiskies, I think, for medicinal reasons only.' Chris was already rooting around for the necessary ingredients in their well-stocked bar, which seemed to have everything. 'Dry your hair or you won't be starting work on Tuesday,' he ordered. 'And get out of some of those wet clothes.'

Lindsay was sitting on the floor, shoes and socks off, drying her hair in front of the huge log fire when he emerged with two cut-glass tumblers full of the warm golden liquid beloved of Dubliners during the winter months, with sugar and cloves and lemon slices. She shivered slightly as she drank the hot toddy. He knelt down beside her, gently took her glass away and put his arms around her, then he rubbed her back and dried her hair and held her until she lifted her face and he kissed her, slowly, a kiss that seemed to go on for ever. And when he stopped and looked at her she kissed him again and suddenly they were lying on the rug, he was peeling off her wet clothes and she was stroking him and kissing him lightly on his neck and shoulders and forehead and loosening his clothing . . . and the hot whiskies were abandoned.

It was dark as they lay, satisfied, in front of the blazing fire, grinning at each other like a couple of school kids.

'Know something? I never thought I'd say this again but I'm starving,' Lindsay announced.

'You've a great appetite, I'll say that for you,' he teased, and she threw a cushion at him, feeling a bit more confident in his company now.

'I'm not one of your usual model types, so I won't be having a salad for dinner.'

'I've never gone out with a "model type" as you put it. I'm well used to real women.' He winked at her knowingly.

They decided to order from room service and eat by the fire, so Lindsay got back into her fluffy white robe and they tucked into fillet steaks with a huge green salad and made no attempt to resist the myriad potato dishes and sauces that arrived with their meal. The waiter even laid a crisp, white tablecloth on the coffee table in front of the fire and lit candles and poured aubergine-coloured wine into tall, elegant glasses. They had skipped starters and decided instead to try a selection of desserts – all now winking at them from a side table, tiny lemon tarts, chocolate roulade, miniature crème brûlées and raspberry meringues. Despite Lindsay's moans about being stuffed, they managed, between chats and sips of wine and gulps of coffee, to polish off the lot. Then they curled up on the huge comfy sofa and watched a movie.

In the break Lindsay phoned Tara, who had indeed rescued Charlie, fed him and walked him and sneaked him in to her apartment where he was now lying directly up against the radiator in the kitchen, refusing to move.

'He thinks it's your version of an Aga.' Lindsay

laughed and managed to avoid Tara's amazed 'You won't be home tonight either' questions with lots of 'talk to you later' type answers.

By ten-thirty Lindsay could hardly keep her eyes open so they watched the end of the movie in bed and when Chris teased her about the 'girlie' ending he found her fast asleep, propped up against the pillows.

She woke early the next morning and this time waking up beside him didn't feel so strange. Before she had a chance to sneak out of bed to see if she looked even half decent, Chris had slipped his arms around her from behind. Once again their lovemaking was different as they teased and explored, with Lindsay marvelling in her new-found confidence as she devoured his body. He told her again how beautiful she was and she believed him because somehow, since Friday, she felt good about herself for the first time in ages. It showed in her eyes, her face and her movements, her whole demeanour.

Chris had ordered all the Sunday papers, Irish and English, with breakfast so they stayed in bed, eating another huge meal and drinking masses of coffee and juice and reading each other bits from the papers aloud, which was one of the things that Lindsay had missed most when she and Paul had split up.

'Tell me a secret.' She looked up to find Chris watching her and something made her hesitate.

'I've no secrets left,' she laughed, not sure she was ready to tell him about her past life.

'Don't be ridiculous, we all have millions of secrets, thoughts we don't share. Go on, tell me a big one.'

She realized that she had nothing to lose. 'I was engaged until a couple of months ago, would have been just about married by now, except that I found out he was going to marry someone else.'

He looked at her for ages, it seemed. 'That's rough. How did you cope?'

'Very badly at the start. My friends mainly pulled me through it. And the new job helped a lot.' She gave him a wobbly smile. 'It was the worst thing that ever happened to me.'

'I'm sorry.'

'I'm OK now.'

'Do you still care about him?'

Lindsay wondered what the honest answer to that was. How to explain that some days she hardly thought about him at all and some nights she cried herself to sleep? How sometimes it just crept up on her and she felt so lonely for him. How she worried that she'd never feel like that again, ever.

'I met him recently in a restaurant and it didn't hurt as much as I thought it would. Then at other times, like reading the papers with you just now, I thought of him and it hurt. So yes, I suppose I do still have some feelings for him. I guess I always will.'

He reached over and pulled her close and just held her for a while, stroking her hair.

'Now, you tell me one.' She looked up at him expectantly.

'Well, this is probably not the right moment to

tell you but, erm, I have a date later with a girl I met last week. She's been working away for the past few days and I had arranged to have dinner with her tonight. I wanted to let you know, just in case . . . Dublin can be a small place sometimes.'

'Oh.' She didn't know what to say to him. It was strange to think of him with someone else, getting to know them, sharing secrets, maybe having sex. Just like the two of them, in fact. She wondered how she'd compare.

Don't even go there girl, a voice inside her head warned. This was only ever meant to be a one-night stand, another notch in the recovery process.

'Thanks for telling me.'

'That's OK. Are you all right about it?' He looked a bit embarrassed and she was glad he'd asked.

'Yeah.'

They went back to reading the papers but somehow she knew that both of their minds were elsewhere.

'Fancy some lunch?' he asked her after a while.

'Definitely not, I ate enough breakfast for three people. Anyway, I suppose we should make tracks and give them back their room.'

'Yeah, it's almost three o'clock, they'll think we've moved in permanently.'

'What will I do about Maurice's clothes? Can I wear them home and have them cleaned and send them back to him in a day or two?' Lindsay didn't feel like getting back into her party clothes.

'Sure, I'll let him know. I'll just take a quick shower and then I'll call him.'

'By the way, I'd like to contribute towards the cost of the room for the weekend.' She was adamant she wanted to pay her share.

'On the house.' She didn't believe him. 'Seriously, I spoke to him yesterday and our only cost is for food and I've already sorted that out. So, you get the next one, OK?' He grinned at her.

'OK.' This was not at all like her. Everything seemed to be 'OK'. She felt very relaxed, as if she'd known him for ages. While he called Maurice, Lindsay showered and combed her hair and re-paired whatever damage she could with her meagre supply of make-up.

They left with more clothes than when they arrived and strolled to a taxi rank together in the late December afternoon. He asked for her phone number and she gave her mobile but not her home number. She'd had enough experience of coming home nights wondering if there was a message. She wasn't ready to go down that road again yet. He gave her his mobile and his home number, which made her happy, although she didn't know why.

He'd decided to walk home as he only lived about fifteen minutes away, near Leeson Street, a very fashionable area of Dublin. It was an apart-ment in a Georgian house, he'd told her yesterday, and she wondered what it was like.

A taxi arrived. Suddenly the parting was awkward, as all first partings are. Each unsure, not knowing quite what to say.

'Take care, I'll call you soon.'

'Or maybe I'll call you,' she laughed as she got into the car.

'On second thoughts no. I made the first move. You call me. Oh, and enjoy your evening and remember, nice girls don't have sex on the first date.'

He was still grinning as the taxi pulled off.

Chapter Fourteen

The house was strangely silent when Lindsay let herself in. She'd grown used to the never-ending buzz of hotel life and Charlie's absence added to the eeriness in the shadowy hall. She phoned Tara.

'I'm back and I owe you one.'

'You owe me the details. I'm on my way and Debbie is probably asleep in her car outside your house. She's been panting since yesterday morning.'

'OK, give me twenty minutes to change and light the fire.'

Lindsay quickly showered again, mainly so she could finally wash her hair and use a good exfoliator on her skin, which felt grimy from lack of proper cleansing. She slathered on masses of body butter and 'rose day cream', her current must-have for her face. She towel dried her hair and got into comfy clothes and had just put a match to the fire when the doorbell rang. Three bodies hurled themselves in the door, Charlie's enthusiasm beaten for once by the eager faces of her friends.

'This'd better be good,' Debbie grinned as she

fished a bottle of wine and a packet of doggie treats from her bag and they settled on the couch with Charlie at their feet.

Lindsay grinned stupidly, wondering how long she could drag it out.

'I spent the weekend in a hotel with Chris Keating. I asked him to have sex with me.'

It was worth it just to see the look on their faces. Debbie almost choked and Tara's mouth opened and closed like a particularly hungry goldfish. They said nothing for a second, waiting for her to call a joke.

'Swear.' She crossed her heart and hoped to die.

Charlie almost ended up in the fireplace with the hullabaloo that broke out. Tara screamed and danced around the sofa and Debbie jumped up and down sending raspberry-red stains flying down her T-shirt.

'Oh, my God. Start at the very beginning and don't leave anything out,' Debbie yelled.

'OK, Friday night, where did you go and what were you wearing?'

Tara, ever the lawyer, wanted it all ordered and neat.

They sat for hours while she told them a very modern version of a fairy tale without the happy-ever-after ending, interrupting only once or twice to clarify a completely insignificant detail, as girl friends do.

'You asked him to have sex with you,' Tara kept repeating until Debbie nudged her impatiently.

'What were your exact words?' Typical Debbie, straight to the core. 'Did anyone else hear? What was his immediate reaction? Were you scared he'd laugh at you, or even worse, say no?'

'I didn't really give myself time to think about it. I just fancied him and I wanted to have sex with someone other than Paul and we seemed to have a buzz going and I just didn't want it to end.'

'Yes, but my God, Chris Keating. Talk about going for gold.' Tara still couldn't take it in.

'Well, no better way to forget sex with Paul than by having sex with one of Ireland's most gorgeous men,' Debbie grinned. 'How did you know he wasn't in a relationship, or did you even care, you brazen hussy?'

It was ages since all three of them had been like this, all girlie and eager and excited and Lindsay was so glad to have them around.

'I kind of guessed he wasn't in a serious relationship cause of the vibe between us, you know. Although . . .' Lindsay couldn't resist a final attempt to show them her new self, 'he does have a date with someone else tonight.'

Debbie might as well have dyed her T-shirt red, with all the wine she'd managed to spill as she jumped up and down again.

'What are you on?' She couldn't believe her ears. 'How did you find that out?'

'He told me.'

'And did you not ask him what he was playing at?' Tara was bemused at this latest twist to the happy-ever-after story, suddenly seeing her dreams of being a bridesmaid go up in smoke.

'Don't be ridiculous. It's got nothing to do with me. He had it all arranged and besides, we've only just met. I don't have any claim on him and I don't even know if I want another relationship.'

OK, that last bit was maybe a tiny little white lie, Lindsay realized, wondering how she'd feel if he didn't ring.

'Anyway, he doesn't know how lucky he'd be to have a girlfriend like me because I have absolutely no intention of falling in love or getting married. Ever again. I think that makes me a very good catch for a guy who must be fed up of women falling for him.'

They weren't fully convinced but sensibly said nothing.

They eventually had to break for food and Debbie rustled up some pasta with the less-than-generous contents of Lindsay's fridge – tomatoes, garlic and a block of fresh parmesan, brought to life with the help of some good olive oil and a pot of slightly wilted basil on the window sill. They talked for hours and were still amazed at her casual outlook.

'It's simple. I really fancied him, we had a great weekend and I don't know if I'll see him again. I guess I hope he calls, but if he doesn't I'll survive. I'm not sorry I did it. OK?'

They left at nine-thirty with lots of questions still unanswered but arranged to have a pizza together during the week to 'catch up on the latest'.

Lindsay was in bed by ten and fell asleep wondering where he was that night.

She opened her eyes at seven a.m. next morning and imagined it had all been a dream.

She was determined to make the most of her last day of freedom, however, so she leapt out of bed, her feet barely touching the cold hard floorboards as she padded quickly downstairs in the chill, dark December morning, grateful as ever for the comfort of the geriatric stove. She was out walking with Charlie before seven-thirty and showered and dressed and juicing by nine. On her way into town to do some Christmas shopping she switched on her mobile. She had a text message.

TANX FOR GT W/END. BED FELT BIG & MPTY LAST NITE.

It had been sent at seven forty-five that morning. Lindsay couldn't keep the grin off her face. Was it his way of telling her that he'd slept alone, in spite of his date, she wondered. She felt happy as she shopped, picking up a fab baby-blue angora sweater for Tara and a brilliant rich orangey-gold velvet scarf for Debbie. Around lunchtime she texted him back.

BED WARMING SERVICE AVAILABLE. RATES REASONABLE. CALL CHARLIE AT 333-1833.

He replied immediately.

GOTTA MEET THIS GUY. SOUNDS JUST WHAT I'M LOOKING 4. WUD U BOTH B FREE 4 DINNER ON FRI?

Her response was even quicker.

CALL ROUND 4 A 'BITE' BOUT 8.30.

She didn't hear anything until later that evening.

ON ROUTE 2 LONDON. C U FRI.

She texted back her address and went to bed with a smile on her face, looking forward to her first day in a new job and wondering what the week would bring.

Chapter Fifteen

On her way to work next morning, Lindsay could barely contain her excitement. She had been awake since six-thirty and had stayed swamped in the huge duvet, thinking about the day ahead. By eight she was showered and dressed, having changed her clothes twice.

She eventually settled on a Lyn Mar long, knitted, aubergine-coloured dress and coat, made funky by the addition of clumpy ankle boots. The dress was very plain and curvy and the coat was thick and chunky and cosy. The rich colouring suited her and she caught her hair back so as not to look too girlie, adding some earrings as a final touch. She felt good and was glad that Chris was in London, not sure that she could cope with the thought of maybe bumping into him on her first day at school.

She arrived at the *Live from Dublin* production office at nine-fifteen and it was already buzzing. Marissa, the production secretary, showed her to a spare desk with phone and computer and explained that the weekly meeting would start at ten. Lindsay sat quietly and made a 'To Do' list – obvious things like 'get stationery' and 'phone IT re computer' – while keeping an eye on what was going on around her. It was a large open-plan office, home to around twenty people. It was easy to spot the researchers – they were already 'phone bashing' and generally getting ready for the meeting. Alan Morland, the Executive Producer, came over to say hello.

'I can't tell you how glad we are to have you on board,' he grinned at her. 'We can certainly use the help. This is a madhouse. Come to the meeting and just get your bearings and then in the afternoon we can have a coffee and I'll explain all.'

Lindsay was grateful that he seemed normal . . . and nice, which was a definite bonus. Television producers and directors were usually creative and artistic, sometimes highly strung and a few were either mad or egotistical, or both. As the meeting got underway Alan introduced her to the team. There were eight researchers, a director, two production assistants (who worked mainly in studio with the director), three secretaries and an assistant to Tom Watts, who had presented the show for the past five years. Tom wasn't at this meeting and Lindsay wondered what he was like. She'd seen the show, of course, and knew he was in his late thirties. On screen he seemed outgoing and charming one minute, cruel and sharp tongued the next. Divorced and reported to have a string of very young girlfriends, the audience loved him although there were rumours that the show was losing some of its viewers to a rival chat show hosted by a drag queen. Lindsay knew that this was one of the reasons she'd been drafted in, to help produce items for the show that might appeal to a twenty- and thirty-something audience. The meeting went on for over two hours and ideas were raised and discussed, with each of the researchers vying to have their particular topic considered. It was healthy competition that could only be good for the ratings, although Lindsay didn't doubt for one minute that the rivalry was real. Anyone working on the top-rated TV show was there because they were very good at their job and fiercely ambitious. A draft running order for Saturday night's show was drawn up and a strategy discussed. Alan decided that they would open with a chart-topping boy band and follow with a discussion on teenage abortion. This was the subject of much debate. Promotions, competitions, audience were all talked through in some detail. Lindsay was exhausted by the time they broke up and it wasn't even lunchtime.

They all went to the canteen for a quick sandwich and everybody was back at their desks in record time. Tuesday was generally an easy day, Alan told her as he invited her for coffee at three-thirty. Most people drifted home early because by Wednesday it was full steam ahead and many ended up working late and of course, they all worked every Saturday from lunchtime until the show came off air at eleven.

Over coffee, they discussed the strategy for the coming months, as the new season would kick off after Christmas and continue until May or June. Alan explained that as they had only three more shows before the Christmas break, he was happy for her to simply observe, lend a hand when needed and generally work on ideas with researchers for after Christmas. He told her he'd been really impressed with her training programme and felt confident that she could bring some fresh ideas to the show. Lindsay was thrilled and asked for feedback on her performance as the weeks progressed.

After coffee he insisted she take a half-day and go home early, which meant that Lindsay was able to get a bit more Christmas shopping done and think about food for Friday.

She was determined not to kill herself cooking and cleaning to impress Chris so after consulting one of her many cookbooks over a cup of frothy coffee she eventually settled on a simple fish dish and decided that she'd get some fresh flowers and light some candles. He'd just have to take it or leave it, she thought, although she suspected that she wouldn't feel so confident once Friday came.

After an hour and a half on the phone to her mother, her sister and the girls, Lindsay retired to bed exhausted and dreamt of disasters on live TV programmes, all of which were her fault.

It was easier next day because Lindsay at least knew the ropes and she was at her desk before nine, determined to jump straight in. Everyone seemed friendly and helpful, although she wasn't quite sure about one of the researchers, a tall thin blonde named Kate. She had been very cool towards Lindsay when she heard that she was the new assistant producer and Lindsay sensed that she'd have to work hard to win Kate over. Still, nothing could daunt her today and she got stuck in with gusto, organizing all her personal needs, making a few contact calls and starting work on a list of ideas which she hoped to present at next week's meeting. The time flew and before she knew where she was it was six o'clock and she had arranged to meet Tara and Debbie at seven in a new café in Temple Bar.

They all arrived within minutes of each other and ordered a huge bowl of spaghetti with squashy, roasted baby tomatoes, basil leaves torn to shreds and crispy, toasted, garlicky breadcrumbs. Just to complete the image of the three little pigs they decided on a large pepperoni pizza with lashings of stringy mozzarella. They savoured the twenty-minute wait for food, enjoying the rich scent of garlic and herbs that pervaded the tiny room, accepting the manic, friendly sounds from the kitchen, anticipating the feast that was soon to be theirs and sipping some nicely chilled Frascati. Bliss.

The girls demanded to hear Lindsay's news first and she happily filled them in on the first two days in her new job. They were intrigued at how easily she seemed to have fitted in and teased her a bit about name-dropping a few of Ireland's celebrities.

'Oh, I see, you just happened to get chatting to Jason Nugent in the lift,' Debbie laughed at her animated expression as she related her encounter with a hot new radio presenter, while Tara remarked that it was a million miles away from the world she inhabited from nine to five, full of grey-haired, grey-suited, grey-faced legal types.

The food arrived in typical Italian style, delivered by two waiters who fought as they noisily arranged the table and presented the food as if it were Babette's Feast. The girls looked on happily. They were ravenous and didn't mind the fuss in the least. It was all part of the Italian experience.

'Guess who rang me the other day and asked me out?' Tara could no longer contain her news. Debbie stopped, fork full of dangling spaghetti two inches from her mouth, head back in anticipation.

'Who?' she asked, sensing something important but not yet sure if it was worth delaying the first bite of spaghetti for.

'Michael Russell.'

The food won because Debbie hadn't a clue who Michael Russell was.

'Michael Russell?' Lindsay was aghast.

'Who's Michael Russell?'

'Oh my God, I knew he was interested in you that day.'

Tara looked mortified.

'Who's Michael Russell?'

'What did you say? Have you met him yet?'

'No, we're meeting for a drink on Saturday night.' Tara grinned sheepishly.

'Will somebody please tell me who the fuck is Michael Russell?'

Debbie, annoyed and ridiculous with lurid green basil oil running down her chin, wasn't going to be left out for a second longer.

'The Course Director,' they chorused, which meant nothing to Debbie for a split second.

'Oh my God, the Course Director.'

Lindsay was intrigued.

'I knew it, that day of my final project, he talked to you for ages and I saw him looking at you as you were serving the wine. Tell us everything, quick.'

'Well, he rang me the other day at work.'

'How did he get your number? He didn't ask me!'

'When I filled in that form for the payment of that vast sum of money that you offered us to be your slaves for the day, I had to give my telephone number, in case of any problem. He seemed kind of shy and worried in case I wouldn't remember him, so he introduced himself and practically gave me his life history by way of introduction, which was kind of cute.'

'And did you know him?'

'Yes, as soon as he spoke I sort of remembered his voice, which is odd.'

'She's getting married in the morning . . .' Debbie sang, and they fell about laughing.

'That's fantastic. He's very cute in a sort of Tom Hanks in *Sleepless in Seattle* way.' Lindsay, as usual, got it in one. Debbie wasn't sure that this was a compliment – it was way too nineties.

They chatted on this subject for at least an hour and eventually got round to Lindsay's date on Friday.

'How do you feel? Are you excited?'

'What are you wearing/cooking/planning?'

'Are you nervous? I wouldn't be.'

'I would, he's sort of famous and eligible.'

'Wrong, he's very famous and eligible. Actually, I'd be scared stiff.'

On and on it went, forcing Lindsay to articulate something she wasn't even sure of herself.

'No, I'm not nervous and I'm not going to go to a lot of trouble. I feel a bit ridiculous, to tell you the truth, as if I'm a child playing a game or something. On one hand I wonder what on earth he wants with me when he can have his pick of women . . . younger, thinner, better-looking. Why did he come looking for me?'

'He didn't. You went looking for him.' Debbie gave her a cheeky grin.

'You're right, I'd forgotten that little detail, thank you for reminding me. But he did make the next move, I mean he didn't have to get in touch. So, how do I feel about it? Well, I'm delighted and a bit excited and I'm dying to see how Friday goes. But you know, if it ended tomorrow, or next week, or next month even, I know I'll be OK. When Paul came into my life, it was the best thing in the world and when it ended it was the worst possible thing that could ever happen and it changed me forever. So I'll go along with this and see where it leads me but I have absolutely no expectation of happy ever after 'cause I don't believe in it any more. And I'm never going to feel the way I felt about Paul ever again so I won't get badly hurt no matter what happens. I'm going to have fun and keep my heart intact. How does that sound?' she asked a touch too brightly.

'Sounds like the best of both worlds to me.' Tara looked at her with a hint of sadness in her eyes. 'I think you're great.'

'Me too.'

Chapter Sixteen

On Thursday morning, Lindsay finally got to meet Tom Watts. The presenter strolled into the office at around midday and everyone jumped to attention in a funny 'I'm not trying to impress anyone' sort of way.

'What's happening?' he asked no one in particular.

Alan Morland immediately went to fill him in on progress for this week's show. Rosie, his assistant, left a couple of folders on his desk and the researchers waited expectantly to be called to discuss their particular items.

'Let's have a quick meeting. All route your phones through to Marissa. Monica, maybe you could take notes of any bits and pieces that aren't being looked after.' Alan Morland was brisk.

Chairs became dodgems as everyone wheeled around in a rough circle. Tom Watts glanced about him, signing post and thinking. He looked in Lindsay's direction but gave no sign of recognition, which she took to mean that it was up to her to make the first move. She knew that he would be fully aware of a stranger in the office, they were an intimate bunch, drawn together in a world that was difficult for an outsider to understand, glamorous, stressful, exciting, pressurized. A world where adrenalin constantly bubbled under the surface, where huge highs and constant lows were part of a day's work and where long hours and shared moments had spawned numerous dangerous liaisons over the years. It all made for an intoxicating atmosphere to an outsider like her.

'Hi, Tom, I'm Lindsay Davidson. I'm the new Assistant Producer.'

Nobody in television land ever called anybody Mr or Miss, all the same Lindsay was nervous as she held out her hand. He was taller than she had expected and slightly chubbier than he appeared on TV. A good-looking man with black hair and sharp eyes and a sardonic grin, she knew he'd worked in America for a couple of years, before he came to the station, although he was Irish, born and reared in a small town in the North West. No traces of his roots were evident, however, he was the all-American high-school graduate, sleek and smooth and very polished. He looked every inch the successful TV host and Lindsay knew he had a huge following throughout Ireland. She immediately suspected that he might be very demanding and play the celebrity card a lot.

'Lindsay Davidson, sounds like a tennis player,' he greeted her with a twenty-kilo handshake.

He was a man who probably indulged a bit too much in the good things of life, Lindsay noticed, but he managed to get away with it, though not for many more years, she suspected. His aura of power gave him an undeniable attraction, and she had no doubt he used it to the full when it suited him, which it clearly did now.

'Alan showed me bits of your training programme. I was impressed.'

'Thank you, I'm looking forward to putting all that training to good use on the show.'

'Great.' Suddenly she knew she was dismissed.

The meeting was short and sharp. Tom Watts seemed to know all the right questions to ask to put everyone under pressure.

'Who's looking after the audience this week? Monica? Last week they were all from a geriatric ward, I'm certain one or two of them even fell asleep during the show. I want to see young faces this Saturday.'

Monica's face resembled a very ripe tomato and Lindsay wondered how she was going to tackle that particular problem because she knew that tickets for this week's show would have been distributed at least a month in advance. There was a huge waiting list, stretching to nearly a year but Lindsay knew Tom Watts was right. The audience were beginning to look a bit too middle aged.

'Who wrote this intro to the boy band? I refuse to call them the Monkees of this Millennium. It's crap and it dates all of us and whatever about the rest of you, I'm in my prime.' He grinned and everyone relaxed a bit. It was going to be OK. He was in a good mood. Even though editorial control for the programme rested with the Executive

Producer, a high-profile presenter such as Tom Watts wielded considerable power and it was clear that he considered this was 'his' show.

The meeting lasted only twenty minutes or so and afterwards no one made any real move to go to lunch. One or two people nipped out to get a take-away coffee and a sandwich, with a quick 'anyone want anything from the canteen?' but as this was Thursday and Tom was in the office, they all knew that they could be called upon at any moment. The pressure was on.

Noticing that Tom and Alan were deep in discussion at one end of the office, Lindsay went to have a quiet moment with Monica about the audience. As she had suspected, the younger girl was in a bit of a panic. She was absolutely efficient and methodical and each person who applied for tickets had to fill out a questionnaire, in order to ensure a good mix of social background, urban versus rural, age, male/female, etc. She had already taken steps to ensure that younger applicants were given priority where tickets were concerned but this would take a few more weeks to show on air, which wouldn't solve this particular headache. There was also another simple problem, difficult to overcome. People lied.

'A lot of people know that if they look for tickets for their granny and grandad they might not get them so they tell us they're for their brothers and sisters, or nieces and nephews,' Monica explained. 'So, even though I think we have a good mix, when they arrive it's clear that a good number of them didn't give their correct ages.'

'OK, let's see if I can help, I've nothing much to do at the moment.' Lindsay knew that Monica was worried. 'For a start, let me have a look at the file on last week's gang, just to get an idea.'

Sure enough, there were lots of applications from twenty- and thirty-somethings but when Lindsay looked at the tape of the programme there were far more of the blue-rinse brigade in the audience.

She discussed it again later with Monica.

'Are the tickets printed with specific seat numbers?'

'No, because it would take too long to seat them, with an audience of three hundred and fifty.'

'How many floating tickets do we keep back each week for guests, friends, etc.?'

'About forty.'

'OK, here's a plan. Suppose we give as many of the spares as we can to younger people, friends of the production team, etc. We could put a special mark on them so that when they arrive we could direct them into studio first and seat them in the front row. Then you and I could mingle with the general audience while they're having their pre-show glass of wine and pick out as many young faces as we can and place them in prominent positions for cameras. That way it might appear there are more younger people present, at least as far as the viewers at home are concerned. After all, that's all that matters.' Lindsay grinned. Monica was delighted and they agreed to rope in any of the researchers they could to help on the night. Lindsay also suggested that Monica draft up

147

a new questionnaire for ticket applicants and include a few trick questions.

They giggled helplessly in the corner as they worked it out.

'OK, let's start by asking them what sort of music they like,' Lindsay reasoned. 'If they list Britney Spears or Slipknot as their favourite performers they're probably still at school, or male, or both. If they mention Perry Como or Doris Day they might live in a nursing home or at the very least the only other thing that occupies them at the weekend is collecting their pension.'

Monica began to get into the swing of it. 'We could ask them what their favourite food is, that's a real giveaway.'

'Definitely. Irish stews and toad-in-the-holes get nothing. Fajitas and lamb vindaloos get extra tickets.' The two girls tried in vain to keep the laughter under control.

'What's going on?' Alan Morland approached Monica's desk.

'Come on, share it.' Two foolish grins stared back at him and he knew it was useless.

'Monica, I need to talk to you about the audience later.' He looked tired.

'Oh, that's what we're working on at the moment.' The younger girl was on the defensive immediately.

Lindsay stepped in. 'Monica already had a plan so I'm just seeing if I can lend a hand, if that's OK.'

'Yeah, great, thanks, I'll leave you to it. Shout if you need me.'

'It'll be fine, no worries.'

Lindsay spent the rest of the day helping out where she could. David, the researcher looking after the boy band, was in trouble. Apart from the intro that Tom hated, the record company involved with the band had sent in a list of requirements for their dressing rooms that would take two days to organize. Also, there were several topics that the band would not discuss. These included the recent suspected drug raid on one of their homes and the question of whether a well-known teenage pop idol in the UK was pregnant by the lead singer.

These were, of course, the very questions that Tom wanted answers to and he was pushing David very hard, while Alan Morland was trying to keep everyone happy.

'I don't care, let's dump them if they won't co-operate. They need us, we don't need them,' Tom insisted as he left the office. Nobody else agreed with him and Alan walked with him to his car to discuss it further. The boys were currently No. 1 in ten countries and having them on the show was a coup. Lindsay suggested that she and David go to the canteen and put their heads together to see if they could reach a compromise with the record company, keep Tom happy and not lose the band.

Lindsay had to drag herself to the shops after work, to organize food for the famous dinner and by the time she let herself in to the house at nine-thirty Charlie was hysterical and she wasn't feeling very calm herself. No amount of hot milk, her mother's favourite remedy, would help tonight, she suspected, as she took off her shoes and ignored Charlie, stretched out on her favourite tapestry

149

cushions on a chair from which he was normally banned. Bed by eleven seemed the only cure for both of them although she knew that Charlie, with his soulful, pleading eyes, would rather have had a walk.

Chapter Seventeen

Friday came at last and Lindsay wasn't sure whether she was thrilled or traumatized. She was awake by six a.m. and despite her intentions, ran around the house plumping cushions and opening windows and generally annoying Charlie, who wasn't used to living with a tornado. By eight-thirty she'd exfoliated to within an inch of her life, flossed and whitened her teeth, applied at least half of her very expensive face mask whilst praying that she wouldn't erupt in an army of fluorescent spots and checked for a suspected cold sore three times.

She was exhausted by the time she hit the office at ten, having nipped in to her local salon for a quick blow-dry. She decided enough was enough and put all thoughts of impending doom in relation to the evening ahead to the back of her mind, giving herself a 'get a life' mental lash. It nearly worked.

Fridays, she quickly realized, are the worst days for a live weekend chat show, the last working day of the week for most people and the day on which things always seemed to go wrong. Today was no exception. Everyone appeared to be working against the clock. Tom Watts was in for most of the day, going through briefs with the researchers. Each one provided detailed notes on their particular guest and tried to make them as interesting as possible. They also offered a suggested introduction that Tom might or might not use and a list of relevant questions. The skill was to get the person to talk about topics that they might not necessarily want to talk about, but which the viewers definitely wanted and even expected them to. This week there was a problem with a former Page Three model who was coming on to promote her book but refusing to talk about whether she'd had her breasts enlarged, a subject that had filled many tabloid pages in recent months. Alice, the researcher, was adamant that she would get up and leave if the subject was raised. Tom, however, seemed determined to do so and tried to rope Lindsay in for support.

'Lindsay, tell us what you think. I say we have to ask her about her boob job, Alice is afraid to push it.'

Lindsay joined them reluctantly, aware that this was one of the calls she would have to make if she were in charge. There was no easy answer.

'I imagine this kind of thing comes up often on live programmes everywhere and it is a dilemma. I think we have a responsibility to honour a commitment not to discuss it, provided it's been made clear to us when the artist was being offered.'

'Ah, that's a cop out,' Tom goaded her.

'Well, I don't think this is a discussion we should be having the day before the artist comes on the show. We should have these things clarified before we agree to have the guest on. In this case, if we had known earlier, we could have incorporated an item on cosmetic surgery into the interview and perhaps have asked her to comment generally, but I don't think we can do anything now, it's too late in the day.'

'Well, I cannot have her without asking her something, we'll be laughed at, it's the only reason people want to see her.' Tom was adamant.

'Can we find out if she'd be prepared to comment generally?' Lindsay asked Alice.

'She would, reluctantly, I think. I did a long phone interview with her last night. She is fed up with the media attention to her breasts and wants to move on and develop her career as a writer.'

'Well, developing her boobs has certainly helped develop her writing career,' Lindsay laughed. 'I think we should take a different approach and ask her about her Page Three days and if it's been a help or a hindrance. We can also ask about the lengths these girls are prepared to go to, to make it onto the pages of the tabloids and take the questioning as far as we can down that road.'

'OK, give me an hour and I'll change the line of questioning.' Alice seemed relieved to have reached a compromise, although Lindsay sensed that Tom Watts was not happy. It would make for an interesting twenty minutes both on screen and off, she thought.

The morning raced ahead like a greyhound, the

atmosphere was tense and Lindsay longed to be in the thick of it all instead of on the sidelines, but she knew her turn would come.

Suddenly it was six o'clock and although everyone was still working, Lindsay, doing her best superwoman impression and fooling nobody, left feeling very guilty.

By seven-thirty the fires were lit, candles lined the mantelpiece and the kitchen and sitting room looked just right – warm, cosy and elegant but well used and comfortable. Most important, the rooms didn't look too set up for an intimate evening. Lindsay loved flowers, candles, lamps and cushions, so everything looked natural.

She had the quickest shower ever, partly because of time but also so as not to ruin her hair, which was soft and shiny and curly, but could become dead and lifeless after about thirty seconds in a steamy shower. She set out her make-up with all the subtlety of Colonel Gaddafi.

First up, Clarins Beauty Flash Balm. None of her friends had ever been able to explain what it did, but applied it lavishly none the less. Then came Laura Mercier Secret Camouflage, quite simply the best concealer in the world. Next her desert island must-have – Touché Eclat, for under eyes, which seemed to lighten the whole eye area, even more so once Geri Haliwell supposedly claimed not to be able to leave home without it. Foundation, luminizing colour powder (great for a touch of sparkle, especially on the cleavage), eye make-up and Posh Spice's favourite lip pencil – Mac 'Spice' – completed the look, not forgetting a dash of

Prescriptives cheek stick, which took her three months to locate once Madonna was apparently spotted with a similar-looking black tube in a posh loo in Los Angeles. A twenty-five-minute military regime involving some fifteen make-up products ensured she looked as if she wasn't wearing any. Well, hardly any. She hadn't really made up her mind what to wear, but eventually settled on her fine wool black pinstripe trousers which were well cut and narrow and slightly flared at the bottom, making her legs look long and reasonably thin when worn over high-heeled boots. On top she wore a fab French blouse, in various shades of blue and grey and inky black. It was quite flamboyant but very delicate and see through. She left enough buttons open to show a generous helping of the matching black, heavily embroidered bra top, which was a feature of the designer. It pushed her boobs up and made her feel very sexy, without being too 'come and get me'.

All the same she closed one button, just in case.

Hell, what am I worrying about, he's already had me, she thought, and opened two more.

She checked the food and opened a bottle of nicely chilled white wine, desperate for a glass herself but deciding that she had to face him sober sometime. She had just decided the top was too much and was standing in her bra and pants when the doorbell rang.

Oscar nomination sprang to mind later as she thought about her performance when she opened the door trying to keep the 'this could all go horribly wrong' look off her face. As soon as she saw him she burst out laughing, partly from nerves but mostly because of what he was holding in his hand – a giant tin of Pedigree Chum with a huge, juicy looking, meaty, smelly bone sellotaped to the top of the can.

'I gathered that the goodwill of this dog of yours might be crucial to the future of our relationship,' he grinned and she wondered for the millionth time how she'd had the courage to do what she did last Friday.

'My friends are usually much more subtle, I'm afraid he'll see through that lot immediately and refuse to come near you.' She grinned back and stepped aside, the awkwardness of the first 'will he, won't he, should I, shouldn't I' moment gone in a whiff of beef marrowbone.

He followed her down the few steps to the kitchen. She had not invited him into the sitting room on purpose. This was where she and Charlie hung out and this was what she wanted him to see and hopefully like.

'Wow, what a great room.' He looked around and earned himself five brownie points in as many seconds. Lindsay loved this room. It was big, open and friendly with an old Victorian fireplace, a big squashy sofa and original beams and wood panelling. It also had a big, old, well-scrubbed table, home to a massive antique jug of flowers courtesy of the market, or her garden, or both. There was no fitted kitchen; the units were all free-standing and individual, which seemed to add to the unstructured look. The original French doors to the garden were intact and the sixty-year-old

Aga, complete with four-year-old Charlie firmly attached, completed the vaguely Shaker style. She sometimes thought the dog would have to be surgically removed if she ever decided to sell the place. At this moment, Charlie was eyeing the newcomer suspiciously. He was well used to Lindsay's friends who all came to tickle his tummy and he usually didn't have to move from his favourite spot. This one smelt different, however, and his nose edged its way towards the source of the best whiff he'd had all day. It took all of five seconds for Charlie to decide that Chris was his new V.B.F.

'Beer or wine?' Lindsay was feeling awkward again.

'Wine would be great, thanks.'

'Red or white?'

'Red if you have some open.'

'Sure.' She poured half a bottle into one of her fat, long-stemmed wineglasses and it still looked like a miserable half glass. She did the same with the white for herself, enjoying the instant sedative as she took a big gulp and sent half of it down her front. Luckily, he hadn't noticed.

He was very impressive, she thought again, glancing at him as she mopped up her cleavage. It wasn't that he was drop-dead gorgeous; it was more the whole package. He was tall, well built and looked really healthy, as if he was about to spring into action at any moment. He had a clean and vibrant smell and tonight he was wearing an expensive black jacket with a grey shirt open at the neck and his hair had that just-washed appeal. She had that feeling of wanting to touch him, again.

'So, tell me about the first week. Was it better or worse than you expected?'

'Oh, no, I expected it to be brilliant and it was. It was also really scary.' She filled him in and he seemed relaxed and happy as she recounted the incident of the former Page Three model.

'I'll have to remember to tape that tomorrow night.'

She wondered if he had another date with the Sunday girl. 'How was your week?'

'Fine, although I'm a bit wrecked. I went to London as I told you and then ended up in Luxemburg, covering a story I've been keeping an eye on for a while now. So, I only got back last night and then Jim Burns, Director of News, rang at eight-thirty this morning. He wants me to do a stint on *Ireland Today*.'

'How do you feel about it?' Lindsay knew that it was the top-rating morning TV programme, on air from seven to nine a.m., with a hard news edge to it and an interesting mix of guests.

'I'm not sure. Personally, I never watch TV in the mornings and I hate the idea of getting up at five. I'd rather it were radio, at least that way I could fall into work with wet hair and wearing jeans. At the moment, it's only for a couple of weeks in January, but you know what they're like, I could be still there next Christmas, which is definitely not my intention. There are too many other things I want to do.'

'Like what?'

'More in-depth news stuff and two projects – documentaries – I'm working on. I've also been asked to do a late-night current affairs type thing on radio, which I'm supposed to be starting immediately after Christmas. It's already in the transmission schedule but I couldn't do both late-night radio and morning TV. Might have a bit of a disastrous effect on my social life.' He grinned and raised his eyebrows.

'Not to mention your sex life.' Damn. She tried desperately to gobble the words back up but they slithered off her tongue like runny yoghurt.

He'd definitely think she was obsessed with it.

'Since you brought it up first, I had a great time last weekend. Sunday night seemed very tame by comparison.'

Great, she thought viciously, struggling not to ask for details. She knew he was laughing at her, she could feel the little jets hitting the back of her neck as she stirred the main course with gusto, ignoring the fact that the recipe had specifically said to stir once only. She'd worry about that later. Still, she could only keep her back turned for so long and after she'd poured wine into her already full glass and petted Charlie twice, she was forced to look at him.

'Well, if you insist on associating with out-spoken, hot-blooded females, you've got to be able to take the consequences,' she mumbled and grinned back at him, knowing her slightly pink face was betraying any attempt at nonchalance.

Chapter Eighteen

Things took off a bit after that. Memories of their illicit weekend sort of bonded them and she was glad he'd brought it up.

Dinner was a success. Lindsay had abandoned her cookbooks and decided instead to consult her current favourite celebrity chef, via his website, and he advised her to 'keep it simple and use only the best ingredients'. The fish dish had gone out the window after she'd spoken to Tara, who insisted that nobody really liked fish. She also mentioned the risk of salmonella, which was the final nail in the fish's coffin. This conversation caused a major crisis and gave Lindsay one more nightmare scenario to dream about. Eventually she decided to fall back on one of her 'tried and tested' – leg of lamb, dusted with seasoned flour and browned on a hot pan, then roasted slowly, for hours, in the company of a bottle of a good robust wine, sweet red onions, bay leaves, thyme and lots of black pepper. What emerged didn't resemble leg of lamb as we know it. It fell off the bone and looked as if it had been put through a shredder and it was surrounded by the most wonderful wine and red-onion marmalade.

It also smelt absolutely wonderful, which helped a lot. The over-zealous stirring hadn't helped the complicated risotto thingy which Lindsay immediately abandoned. It was the wrong thing to cook anyway. She had been trying to show off and as usual, it didn't work for her. The flavours were too rich for the lamb, she consoled herself as she mentally consigned it to Charlie. She wasn't in the least thrown by this, however, because she was a confident cook. She had a tray of crunchy roast potatoes almost ready so she simply popped on some green beans and made a colourful organic leaf salad from the various plastic bags she always kept in the bottom of the fridge. She liked to cook and chatted happily to Chris as she worked, explaining how the Aga worked and telling him about her dream to be a chef in Ballymaloe, the world-renowned cookery school in Cork. He washed the salad leaves and told her a bit more about his family, how his mother loved messing about in the kitchen and could entertain twenty people effortlessly.

She had apparently passed on at least some of her knowledge to her offspring, all of whom could conjure up something in the kitchen, although Chris doubted he could beat the smells that were wafting around the place tonight, he teased her. She hadn't bothered with a starter, another attempt to be casual about the night, so when it was all ready she simply put everything in the middle of the big, worn table – an old-fashioned platter of aromatic lamb with the gorgeous sauce, a well-used wooden salad bowl and a couple of old porcelain dishes with the roast potatoes and green beans. It all looked delicious and Chris tucked in as if he hadn't eaten all week. He seemed relaxed and happy and not a bit 'famous'.

'This is fantastic, I'm afraid I couldn't compete,' he laughed and sat back to take a break, having demolished his first portion. They chatted as they sipped their wine. He liked the feel of eating in the kitchen, he told her, and Lindsay explained that as the room was always warm, courtesy of the Aga, people seemed to gravitate towards the kitchen and so it had seemed sensible at the time to get a big, old table and make the most of the atmosphere. The comfy sofa and fireplace helped during winter, making it all seem very homely, the ultimate country kitchen. It was the best thing about the otherwise tiny house and the reason she'd bought it. In summer, she simply left the French doors open to the garden and ate outside as often as she could.

'It's very different to my place,' Chris explained as he helped himself to another huge plateful. 'I bought it because it was close to the city centre and I wanted an apartment in an old building, instead of in one of those characterless new developments. The house itself is really great, with all the original Georgian features intact. Then when I moved in I wanted to go against the trend so I opted for a very modern, sort of minimalist look, with the help of a friend of mine who's an interior designer.'

'What's her name?' Lindsay asked, explaining that she had been an interior designer before taking up her current job.

'That explains it – I knew you must have had some training as soon as I walked in here. Your colours are terrific. My friend's name is Catherine Hickson.'

'Yes, I know her, she has a place in Blackrock. She's very good, I'd be interested to see what she's done with your place.' Once again Lindsay wished she hadn't said it, it sounded as though she was angling for an invite.

'Well, I was going to offer to cook you dinner next week, but after this I'm not so sure.'

'I'm a dustbin, really, so don't worry. Besides Charlie will eat anything I can't manage and he's very easily impressed.'

For dessert Lindsay had made a warm lemon sponge pudding with a big jug of cream.

'It's real comfort food', she half apologized. 'I think it's a carry over from my childhood, a sort of adult version of Liga.'

'You're mad,' he laughed as he shovelled it in.

'I think I am, a bit. I eat masses of this kind of food when I'm feeling a bit down in the dumps.'

He was still laughing as they sat down on the couch to finish their wine. All of a sudden it felt funny to be so close to him. She wondered if he expected to go to bed with her. Oh God, I forgot to change the sheets and Charlie was up there rolling around earlier, she thought, her eyes mentally darting about the place, wondering if she should escape and do a quick clean up.

'Mind if I check out the late news heads?' He seemed oblivious to her discomfort.

'Sure.' She handed him the remote control and relaxed a little.

But not for long.

Maybe he intends to stay the night. I didn't even attempt to clean the bathroom.

'You OK?'

'Yeah.'

'Tired?'

'A bit, I haven't been this energetic in the evening for ages,' Lindsay told him, realizing that she had become used to just coming home and vegging with Charlie. 'When the girls come round they're more interested in wine than food so if we eat at all it tends to be takeaway.'

'You're very close then?'

'Well, they either keep me sane or drive me insane.'

'And they're the ones who helped you when you split up with your . . . erm, the guy you were engaged to?'

'Yeah. They were brilliant, I don't think I could have done it without them.'

'Do you see them often?'

'Probably only once or twice a fortnight, but we talk almost every day. Debbie works for Aer

Lingus, so she travels all the time. She's feisty and impulsive and either loves you or hates you. She makes me laugh all the time. Tara is quite different. She's a lawyer, much more level-headed, always sees the other point of view. Loves animals and children. Very soft. Actually Debbie's as soft as butter too and the sort of person you could call on 24/7.'

'I envy women their friendships, sometimes. Men's relationships are so different. Even with close friends, we tend not to really say what we feel, it's all hidden behind football or rugby or politics or pints.'

'Well, it doesn't have to be, you've just got to allow yourself to be vulnerable, tell some secrets.'

'Speaking of secrets, tell me one.' She'd walked into that one for sure.

She hesitated and then decided that plunging straight in had worked so far.

'I was a bit apprehensive about tonight, it's very different to how we spent last Friday night.'

'Are you still worried?'

'I did wonder if you'd expect to have sex or stay the night, and I guess I'd be disappointed if I thought that sex was all we had in common.'

'You know, sex in a way is the easy part.' He looked thoughtful. 'It either works or it doesn't. Sometimes it's really great and other times it just doesn't gel and you know it pretty quickly. The rest is more complicated. Actually, I think I can be quite selfish. If I lose interest after a while, I don't even bother trying to get to know someone. I think that as you get older you become less tolerant. In my twenties I just wanted a great time, now I'm less likely to waste time on a relationship that's not working.'

'Relationships are very fragile, though,' Lindsay was speaking from personal experience, 'especially at the beginning. They break easily. You have to mind them. And I think you have to be honest, even if it hurts. So, you tell me a secret.'

'I knew you wouldn't let me get away with it. Well, let's see, I lived with a girl for about two years. It finished last year and I haven't really seen anyone else since, at least not seriously. She was, and still is, a great person, our sex life was everything I could have hoped for but something wasn't quite right. I thought we loved each other and I think even now that I did love her but at the end of the day we discovered that we didn't like each other enough. Does that sound strange?'

She shook her head.

'It ended badly. My family were very disappointed, I think they had great hopes for it.'

'I'm sorry.'

'Don't be. I think I realized before she did that it was over. By the time we eventually split I had mentally moved on. I don't believe she ever really admitted it to herself until the end, so it came as a shock.'

'What are we like? Not a great ad for happy ever after.' Lindsay was glad he'd told her.

'I don't know whether I believe in till death us do part.'

'Me neither,' she smiled sadly.

Without her anticipating it, he leaned over to kiss her. It was different, soft and slow, sensuous and exploratory, as if it were the first time. It went on for ages and made her feel funny and suddenly she didn't feel sad any more.

Chapter Nineteen

Lindsay called Tara as soon as he'd left. It was twelve-thirty. She needed to talk to someone.

'How did it go?'

Tara took the call as a bad sign.

'Do you know something, I honestly don't know. It felt a bit awkward at the beginning, when he arrived, but then it settled down and I really enjoyed it. Then after dinner he told me about a girl he'd lived with for two years and he went a bit quiet, even though he implied that he'd been the one to end it. I got the feeling he's a bit wary of relationships.'

'Aren't we all? Did you have sex?'

'No, I thought he might expect to and it wasn't really that sort of night, so I said that to him, but he said sex was the easy part of a relationship.'

'It probably is for him, I'd say he has no shortage of offers. What did he say when he was leaving?'

'He kissed me and said he'd call me over the weekend and that he'd cook me dinner. I don't know why I feel he won't call, he just seemed sort of distant. I can't put my finger on it.'

'I think you're reading too much into it.'

'Yeah, maybe. It's just that after he left I realized the night was quite ordinary, not very exciting. He asked if I was tired and I said yes, I mean, how boring is that for a Friday night?'

'You're being paranoid.'

'I suppose I am. So I am definitely not going to let it take over the weekend. If he calls, he calls.' She could feel Tara smiling.

'I'll remind you of that when you're going mental by Sunday.'

'I hate waiting for the phone to ring. Maybe he was just bored and couldn't wait to get the night over with.'

'Stop this now. It's ridiculous. Oh my God, listen to me preaching, I'll be the exact same after tomorrow night.'

'Yes, I want to hear everything. What are you wearing? Will you invite him back to your place? Hang on till I get my glass of wine.'

Lindsay settled herself on the couch and listened to Tara agonize over what she'd wear.

Next came the age-old problem of whether to invite him back or not.

'Don't make any decision now, see how the night goes. Besides he might not drive, in which case you'll both probably get separate taxis.'

'I hope he takes things slowly, doesn't expect too much.'

'Tara, the man has just come through a painful separation. He hasn't dated in years. He's hardly going to jump on you. He's probably just as nervous as you are. Besides, you'd put anybody at ease, you're great with people.'

'Thanks. Yeah, I know you're right. I'm glad I talked to you. I was working myself into a right panic.'

'We're all the same.' They chatted for nearly an hour and Lindsay felt better as she climbed into bed, tired but less emotional.

She woke early and decided to have a lazy morning. She went for a quick walk with Charlie. It was a freezing, grey December morning and the sky was low and threatening. Lindsay stopped at her local mini-market and bought some croissants and fresh OJ.

Debbie phoned at nine-thirty and called around for breakfast. Their conversation was a rerun of the one she'd had with Tara, although Debbie was more forceful.

'You're an eejit. He'd hardly have offered to cook you dinner at his place unless he really liked you. Men don't do that.'

'I guess so. Well, let's wait and see and meanwhile I'm not staying in waiting for the phone to ring. I'll be working tonight but how about a drink tomorrow night?'

'Sure, then we can assess Tara's date, rehash yours and get all the gossip from the show. Perfect. Shame I haven't got a bit of juicy stuff myself.'

Lindsay laughed. Debbie was always so positive and she loved her for it. They spent a relaxing two hours catching up before Lindsay had to jump into the shower and get ready for work.

On her way out the door she switched on her mobile. She had a text.

REALLY ENJOYD LAST NITE. SORRY IF I WAS A BIT QUIET. MALE INSECURITIES! DINNER WED?

Lindsay laughed. She knew it was OK.

When she hit the studio, it was organized chaos. The first band had lost their drum kit so they couldn't rehearse. David the researcher was tearing his hair out trying to locate it and chase up the boy band who were stuck in a record store downtown in the midst of thousands of hysterical fans. Lindsay offered to help and made her way to the office. All was calm. 'Don't worry,' Alice told her when she mentioned the drum kit. 'This happens every week, or at least something similar. No matter how much you plan everything down to the last detail, something always goes wrong. And it always seems to work out in the end. So, save your energy for a real crisis.'

'Good advice, thanks. Is everyone in?'

'Yeah, at least those who need to be. Alan won't come in until about four and Tom doesn't appear until the full dress rehearsal at seven.'

'OK, I'm going over to studio again, to sit in the box.' The production control room, or the 'box', was a glass-panelled room located above the studio, suspended, as it were, in mid air. It was the nerve centre for all operations for the live show. Lindsay had loved it from the moment she'd walked into the control room in the Training Centre. It had an electrifying atmosphere.

Everything happened there. Ultimately, whoever was directing controlled the live show – cameras, sound, lighting – phone calls, reaction, competitions – decisions were all made here first. Geoff, the director today, was brilliant but mad and he survived by abusing everyone. Assholes and idiots featured bigtime in his life. He was still suffering the fall out from the lost drum kit. Rehearsals were now running half an hour late and this was bad news as it all came off at the other end. Ultimately, at nine o'clock they were live on air, whether they had finished rehearsals or not. This put extra pressure on the entire crew. Today, through no fault of the production team, they had got off to a bad start and Geoff knew from experience that they wouldn't recover. Everyone was on their toes, knowing they couldn't afford another mistake. Lindsay sat, fascinated, remembering why she'd been attracted to this job in the first place.

At five-thirty they broke for tea and the production team assembled in the office for a quick meeting with Alan Morland.

'All OK?'

'So far so good,' Geoff murmured and everyone else nodded. 'If it wasn't for those imbeciles who forgot that they needed a drum kit to rehearse, we'd be right on target.'

'Our Page Three model missed her flight but I've got her on to the next available one, which should get her into Dublin at seven.' Alice looked a bit uncomfortable. 'I'll have a car waiting at the airport so she'll be OK, but I gather she'll need some pampering. Seemingly, she was besieged at Heathrow by photographers so she's not in the best form, so my time will be completely taken up with getting her to perform. I need someone to look after my band, anyone except David, who has two on his hands already,' she grinned at her colleague, knowing he'd had a tough afternoon. Nobody offered.

'I can do it.' Lindsay smiled. Alan Morland nodded gratefully. 'I just need help with the audience and then I'm free to mind them.'

'Thanks.' Alice looked relieved.

They all adjourned for a quick tea and it was back for the dress rehearsal. Things really started to hot up.

Tom Watts wanted everything and he wanted it now. He clearly wasn't in good form and the researchers bore the brunt of it. Nothing seemed to be going right. Tempers were becoming frayed. Tom barked at every one of the production team he encountered, who in turn barked at everyone else they came across.

Lindsay hovered, taking it all in, helping out where necessary, learning what the hiccups were.

At eight the audience arrived and they were treated very well from the moment they stepped into TV reception. For most people it was a once-in-a-lifetime experience and they were very excited.

Each week, one of the researchers did the introduction, outlining the format of the programme and asking for the audience's help, explaining that they were the vital ingredient in the show and it was really important that they were lively and interested and up for anything. Members of the team who were available mingled and tried to answer any questions. Monica and Lindsay had their plan and they roamed around looking for young faces. Once they spotted someone they approached them and asked if they were willing to help. They always were. The two girls then brought them into studio and sat them in prominent positions. As a reward they were invited for a drink with the crew after the show, which was the icing on the cake as far as they were concerned: a chance to really mingle with the rich and famous. Lindsay noticed that time, as usual, was against them so she looked to Kate for help.

'Kate, would you have time to help us with the audience?'

'Not really, Tom wants me to sort out his cards.' Kate was cool. No, she was icy.

'OK, well as soon as you can, I need help and as you're the only researcher who doesn't have a guest tonight, I'd be really grateful.' It was the wrong thing to say.

'I said I was busy, Tom comes first.' Kate swanned off.

Lindsay was furious but kept her temper, not wanting to make an enemy of anyone at this stage. She followed her.

'All right, that's fair enough, but if you have any time at all between now and the beginning of the show, I could really use a hand. OK?' Lindsay stared at her then returned to the task in hand, knowing she wouldn't get any help from Kate.

It seemed they got the audience in with seconds to spare. Suddenly the atmosphere changed. Tom Watts appeared to tremendous applause, his earlier mood forgotten. He did a quick warm-up, explaining what would happen, hinting at special guests and generally working the audience into a frenzy.

Within minutes, the sound of the opening animation filled the studio; the floor manager announced 'We're on air' and suddenly all the tension evaporated. Everyone was too preoccupied with keeping it all running smoothly. 'Live' meant that any mistake was seen by the viewers and everyone was determined to do their utmost to ensure it was perfect. It felt wonderful to be part of it all and Lindsay's heart raced and didn't slow down until the credits rolled at the end of the show.

The boy band performed to a rapturous welcome. The Page Three model was booed at every opportunity. It made for great television. Tom Watts, however, clearly didn't think the interview was worth doing and Lindsay wasn't sure about his approach. He constantly made references to cosmetic surgery and the model became more determined not to talk about it and clammed up entirely in the process. It was fascinating to watch. Towards the end of the interview Tom invited questions from the audience, which hadn't been agreed with anyone in advance. Alice panicked. 'I wish he'd told me he wanted questions, I could have put in a few people with strong views on both sides.'

A good-looking twenty-something guy, wearing

an earring and grinning, asked the obvious question, which clearly was what Tom Watts had intended.

'I'd like to ask you, like . . . have you had a job done and if so, what size are you now?' The audience burst out laughing.

'I do not wish to discuss that, it's personal and I refuse to comment.' She was clearly furious.

'Well, whether you have or haven't, I think you've got great knockers.'

Alan Morland, standing beside Lindsay, nearly had a heart attack, knowing they'd come under fire for that remark. He signalled to Tom Watts to move on. Tom ignored him.

'How many people in the audience would have cosmetic surgery, if money were no object?' Only a handful were prepared to admit to it.

'The lady in red in the second row with her hand up, what would you like to have done?'

'I'm a size 36 double D so I'd have my boobs reduced. I'm fed up with men making suggestive comments every time I pass by.'

'Is this a problem you have?' Tom asked his guest.

'No.'

'But surely, you must have comments made about your appearance all the time?'

'Nothing I can't cope with.'

On and on it went until Tom was forced to end the interview and go to a commercial break. His guest didn't even wait for the applause, she stormed off and Lindsay knew there would be a row. She saw Alan go to talk to Tom, who looked very pleased with himself. She knew it would be strictly business until the show was over. Repercussions would come later. It seemed like only ten minutes before Tom said good night and the credits rolled. It was eleven o'clock and everyone breathed a sigh of relief. It had gone relatively smoothly, except for the Page Three model who'd had a screaming match with poor Alice before storming off.

The guests and crew adjourned to the hospitality room for a drink. Lindsay spent another half-hour making sure all her audience members who had been promised a drink were looked after. Suddenly she realized she was absolutely whacked.

'It's the same every week.' Geoff saw her yawn. 'You're on a high and then suddenly you're knackered. Then, when you get home, the adrenalin is still pumping and you can't sleep. Have a drink and relax.' Lindsay knew he was probably right so she headed for the bar.

'You look like you need a large glass of wine. Red or white?' Julie, one of their hostesses, grinned at her.

'White would be great. Is it always so busy after the show?'

'It's actually very quiet tonight, almost too civilized.' Julie smiled as she handed her a large glass of chilled white wine, which was surprisingly drinkable, Lindsay thought. She had been told to avoid the wine at all costs. 'It's usually plonk and it's always warm,' were Geoff's parting words, but in fact tonight it was neither. Anyway, she couldn't have cared less. This was fun.

Alan spotted her and came to chat. 'You were a great help, took a lot of pressure off me and thanks for all you did with the audience, it really made a difference.'

'No problem.'

'Here comes Tom, I need to talk to him before we all have a few drinks. I'll catch you later.'

Lindsay was content to sit and watch and relax. It had been an exciting day. It was her first real programme and even though she hadn't been given a credit at the end of the show, she felt part of it and was happy.

Chapter Twenty

Lindsay left the studios at twelve forty-five, having polished off a second glass of wine. She stopped at her local service station and bought all the papers she could find. She loved getting the Sundays on Saturday night on her way home, it always made her feel she had a head start on the coming day. Charlie was very pleased to see her and lay beside her in the bathroom as she removed her make-up, something he didn't normally do. He even accompanied her to the loo, sniffing at her bottom as she sat down, making her laugh so much that she couldn't go. She put on her childish, fleecy PJs and curled up on the sofa, not in the least bit sleepy, exactly as Geoff had promised. She skimmed all the papers and drank a mug of hot milk to help her on her way. She was laughing to herself at a funny article when she remembered that last week she would have read it aloud to Chris.

What a strange few weeks it's been, she thought and suddenly remembered Tara's date.

She dialled quickly, glancing at the clock. It was one-thirty.

'Hello,' a sleepy voice answered.

'It's me, can you talk?'

'Hi, Lindsay.'

'I'm just in, are you in bed?'

'Yeah.'

'Are you alone?'

'Yeah.'

'Are you asleep?'

'Yeah.'

'Right, just tell me did it go OK?'

'Yeah.'

'Good, call me first thing, hon. Nite nite.'

Typical girlie conversation.

After half an hour Lindsay gave in and went to bed herself and was soon dreaming of more television disasters, in which she played a starring role.

She woke to the phone ringing. It was eleven-thirty. She struggled to answer it, knowing it had to be Tara.

'I want to hear everything, but wait till I put some clothes on,' she laughed as she answered.

'If you insist, but as I can't see you what difference does it make?'

'Hello?'

'Hi, it's Chris.' Cue stomach flutters.

'Oh, hi, I was sure it would be Tara. I phoned her at one-thirty last night and I thought she might be getting her own back.' She spoke fast because she felt nervous and didn't know why.

'Want to call me back later?'

'No, hang on . . . now, that's better, I'm back in bed so I'm not freezing my ass off. Thanks for your text, I was going to text you back this morning.'

'That's OK. I really did enjoy Friday night. It was very relaxing.'

'I thought maybe you'd been bored to death. Not a very exciting night, when you think about it.'

'Well, it would be hard to top the Friday before for excitement, but no, it was exactly what I needed. I never seem to get time these days to just sit and relax, with no pressure. So, thanks.'

'My pleasure.'

'How did last night go?'

Lindsay made him laugh telling him of the drama behind the scenes.

'Did you see our Page Three girl?'

'No, I was out but I taped it and I'll run it while I read the papers later.'

Another date? She wondered but didn't ask.

'What are you up to today?'

'Nothing, except a walk with Charlie and a drink with the girls later. I intend to have a long bath and be lazy. How about you?'

'My mum's in town so I'm taking her to lunch in Café Caprice. Then a friend's having a dinner party later and I'll probably go there for a few hours. Apart from that, not much, might go to the gym and I have to swing by the office later.'

'Wow, sounds like a lot to me, I'm tired just listening to you,' Lindsay grinned. 'I think I'll have a cup of tea and go back for a snooze.' She realized it was the first time they'd talked on the phone. It made him seem more real somehow and she felt close to him. She still had this mental image of a 'celebrity' and was always surprised to find that he was quite ordinary really. He was also a nice person; you sort of knew he cared about people. He didn't seem to be self obsessed, like most good-looking men. Hell, like most men, in fact.

'Lazy thing. Listen, about Wednesday, could we put off the cooking till another night? I have to go to London again tomorrow and I might not get back until Wednesday evening.'

'Yeah, sure. Want to give me a call during the week?' Lindsay was proud of herself for keeping it cool.

'Well, we could go to the movies on Wednesday evening anyway and then I could cook another night. How does that sound?'

'Great.'

They arranged to meet in town at seven on Wednesday as he was coming straight from the airport. Lindsay hung up and snuggled down under the sheets, glad he'd called.

She was suddenly awake.

The phone rang again.

'Hello.' She was less sure this time.

'I can't believe you rang me at two o'clock in the morning, I was fast asleep.'

'It was only one-thirty. Tell me all. No, wait, let me get up and put the kettle on. I'll ring you back in five minutes.'

'No, because we'll be on the phone for an hour at least, then I'll have to do the same with Debbie and then you'll both want to hear it all again tonight anyway. So, you'll have to wait until later.'

'Bitch.'

'I know, see you half-eight in McGivneys.'

True to her word, Lindsay did absolutely nothing all day, except veg and watch TV and read and nibble. It was heaven. Charlie made several attempts to interest her in a walk, then gave up and simply sat by the back door for an hour, hoping she'd notice. She resisted all his efforts at emotional blackmail – holding the ball in his mouth, chasing around under her feet and nibbling her toes, looking longingly at the hook where his lead hung limply.

After a snack of chocolate biscuits and crisps, she adjourned to the bath where she soaked in juniper berry and ylang ylang essential oils then did her nails and applied moisturizer lavishly to her lazy body, revelling in the luxury of time off. She refused to even think about Christmas, which was almost here. Somehow it didn't matter so much this year, because of all that had happened. She wondered what Paul would be doing and felt the old familiar longing, but for the first time thinking of him didn't bring him close. Somehow he'd slipped out of her net and he felt far away.

At eight-thirty she met the girls in one of their locals, near enough for Lindsay to walk to, snuggled into her sexy black shearling coat, which had cost a bomb but made her feel filthy rich.

They were waiting, Debbie almost hysterical because Tara wouldn't say a word until the three of them were together.

'Sorry, sorry, just let me get a drink and I'm with you.'

'You don't need a drink – here, have half of mine.' Debbie was desperate.

'What are you on? I'll only be a second. Anyone want anything?'

Lindsay was already halfway to the bar.

Three minutes later they were ensconced in the corner, deep in conversation, oblivious to everyone.

'It went well, we had a few drinks and just talked—'

'Whoa, girl, don't do this to me.' Debbie had missed the build up because she'd been flying for the past two days. 'Start at the beginning. What were you wearing? Did he collect you? How did you feel when you saw him . . . ?'

It transpired that Tara and Michael had a lot in common and he was quite shy. 'He asked me a lot about myself, which is almost unheard of, if the guys I've been out with are anything to go by. Normally they talk about themselves or sport or politics.'

'Or sex,' Debbie laughed. 'Honestly, the number of guys on my flights who talk about women and getting laid . . . I swear they're obsessed.'

'Well, I'd say he hasn't even thought about sex since he and his wife separated,' Tara said naïvely and the other two howled.

'God love your innocence. He might not have

mentioned it to you but he has definitely thought about it, maybe even done more than that,' Debbie winked. 'How's his eyesight?'

They fell about laughing, getting some very odd looks from the regulars.

'Every ten seconds, that's how often men think about sex.'

Suddenly, they were off on another tangent, the drinks flowed and the three of them revelled in the gossip and scandal and companionship. They were very impressed with Chris and his text and awarded him another ten brownie points. They had a long discussion about breasts, brought on by an argument about whether the pair at the next table were Jordans or genuine.

They finished up at eleven-thirty, having discovered that Michael had left Tara to her taxi and kissed her briefly.

'On the cheek.'

'What?'

'I liked it, it was sort of sweet and I felt really comfortable with him. Safe, I suppose. But nicely safe, not boringly safe.'

'God, how did I ever end up with you two as best friends?' Debbie wondered. 'One likes a kiss on the cheek on the first date and the other bonks her guys senseless.'

They kept it up as they walked back towards Lindsay's house, from where the other two would call a taxi. They stopped for fish 'n' chips en route, resolving to keep them until they reached the warmth of the kitchen but unable to resist the salty, sodden potatoes as soon as they caught the smell.

They had very little left by the time they reached their destination but tucked into the remains and drank copious amounts of hot tea and kept the buzz going. It was warm and easy.

Thirty minutes later Lindsay was in bed, as tired as if she'd worked all day.

Next morning, Lindsay was glad not to have to go into the office, as the team worked from Tuesday to Saturday unless there was an emergency. She checked in by phone just in case she was needed, then gave the house a minor tidy up, did some more Christmas shopping, met Debbie for a quick lunch and called to see her Mum on the way home. Miriam Davidson was rushing around as usual, but she wanted to hear all about the new job. Lindsay chatted freely, but somehow didn't mention Chris, even when her mother remarked on how well she was looking. This was most unusual. Her mother was normally too preoccupied with everything, well mostly herself. She didn't notice much about her children or grandchildren, which sometimes let them off the hook and other times hurt a bit.

'I don't suppose you've heard anything from Paul?'

'No.'

'Pity. I always liked him.' Lindsay somehow felt it was her fault that he'd left.

'So did I.'

'No need to be sarcastic, I was only asking.'

'I wasn't. I just feel you think it was somehow my fault that it ended.'

'Don't be ridiculous, of course I don't.' Somehow the words and the tone of voice didn't fit and today it rankled.

'Well, it turns out he didn't want to get married after all, at least not to me. But he had met someone else and he's going to marry her.' There, it was out.

Lindsay turned away, feeling the familiar feelings rush in, but not before she'd seen the shock on her mother's face. For a second, she wanted to collapse into those strong arms, but she wasn't used to it and it didn't come easy at this stage in her life – odd really, when you considered her other close relationships. Instead she turned back towards the older woman. 'Anyway, it's over and I'm getting on with my life and I feel quite good about things at the moment.'

'I'm sorry, it must have been hard, I wish you'd told me sooner.'

'You're always busy.' It was said matter-of-factly, no blame attached.

'I'm always here if you need me.'

'OK thanks.' She saw the look of sorrow on her mother's face and knew it was genuine. She suspected neither of them knew what to say next.

They had a cup of tea and Lindsay made some small talk and left. Later she thought about their conversation and felt a bit down, knowing they needed to talk a lot more about a lot of things.

Tuesday morning was the weekly meeting and it was fiery. The ratings had just come in and the show was down on the previous week. They had started on a high and held their viewers until after the Page Three girl, but lost out to a rival chat show after ten-fifteen.

Tom Watts wasn't shy about where the blame lay.

'We're all becoming too complacent. I don't want anyone else on the show pushing a book.'

Alan steered the discussion around to the last two programmes before Christmas. It had been agreed to keep the last show light, full of bits 'n' pieces – competitions, music, celebrity presents, etc. Lindsay thought this was a mistake, because it was precisely what every other daytime show would be doing that week. She felt the audience would want a more meaty show and said so.

Tom Watts shot her down immediately. 'Anyone at home on the Saturday before Christmas wants to be entertained, not depressed by debates on abortion or suicide.'

'It doesn't have to be either Christmas presents or suicide. I think there's a fairly large middle ground.' Lindsay was not about to be intimidated. A couple of the researchers agreed, although all admitted that finding celebrities willing to travel so close to the holiday period was a problem.

They tossed the ideas round for an hour and agreed to have a further meeting later in the week. Meanwhile this week's show needed attention, if the ratings problem was to be addressed. They all set to work.

On Wednesday morning Lindsay got a text from Chris.

SORRY, WILL B IN LONDON TILL THURS. C U AT
W/END?

It took her a few moments to realize how much
she'd been looking forward to seeing him. She
went ahead with her hair appointment just to convince herself it wasn't for him.

Chapter Twenty-One

On Wednesday evening, Lindsay didn't feel great and by Thursday she had all the symptoms of flu. She woke with a terrible headache and a temperature, feeling as if she had been put through a mangle. Even getting out of bed was a struggle. She swallowed some tablets and sat in the kitchen, shivering in spite of the warmth.

Maybe a shower would improve things, she thought wearily, then suddenly realized that she couldn't do it. Her body felt heavy, yet had the consistency of a bowl of jelly and she knew she'd have to go back to bed, feeling guilty as she always did when she got sick, as if it was her fault, somehow.

She rang the office and spoke to Alan Morland, who was working although it was barely eight-fifteen. He assured her that they'd survive without her.

She made a warm lemon drink, filled two hot-water bottles and crawled back to bed. She slept on and off all day, got up for an hour or two and made some soup, then tossed and turned all night.

Friday morning was the same, except today her legs wouldn't support her. She rang her local doctor's surgery. They were inundated with patients, mostly with the same symptoms. Could she come in? 'No, I feel too weak.' Best they could offer was a visit from a locum who would give her a prescription for antibiotics. She accepted.

She struggled downstairs for tea and toast but couldn't taste either, so she crawled back to bed for the second morning, deciding to ring Tara and moan.

'What will I do about Chris? I'm supposed to be going to his house tonight and I look like a witch!'

'Don't be ridiculous, call him and put it off. I'll ring Debbie and one or both of us will be round after work. Meantime, do you need anything?'

'Arsenic would be good.'

'Stop feeling sorry for yourself, you'll survive. It usually takes three days to hit, then three days when you feel like dying then three days to go.'

'In that case I should be OK by January. Thanks, I really needed to hear that.'

Tara laughed. 'I'd forgotten what a grumpy old cow you are when you're sick. Tuck yourself in and I'll see you later.'

Lindsay couldn't sleep. She didn't want to phone Chris because she felt so awful. Texting was the only option.

I'VE GOT FLU. WON'T MAKE IT 2NITE. REALLY SORRY.

She got a reply an hour later.

I'M IN PARIS. WON'T GET HOME 2NITE. WAS
JUST ABOUT 2 TEXT U. SORRY UR SICK. SPEAK
2 U 2MORO. XX

She was disappointed and relieved. One look at
her blotchy skin, greasy hair and goose pimples
should see him off in record time, yet she wished
he would just call in and give her a hug. She dozed
on and off and rang her mother.

'Oh dear, I am sorry. I'm just off to play golf. Will
I get Anne to drop by?'

Thanks a million.

'No, I'm OK, don't worry.' She clearly wasn't
worried in the slightest.

Anne rang. 'Are you OK? Want some company?'

'No thanks, but I may need someone to get a
prescription later. Meantime, I think I just need to
sleep it off.'

'No problem, just call when the doc's been. I'll
be round in a flash.'

The afternoon dragged by and she couldn't even
watch TV. Her eyes hurt. Her bottom was sore.
Every single bit of her had something wrong with
it. The doctor was in and gone within five minutes,
no sympathy, which didn't help. The girls arrived
at seven with flowers and Lucozade and grapes
and a bottle of whiskey 'for medicinal purposes
only'.

'God, you look awful. Be very glad Chris is not
in the country.'

'Thanks, I really needed that.'

'I'll make some soup,' Tara said kindly.

'No, please, I can't face any more soup.'

Anne dropped in briefly to collect the prescription. 'God, you look awful.'

'Go to hell and take Debbie with you.'

Her sister left, grinning sheepishly, promising to drop the tablets through the letter box on her way home from the late-night pharmacy, after another round of shopping.

'Let's order in Chinese,' Debbie grinned, ignoring the jibe. Lindsay wanted to throw up.

They eventually settled on pizza – again, vile smells forgotten. Lindsay sat in her dressing gown beside a roaring fire and shivered as she nursed a hot lemon drink.

Charlie glued himself to her feet, sensing her unhappiness. Tara had been out with Michael again, this time for dinner and he'd dropped her home.

'Yes?' Debbie was all ears.

'Nothing happened, although he did kiss me good night.'

'Yes?'

'That's all.'

'Good kisser, bad kisser?'

'Very good kisser.'

'Whoopee, I see bridesmaids' dresses.'

They all laughed, even though it hurt Lindsay. By ten o'clock she was exhausted and they trooped into her bedroom where they watched a movie, all three of them curled up in bed with Charlie on their feet. It reminded Lindsay of the last night they'd stayed with her, after she'd bumped into Paul. They were still laughing as they tucked her up and left,

193

promising to check-in in the morning. She slept for a couple of hours but woke early, feeling dehydrated, her skin even blotchier, if that were possible.

Even the girls couldn't cheer her up and she refused all offers of help.

She got another text at lunchtime.

ON MY WAY 2 MANILA! PROBABLY NOT BACK 4 A WEEK. R U OK?

She didn't even trust herself to reply, she felt so full of self-pity.

Luckily, she slept most of the day. Alan rang to check on her progress and left a message reminding her that she was invited to Christmas dinner the following night at Tom's house.

She rang him back late that afternoon, but got his answering machine.

'Alan, it's Lindsay. I'm still the same. Sorry but I won't make dinner tomorrow. I'll talk to you on Monday.'

The truth was, she felt she wasn't really entitled to be at the dinner but suddenly it only added to her misery. Besides, she would have loved to see where Tom Watts lived. She decided to sleep for another while then get up and watch the show. She woke at midnight, and then burst into tears because she'd missed the entire programme.

Another text message.

JUST ARRIVED. GORGEOUS WEATHER. GOING 4 SWIM LATER. R U FEELING ANY BETTER?

Her reply was brief.

I'M OK. STILL IN BED. TALK SOON.

Her phone rang.

'Hi Rudolph.'

'That's not even remotely funny. Besides it doesn't adequately convey to you that besides my gorgeous red nose I have the cutest blotchy, pasty face and particularly attractive hair that you could fry an egg on.'

'Just as well I'm in the Philippines, so. I suppose sex is out of the question?'

She burst out laughing.

They chatted for ages. It turned out he was following up an international drugs scandal that appeared to have its roots in Manila, so he expected to be there for a while.

Lindsay felt a bit better having talked to him. She abandoned what was left of the night and went back to sleep.

Her sister did some shopping the following day and the girls arrived with more fruit and magazines. It was Tuesday before Lindsay even began to feel normal enough to phone the office. Alan insisted she stay at home for the rest of the week: she suspected he just didn't want anyone else infected and she was not really essential to the production yet.

'No point in giving us your germs for Christmas.'

'Thanks, it's nice to feel needed.'

'Don't worry, I intend to work you to death in the New Year. Get all the rest you can.'

*   *   *

Suddenly, it was Christmas Eve. Lindsay still hadn't got her energy back, despite gallons of juice and masses of fresh food. She knew Chris had hoped to get home the previous night but hadn't heard from him.

She had lunch in town with the girls before they all departed, Tara to her parents in their lavish country home in Wicklow and Debbie to her mum and brothers by the sea near Wexford, further down the east coast. They exchanged presents and drank hot chocolate. To their surprise, Tara had invited Michael Russell to spend Christmas with them and he'd accepted.

'Well, he doesn't have any plans.'

They teased her mercilessly but they were secretly chuffed. Lindsay felt a bit lonely, thinking of how close her friend was to someone she'd met only a few weeks ago.

She'd hardly seen Chris.

After lunch she got her hair blow-dried, packed a bag, gathered her presents and Charlie and headed for her family home. Just as she was leaving she got a text.

WHERE R U? HOPING 2 C U B4 I GO HOME.

ON MY WAY 2 MUM'S. CALL ME IF U CAN.

CAN I CALL ROUND ON MY WAY?

I'D LIKE THAT.

She gave him the address and headed off, happier than she had been earlier. She'd missed him, she realized suddenly. It had felt odd seeing him one night on the main news bulletin, via satellite phone. He looked tanned and healthy, his blue eyes intensified by the background of the bright sky and she'd felt a bit lonely for him, which was stupid as she barely knew him. He'd been away for nearly two weeks.

She felt the familiar little-girl feelings she always experienced as she drove up the driveway of her family home. It looked great, a large double-fronted Edwardian house with imposing bay windows and beautiful grounds. Her parents had bought it for a song more than thirty years ago. They'd renovated it completely over the years and when her father died Miriam Davidson had thought about selling up and moving to an apartment, but thankfully decided against it. Lindsay loved this house, especially in winter with the vanilla-pod scent of jasmine and winter box and the magnificent variegated holly guarding the entrance.

As usual the Christmas tree was in the front window and the hall door was weighed down with an oversized crown of greenery. She missed her father very much at this time of year. Lindsay's mum was busy in the kitchen and greeted her enthusiastically.

'Can you light the candles on the mantelpiece in the drawing room? It's almost dark.'

'Sure, just let me dump my bags and Charlie. By the way, a friend of mine is calling in for a drink on his way home.'

'Fine, Anne and the gang will be here soon and I've got a couple of my golfing chums popping in.'

'Will I do my usual job on the fireplace?'

'I don't think I could stop you.'

Lindsay laughed and set to work, raiding the huge bowl of satsumas and studding a dozen or so with cloves, which she then placed on the mantelpiece in the big room. She could still remember seeing an American family on TV do it when she was about five years old and the tradition had stuck in the Davidson household, although Miriam felt it looked cheap and home-made. Lindsay loved the smell of the oranges and cloves that seemed to intensify with the heat of the blazing fire. She searched for her tiny little bottle of oil of orange, which her father had bought for her and which she'd kept hidden for years on the window sill behind the drapes, sprinkling it carefully over the log basket as she always did, enjoying the fact that nobody could work out how the smell became almost overpowering when a log was thrown on the fire. She'd giggled every year with her father over this, it became one of their many secrets. Now she laughed as Charlie settled himself in for a long, cosy evening, licking her hand to let her know that her secret was safe with him. The room looked perfect, yet somehow Lindsay had never really liked it. It had been furnished by an interior designer years ago and Lindsay had waited to be asked to re-do it when she took up her design job but the invitation never came. The room had everything yet lacked warmth and atmosphere, although Lindsay knew that the huge tree, glowing fire and candles (bought by her because Miriam thought them too messy) showed the room off to perfection. She ran upstairs and fixed her make-up. She was wearing her favourite black leather trousers with a tight black sweater, the severity of the look softened by a huge studded cross which nestled somewhere in her cleavage and gorgeous earrings, a last present from Paul. Her hair was wavy and shiny and she felt good, partly because she'd lost over half a stone during her illness.

The doorbell rang: her mother's friends who thankfully adjourned to the kitchen. Lindsay felt herself getting excited at the idea of seeing Chris again and by the time the bell chimed a second time she had to stop herself dashing to open it. Unfortunately, her nonchalant approach meant her mother got there first.

'Hello.' Lindsay could sense immediate interest.

'Hello, I'm Chris.' He held out his hand.

'Hi.' Lindsay lunged forward, almost tripping in her eagerness.

'Hi, how are you?' That smile again.

'Come in, please. I'm Miriam.'

Lindsay could hear her mother's brain ticking over. Please don't let him know how grateful you are for his interest in your spinster daughter, Lindsay pleaded silently, fixing her mother with what she hoped was a 'back off' stare. So intent was she that she didn't see Chris lean over to kiss her – on the lips – which sent her stomach crashing and her mother's antennae soaring.

He grinned at her discomfort as all three of them entered the drawing room.

'Now, would you like a glass of champagne?'

Oh oh, he's getting the full treatment, Lindsay thought maliciously, wishing her mother would just leave them alone.

'Actually, a beer would be fine, if you have one.'

'Lindsay?'

'I'd love a glass but don't worry, Mum, I'll organize it. You go back to your friends.' Lindsay headed for the kitchen with her mother's sleeve firmly in her hand.

'Why didn't you tell me HE was coming?'

'You know him?' Lindsay was amazed, her mother had no interest in television.

'Not exactly, but I know he's somebody. How long has he been your boyfriend?'

'He's just a friend.'

'But—'

'Mum, back off.'

You're only interested because of who he is. Bet he makes up for me losing Paul, Lindsay wanted to say but held back. It was Christmas and anyway she was probably being a bit unfair. Her mother had always made her friends welcome, no matter who they were.

Lindsay got the drinks, leaving her mother name-dropping, no doubt, and returned to Chris.

'What's the smell in this room? It's great.'

Lindsay laughed out loud and told him her secret recipe for creating Christmas.

Charlie came in to check out the intruder and received a present for his trouble.

'What is it?'

'Open it, I bought it in Paris in a dog boutique. Can you believe it?'

'A dog boutique, now I know you're definitely mad.'

It was a sun visor for dogs, in lurid lime green. The idea was that it was kept on with Velcro, behind the ears, and it came complete with a pair of sunglasses, clipped on to the visor. Lindsay couldn't stop laughing as they tried it on. Charlie pranced around the room, trying to eat the glasses, a bit like trying to bite his tail. It was hilarious.

'And these are for you and I promise they came from a slightly more tasteful shop.'

Lindsay was mortified. 'I didn't get you anything, I didn't expect to see you over the holidays. And I was sick,' she added lamely.

'No problem, it was easy for me, I was in London AND Paris. I spent lots of time hanging around waiting for interviews so I did all my Christmas shopping. Only thing is, it stays under the tree till tomorrow morning.'

'No way.' She had already started on the packaging.

'That's the condition on which you get it, so stop acting like a spoilt brat.'

'OK.'

'Happy Christmas.'

He suddenly came closer and took her glass and pulled her towards him and kissed her – a long, slow, wet kiss that lasted for hours.

'I missed you.' Cue heart thumps.

'I missed you too.'

'Good. Now . . .' He sat on the couch and pulled her down beside him. 'Tell me your news. How's the flu?'

They chatted for ages, then he had to leave in order to arrive in Galway for the family celebration. Apparently they always had a big party on Christmas Eve.

'I'll call you, give me your number here.'

She did and he gave her his and she walked him to his car and waved him off, happier than she'd been in a long time.

Chapter Twenty-Two

The rest of the day was spent in perfect harmony, relaxing, sipping champagne, bathing and putting her nephews to bed. Her sister Anne looked exhausted but assured them it was just overwork. Anne's husband David ran his own marketing company and often worked late, leaving Anne to run the house and manage the kids. She also worked part time as a teacher and complained, like most mothers, of being constantly exhausted. Lindsay made her put her feet up and relax with a drink, which she said was the best Christmas present ever.

At ten, mother and daughters walked up to midnight Mass, another Davidson tradition, while David babysat and got the Santa presents ready. They had a light supper of baked ham and crusty bread and cheese and Lindsay was asleep seconds after her head touched the pillow.

As with millions of houses around the world, Christmas morning started ludicrously early. Jake, her youngest nephew, crept into Lindsay's bedroom on the basis that she was the only one who wouldn't try to persuade him that Santa was still in Sweden and had to get to all the countries in between before he hit Ireland.

'Has he come?'

'I don't know. Let's take a look out the window and see if there are any sleigh marks.'

'Yes, I can see them, there they are and there's Rudolph's paws.'

'Well then, we'd better just listen for a minute at the top of the stairs to make sure he's not still here.'

'OK.'

Lindsay crawled out of her haven, wiped away the remnants of sleep and followed the excited little boy.

He was wedged between the banisters, listening intently.

'Any noise?'

'No, he must be gone. Will we check the carrot?'

'Yes, we'd better, because Charlie usually barks when he arrives and I didn't hear anything.'

'Is Charlie afraid of Santa?'

'No, I think he's a bit jealous cause of the cake and the carrot.'

They padded down the stairway and into the kitchen. Sure enough, the glass of sherry had been demolished and the carrot was a stump.

Jake fell over himself trying to get to the tree and they spent a very happy hour opening all their presents, joined almost immediately by Luke, who of course had heard the commotion that the adults amazingly had not.

Lindsay opened her present from Chris, a pair of

gorgeous antique garnet earrings, long and glamorous and exactly right. She was delighted and mentally consigned the pair on her dressing table to charity or Debbie.

Breakfast was prepared – fresh rolls, juice and a big fry-up – and the table set by the time the other adults were tempted out of oblivion.

Afterwards, they all went to visit the usual collection of relations, returning home about three. Everyone helped with dinner, a big formal affair in the dining room with cut glass and good silverware and real napkins and a blazing fire, another Davidson tradition.

They'd all adjourned to fight over the TV when Chris phoned. Her mother greeted him like a long-lost friend and Lindsay knew she was filling the others in as she took the call.

'Hi, how are you?'

'Fat as a fool and the proud owner of six new pairs of navy socks and three bottles of Old Spice. You?'

'I was obviously a much better person all year because Santa brought me the most amazing pair of earrings that suit my colouring perfectly and are dangling in the light as we speak. Thank you.'

'Pleasure. How did the day go?'

'It was great. Jake had me awake at five-thirty and we had a ball. Later we visited lots of elderly aunts, then my father's grave, which is always a bit sad. But we've just finished a gorgeous dinner and are fighting over which movie to watch.'

'Sounds just like us. Our party went on till four so no one got up early and we haven't eaten yet.

Knowing my mother it will be at least nine o'clock although she always plans it for five and we end up tearing the turkey to bits while we wait.'

They swapped more horror stories for a while then Chris was called away as one of his friends had arrived unexpectedly.

'I'm coming back to Dublin on the twenty-eighth because a friend of mine is getting married the next day. So how about I cook you that famous dinner the night after? Although I can't promise not to be hungover. Weddings aren't really my thing.'

'OK, fine.'

'What are you doing on New Year's Eve, by the way?'

'Debbie's having a party and I've been roped in to help with the food. How about you?'

'My sister's doing the same and I've been roped in to be a spare male. I think I'd rather be in your shoes.'

'You haven't been to one of Debbie's parties. Lots of pilots who think they're God's gift trying to feel you up.'

'Tell them I said to leave you alone.'

'Yeah right, that'll frighten them all right.' They laughed and chatted easily for a minute or two longer and she felt close to him.

'OK, gotta go. I'll talk to you before that anyhow.'

'Enjoy the madhouse.'

Lindsay came back and knew they'd been discussing her but she also knew her sister would wait to be told.

St Stephen's Day or Boxing Day, depending on

where you lived, meant a long walk and lots of reheated food and too many chocolates so Lindsay was relieved to return home the following day. She wanted to get organized so she called into the office to check her e-mails and take home a few files.

Debbie and Tara were still away and she had a message from her new friend Carrie, wondering when they could meet for a chat. Carrie had been working outside Dublin for the few weeks before Christmas and she refused to tell Lindsay what had happened between her and Dan Pearson 'until I have a pint in my hand'. Lindsay left her a message begging her to call as soon as she got back to town.

She spent the rest of the day clearing up the debris from her flu – mouldy grapes and mounds of tissues and empty bottles and too many magazines – then flopped on the couch with the remote and Charlie. Not very exciting.

Around nine o'clock she had a sudden urge to ring Chris. She dialled the number he had given her. She felt a bit apprehensive but wasn't sure why. She needn't have worried, he wasn't home. 'Try his mobile,' a vague-sounding girl offered, putting paid to her hopes that he'd mentioned to anyone that she might call. She gave up, sent him a text and then regretted it, in case he thought she'd nothing better to do, or was checking up on him. Ridiculous, this constant insecurity. She had a long soak and went to bed.

She didn't hear from him until the following evening.

ON MY WAY BACK. R U SURVIVING?

BACK HOME SO NEARLY NORMAL. WORKING 2MORO. NJOY THE WEDDING.

STILL ON 4 DINNER FRI?

I'M HUNGRY ALREADY.

WILL U STAY OVER?

I'LL HAVE 2 ASK CHARLIE.

BRING HIM ALONG.

HE'S FUSSY BOUT WHERE HE STAYS.

TELL HIM I LIVE NEXT DOOR 2 AN ORGANIC BUTCHER.

HE'S PACKING.

C U ABOUT 8?

I'M PACKING 2.

U WON'T NEED ANY CLOTHES.

NOT EVEN FISHNET STOCKINGS AND MY NEW CROTCHLESS KNICKERS?

MAYBE JUST A SMALL BAG THEN.

On and on it went, until he told her he was no longer able to concentrate and she texted good night, still smiling. She felt very much at ease with him although talking to him face to face was somehow less easy. Still, she knew they were becoming closer.

The girls came back the next day and life returned to normal. They spent hours on the phone planning what to wear, drink and cook – in that order – for the famous party. Lindsay and Tara had agreed to do the shopping, on the basis that they were far more organized. Debbie set about cleaning her little house, moving furniture upstairs and removing any delicate objects.

The other two were to be at her house by lunchtime on New Year's Eve, to start cooking. Charlie was designated official party animal so Lindsay decided to pack all her stuff when going to Chris's house and head straight for Debbie's from there the next day. Friday was lurking in the back of her mind and just thinking about it filled her with delicious anticipation. She found the idea of knowing in advance that she would be spending the night with him very erotic and suddenly she began to think of the two of them together at the oddest moments, like when she was washing the car. It hung around her like a sinful, guilty secret, haunting her in a very pleasurable way.

She had already decided what she was going to wear – her gorgeous black Joseph suit, which had cost a fortune, even in the sales in Brown Thomas. It was the softest material, very simple, but cut magnificently and it hung perfectly, the long tapered jacket fitted at the waist and the skirt short. She planned to combine it with sheer black stockings and black suede knee-high boots and wear nothing underneath on top except a gorgeous black, lacy bodice, which would remain hidden until the jacket was unbuttoned and then reveal a very voluptuous cleavage that owed more to padding than nature. Hopefully, by the time he got to the foam filling he'd be sufficiently interested anyway. She would get her hair blow-dried but then tie it back so that the whole look was understated with just a hint of sexiness on the outside, only to reveal a complete slut, vamp, tramp, or sex goddess – she still wasn't sure which – underneath. She knew she would never be considered a sex goddess, but liked the feelings just thinking about it aroused.

Chapter Twenty-Three

The flutters had already started by the time she rang the doorbell at ten past eight on Friday night. Charlie was hysterical, being out on a 'midnight' adventure was a relatively new experience and she had a hard job keeping him – and his hair – off her suit. He just loved the smells that darkness seemed to create and darted about everywhere. She was glad Chris had buzzed her in rather than let her in himself because she sort of fell in the door, complete with thrusting dog, flowers and overnight bag.

He leaned over the banisters and grinned at her and she suddenly felt overdressed and foolish, especially since he was in jeans and a T-shirt.

'Hi, come on up, my mother just called in for a second.'

'Oh, right, OK.'

Fabulous. She tugged at her skirt and held the flowers close to her chest.

'Hi, Charlie.' As soon as he heard a friendly

voice, particularly one that had provided him with the juiciest bone ever, Charlie took off, taking Lindsay with him so that she arrived at his door covered in dog hairs with her own sort of 'looser' than she would have liked.

'Hi.'

'Come in, you look like you could do with a drink.'

'Remind me never to bring my dog to dinner again, especially to one that smells as good as this.'

She followed him in to the most fantastic apartment, completely unlike her house. It was all wood and stark walls and gorgeous artwork, with oversized windows and ceilings that reached the sky.

'This is my mother, Nina. She's in town for the weekend and just dropped in on her way to dinner.'

'Hi, I'm Lindsay.' She shook hands with a tall aristocratic-looking woman with a warm smile who looked at her kindly.

'Hello, Lindsay, what a gorgeous dog.'

The said gorgeous dog was lying on his back, everything exposed and dangling, waiting to be stroked. Lindsay sort of nudged him – no, kicked him – and he yelped and looked offended. She thrust the ginormous bunch of Casablanca lilies at Chris and folded her arms tightly.

'Thanks, I don't think anyone's ever bought me flowers before. They're great.'

She tried desperately to think of some witty reply but just grinned stupidly.

'I'm very impressed with the smells coming from the kitchen. Lindsay, I'd be careful, he's obviously very keen.' Nina winked at her and picked up her bag. 'Well, I'll leave you to it, enjoy your evening. I hope I'll see you again sometime.'

'Talk to you over the weekend,' she told Chris and was gone.

Why can't all mothers be just that interested, Lindsay thought unkindly.

'Glass of wine?'

'Yes, please, white if you have it. Your apartment's really great, by the way.'

'Thanks, I'm never quite sure. Sometimes, when I've been away I come home and I think, yes, I absolutely love it. Then when I've been here for a while I wonder if it's not a bit cold.'

'Oh no, on the contrary, I think the wood and the amazing colours of the art really add warmth.'

'That's good coming from you. There you go.' He handed her a glass of wine. 'You look great, by the way.'

She had perched herself on a high stool in the kitchen, feeling a bit self-conscious when she saw him looking at her. The outfit had definitely been a mistake. He looked relaxed and she looked like a high-class hooker.

'Thanks. Charlie's made himself at home anyway.'

The dog was stretched out in front of a very modern stove, lying on the softest creamy-white rug.

'Good, you do the same.'

'What, lie on my back with my legs in the air?' She was sorry as soon as she'd said it. What was wrong with her, she wondered. She seemed to

213

be always making too much of the whole sex thing with him and her attempts at seduction had seriously backfired.

'Well, yes, if you really want to, but I meant make yourself at home. Want me to take your jacket?'

'Er, no thanks, I'm fine.' She felt completely foolish and wondered if she could put a pin in her jacket when she realized he was standing beside her.

'What's up?'

'Nothing, why?'

'You look uncomfortable.'

'Actually . . .' She made an instant decision. 'Would you mind if I changed? I brought jeans and a T-shirt in case I . . . erm . . . stayed over and er, I'd be more comfy, I think . . . maybe . . . I might . . .'

'Sure. I'll show you the bedroom. Although if you do change, does that mean you keep on whatever that bit of black lace is that I can't help noticing at the top of your skirt.'

'Well, I don't know too many women who wear stay-ups with jeans, but . . .'

'Come on'. He was laughing at her as he led the way into an oversized room, almost entirely white, dominated by a huge bed with a soft, chocolate leather headboard and base and the most amazing, bright yellow bedclothes. On the wall behind the bed there was an enormous painting in various shades of yellows and oranges. Everything else was hidden behind anonymous white doors.

A long, sleek leather recliner and a TV, video and DVD were the only other items visible. The effect was tranquil and cool, with the yellow providing the sunshine.

She decided to come clean.

'I think I got it all wrong tonight. You see, the fact that we've already had sex made me think I needed to spice it up a bit so I sort of went for the prim schoolteacher look, you know . . . sexy underneath sort of thing.' She could feel a slight heat moving up her neck. 'It all went wrong when Charlie propelled me up the stairs, with my hair falling down and my boobs hanging out. God, what must your mother have thought?'

He was showing her the bathroom and she was behind him when she blurted this out to his back. He turned to look at her and burst out laughing.

'What are you on about? You're mad.' He stopped when he saw that she was embarrassed.

'Come here.' He lifted her up onto the counter top at the basin, which was the only available place to sit and stood in front of her and took her hands in his. He tilted her head, forcing her to look at him.

'First of all, my mother wouldn't care if you'd been naked, she takes people as she finds them and doesn't judge. So stop worrying. Secondly, what's all this about having to spice things up for me? I asked you to stay tonight because I wanted to spend some time with you, after all the running around I've been doing lately and then Christmas and everything. Sex between us so far has been fantastic and I'm looking forward to lots more but I want to get to know you as well. OK?'

'OK.'

He kissed her then, a kiss that started off gentle

and barely touching and somehow became much more intense. He moved even closer and she wound her legs around him as he pulled her to him. She arched towards him and her skirt rode up and he ran his hands over her body, feeling the silk of her legs, then the lace, then bare skin.

'You're beautiful and funny and smart and mad and I'm mad about you and you don't have to dress up for me although I love that you did.'

'I couldn't take off my jacket, even though I was roasting, cause I didn't have very much on underneath.'

'Show me.'

She slowly unbuttoned the garment, looking at him as his eyes followed her fingers. When she'd finished he lightly moved it back so that he could see her breasts, pushed up and not very well hidden, and she sat there with her skirt up around her waist and her legs wrapped around him and they tortured each other with lips, tongues and touches, tugging at clothes. On and on it went until neither wanted to stop, then he entered her and she thrust forward and they made love on top of the wash-hand basin with their clothes half on and it was one of the most erotic experiences – partly because it was so unexpected.

Afterwards, he took her to lie on his bed and they held each other and said very little until she asked, 'How's dinner? I'm starving.'

'Dinner might have become a takeaway at this stage I'm afraid.'

'No way, you're not getting off that easy. Go rescue.'

He kissed her on the forehead. 'Why don't you change into something comfortable – there are lots of clothes in the wardrobe – and I'll go check on the food.'

Her overnight bag was still at the front door so she searched in his closet and smelt the almost familiar scent of him and found a pair of jeans and one of his big white shirts. She liked knowing she was wearing his clothes. The shirt was miles too long so she tied it at her waist – abandoning the heavy bra and pinching stay-ups with glee.

Back in the bathroom she laughed when she saw her hair so she unpinned it and left it loose and decided against applying more make-up, even though the original had been seriously damaged in the earthquake.

When she reappeared in the kitchen he was indeed busy rescuing the food.

He handed her a fresh glass of wine, which she gulped thirstily as she resumed her position on the stool and watched, much more relaxed with him now.

'You look about fifteen.'

'I wish. How's the food?'

'Well, it's pasta and I had only done the sauce so I think we'll be OK.' He was boiling the kettle and opening some vermicelli as he spoke. 'Are you hungry enough to risk it?'

'Definitely.'

She set the table while he put the finishing touches to the meal and they ate in the kitchen with the help of a creamy, fat candle and a paper-thin, fingernail moon and it all tasted delicious, their appetites improved by the spontaneous exercise.

Dessert was simply fruit and cheese. They sat and chatted for ages, sharing stupid little nothings and being giddy. Afterwards, they cleaned up together and forgot to walk Charlie because they both wanted to go back to the closeness of the bed, where they watched TV in the dark, kissed and touched, and generally behaved like lovers.

Eventually Lindsay got up, removed what was left of her make-up and cleaned her teeth, and Chris got the house ready for bed. They tried to sleep but ended up talking for ages. She told him more about Paul and how she feared at the time they broke up that she would never be happy again.

'And now look at you, new job, new life, everything going for you.'

'Yeah, I don't think he'd even recognize me, I've changed so much.'

'How do you mean?'

'I dunno, I've just become more laid-back, less of a worrier, I live life more day to day now. I seemed to be always rushing around, wanting more, trying to manipulate things to go my way. Then, when the break-up happened it taught me that you can't always control things. I also became so self-obsessed, I don't know how the girls put up with me. I kind of prefer the new me, I'm a bit softer, all my hard edges have been chipped away.'

'Thanks for telling me.'

'Have you ever felt like that?'

'Sure, I think being in this business, especially when you're in the public eye, makes you go into yourself a bit. Sometimes, it feels like people expect you to be a certain type of person, because you're a "celebrity". At times I find myself performing and then I get really annoyed so I sort of retreat back to my small circle of friends who know me, so I can be myself. I've had my share of knocks too.'

'Like what?'

He hesitated, but only for a second.

'I went out with this girl once, a good few years ago. I really liked her, introduced her to all my friends. She'd even come home with me several times to meet my family. She seemed to be mad about me, then I discovered she'd slept with me for a bet. That did my ego a lot of good, I can tell you.'

'How did you get involved with her in the first place?'

'I met her in a nightclub. I wasn't very well known at the time but her friend recognized me and bet her £500 that she couldn't get me to sleep with her. I found out months later when the same friend got drunk at a party and thought it would be hilarious to tell me all about it.'

'And were you still going out with the girl at the time?'

'Sure was. She swore that she hadn't taken the money and that she really loved me but do you know something, I didn't believe her and there had been lots of other, little things . . .'

'I'm sorry that happened to you.'

'I got over it but it made me much more careful of people. And in a funny way I suppose that's what I was saying to you earlier. You see, she was absolutely stunning to look at and the sex was amazing and I thought I was really lucky to find her. But as it turned out she wasn't so nice after all. It taught me a lesson.'

'What?'

'That looks aren't really that important . . .'

'That's easy for you to say . . .'

He looked a bit sad for a moment. 'But relationships aren't really about looks or sex, although looks are the initial attraction and of course sex is very important. You have to really like the person, be able to trust them, know they're honest with you – otherwise it's all pointless really.'

'Thanks for telling me.'

'So now you know. And that's one of the best things about me now, funnily enough. I won't lie to you and I won't cheat on you and I'll always be honest with you, even if it hurts. I think it's the only way for a relationship to have any chance of surviving.'

She held out her hand. 'It's a deal.'

Chapter Twenty-Four

Lindsay woke to find two mouths very close to her face. One kissed her and the other one licked her.

'I was very relieved when I woke up and found it was your dog on top of me and not you, otherwise I'd have had to tell you about your weight problem.'

'Well, I thought you had very bad breath for a moment there. How the hell did he get in here?'

'The door was open. I heard him around four and he was on the floor. At five he was at the end of the bed, snoring. By seven he was trying to have sex with me.'

'Get off, you big oaf, you're not allowed on the bed.'

Charlie ignored her, rolling over and demanding to be played with.

'I'm really sorry.' She heaved her body and threw him off the bed.

Chris was already up. 'I think the poor dog is trying to tell us he needs to pee. So I'll put on the kettle and dash out for some croissants and papers and bring him with me, how does that sound?'

'Too good to be true. What's the catch?'

'You're making breakfast AND cleaning up.'

'Done.'

Lindsay lay there when they'd gone and savoured the moment. It had been a funny night and she was happy that it had happened the way it did, glad she'd allowed herself to be vulnerable with him and that he'd paid her the same compliment. Funny how admitting your weaknesses makes you more attractive to another person, sometimes, she thought, as she hopped out of bed and went to make some coffee.

She was standing in the kitchen in his white shirt, all legs and hair when Charlie bounded into the room, sending a book flying with a swish of his tail. Chris followed, grinning.

'What?'

'Nothing.'

'WHAT?'

'You snore.'

'I DO NOT.'

'You do – you did in the hotel but I didn't know how you'd take it if I told you. And you did it again last night.'

'Oh my God, that's impossible. It must have been Charlie.'

'Nope, sorry. Anyway, it was kind of cute. You sort of make little whale noises, all puffing and blowing with a big round mouth.'

'I'm leaving now.'

'You are not, not until you've made breakfast and cleaned up.'

They slagged each other for the next ten minutes but she was secretly mortified. Nobody had ever said that to her before. How come Paul had never told her?

Just another thing he never said, a little voice reminded her as Chris came up behind her and gave her a hug. 'Want to have breakfast in bed?' she said. He kissed the back of her neck.

'Only if you lock that animal up.'

'I will if YOU promise to get on top of me instead.'

'OK, but one lick and you're history.'

The morning passed far too quickly and it was time to leave and start cooking for Debbie. Lindsay phoned her friend before she left to see if anything was needed.

'No, just get over here as soon as you can. Tara is trying to organize me to death and I need back-up fast. Where are you?'

'I didn't go home last night.' Lindsay was trying to be diplomatic because Chris was reading the papers beside her.

'I know that, idiot, didn't he ask you to stay? Are you still there?'

'Yes.'

'Damn. I need more glasses. I don't suppose he'd have any.'

'I'll try.'

'Great. Get here as soon as you can.'

'Well, is she all set for the party?'

223

'No, Tara is trying to organize her. She needs some glasses. I don't suppose you have any you wouldn't mind lending?'

'Have a look over there, I'm afraid glasses aren't my strong point. I think I only have the few I bought when I moved in.'

'No, I need a couple of dozen, I'd say.'

'I could go and borrow some from Maurice, if you like. The hotel must have hundreds.'

'No, that's too much trouble.'

'No problem, if he has them. I'll ring him while you're in the shower.'

'Great, thanks.'

Lindsay washed and changed into her own clothes and was sorry to be leaving him, especially on New Year's Eve. He walked with her to her car and promised to see her later.

Tara was organizing and Debbie was resisting so she had arrived just in time.

'Did you get the glasses?'

'Chris is borrowing some from Maurice and he said he'd drop them over later,' she replied nonchalantly although she didn't feel in the least bit nonchalant.

'Whoopee, we get to meet him at last.' Tara and Debbie did a little dance, animosity forgotten. 'We'd better get into our glad rags before he arrives.'

They worked like mad and soon there were plates everywhere. Debbie made lots of spicy samosas and spring rolls and Tara took care of desserts. Lindsay did the main course – two huge

224

casseroles of coq au vin and a vegetarian lasagne, rice to be organized later. They made popadoms to go with the dips and ate most of them, then got together for a massive clean up, dishes first and then themselves.

They were sitting in Debbie's bedroom, drinking champagne and doing their make-up when the doorbell rang. Lindsay felt funny. It was the first time he'd met any of her important friends and it made their relationship seem real.

She ran downstairs, closely followed by the other two. 'We'll be in the sitting room, pretending not to be interested.'

'Hi, you found the house.'

'Yeah, no problem.' He kissed her and grinned. 'How's it all going? You've got flour on your nose.'

'You say the nicest things. I wasn't allowed a shower because I'd already had one in your house. Then by the time I got to do my make-up the others had hogged the mirror.' She had changed, however, into a new black dress – tightly fitted, strappy bodice top with a silk skirt that flowed from just below her boobs, the entire thing covered by another long-sleeved dress in really fine fishnet. It revealed a lot of skin through the net and it looked expensive and sexy, especially with the sheer stockings and high, black heels and she felt great that he'd seen her in it.

'You look gorgeous, far too good to be out on your own.'

They seemed to be occupying a little world of their own when Debbie and Tara 'casually' emerged, terrified in case he just dropped the glasses and left.

'Hi. Come in.'

Debbie had decided to be the perfect hostess, in black leather and masses of copper curls.

'Hello, I finally get to meet you two. God, I'd say you're a dangerous threesome when you get out together.'

'Nonsense, we're pussycats. Well, I am anyway and I try to keep them in check.' Tara looked brilliant in a tight, blue, knitted dress, all blond hair and big eyes. They made quite a picture as they unknowingly posed together and grinned at him.

'Glass of champagne?'

'I'll tell you, I've had more champagne since I met Lindsay . . . Yes please.'

He came and chatted and Lindsay watched him and her stomach lurched. He looked fantastic in a big, soft, dark grey suit and white shirt that showed off his tan. He'd showered and he smelt great and his hair was wet and she wanted a repeat of the bathroom scene. He caught her eye and winked at her and for a second she thought he could read her mind and she turned puce.

'I'd better leave, I've got to go home, dump my car and get to Sandycove. I hope the night goes well. I'd say the guys haven't a chance.'

'We'll try.'

They made themselves scarce while she led him to the door.

'What were you thinking of that you blushed as soon as I caught you looking at me?'

226

'Mind your own business.'

'Bet it was the same thing I was thinking when I saw you at the door.'

'You go first.'

'Bathroom.'

'Bingo.'

'Let's do it again soon. I'll call you next year.'

'Better make it early in the New Year. My diary's already pretty full.'

He laughed and was gone and she rushed back in to hear their reaction.

'My God, he is seriously gorgeous, much better than he looks on telly. Why didn't you tell us?'

'Now I understand why you couldn't wait to get his clothes off.'

'He kept looking at you and grinning.'

'He did not.'

'He did and you were being all girlie.'

'I was not.'

'He's so . . . I dunno, normal. Not like you'd expect.'

'I know, that's what I thought.'

'He's really nice. Oh, I'm so happy for you, you deserve it.'

They danced round the kitchen hugging and laughing and the night continued as it had started, with music, mayhem and mirth. The house was soon crammed and the party took off.

By midnight it was heaving. Even Charlie looked the part, in a ridiculous, cone-shaped, paper hat with streamers flowing from his collar. Like millions of others they took their countdown from TV then made complete fools of themselves by forming a snake and zigzagging up and down the road, kissing everyone they met.

As soon as they got back into the house Lindsay went to ring her mum and sister and chatted to them for ages. Then Tara borrowed her mobile because she couldn't find her handbag and the house phone was ringing non-stop.

It was after one by the time she got her mobile back and she had a text.

H.N.Y. ANY CHANCE OF A DATE B4 OCT?

She was delighted and dialled his number.

'Happy New Year.'

'Hi, same to you. How's it going?'

'Great. I miss you.' Oh oh, that was definitely the champagne talking.

'Me too, I keep thinking about that dress and what you're wearing underneath.'

'Nothing.'

'That's what I was afraid of.'

'I'll save you a sneak preview.'

'You'd better and keep away from those pilots.'

The noise was deafening on both ends of the phone so they agreed to talk in the morning. She hung up and went back to the party, hugging everyone again. It was the first big occasion that she hadn't thought of Paul.

It was five-thirty before Lindsay decided she couldn't take any more and crawled into bed in Debbie's spare room. Tara joined her almost immediately and tried to chat. They were both asleep within minutes.

Next morning, very late, Lindsay woke to find Tara standing over her with a mug of coffee.

'Debbie never went to bed. There are about five of them downstairs making pancakes for breakfast.'

'OK, come on, let's go down, we might as well see this thing through.'

It was four in the afternoon before a weary Lindsay and a bleary-eyed Charlie – still wearing the hat – arrived home. She forced herself into the shower, changed into her comfiest stretch jeans and tight red cashmere top, tied her hair back with a ribbon and drove out to see her mum. Charlie was flat against the Aga when she left and hadn't moved an inch when she returned two hours later.

Chris rang just as she arrived home.

'Hi, it's me. How did it go in the end?'

'I'm wrecked.'

'Me too, and I've another drinks party to go to this evening. Actually it's just around the corner from your house. Do you fancy popping in or are you doing something?'

'No, I'd planned to go through some stuff for work tomorrow. Anyway, I couldn't simply arrive at a drinks party, I won't know anyone.'

'You'll know me. Listen, no pressure, why don't you see how you go and give me a call. You could walk round for an hour, it's literally the next street to yours.'

'I think I'll stay put, thanks anyway. If I don't see you I'll talk to you tomorrow.'

'OK, I may have to go back to London but I'll let you know. Take care of yourself.'

'You too.' Lindsay hung up and settled herself down with her files and a glass of wine. She just about had the energy to put a match to one of those instant bags of coal and she sat and stared at the hot orange icepops, wondering why she'd suddenly felt too shy to walk into a party and announce that she was with him. It was still all so new and flimsy and delicious and she hugged it to her. Don't be greedy, she warned herself. Don't want too much. She was very happy with what she had. Plenty of time for confidence and showing off later. Contentment was not something she'd felt often in a relationship, but now she savoured it, even more so since she'd spent the night at his place. She knew they'd taken things to a different level.

She settled down, half hoping that he'd phone and ask her again to call round to the party. She changed her clothes and redid her make-up, knowing she'd be there like a shot if he asked again. Maybe she should ring him back. No, better wait and see.

The doorbell rang. She wondered. She ran. She smiled.

'Hi.'

Paul stood there.

Chapter Twenty-Five

It was pitch-black outside. Lindsay blinked, convinced it was Chris and that her mind was playing tricks. Then he spoke and she knew.

'Can I come in?' A voice like velvet that she thought she'd never hear again.

The old half of her wanted to grab him and drag him inside, in case he got away. Again. The other half wanted to kick him back down the path, roll him out onto the street, directly into the path of an oncoming bus.

She stood back, silently, hating herself for her unspoken enthusiasm.

'How are you?' asked eyes that could melt ice at twenty paces.

'Great,' a pair of too bright, confused ones answered.

'I wanted to talk to you. But first can I use your loo?'

Hardly the most romantic of introductions but she stood back anyway, helpless as usual, it seemed. He bounded up the stairs, well used to this space. She followed, unsure why, and went into the bedroom.

Flicking on the light, she checked herself in the mirror, foolishly glad she'd changed out of her comfies. Her face looked washed out. She felt sick. He, on the other hand, looked his usual polished self, although he'd put on a bit of weight and his face was fuller, even a touch jowly.

Suddenly he was beside her.

'God, we had some good times in this room, in this house. I've missed them.' He stood directly in front of her and touched her arm. He was close, very close and she could smell alcohol although he didn't look drunk.

She reached over and pulled down the blind, not wanting to be seen.

She was too late.

If she hadn't been so preoccupied she might have noticed Chris standing beside his car, on the other side of the road, staring directly at the two of them.

'Come down to the kitchen.' She felt uncomfortable and she didn't fully understand it. God knows she'd imagined him back in this room many times over the last few months, holding her, kissing her, telling her it was all a mistake. How many times had she woken and pictured him standing exactly where he now stood, watching her, undressing her with his eyes?

She flicked off the light and he followed her downstairs.

Charlie looked at him but didn't move and he made no attempt to greet the animal.

'Why did you come?' She needed to know. Quickly.

'I'd love a drink. Any chance?'

Automatically, she poured him a Scotch, glad to be busy for a moment, delighted to have an excuse to turn her back on him, afraid of the power he still had over her. She handed him the tumbler and finished her own glass of wine in a swallow, topping it up with more than she wanted and less than she needed.

He sat down on the couch and he wasn't as powerful as she'd imagined, in fact he'd definitely let himself go a bit, she thought. Or was she just seeing him as he really was? She deliberately didn't sit beside him, curling herself instead in a protective ball on one of the big squashy armchairs.

'I've thought about you a lot these past few weeks, especially over Christmas. We need to talk.'

'We needed to talk months ago but you never gave me the chance. Why now? What's changed?'

He knocked back the burning liquid and kept his eyes on her as he did so. Suddenly she saw he looked really tired, maybe that was what was different.

'I miss you.'

She didn't know whether to burst out laughing or burst into tears, but knew the former was based on hysteria and suspected the latter was much closer to how she was feeling.

'I missed you for months. It would have been easier for me if you'd died. It would have hurt a lot less.'

He was uncomfortable and she was glad. He

indicated his glass and she knew he needed to get away from her unforgiving eyes.

She gestured towards the bottle and he escaped for a refill.

'It was all a misunderstanding.' He was beside her again.

'What exactly did I not understand? The bit about you getting married, only not to me?'

'I panicked, I wasn't sure, it was nerves . . .' His voice trailed off.

'You were nervous so you asked someone else to marry you, while you were engaged to me?' She was convinced she must be going mad.

'I hadn't actually asked her to marry me, I just said that to make you back off for a while.'

'What?' She was definitely going bonkers.

'I'd met her and we'd seen each other for a drink after work, that sort of thing. I felt trapped with you and she didn't ask anything of me.'

'No.'

'I never intended it to go as far as it did . . .'

'You never even tried to contact me, to explain . . .'

'I was afraid to.'

'OK, let me get this straight. You lied to me, put me through all that, because you didn't want to tell me you needed a bit of space.'

She looked at him as if she'd never seen him before. 'How could you do that to me? What did I ever do to you to make you want to hurt me that badly?'

He drained and refilled his glass again, anything to avoid looking at her.

'Our break-up was the worst thing that ever happened to me. I nearly didn't make it through.' She was crying now, but not by choice. Big, wet, silent tears that might have gone unnoticed in the lamplight, except for the noisy dribbles and snuffles that gave her away. They were tears of frustration, anger, vulnerability.

'I'll make it up to you.'

'You couldn't.'

'Give me another chance.'

'I gave you everything I had and it wasn't enough. I've nothing left to give to you.'

'Look, let's go out somewhere, get something to eat, talk—'

'No.'

'I want us to get back together.'

'There is no us.'

'Look I've changed, I'll—'

'So have I.'

'I can explain, it wasn't as bad as it sounds . . .'

He was refilling his glass again and she realized he was quite drunk. In fact, he was starting to slur his words and as he poured another she noticed he'd had nearly half a bottle.

'Why are you drinking so fast?'

'Dutch courage.' He grinned and she remembered it and it hurt all over again.

'How much Dutch courage did you have before you came here?'

'One or two. I wasn't sure you'd talk to me but I knew I had to try and see you.'

'Why now? We've both changed . . . I've come a long way . . . I'm not the same person.' She

235

stopped, suddenly afraid that he could still hurt her. 'Why now . . . ?' It was the million-dollar question.

Just when it no longer kills me to hear your name, when I don't think about you every second any more, just when I've met someone else that I might be falling a little bit in love with. But she didn't have the courage to say any of it, or else didn't want him to know, afraid he'd spoil it like he'd spoilt everything else in her life.

'I want you to go.' She'd only just realized it.

'Can we go out tomorrow night, somewhere quiet, just to talk . . . Please?'

'No.'

'Think about it. I'll call you.' He stood up and swayed slightly.

'You can't drive like that, you'll kill yourself.' What the hell did she care?

He read her mind. 'Would you care?'

'I'll call a taxi. She dialled quickly, afraid of her answer and what it would do to them both.

In what can only be described as an act of God, the cab arrived within minutes, unheard of in the tiger economy that was modern Ireland.

'I'll call by in the morning to collect my car. Maybe we could have breakfast?'

'I have to be in work early, I have a meeting.' She lied easily.

He was at the door. 'I still love you, you know.' He delivered the final blow and for a second it punched her in the stomach and then, like a bolt of lightning, she realized that she didn't love him.

Not any more. It should have freed her but right now it was still too raw.

She closed the door quickly and just as she had all those months ago she slithered onto the cold, hard floor in the draughty hallway and cried for what might have been.

Chapter Twenty-Six

She didn't move for ages. Huddled against the wall like a well-dressed down-and-out seeking shelter, she didn't notice that Charlie was beside her until she eventually realized that something was saving her from the icy wind blowing in under the badly fitting front door. She got up because she had to, forcing her body out of its unnatural contortion, jerking as she put her numb foot to the floor. The hall was dark and the floorboards squeaky as she made her way slowly to the kitchen with her dog padding along, minding her.

The room was warm and cosy, the fire still doing its job. She shivered and sat down. Charlie hopped up beside her, ignoring the house rules. She stroked him because she knew it would keep him close and she needed the comfort. After a while she poured herself a brandy, trying to get the warmth back into her stiff, numb body.

For once, she didn't want to talk to anyone. She simply sat, nursing her drink and her dog, staring into the now dying flames as one might watch a not very good movie. Sometime later she saw the clock and discovered that it was well after midnight – almost three hours had passed since her visitor left. She turned out the lights and went to bed, stopping only to check her answering machine – the phone had rung a couple of times during the evening. No messages. She didn't care.

Ten minutes later, teeth brushed, hollow face washed clean by all her tears, she filled a hot-water bottle and climbed into bed where she clutched the warmth and curled up, foetus-like, and tried to protect herself until morning.

When it came it brought little relief to her aching body and throbbing head. She rose at seven and got a fright when she saw the grey face and lifeless eyes and black circles. She dressed and pounded the streets with Charlie, hair scraped back, dark glasses protecting her from prying eyes. She walked for over an hour and tried to make sense of it all, wondering why he still had the power to hurt her if she didn't care any more.

When she got back to the house she phoned Tara but she'd left for work and her mobile was off. Desperate, she tried Debbie, who was on her way home from the airport, having just got in on an early morning flight from London.

'What's up?'

'I need to talk to you, but I have to be in work by ten at the latest.'

'The traffic is terrible so I probably wouldn't get to you until after nine. What about lunch?'

'OK, see you at one in O'Shea's.'

'Are you OK?'

'Not really.'

'Is it Chris?'

'No.' Long pause. 'Paul called last night.'

'Called where?'

'At the house.'

'Were you there?'

'Yeah.'

'Did you let him in?'

'Yep.'

'What did he want?'

'Me. Back.'

'Jesus fucking Christ, the nerve of the bastard. Are you OK?'

'I dunno, I think so. I need to tell somebody.'

'Right, you hang on till lunchtime, OK babe?'

'OK.'

She showered and dressed and heard the phone ringing but didn't answer it. When she left for work at nine-thirty his car was gone.

'You look terrible,' Alan Morland greeted her as she entered the office.

'Happy New Year to you too,' was the best she could manage.

They had a meeting at ten but Lindsay couldn't remember a thing that was said. At eleven-thirty one of the secretaries arrived into the office completely hidden by a huge bunch of roses, which she handed to Lindsay. She couldn't bring herself to examine the card, hoping they were from Chris but afraid to risk it, at least until she was alone.

At twelve Alan sent her home, despite her protests.

'I swear I'm OK, I'm over the flu.'

'Well, then you need another day or two to rest. Go home, take it easy on your first day back and see how you feel in the morning.'

She gave in and rang Debbie, who insisted she come round to her place for lunch instead.

She arrived to a huge bowl of home-made soup and fresh, nutty brown bread, which Debbie forced her to finish.

'No point in making yourself ill again,' she advised.

Afterwards they went for a drive to the beach at Dollymount and Debbie parked the car and Lindsay poured out her short but eventful story.

'I don't believe it, I just don't fucking believe it,' was all she managed to say. Several times.

Tara rang at four. She'd been in court all day and had just been given Lindsay's message.

'We're heading for McGivney's. Call by on your way home and cancel any plans for this evening. It's an emergency.' Debbie was her usual straight-forward self.

'Are you OK?'

'It's Lindsay.'

'Is it Chris?'

'Paul.'

'Paul?'

'Fraid so and believe me you'll need a drink to stomach this one.'

'I'll be there in half an hour.'

So they sat and talked for the millionth time in this particular scenario and still didn't understand it, although Lindsay found it helped her greatly. Suddenly she began to thaw out and see things clearly, with the help of some obscene language from Debbie and a few hot whiskeys from Tara. They were shocked by his callousness, Tara more so because she was hearing it for the first time.

'Let me get this straight, he wasn't getting married at all . . . but why . . . ? How?'

'He said it was nerves, he wasn't sure he could go through with it and needed some space.'

'That I can understand but what a cruel fucking way to get it.' Lindsay realized that Debbie had gotten straight to the heart of things, as usual.

'I know, that's what I keep thinking. What did I ever do to him to make him treat me so cruelly and with so little love or compassion?'

'Listen, don't fool yourself. Whatever other good points he may have had, compassionate he wasn't.' Debbie was not in the mood to be tactful.

'This has nothing to do with you. It wasn't your fault.' Tara knew how hard this was for her.

'I feel used. I feel dirty. I feel as if I deserved it somehow.'

'You didn't.' Tara looked sad.

'Imagine that he could do that to me, though. And then, come back months later and expect to pick up where we left off. He didn't even ask me if I had met anyone, didn't even consider what effect all of this would have on me.'

'Please, before I slit my wrists, then yours, tell me you're not considering taking him back.'

'No.' She managed the tiniest grin.

As soon as she said it aloud she felt better, helped by their whoops of delight.

'Thank God, otherwise I'd have had to commit you.'

'I feel like having champagne as a treat.'

'No, please, I'm not even nearly at the stage of celebrating yet. I don't even feel relieved. I feel numb. I feel as if I've done fifteen rounds in a boxing ring. Somehow, I can't shake the feeling that I did something terrible for him to have treated me so badly.'

'You did nothing. This is not about you. Just thank God you didn't get as far as marrying the bastard.'

'Have you told Chris?' Tara wanted to know.

'No. I haven't talked to him. I think he may be in London.'

'Will you tell him?'

'I don't honestly know if I have the courage. I'm ashamed of it – ashamed that Paul cared so little for me that he treated me like that.'

'He'd understand. It could happen to anyone.'

'Yeah, I suppose so. I'm sure I will tell him – next time he asks me for a secret I'll probably just blurt it out.' She smiled, suddenly feeling close to him, even though she hadn't a clue where he was in the world or what he was up to. She'd call him later.

They ordered pub food – big juicy steaks with home-made chips and salad – nothing fancy but very tasty.

Lindsay felt almost human again as they walked

back to her house at nine. She'd forgotten to tell them about the flowers and handed Tara the card to open.

'Maybe they're from Chris.'

'I wish, but no, I don't think so somehow. I never did like red roses anyway.'

'Forgive me, I'll make it up to you,' Tara read and made one of her favourite 'I think I'm going to throw up' gestures.

'I don't think he'll give up too easily. You're going to have to spell it out to him.'

Lindsay was already checking her messages and there were two from Paul, asking her to call him.

'Do it now, get it over with.'

'No. He didn't show me that courtesy. Let him sweat.'

This wasn't like her at all and the girls were thrilled. They sat around and drank tea and kept her company but by ten o'clock she needed to go to bed. Last night's escapades had suddenly caught up with her.

She scrubbed her face and sloshed on lots of moisturizer and went to bed with her mobile phone. No messages. She sent a text.

HOW DID LAST NITE GO? R U IN DUBLIN?

She got a reply just as she was dozing off.

IN LONDON. U DIDN'T MAKE IT 2 PARTY.

NO. DID SOME WORK. WENT 2 BED EARLY. WHEN R U HOME?

It wasn't really a lie, she reasoned with herself. It was all still a bit too raw to talk about.

NOT SURE

He must be tired, she thought and just then her phone rang. She was delighted he'd phoned. She needed to feel close to him tonight.

'Have you forgiven me?' was not what she expected to hear.

Chapter Twenty-Seven

The conversation turned out to be much more difficult than she'd imagined. She decided to cut straight to the chase, explaining that it wasn't a question of forgiveness, it was all about trust – something she'd never again have with him, she didn't add. He clearly thought she was open to persuasion. It went on and on and it ended badly and she hung up, exhausted but relieved, hardly able to believe that she had reached a point where she was refusing his advances.

When had this happened, she wondered as she settled down and tried to sleep. She hoped she'd done the right thing, was scared at the finality of it all, but knew deep down that there had never been any future anyway. It would have ended, sooner or later.

She wondered how much Chris had helped in her recovery and considered what he'd say when she told him. If she told him, she thought, but knew she would. Eventually. Funny how she felt she could trust him.

She thought about the decisions, some our own and others thrust upon us, that take us down a certain route and shape our lives. Meeting Paul, marrying him, would have taken her in a completely different direction; losing him had altered her perspective irrevocably and changed her course dramatically. Although she wouldn't wish what she'd gone through on her worst enemy, she knew the experience had made her a different person and she sort of liked who she was now.

She slept soundly, which was odd in the circumstances, and woke feeling tired but much better. She showered and went in to the office early, determined to make up for lost time.

This week's show was weak, Lindsay felt, with no major names on the running order. Alan was worried and Tom Watts was in a foul mood, unhappy with the look of the programme on paper.

'We need a big name,' he announced as soon as he walked in. They had already had a quick meeting and everyone was phone bashing. Lindsay set to work on some ideas for an interesting debate, in case one was needed if they didn't get the hoped-for celebrity. The researchers were tearing their hair out. Alice had an offer of a new, hot Latin guy who'd taken the British charts by storm, but he'd pulled, just when she'd told everyone she had him, which didn't help Tom's mood. A horrible but fashionable celebrity chef had also looked likely but this morning's tabloids had announced details of an affair with a sixteen-year-old – while his wife was six months' pregnant, and he had, naturally enough, gone to ground.

They all worked tirelessly, not even stopping for lunch but nothing paid off and one by one they left feeling deflated. Lindsay stayed until seven, then rang Tara and Debbie to say hello and tell them of her late-night phone conversation. Tara had a date with Michael Russell and Debbie immediately offered to call round but Lindsay assured her she was OK. She went home and took a long bath, rang her mother and then curled up on the sofa, wondering where Chris was. Her phone rang around ten and something stopped her answering it. It was Paul, asking that she ring him whenever she got in. She unplugged the main line and went to bed early, checking again for a text from Chris. Nothing.

Next day in the office the atmosphere was even worse. They had resorted to C-list celebrities and nothing interesting was coming back. Alan called a meeting before Tom came in.

Lindsay proposed that, in view of the dearth of stars, they opt instead for a good discussion. She had done some work on the spiralling rate of suicide amongst young men and had the mother of a twenty-year-old victim willing to come on. There was also the possibility that a guy who had attempted suicide would be willing to talk, although Lindsay had not made contact with him directly as yet.

Tom Watts arrived in the middle of the meeting and was scathing about the idea. He acted as if

Lindsay was trying to sneak in a discussion item behind his back, which was ridiculous. A heated argument ensued, with most people shying away from getting involved, sensing Tom's mood. Alan, who should have taken the reins, didn't and Lindsay decided to back off, but not before making it clear that she thought a good discussion was better than a list of mediocre interviews that wouldn't hold anyone's attention. The only option, without Alan's back-up, seemed to be to go for the show as it stood and hope the viewers remained loyal.

On Thursday evening Lindsay went to her sister's for dinner, to celebrate Jake's birthday. He'd already had a party in the afternoon and was waiting at the gate for Lindsay, determined to tell her everything in minute detail. She smiled as she listened to how the fairy cakes all had sparkly bits that you could eat, 'silver and gold and brown bits that made your fingers sticky and tasted yummy'. She had bought him a video, a book and new jeans, and he skipped along beside her trying to hold her hand and clutch his presents and a goody bag at the same time.

Anne had invited a couple of friends around and they sat and chatted and relaxed and in the background she saw Chris on TV, doing an interview from Paris on one of the major current affairs programmes.

'Oh look, there's Lindsay's new boyfriend,' Anne screamed and ran to turn up the sound. They were all very impressed and Lindsay felt funny and happy at the same time.

He looked tired but gorgeous, she thought, and wondered for the hundredth time how she'd managed to get so lucky.

'My God, he's some catch. What's he like?' Anne's best friend Dorothy asked in admiration.

'The find of the century, if you believe Mum,' Anne laughed.

'He's not really my boyfriend, I've only been out with him a few times,' Lindsay felt compelled to confess, 'but he's a lovely guy and I really like him.'

They cheered and toasted and slagged her and she realized she missed him a lot.

Later, at home, she tried his mobile but it rang out. It was funny that she hadn't talked to him for a few days – didn't even know he'd gone to Paris. She sent him a text and waited.

SAW U ON TV. ALL OK? RING WHEN U CAN. MISS U.

No reply and next morning she checked, sure there would be a message, but there was nothing, which she found strange. She arrived in the office to find an enormous yellow bouquet on her desk. She opened the card eagerly and was disappointed to read the message. 'Let's start again. Please?' She dumped the card and felt like doing the same to the flowers.

She worked late, helping to inject as much life as she could into a lacklustre show. Alan stayed with her, admitting that he didn't feel great when they stopped for a pint together on the way home. Apparently, he'd been having stomach pains for a couple of weeks and hadn't had time to go to his G.P. which Lindsay told him was downright stupid. They parted and he promised to have a check-up early the following week. When she arrived at her house there was a note in the door from Paul, asking her to call him. She tore it up.

Later, Lindsay left a message at home and on Chris's mobile and waited expectantly. She began to feel uneasy but didn't know why.

He rang on Saturday morning, just as she was rushing out to work.

'Hi, it's Chris.'

'Hi there, stranger. When did you get back?'

'Late on Thursday night. I ended up in Paris.'

'I know, I saw you on TV. How have you been?'

'Fine, you?'

Something didn't feel right about the conversation but Lindsay, not knowing any better, barged ahead as normal.

'I'm good. Busy week, not-great show tonight so the pressure's on.'

'You didn't make it to the party after all the other night?'

'No, I felt a bit awkward, to be honest. Silly, I suppose?'

'So what did you do instead?'

'Nothing much. Stayed here, worked, went to bed early.'

'Any callers?'

'Er, no, no.' Why was he asking? Did he know something?

Stop it, she chided herself, you're being paranoid. 'So, was it a good night?'

'I got pretty drunk actually. Have you been out anywhere since?'

'No. Jake's party was the highlight of my week. So, when am I going to see you again?'

'I'm not sure, I've a bit of a mad weekend. I'll give you a call.'

'Oh, right . . . Chris, is everything OK?'

'Fine, why?'

'You seem . . . I dunno, distant. Is it something I've done?' She hated herself for asking. Funny how the old insecurity crept in immediately.

'You tell me.'

'What's that supposed to mean?'

'Nothing, listen I've got to go. I'll talk to you again.'

'OK, bye.'

'Bye.' Click. He was gone.

She was afraid.

Everything that could go wrong did, most of it live on air on the show that night. They lurched from crisis to crisis. Tom was livid. Tempers flared. Everyone suffered.

As soon as he saw the audience, Tom attacked Monica and Marissa. 'It looks like a geriatric ward. This is not good enough, if you two can't manage a simple task like that we'll have to find someone who can.' Marissa hung her head and Monica was almost in tears. Lindsay was upset that others could overhear, but said nothing, afraid to aggravate an already fraught situation.

It got worse. As soon as they went on air, with a top-ten female solo artist – the best thing on the show by a mile – sound had a technical problem and the backing track failed in the middle of the song, leaving her miming to nothing. She stopped dead. The floor manager cued manic applause, Tom apologized but the artist was furious and barely spoke during the interview. Then Tom got annoyed and cut it short, leaving them with ten minutes to fill later and a handful of mediocre guests, one of whom turned up late and had to be dropped and another who was so boring that even Lindsay had trouble staying awake. Alan looked grey in the face and she felt really sorry for him. He was a nice man but not strong enough for their heavyweight presenter.

After what seemed like an eternity the final music sounded, but not before one final disaster – a 10,000-euro Greek holiday giveaway to an obnoxious woman who acted as if she was allergic to everything Greek and asked for the money instead. Tom nearly hit her and Alan cued the credits immediately, cutting off his good night, which irritated him even further, if that were possible.

The atmosphere in the hospitality suite was tense. Tom was ignoring the entire team and Alan looked like he hadn't the energy to deal with it. None of the guests had hung around, which was unusual and Lindsay had one quick drink before she made her escape, feeling down about the show and worried about Chris.

Chapter Twenty-Eight

Next morning Lindsay decided to ring Chris, then worried about his reaction. Without thinking, she jumped up, showered and dressed in her favourite denim jacket, white T-shirt and long floaty skirt. She wanted to appear casual, so she tied her hair back in a blue ribbon, applied only a little make-up and raced Charlie to the car. There was only one way to tell if her hunch was right – see him face to face and talk to him and sort it out, what-ever it was. She'd decided to surprise him with breakfast so she stopped off at a good deli and bought flaky croissants and soft muffins and warm, nutty rolls. She also got all the Sunday papers, even though he would probably have them already – picked up some fresh juice and headed for his apartment, not sure what she would do if he wasn't home.

His car was there so she bounded up the steps and waited, not wanting to let him know in advance she was there. Sure enough an unshaven, sleepy-looking, twelve-year-old carrying BMW keys came out shortly afterwards and held the door for her. Those IT millionaires are getting younger looking every day, she decided.

Charlie dashed up the stairs ahead of her and she smiled as she remembered her last visit to his home. She couldn't wait to see him again and grinned as she settled Charlie down outside his front door, surrounded by papers and pastries – which he kept trying to sniff at. He looked comical and she was laughing as she rang the bell and crouched down in the corner, looking like a two-year-old in her trainers and long, flowery skirt.

'Hello, who are you?' She was amazed to hear a woman, thinking it must be his sister, the younger one, by the sound of the husky voice. She jumped up, red-faced, about to apologize when she came face to face with a young woman she knew wasn't his sister.

She's wearing my shirt, was her first ludicrous thought as she stared stupidly at the blonde girl with the tousled hair. Carefully tousled hair, wearing make-up, high heels and his shirt. Her shirt. Her heart started pounding and her head felt noisy. She said nothing.

'Hi, are you looking for Chris?' She seemed very nice, which made it worse, if that were possible. She had a friendly grin and big boobs.

What is it with men and blondes with big boobs she asked herself, remembering Paul in the restaurant.

'No, sorry, I must have the wrong apartment.' She didn't know how she managed to make sense in her stunned state, but somehow the words tumbled out and she grabbed Charlie's lead and dashed back down the stairs, convinced she was going to have a heart attack and die on his doorstep.

'Excuse me, you've forgotten your things . . .' the girl had bent down to pick them up and Lindsay turned, noting long legs and red nails, then blue eyes and Chris all in the same split second.

She turned and fled and she heard him coming after her and knew she had to get away fast. Just as she got to the outside door he sprinted ahead of her, throwing his weight against the heavy wood and blocking her way.

He had just showered and she could smell him and she wanted to slap him.

'Why didn't you tell me . . . ? You promised me, remember?'

'Why didn't YOU tell me?'

She said nothing, not knowing what he was talking about, concentrating as she was on not letting him see her cry.

'You said you wouldn't cheat on me . . . Why? I don't understand . . . even if you had lost interest you could have ended it before . . .'

He stared at her with the same cold eyes she'd seen that night in studio, although now that she knew him better she recognized the shadings – then he'd been wearing the icy-blue angry ones whereas now he had on the newest pair of grey, distant ones.

His lip curled and he sort of smirked and she didn't like it.

'I saw you the other night. I called to see if I

could persuade you to join me at the party. Was he who I thought he was?'

She could feel the hot, blackberry colour starting in her chest, staining her neck and her ears and her face. He laughed but it wasn't pleasant.

'It didn't take you long to forgive him, did it?' The grey turned to the coldest blue she'd ever seen and she shivered. 'So don't you dare lecture me about cheating.'

'Nothing happened.'

'Don't lie. I saw you. I was standing outside when you were in the bedroom. You make up pretty quickly.' His voice was a sneer.

'I didn't do anything wrong.'

'You didn't even have the courage to tell me. I asked you. Specifically. Twice.' He almost spat the words and it made her feel cheap and nasty.

They stared at each other, full of animosity and hostility, for what seemed like ages.

'I hate you.' She didn't mean it, life would be much simpler if she did, she realized sadly. It tumbled out like so many other things she'd told him since they'd met.

What she really hated was what he'd done to her, what he'd given and taken away so quickly. She hated him for not trusting her and mostly for not even giving her a chance to explain. Hated him for looking so normal while she was falling apart. Hated him for replacing her so effortlessly.

She made to push past him but he grabbed her arm and held it too tightly. 'You fooled me. I thought you were different.'

'Let go of me.'

Suddenly she was out of control and she screamed and lashed out at him, punching him in the stomach in an effort to loosen his grip. Charlie started barking quite viciously and the girl in the shirt and high heels came running down the stairs.

'Chris, what's going on?'

Lindsay pushed past him, crying openly now, wanting desperately to escape, her breathing heavy and her heart pounding. He grabbed her and twisted her round to face him.

'You can't even admit it now, can you? I rang several times during the evening, just in case. But you were obviously too busy to answer the phone.' He moved very close, his face inches away from her. 'I know he stayed the night and you didn't even have the guts to tell me.'

'He didn't.'

'You're a liar.' It was the final nail in an already sealed coffin.

'Let me go.' It was a pathetic, whispering plea. He looked as if he was either going to ignore it or slap her and then he silently stepped out of the way and she passed him as if in slow motion, hair flying and dog bounding. She didn't look back.

She ran, past her car, the houses, the sleepy Sunday traffic.

Charlie loved it and he was laughing at her as they sped along the still snoring streets.

She had to stop eventually, but she couldn't let anyone see her distress, so she put on her sunglasses and walked as fast as her unfit body would allow, wiping her streaked face and runny nose on her sleeve. Afterwards she didn't know how she got home. It was a good hour's walk and she remembered absolutely nothing of it.

Once in the door she didn't cry, just sat in the chair and tried to decipher it all. None of it made sense. If he had seen her, why hadn't he just knocked on the door? Why had he stayed outside, spying on her? What did he mean when he said he knew Paul had spent the night? Unless he'd somehow seen his car still there next morning? But he didn't know Paul's car, did he? Why had he looked at her with such hatred? Why had he made no effort to let her explain? And worst of all, how could he go off with someone else before they'd even had a chance to talk?

When she couldn't stand it any longer she grabbed Charlie's lead again and went out and walked the streets once more. Anywhere, she didn't care, just as long as she was moving. She felt nothing like she'd felt when Paul had left her – perhaps it had been more of a shock then, whereas with Chris she'd never really anticipated a future. Still, she felt lonely for what they'd had. Hollow, as if a bit of her had gone missing. Cold. Add to that angry, confused, stunned and wanting to kill him and it just about summed up how she felt. The only thing she knew for sure was that she wasn't going to let it destroy her.

She walked for miles, until the back of her legs hurt and Charlie was like an old-age pensioner limping along beside her. She thought about going straight back to his house, pounding on his door, demanding an explanation, but knew it wouldn't do any good. He'd already moved on and that's what hurt the most. She was still confused, couldn't make sense of some of what he'd said, but knew from bitter experience that she could be analysing this till the cows came home and it wouldn't make a shred of difference. She knew it was over.

In the midst of all this it was funny to realize that he'd come to mean more to her in a few short weeks than anyone else, including Paul. It was a relationship based on talking and sharing and laughing and being friends and being vulnerable. A real relationship. Not like with her and Paul, where she was the lover and he was the loved – she knew that now. This was a coming together of two equals – despite his celebrity status. And the saddest thing of all was that it had so much potential, so many possibilities and that was what she was grieving for now.

In fact, when she thought about it, she realized it must have been love.

Chapter Twenty-Nine

When she let herself into the house it was almost dark and the phone was ringing. She answered it without thinking.

'Lindsay, hi, this is Alan Morland. Sorry to disturb you at home.'

'Alan, hi, no problem.' She tried to sound cheerful. 'What's up?'

'I was wondering, would you be able, by any chance – and please say if you're not – to meet for a drink this evening?'

'Sure.'

'Em . . . would you mind calling round to my house? It's a bit complicated. I'll explain when you get here. I need to talk to you about something to do with the show. It should only take an hour or so.'

'No problem, give me your address.'

'You're sure?'

'Yep, I'll be glad to get out of the house for a bit.' If he only knew.

'Great, thanks. I really appreciate it. Say around seven-thirty?'

'See you then.'

She peeled off her clothes and climbed wearily into a hot bath, feeling as if she'd severed all her nerve endings. Charlie had refused to make even the short journey down the stairs and lay stretched out at the front door, where he seemed intent on remaining for several hours, or at least until he'd recovered from the London marathon.

She refused to think any more, except to decide that she was going to handle things differently this time.

Actually, I'm becoming quite an expert at surviving, she thought bleakly, as she soaked in the hot, steamy suds. One or two more and I'll be setting up a support group and making a name for myself.

She decided she wasn't going to talk about it – to anyone – for the next few days. Not even the girls. She just didn't have the energy for it and she now knew that she couldn't go through it all again, in the same way as before.

No more self-indulgence, she lectured herself. I'm not going to think about it or him again. I'm simply going to forget I ever met him.

If only it were that easy, a little voice jeered.

She took the answering service off her mobile and unplugged the phone at home. At seven she dressed in jeans and a big comfy sweater and took a taxi to Alan's house a couple of miles away. She stopped to buy a bottle of wine and then wasn't sure. He was her boss, after all. She decided against it, although she badly needed one herself. It won't solve anything, you've already learned that the hard way, she thought cynically as the cab pulled up outside the modern apartment block in fashionable Dublin 4.

Alan greeted her warmly. 'Thanks for coming, I'm sorry to break up your weekend but I needed to talk to you before Tuesday and I won't be available tomorrow.'

She was intrigued. 'I wasn't doing anything anyway.' She gave a weak smile. Not unless you count trying to scratch the eyes out of one of our top stars.

'Glass of wine?'

'I was going to bring a bottle but thought you mightn't like it as this was business.'

'God, do I look like that kind of guy?' He was horrified.

'No.'

'My girlfriend is always telling me to loosen up at work, so maybe I am that kind of guy. Now that would be gruesome.'

'I promise I'll let you know if it happens. I'd murder a glass of white if you have one.'

'So would I. Sit down.'

It was a typical modern apartment – bright and stylish with incredibly little space, even though it was two-bedroomed and had probably cost almost half a million euro, given its location. Very male. She wondered about his girlfriend, but didn't like to ask.

He returned with two very civilized crystal

glasses – nothing like her balloons, which was just as well given her new-found sobriety.

They made chit-chat for a couple of minutes and then he told her.

'Remember I wasn't feeling well?'

She nodded, sensing something immediately.

'I had stomach pains in the middle of the night last night and had to call my doctor early this morning. The pain was bad enough that I couldn't drive. He came round here and examined me. He wants me to go into hospital in the morning.'

She tried not to show too much concern.

'What does he suspect?'

'He honestly doesn't know. The pains had gone by the time he arrived but he doesn't like the tiredness and lack of energy so he wants to run some tests. He says I'm not to worry.' He grinned at her, a very weak one. 'Why do they bother telling you that?'

'I know, but at least you're doing something. I'm the type who runs to the doctor with everything. If something's wrong with me I want it caught very fast. It's the only option, believe me. I cannot, for the life of me, understand people who won't get something checked. What does that achieve? You still have the pain and you're worried sick as well.'

'I know, but I'm a big coward. My girlfriend's a doctor and she's the same as you. She's in London working for six months. I haven't told her yet because she'll be on the next plane home.'

'If it were me I'd want to know.'

He smiled at her, looking like a little lost boy and

she wanted to hug him but didn't know him well enough.

'I'll wait till after tomorrow.'

She nodded knowingly.

'So, basically, I need you to take charge. I'll be on the other end of a phone and hopefully I'll be back in the office in a couple of days. I've spoken to the Head of Programming and he's a bit reluctant, to be honest, as you're so new to the job, but I've assured him you'll be fine and, just between you and me, there's no one else. All the good people are already assigned to other programmes. How do you feel about it?'

'Nervous, excited, terrified, elated and scared stiff,' she smiled. 'But I'll do it.'

'Good girl, I knew you would. It's a great opportunity to get noticed by the powers that be and remember, I'll be around.'

'I'll be your most frequent bringer of grapes,' she grinned at him half-heartedly.

They chatted for a while about the items on the agenda for this week and agreed to wait until she saw the Saturday figures before making changes. Lindsay knew he was unhappy with the way things had gone and she was sorry he now found himself ill in the middle of all this.

'Don't let Tom order you around. Stick to your guns.'

'I will.'

They talked some more and drank another glass of wine, then Lindsay left to get some sleep and give him time to get organized for the day ahead.

'If there's anything I can do, call me in the office,

I'll be in early.' She couldn't resist hugging him as she left and she sensed he was embarrassed and touched at the same time.

'I'll be OK, ring me whenever and leave a message and I'll call as soon as I can.'

'Good luck.'

'Thanks.'

She asked the taxi to drop her at Chris's house to collect her abandoned car. His was nowhere to be seen and she was glad, because she didn't quite trust herself yet.

She drove home thankful that she at least didn't have Alan's problems and grateful to have something to keep her busy for the week. It helped in her new plan not to think at all about her own problems. The plan worked until she tried to sleep and kept seeing Chris's face.

She woke at six, feeling as if she hadn't slept at all and after several cups of coffee and a ton of make-up she was at least ready to face the world.

She arrived at the office at seven-thirty and immediately called up the viewing figures on her computer. She stared at the screen for ages, convinced she was reading it incorrectly. A glance over the previous week told her she wasn't. Saturday night had been the worst show this season. The figures had started off as normal but the graph had gone sliding steadily downwards, losing thousands of viewers every fifteen minutes. The final result was that they had dropped out of the top-ten programmes for the first time in years. Lindsay shivered, suddenly aware of the responsibility.

After a quick visit to the canteen for coffee and brown toast with honey – which she didn't really want, but it was part of her newly established health kick – she settled down and drew up a comprehensive list of possible guests and topics for the next four shows. Although Monday was officially their day off, she was surprised and pleased to see that most of the team popped in at some stage during the day, as if aware that this week was going to be extra tough. David and Alice spent a couple of hours on the phone and Kate was the only researcher who didn't appear. Lindsay worked hard until eight that night and went home and fell into bed, exhausted. There was only one message, from Alan, to say that he had no news but would ring her the next day. He hoped things had gone well for her.

Lindsay was awake by six again on Tuesday and took Charlie for an early-morning walk, purely out of guilt. It was still dark and it felt odd, as if she was out and about at the wrong end of the day, but he bounded along happily, knowing no different. She showered and dressed in her best black suit, which gave her an air of authority and at the same time matched her mood. Not even her newest gipsy top could disguise the lack of sleep, although she barely noticed this in her haste to get to work and keep occupied. By the time the others drizzled in at around nine-thirty she was prepared. She was also nervous.

At ten she asked if everyone would be happy to meet at ten-thirty.

'Shouldn't we wait on Alan?' David asked curiously.

'He won't be here so he's asked me to take the meeting. Grab a coffee everyone and get your stuff together.'

By ten thirty-five all phones were on voice mail and Lindsay explained briefly that Alan was off sick for a few days, leaving out the details as he'd requested. She'd printed off copies of the figures and there were groans and gasps as they were digested. Calmly, she told them that they needed a very strong show this week and distributed a suggested running order based on the best and worst scenarios.

'First up, Alice, how are we doing with our Latin heart-throb?'

'Well, you know what happened last week, but I talked to his manager last night and he's confirmed him again for this week. I think it'll be OK.' She smiled nervously.

'Great, well done. I know how hard you've worked on it.' Lindsay smiled and Alice glowed.

'I also have Colin Quinn for this week,' the younger girl said shyly, not quite managing to hide her triumph and turning pink in the process. The news was greeted with murmurs of 'nice one' and 'cool' – compliments indeed from the competition.

Colin Quinn was one of Ireland's top actors, having made it big in America about ten years ago at the age of twenty-eight. He now commanded millions of dollars per project and was considered one of the hottest properties on the movie market. He was also, if the gossip columns were to be believed, one of the nicest guys in the business. He rarely gave interviews, unless promoting a movie and even then almost never commented on his private life. But what was really interesting and the absolute coup about getting him now was that he had just come back on the scene after almost two years of solitude, following the untimely death of his wife, which had left him with two young children. Everyone wanted to hear him, wanted to see how he looked, wanted to know what had happened.

'Wow, how did you manage to keep that so quiet?' Lindsay tried to hide her elation. This was exactly what the show needed.

'I've been working on it for weeks, months even, but I didn't know if it would really happen, because he's apparently quite shy and avoids the media like the plague. But, for some reason his agent liked me and I assured her we wanted to do a serious interview and not a tabloid piece and he's decided it's time to come home to visit his parents and face everyone again . . . so . . . they've said he'd do the show this week.'

'That's fantastic. You are an angel; it's just what we need.' Everyone agreed and Alice basked in the glory.

'Er, I've got the celebrity chef back on,' David blurted out, presumably wanting a bit of the warmth himself. They all burst out laughing.

'And, he'll say the sixteen-year-old threw herself at him and that he loves his wife and wants to be a good father.'

'Brilliant, well done, David. That means we've

got a heart-throb for the teenagers, a good old gossip for the tabloid readers and hopefully a serious and meaty interview for our regulars. Anything else? Kate, anything on the horizon?'

'I'm working on a couple of big names.' Kate was immediately defensive and Lindsay wondered why the other woman seemed to resent her so much. 'OK, well, why don't we talk separately later in the week and you can bring me up to date if Alan's not back?' Lindsay smiled and refused to be drawn into the chiller cabinet.

'Now, anything else? Let's see, we need to talk about other, smaller items, as well as the audience. And by the way, I don't think I want any "bits" in the show this week, no competitions, demonstrations, etc. We've got a really strong line-up so let's give it to them hard all the way. No fillers. OK?'

They chatted on for another half-hour and the meeting had just broken up when Tom Watts phoned.

'Lindsay, I've just got a message from Alan. What the hell is going on?'

Lindsay was unsure from his tone what he meant and played for time.

'What did he say?'

'Just that he was sick and wouldn't be around for a couple of days and that you were in charge.'

'Oh, right, well yes, but it's all under control, don't worry.'

'I am worried. Quite frankly, we need a producer, no offence meant.'

'None taken. Well, I know he talked to the Head

of Programming and there is a shortage of people available and—'

'That's bullshit, we're the top-rating show in the country.'

Not any more . . . She held her tongue.

'I want a top producer, I need one. I'll talk to him.' Tom Watts was furious.

'Are you coming in today? I'd really like to go through the running order with you. We actually have a very strong show lined up for—'

'I'm not coming in until I get to see Jonathan Myers. I'll ring him now on his mobile and talk to you later.'

'OK, then, bye.' Lindsay said to a dead phone line. She went for a takeaway coffee to clear her head and cool her burning cheeks. It was clear that Tom Watts had absolutely no confidence in her and it bothered her but there was nothing she could do. He was perfectly entitled to go straight to the top – after all, he was one of the biggest stars in the country and she'd done nothing to prove herself. Hell, she'd never even met the famous Jonathan Myers.

That was about to be rectified because as soon as she returned to the office there was a note on her desk to call Aoife, P.A. to the Head of Programming.

It seemed the great white chief wanted to see her at five this afternoon if she was free. She agreed and spent the rest of the day preparing her defence, feeling she was getting ready to face the hangman.

Chapter Thirty

At exactly five minutes to five that afternoon, Lindsay presented herself at the very luxurious penthouse offices of Jonathan Myers, feeling nervous, even though she knew she had done nothing wrong. She desperately wanted a chance to prove herself and knew that this man had the power to give her that chance.

He came to meet her and she was surprised to find she liked him immediately. He smiled and held out his hand.

'Come on in, I'm sorry I haven't had an opportunity to meet you before now. I've heard a lot of good things about you.' This, of course, completely disarmed her and she felt her resentment fade, which was not what she needed right now. She wanted to remain indignant, in combat mode, but his grin made it impossible.

'Well, I sure as hell had the ear chewed off me this morning by Mr Watts,' he said with a slight American twang, 'and I suspect you had your share too?'

Lindsay grinned and nodded.

'To be fair, I see where he's coming from. The show is obviously very important to us and it needs a really good producer. The problem is that there are really only two or three people who could handle it and at the moment they are committed elsewhere, and the soonest I could free one of them would be in about six weeks' time and even that would present me with a whole new set of problems. I could bring in a good freelancer but he or she would be starting from scratch in the same way as you are and would have little experience of the show, which has a very particular style as well as a, shall we say, challenging presenter. Anyway, tell me how you feel about being asked to cope on your own?'

Lindsay knew she had one chance to convince him. She chose her words carefully.

'I think it's a fantastic show and an amazing opportunity for me but I would only want to do it if I thought I could bring something to the show. And I think I can. I feel the format is a little tired at the moment and the competition for guests is getting tougher. We need to go after the top names but also bring another dimension to it, generate some Irish items, good interviews, interesting discussions – maybe tackle issues that haven't been done before in an Irish context. We have to keep our viewers glued to the show and we won't do that with mediocre names, just because they're on the publicity trail. Also, I feel Irish people like to see other Irish people talk about difficult, thorny subjects. I realize I have relatively little experience in TV but I know a good programme when I see one. I've watched enough – good and bad – over the years. Also it's an area that I'm really interested in and I'm prepared to work my ass off for the next few weeks or months or whatever. I do have Alan, hopefully, to bounce things off and that would be a help also.' She paused for breath and knew he was looking at her intently.

'How do you get on with Tom?' She knew it would come and answering it was not going to be easy.

'I have a great deal of respect for him, I think he does a very good job. Sometimes, I think he's too close to it all and that's where I see my role. He gets a bee in his bonnet and can be stubborn and he is resistant to change, which I think is needed in certain aspects of the programme, but overall I think he's very intelligent and highly capable and sometimes he's superb.'

He looked at her for a long moment.

'Well, I've talked to a number of people about you and they all tell me that you too are intelligent and highly capable and your training programme was described as superb by one or two of them.' She turned purple with pleasure. 'So, I'm prepared to give you a chance. But there are a couple of things you need to be aware of and obviously this is completely confidential. Firstly, I agree with your assessment of Tom Watts and he is a very important part of our television schedule right now, but I also know that he can be extremely chauvinistic and a bully. He gets his own way a lot of the time because he shouts very loudly and he's known to be aggressive at times. Secondly, we are a little concerned about the direction of the programme and the reason I can talk to you about it is because I've already had this conversation with both Alan and Tom and it is, in fact, one of the reasons you were assigned to the show in the first place. Last weekend's ratings were diabolical and I think we need to take urgent steps and make whatever changes are necessary. Thirdly, I will act as Executive Producer in the absence of Alan. I will give you my direct line, my mobile and home numbers so that you have access to me at all times and I am available to attend your weekly meetings. How does all that sound?'

It sounded like more than she could have hoped for.

They ran through her plans for the next show and he seemed very impressed at the line-up.

'If that doesn't win back a few viewers then nothing will. Well done.'

'I also intend promoting the show more. From tomorrow we have promos on the hour on radio and TV kicks in tomorrow night as well. I've also "leaked" it to the papers that we have Colin Quinn and a couple of them have promised to hint at it on Saturday and give us the "pick of the day".'

'Great. And listen, I really appreciate you taking this on and we'll look at somehow reflecting our appreciation in the form of a bonus of some kind.' He stood up and walked her to the door. 'By the way, I'll speak to Tom at home tonight and tell him you have my full backing. Me being Executive Producer will keep him sweet but this is your project until we know how Alan is, so go for it and don't hesitate to run things by me if you need another opinion.'

It was six-thirty when Lindsay emerged and she felt shell-shocked, but for the first time in days she had something to look forward to and she knew this was exactly what she needed to keep her mind off her problems. She returned to the office and worked for another hour or so and then decided to call it quits. She felt lonely and would have loved to be able to tell Chris all about it. This was a big chance to develop her career and she had no one to share it with. Refusing to go any further down that road she picked up her bag and headed for home. In the car park she met Michael Russell.

'Hi, stranger.' He was still quite shy with her because of Tara. 'You look a bit lost. Are you OK?'

'Yeah, fine. It's just been one of those days, you know?'

'Well, I'm just on my way to collect Tara and treat her to a pizza and a glass of wine. Want to join us and tell me all about it?'

'Oh, no, thanks, I couldn't. I'm not much company tonight anyway.'

'Well, I'd really love to chat to you, and Tara spends all our dates going on about how wonderful you are anyway,' he grinned, 'so, what's the difference?'

'I don't know . . .'

He sensed something was wrong and seized the opportunity.

'Listen, leave your car here and come with me. We'll drop you home. That way you can enjoy a few drinks. Hop in, I'm parked over here.'

Before she knew what was happening she was being driven to collect Tara, who was thrilled and surprised when she saw her friend. 'I've left you two messages today. What's wrong with your mobile?'

'I dunno, it doesn't seem to be taking messages.'

'What's up? You look all in.'

'I'll tell you over a glass of wine, if you can bear to listen to an account of my day.'

'Sure. Driver, take us to the restaurant.'

In the end it turned out to be exactly what she needed. Once again her friends had saved the day. Michael whistled when she told him about her meeting with the Head of Programming.

'Wow, Lindsay, that's brilliant. But it's happening very fast and you need to remember that it would be a big knock if it all came tumbling down. So do use Jonathan and run anything by him that you're not sure of. That way, he has to take some responsibility. Don't let him off the hook because if it goes well you can be sure he'll take part of the credit.'

'Yeah, I know, thanks.'

'And listen, I'm available any time you need a second opinion. And I think you've done amazingly well so far. Congratulations.'

Lindsay smiled and changed the subject, more relaxed than she'd been all day. Tara told her they were going for a weekend to Prague and Lindsay teased them about being a couple of lovebirds and they both blushed and grinned and she knew they were happy.

'How's Chris?' Tara asked between mouthfuls of pizza.

Lindsay was prepared.

'I haven't seen him. He's in Paris. I've spoken to him, though, and he's OK.' It wasn't really a lie, she consoled herself. She just wasn't ready to tell them.

They dropped her home at midnight and she realized she was a little bit drunk and so was Tara. They giggled and Michael thought they were hilarious. She was very glad she'd met them. She checked her mail and fell into bed, glad at least that Paul appeared to have given up ringing and leaving notes.

Chapter Thirty-One

On Thursday they had a bit of a crisis. Lindsay was working away checking research briefs and questions, wanting everything to be perfect for Tom Watts, who had calmed down considerably since talking with Jonathan Myers. He chilled even further once Lindsay ran through the running order with him. He was delighted they had Colin Quinn, the man who was now providing Lindsay with her first real crisis.

Alice had told Lindsay during the afternoon that his agent wasn't returning her calls, always a bad sign. 'I'm trying to confirm flights and find out if he needs a hotel but suddenly she became all vague and hasn't responded to my messages this afternoon.'

'What do you think is the problem?'

'He's filming somewhere near Mexico and they seem to be keeping a tight rein on him. I'm just worried that they won't finish on schedule and he might not make the connecting flights to get him here in time for the show.'

'Want me to talk to the agent?'

'Yes, it might just help. Thanks.'

Lindsay made the call with some trepidation, knowing that some New York agents had little time for small TV shows in Europe, and especially those outside of London and the BBC. This one, however, was very pleasant and Lindsay liked her immediately.

'Hey, Lindsay, nice to talk to you. How's the weather in Ireland?'

'Gorgeous, it's a perfect weekend for an Irishman to come home.' Lindsay decided to cut to the chase. 'I just wondered if there was anything we could do for him, anyone he'd like to bring to the show, any special requests for his dressing room, etc.?'

'No, to be honest, the movie company are giving me a lot of shit and that's my priority right now. My other worry is his folks. He's been trying to reach them but he's in a very isolated location and there's a storm brewing. I know he's anxious to see as much of them as possible, but I can't get hold of them so I don't even know if they know he's coming.'

'Can I help? I could call them and invite them as our guests anyway, send a car to collect them, whatever?'

Shirley, the agent, wasn't buying it.

'Lindsay, I know you really want him and I'll do all I can, because I really think he could do with a trip home right now, but I'm afraid I'm not at liberty to give out his home number in Ireland.'

Nice try, Lindsay, she thought to herself, hoping to somehow get to speak to his mother or father and put a bit of pressure on from this end.

'I'll tell you what, though, I will somehow get hold of them tonight and I'll give them your number, if that's OK, in case they want tickets or something, because one way or the other it's going to be quite tight getting Colin there.'

'OK, please do, I'll be happy to help. Give them my mobile and tell them to call me anytime, if they need anything.'

Alice and Lindsay went for tea in the canteen, treating themselves to lasagne and chips. Lindsay could only manage half of it but at least they were able to put their heads together and come up with a plan.

They worked until nine o'clock and then had a pint on the way home. Lindsay arrived in exhausted at ten-thirty to find two messages from Alan. She got into her dressing gown, calmed a delirious Charlie and settled down to ring him back. They chatted for half an hour. He was still in hospital but hoping to go home the following morning. So far, they'd found nothing but it would take ten days before all results were back and he'd been ordered to rest. She assured him that all was OK, recounted part of her conversation with Jonathan Myers and agreed to talk to him the following day. Next up she dialled Debbie.

'Hey babe, what's happening? You've been avoiding me.'

'No I haven't, it's just been manic.' Lindsay told her about the show and Debbie was seriously impressed.

'You, in charge, oh my God that is so cool. What sort of credit will you get? Producer?'

'I haven't even thought about it but no, I'm not a producer so I can't call myself one. Besides it wouldn't endear me to the producer grade. Honestly, I don't care, I just want to prove I can do it.' Suddenly her mobile rang so she hung up, promising to meet Debbie for breakfast on Sunday, once it was all over.

The caller turned out to be Colin Quinn's father and Lindsay was delighted.

'Hello, my dear. Shirley asked me to call you. I was just wondering if I could possibly have four tickets for the show on Saturday?' He sounded positively charming with no air of importance.

'Yes, of course. Give me the names so that I can make sure you're met and looked after.'

'Well, it will be myself and my wife and then, well we tossed a coin, because we couldn't decide which of our friends to invite, but in the end we decided on my sister and her husband, that's Anne and Tom Tierney, because Colin is very fond of them. Is four too many to ask for?'

'You can have as many as you like,' Lindsay said simply.

He sounded flabbergasted. 'You mean we could have six?'

'Certainly.'

'But I know they're like gold dust and I don't want to be greedy.'

'It's no problem, honestly.'

'And if he doesn't make it home would we have to give them back? It's just that my wife loves

Tom Watts and wants to see him more than she does Colin.' Lindsay burst out laughing. Typical mother.

'Of course not. We'd love you all to be our guests, whether your son makes it or not. Now, would you like me to send our limo to collect you so that you can all relax and join us for a drink before the show?'

He seemed amazed that anyone would be so nice to him and he agreed to call Lindsay the next day to finalize things. She didn't like to ask for his home number after what Shirley had said.

Next morning, Lindsay dragged herself out of bed and into the shower. She was in the office by eight-thirty. Alice had still not been able to book flights and she was getting very nervous. So was Lindsay, knowing she'd told the Saturday papers of their star guest. They'd look like right wallies if he didn't show and it was getting close to the deadline if she wanted the papers to pull the story. Alice was beginning to wonder if she shouldn't start looking for another guest just in case, but Lindsay knew they needed Colin Quinn badly. All the radio and TV promos had promised the 'interview of the year' and they had to deliver a major name. Two B-list celebrities wouldn't do this time. Besides Tom Watts was really looking forward to this one and telling him didn't bear thinking about, so Lindsay had kept quiet so far. No point in worrying him unnecessarily, she told herself. Still, it was almost lunchtime on Friday and they had no confirmation as yet.

Just as they were about to make the tenth call to his agent, Lindsay's mobile rang. It was Mr Quinn.

'Miss Davidson, I just thought I'd give you our address. We'd all be delighted to accept your kind offer of a lift. My wife is very excited.'

'Great, I'm looking forward to meeting you and please tell your wife that Tom would love to meet her after the show.'

'I'm afraid that might be too much excitement for her right now. I have to live with her, you know.' Mr Quinn laughed.

'By the way, Colin left a message while we were at Mass to tell us not to worry that he was definitely coming home. He wanted his mum to cook roast beef for Sunday lunch and make an apple pie. So that will make tomorrow night really special for us, and I'm sure your viewers will enjoy him. He's a lovely boy.'

'I'm sure they will and thank you so much for the call. I look forward to meeting you all tomorrow evening.'

Lindsay hung up and punched the air. 'Yes,' she grinned at Alice, 'we've got him.'

Jonathan Myers dropped in unexpectedly late that afternoon and the office was a hive of activity. Lindsay was buried in paperwork, the researchers were all tying up last-minute details and Tom Watts had his feet up on his desk reading everything on Colin Quinn.

'Just checking, how's it all looking for tomorrow night?' He strolled over to Lindsay and Tom Watts immediately intercepted him.

'Great. It's all under control. It's going to be a good show. Fancy a coffee?'

'I'm due at an editorial in ten minutes so I'll pass, but I might drop in tomorrow night after the show so you could buy me a beer then?'

'Sure, great.'

'Lindsay, all OK from your end?'

'Yes thanks, we're getting there. I'm just looking forward to waking up on Sunday morning and watching it all over again in my pyjamas.'

'You're a glutton for punishment. Don't forget to call me at home if there are any problems. And good luck.'

Somehow, Lindsay didn't think they'd need it. Shirley had just confirmed flights for Colin Quinn and barring an earthquake it was going to be great.

Chapter Thirty-Two

As soon as she woke on Saturday morning Lindsay hopped out of bed, pulled on some sloppy clothes and went to buy the papers, grateful once again to be busy and able to push her own thoughts away. Sure enough they'd got a couple of mentions and were the 'pick of the day' in the two main ones, which should definitely help their ailing figures.

She took Charlie for a walk but found herself thinking about Chris. She knew she'd half expected to hear from him. Surely he couldn't just leave things as they were? She missed him so much. Suddenly, she began thinking about what might have been so she cut the walk short and returned a sullen-looking animal to the garden in under half an hour. Without stopping for breakfast she showered and dressed in her soft dark grey DKNY trousers, funky white T-shirt and pale grey cashmere wrap-around cardigan, which had cost a fortune but was soft, clingy and emphasized her waist and boobs.

She applied her make-up carefully, wanting to look young, yet authoritative, and at the last minute she decided to call and have her hair blow-dried on the way to work.

She bought a couple of healthy snacks and some fruit juice in case she didn't get lunch and was still first to arrive in the office, a good two hours before rehearsals, just in case there were any last-minute panics.

The day passed off smoothly enough, with the Latin heart-throb keeping everybody entertained during the soundcheck – especially the females. He was almost too good-looking with black eyes, and legs that went on forever, clad in painted-on leather trousers that left nothing to the imagination. He smiled and teased, leaving Lindsay in no doubt that his performance on the night would be brilliant. They had spiked the audience with teenagers, all carefully chosen fans, so he should get a rowdy Irish welcome, Lindsay hoped.

The day flew. Alan telephoned and wished her luck and told her it felt funny to be at home watching TV on a Saturday evening. He'd finally told his girlfriend the news so at least she was with him.

'Well, I hope you'll be proud of us when you see it.' Lindsay knew he was delighted with the line-up. 'Gotta go, I see Tom arriving.'

'Well, what disasters have befallen us?' Tom Watts greeted them as he entered the studio.

'None, so far.' Lindsay searched for wood to touch.

'Has Colin Quinn arrived in the country?'

'We haven't heard, all their mobiles are off. But, no news is good news.'

'What's our plan if he's delayed?'

'I've a discussion item standing by, notes are on your desk along with a new running order, just in case. But I don't expect we'll need it. We'd have heard by now if he hadn't made his flight from the States and all flights from London are on time, so he should be here around seven-thirty.'

'I hope you're right.' He walked off towards his dressing room, leaving Lindsay saying a mental prayer.

Mr and Mrs Quinn and friends arrived shortly before eight and Lindsay greeted them warmly and showed them to the hospitality suite.

'Has our son arrived yet?' Mr Quinn enquired.

'Not yet,' Lindsay said a touch too brightly.

'Is Tom Watts here?' Mrs Quinn wanted to know.

'Yes, he's in studio rehearsing, but he's looking forward to meeting you after the show.' Lindsay knew Tom Watts would not want to be bothered with any of this now. Afterwards, if it all went smoothly, he'd be utterly charming.

They went on air without Colin Quinn, which was not unusual, given that he was the last item in the show and wouldn't be needed until around ten-thirty, but still, Alice was panicking and Lindsay wasn't too far behind, although she tried to look calm.

'Give it another fifteen minutes, then we call the stand-by guests. God damn them, why don't they turn on their mobile phones?' Lindsay wondered in frustration. 'You keep trying to make contact and I'll hover between studio and TV reception.'

They opened with the Latin lothario and he went down a bomb. In the audience, women of all ages went wild at his act and practically mobbed him when he finished, which nearly caused a major problem for security, not to mention the camera crew, who had difficulty getting shots. Luckily Tom calmed things down and insisted that unless they all returned to their seats he wouldn't be able to chat to the object of their desire.

He was absolutely charming and spoke in a broken English accent that merely added to his appeal, although Alice told her his accent had been nothing like it was now when she'd first spoken to him.

'Hell, he's probably from Blackpool originally,' Lindsay laughed in delight.

The interview was terrific, punctuated by screams from the fans each time he spoke. His answers became more and more double-meaning and he worked the audience into a frenzy.

'They're here.' Alice was suddenly beside her. 'They're just getting out of the limo. I have to stay here to make sure Romeo gets off safely. Could you meet them?'

'Sure, just page me if there's any problem. I normally wouldn't leave studio but I won't rest until I see this guy for myself.'

Lindsay dashed out to reception where their hostess was already taking coats. She couldn't see their star anywhere, which was a bit worrying. A tall blond lady seemed to be in charge and there were seven or eight of them, doing what she had absolutely no idea.

'Hello, I'm Lindsay Davidson. I'm in charge of the show tonight.' She held out her hand to the blond woman.

'Hi, Lindsay, nice to meet you. I'm Shirley. I told you it would be tight but we got here.'

'Great.' Where the hell was he? Lindsay looked around the group and smiled, still not seeing him.

'We'll go straight to the dressing room for a few minutes so that Colin can relax.'

'Sure.' She couldn't think of anything else to say and led the way silently. As she held open the security door to let them through she noticed someone who looked vaguely like him, hovering uncomfortably on the edge of the group.

No, it couldn't be, she decided as he gestured for her to go through before him.

It had to be him. There was no one else.

Lindsay couldn't believe it. On screen he looked taller, broader and had a huge presence. In the flesh he was smaller, only a couple of inches taller than she was and he was thinner. His blond hair was cropped very tight and the only thing that resembled his movie-star image was his eyes.

No, it wasn't him, she decided.

He grinned at her shyly, as she stood back and waited for him to come through to the next security checkpoint. 'Thanks', as she held the door.

'You're welcome.' She still wasn't sure.

'Actually, Shirley, I think I'll go straight to make-up, then I can change and relax.' Even his voice sounded different, quieter. But it had to be him, there was no one else.

'I'll show you the way.' Lindsay was still convinced she had the wrong guy, until she got to make-up.

'Colin, hi. Nice to see you again.' Sara, the chief make-up artist, was over in a flash, closely followed by a couple of the juniors.

'How'ya, Sara, you're looking great.' So he even remembered names. Lindsay was impressed. He grinned and gave Sara a hug and Lindsay watched in amazement as six fully grown women attempted to make up one man's face. His two minders watched helplessly. Lindsay dashed back to studio, almost colliding with Alice.

'All OK?'

'Yes, we're just on a break and Romeo is skulling beers in the green room and looking for "hot-blooded Irish pussy".' The two girls collapsed.

'Well, you ain't seen nothing yet. I've just left Colin Quinn in make-up and the only way you'll recognize him is by the amount of women fussing around him. He looks completely different, not at all the heart-throb he appears on screen. He's tiny and skinny. No, that's unfair. He's small and slim.'

Alice guffawed. 'Well as long as he can talk I couldn't care less what he looks like. Maybe he's fading away, pining for his dead wife.' She looked all gooey. 'Anyway, you go. Tom is looking for you. I'll take over.'

Lindsay dashed back into studio. Tom needed reassurance.

'How is it going?'

'Great. Thanks for keeping that lot under control at the start. We could have been in trouble. The interview was fab. Colin Quinn is in make-up. Seems in good form but go easy, I'd say. By the way, his parents are in the audience. I don't know if he knows but it might help him relax.'

'Thirty seconds to air,' announced the floor manager and after a few words about the next item Lindsay stepped quietly to the side of the set as the music pounded her ears.

The celebrity chef had an ego the size of a watermelon and the audience were fascinated. He was a complete fake with dyed hair and orange skin. After plugging his new TV series Tom led him skilfully into talking about the sixteen-year-old who supposedly 'threw herself' at him. He was so thick that he didn't even notice the audience gasping at his lack of respect for women in general and when they eventually booed at him he looked stunned. Tom wound him up and flattered him at the same time and he lapped it up. It made for entertaining television.

The show flew after that and suddenly they were on the music item prior to Colin Quinn. Lindsay saw him standing at the back of the set alone, waiting. She wasn't sure whether to approach him but he looked a bit lost.

'Can I get you anything?'

He shook his head and she was about to move away when she heard him say quietly, 'Can't say I'm looking forward to this but I'll be fine once I get on.' That shy grin was back. 'Hard to believe,

I'm sure, but I actually hate personal publicity.'

'Why did you agree to do it?'

'It's part of every actor's contract with the movie company. They want publicity for their product. Unfortunately, the people who give them that publicity all want to know about your private life. Normally I've nothing to say about myself but this time, because I've been off the scene, they know there's a story.'

'That's hard.'

'Yeah, but if I have to do a big interview I'd rather do it in my home country where at least people care about me. I got thousands of cards and letters from Ireland when . . .' He stopped abruptly.

They stood in silence for a moment as the applause died and Tom Watts' voice came over the speakers. 'My next guest needs no introduction because he is arguably this country's most successful export and a major international star to boot, but having just come through a huge personal trauma I'll bet he'd appreciate knowing how much we've missed him. Let's welcome home Colin Quinn.'

'Good luck.'

'Thanks.' He gave her a wistful smile and walked swiftly towards the lights and when she looked at a monitor nearby he was smiling broadly as he strode over to shake hands with Tom.

The audience went mad as soon as they saw him and gave him a standing ovation. He looked taken aback and touched and slightly embarrassed. Lindsay looked at his parents and saw that his mother was almost in tears, clapping loudly to hide her feelings. She felt like crying herself. It was an emotional moment.

The interview was riveting. Both men clearly knew and liked each other and laughed and joked for a while, until Tom asked the question everyone wanted an answer to.

'Almost two years ago now you lost your wife and you've been away from your work ever since and I know this is your first time home since it happened. How are you now and how are the children?'

Colin Quinn paused for an instant. 'Well, I'm OK now, in fact I'm doing fine, but I cannot tell you anything other than it's been the hardest four years of my life.'

'Your wife was diagnosed with cancer shortly after she gave birth to your daughters?'

'Yeah.' He let out a long sigh and everyone could see he was still raw. 'We had twin daughters just over four years ago and Megan wasn't really recovering as well as expected. We put it down to a difficult birth and the stress and tiredness of having two babies, but after six months or so she was diagnosed with leukaemia. It was the worst moment of our lives. She held on as long as she could to see her babies walk and talk and become little girls really.' His voice was barely a whisper. 'She died on their second birthday.'

He looked very tense as he spoke and people in the audience could be seen wiping away the odd tear. Tom and Lindsay had discussed a strategy if the interview got to this point, anxious to maintain the momentum, yet not be seen to be voyeuristic.

'How are the children now?'

'You know something, they're absolutely fantastic.' He smiled slightly and seemed to relax. 'They really are the best things in my life. Through them I found the strength to go on, even though that sounds like the worst cliché. They laugh and chatter all day and they've really become little women. And they had those two precious years with their mother and they still talk to her all the time. They say good night to her every night and tell her how much they miss her.' His voice broke only slightly, in sharp contrast to the audience, who were mostly in floods of tears. He looked so lost and lonely that Lindsay wanted to hug him, along with every other woman watching, she suspected.

'Speaking of mothers, did you spot your own mother and father in the audience?'

'No way, where?' He scanned the faces and found the two he wanted. 'Jesus, Ma, you'd get in anywhere,' he announced in his best 'Dublin' accent and the mood changed and the audience roared. Suddenly he stood up and ran down to the audience where he enveloped his mother in a bear-hug. It was a very special moment, with all seven cameras vying for the best shot of mother and son.

Chapter Thirty-Three

By the time the closing music had faded Lindsay's mobile, which she'd only just switched on, rang.

It was Alan Morland.

'That was one hell of a show. Colin Quinn was amazing, the best interview I've ever seen him give.'

'Well, Tom was very good with him.' Lindsay was delighted.

'Yes, but he was very restrained and you could see he had a plan. I suspect that was your influence.'

'Only a little.'

'By the way, you gave me a credit, what was that about? I didn't work on the show.'

'You're still Executive Producer, I just added Jonathan Myers to the credits as well. Otherwise nothing's changed.'

'Lindsay, you produced the show tonight.'

'Technically, yes. But I'm still Assistant Producer and I'm happy with it.'

'Thanks. I owe you one.'

'Pleasure. Talk to you on Monday. Go back to bed.'

There was a terrific atmosphere in the green room; everybody knew the show had been great. Lindsay had a quick word with Tom, who introduced her to his latest squeeze, Danielle – a nineteen-year-old dancer with flaming red hair, supposedly fresh from one of the huge Irish dance musicals currently taking the world by storm.

'She looks like she's danced round a few poles to me. Irish dancer my ass,' Geoff winked at Lindsay as he came to say well done.

Jonathan Myers appeared and pumped Lindsay's hand.

'Great show, well done. Colin Quinn was superb.'

'Thanks. Come on, I'll introduce you.'

Colin Quinn was surrounded by fans and was still trying to enter the green room, hotly pursued by half the audience. Security were definitely earning their money tonight. Lindsay introduced the two men and decided to leave them to talk.

'Are my mum and dad coming back here?' Colin wanted to know as she moved away.

'Yes, as well as your Auntie Anne and Uncle Tom and some other relations, all of whom are signing autographs as we speak.' Lindsay laughed and went to rescue them.

'This is a wonderful night. Thank you, my dear.' Mrs Quinn hugged her as she looked around the green room. 'Oh look, there's that lovely chef. I must ask him about his recipe for roast lamb with anchovies.' The others watched in astonishment as she took a glass of wine from a passing waiter and headed straight for their guest.

'I warn you, you'll have to drag her away from Tom Watts once she spots him,' Mr Quinn laughed.

Mrs Quinn, however, did know when to stop and she joined Lindsay and Mr Quinn in a corner, having said hello to everyone including her hero. 'We even had our photo taken by your staff photographer.'

'You must give me your address and I'll send you a copy,' Lindsay smiled at her enthusiasm as Colin joined them. She stood up quickly, not wanting to intrude and left them alone.

Later on, she saw them again and they looked a bit lost so she joined them once more. They were a terrific couple, full of life. Colin appeared for a second time and again she made her excuses and left. She was at the bar getting a much-needed glass of wine when he appeared at her side.

'I think you're trying to avoid me. I wanted to say thanks.'

'What for?' She was intrigued.

'For saying just the right thing back there. I hadn't realized I was going to be so nervous.'

'I'm surprised no one stayed with you. Normally—'

'No, please, I asked to be on my own. Don't blame anyone. But I was glad of the company in the end.'

'It must have been difficult for you.'

'No, actually it was OK and do you know something, I feel better now that I've come home. It was time.'

'I'm glad. And thank you for doing our show. It was a big coup for us to get you.'

'I like Tom Watts, always have. Listen, we're going to dinner now in some very posh restaurant. Will you join us?'

'No, I couldn't. I wouldn't want to intrude.'

'I'd like you to.'

'But I don't know anyone.'

'You know my folks and they've been raving about you since I met them tonight. Please?'

She didn't know what to say. 'OK.'

'Great, let's go.'

Half an hour later Lindsay found herself sitting beside Colin Quinn in one of Dublin's most exclusive restaurants, surrounded by his family, Shirley and the rest of his entourage. The attention lavished on them was astonishing. Waiters hovered everywhere and the owner watched anxiously nearby. They'd been ushered in, past a room full of people all eager to catch a glimpse of the star, to an area reserved for them only. The champagne flowed but Lindsay noticed Colin was quiet and drank only a little.

Afterwards, everyone insisted on going to a nightclub and Colin had his driver take the older people home, assuring his mum he'd be round at three for her famous roast dinner.

Again, they were greeted with reverence and

ushered in to the V.I.P. room. Lindsay felt a bit shy and chatted to Shirley, who seemed much more relaxed.

'It's been a tough week getting him here, but the difference already is amazing. He needed to talk about it and most of all he needed to come home to his mum.'

'He still seems awfully quiet.'

'No, he's fine, believe me. I think tonight was good for him.'

Colin came and joined them and Shirley was dragged onto the dance floor by a very camp hairdresser, part of the entourage.

Lindsay wasn't sure what to say to him and asked him about the children, then felt she'd said the wrong thing as his face clouded. But then he seemed happy enough to talk about them.

'They're in New York. I have a brilliant nanny and she's been on location with the kids for the past month, so I've been with them as much as I could. I've got a week here in Ireland, then three weeks off so she's going home to Australia and I'll take care of them full time. They start school this year so I won't be able to take them with me as much so I'll definitely cut back on my work.'

'Have you any photos?'

'Yep.' He took a photo of two adorable little girls out of his wallet. All three of them were tucked up in bed watching TV and the three faces were so alike, it was incredible.

'They're the image of you.'

'That's what everyone says but they're like their mum as well, especially in this one.' They were gorgeous in scarlet winter coats and hats, all ringlets and ribbons, playing in the snow.

'You must be very proud of them.'

'I am.'

'You're lucky to have them.'

'You're right. I forget that sometimes, when I'm feeling sorry for myself.' He grinned and she understood the screen presence for the first time. There was something about him, with his shy smile and tightly cropped blond hair and blue eyes and rugged skin.

They chatted for ages and suddenly it was four a.m. and they were last to leave the club.

'I'll say good night,' Lindsay said to no one in particular as they emerged into the clear, cold night air.

'We'll drop you home,' Colin said. 'The car's here waiting.'

'No honestly, I'm going in a different direction to all of you, I'll grab a cab.'

'Don't be ridiculous.'

'Honestly, look there's a taxi rank right here.' She pointed to the other side of the road and made her way across, waving good night to them all as they climbed in to the waiting limo. Colin ran after her. He took her two hands in his.

'Thanks.'

'For nothing.'

'I enjoyed myself.'

'Me too.'

He reached over and pulled her to him and wrapped her in his arms. It was a friendly hug and she hugged him back fiercely. She was vaguely aware of a flashbulb going off but he didn't seem to notice.

'Take care of yourself.'

'You too.' She hopped into a taxi and watched him rejoin his friends and minders, who were hovering anxiously in the background.

What a nice man, she thought as the taxi sped through the empty, black streets. Being close to someone else made her feel very lonely for Chris and she wondered for the millionth time where he was.

It was nearly three by the time Lindsay climbed into bed and she awoke to the doorbell ringing at eleven. Debbie and Tara stood there, arms full of newspapers and breakfasty things, as she tried to focus her tired eyes.

'Great show. We want to hear everything.' They pushed past her and headed for the warmth of the kitchen, Debbie already biting into a moist, flaky croissant.

'What was Colin Quinn like? He looked quite ordinary really, not as handsome as in the movies,' Debbie waffled, her mouth full.

'We got you the papers.' Tara threw them down on the kitchen table as Lindsay appeared in her dressing gown trying to secure her hair in a scrunchy.

'Oh my God.' Tara picked up one from the pile.

'What?' Debbie took a quick step towards her. 'Oh my God.'

'What is it?' Lindsay asked. They both looked at her in amazement.

She was still half asleep as she looked at the front page of one of the most popular newspapers. She stared and it took her a moment to take it in and even when she did see it properly she couldn't believe her eyes.

Under the heading 'Learning to love again?' were two photos of herself and Colin Quinn, one of him holding her two hands in his and the other of them hugging. The caption underneath read, '*Actor Colin Quinn and TV producer Lindsay Davidson leaving a Dublin nightclub early this morning.*'

'Oh my God.'

Chapter Thirty-Four

'This gets more and more complicated.' Debbie looked at her friend in astonishment twenty minutes later when she'd brought them up to date after they'd both laughingly insisted, 'What's Chris going to say?'

She'd made herself a strong black coffee and told them the whole story. They found it hard to take it all in.

'Chris saw you with Paul? You tried to explain and found him with another woman? And there's nothing going on with you and Colin Quinn? You'd better start at the beginning.'

For the rest of the morning they tried to work it all out, while Lindsay's phone rang incessantly. It seemed that everyone she'd ever met had seen the picture, including her mother, who left three messages demanding an explanation and her sister, who pleaded for the real story. Finally, she couldn't stand the ringing any longer and snatched up the receiver and snapped, 'Hello.' It was Paul.

'Why didn't you tell me you were seeing someone else?'

'Well . . . I . . .'

'It won't last, you know. Men like him can have anyone they want. How long has it been going on?'

'Well, actually—'

'Don't think I'll be waiting. You've wasted enough of my time already.' He hung up, leaving Lindsay speechless. She decided not to confuse the girls further by explaining.

They ate their way through a bag of croissants, bagels and muffins and drank gallons of juice and coffee and tried to work it all out.

'Why didn't you tell us?' Tara kept asking, obviously upset about Chris.

'I couldn't. I'm sorry. I'd have told you eventually but I needed time. I had to learn to cope with it first myself.'

'I knew there was something wrong the other night at dinner.' Tara was upset with herself for not realizing.

'I'm sorry I haven't seen more of you this last while,' Debbie wailed. 'You poor thing, you've been through the mill and now this.' It was almost too much for Lindsay.

'Listen, I really need your help to move on with my life. It's just that, when things went wrong with Chris, and especially after I saw him with another woman, I realized that he really was the one. Isn't that funny, after all the stuff with Paul? But Chris was different. We had something special, I sort of felt we were soulmates. I know that sounds really stupid cause I'd only known him for such a short time. But I made up my mind, that Sunday after I called at his place, that I wasn't going to let it destroy me and I still feel the same way. And that's the most valuable lesson of all that I learned from Paul.'

'You have to try and talk to him again,' Tara was adamant.

'Well, whatever hope there was has presumably gone out the window if he's seen this. Jesus, I wonder what Paul will make of it as well? I hope he's gutted.' Debbie gave a half-laugh.

'Actually, that was Paul on the phone just now and he sounded furious.' The look on their faces was priceless.

'Listen, it's over with Chris. I don't want to talk about him any more, OK. He said some terrible things to me and he hasn't tried to make contact since to even ask me for answers. And he's obviously with someone else. I have to get on with my life. Now, could you bear to watch last night's show with me again? I really need to see it coldly and work out if there was anything I could have done better.'

So they sat around and ate some more, Lindsay still in her PJs at three o'clock on a bright Sunday afternoon. Eventually, they fell into their normal routine and she got dressed and they headed off to Howth with Charlie, for a meander along the cliffs. They called in for hot chocolate on the way home and dropped her off at eight-thirty and she washed and went straight to bed, exhausted.

*   *   *

Next morning after a late start, Lindsay dressed in black jeans and a white T-shirt and her favourite black jacket and headed into the office, to clear up and start all over again. There were several messages from newspapers wanting to talk to her. She ignored them and rang the Press Office, who agreed to fend off any calls they could. She put her phone on voice mail and set to work. As soon as she checked the ratings she relaxed a little. The figures were the best of the season so far. They'd started off well and had built steadily so that by the end of the show, for the Colin Quinn interview, they had seventy per cent of all available adults watching their programme and they were back in the top ten.

Checking her e-mails she found a note from Jonathan Myers, offering his congratulations on the viewing figures.

She rang Alan and he was delighted. 'Are you OK? I, erm . . . saw the pictures yesterday.'

'Yeah, it wasn't what it seemed.' She laughed at the irony. 'Although I bet that's what they all say. He invited me for dinner with his entourage. We talked. I got a taxi home. He was simply thanking me for being good to his mum and dad.'

'Well, I hope it didn't upset you, that's all.'

'No, I'm fine, talk to you tomorrow.'

About one-thirty TV reception rang and an excited voice announced, 'Colin Quinn is here to see you.'

Lindsay was staggered. What on earth did he want? Famous actors didn't even telephone afterwards. In fact, nobody ever really said thank you to TV shows, all felt they were the ones doing the favour, which was mostly true.

Cursing herself for looking worse than Charlie on a bad hair day, she made her way gingerly to reception.

'Hi.' He peered out from behind the biggest bunch of flowers she'd ever seen and grinned shyly while the receptionist made whale noises in the background, trying to keep her mouth shut.

'Hi.'

'I wanted to say thanks and sorry about the pictures and are you free for lunch?' He thrust the flowers at her just as the doors opened and Chris walked in.

Lindsay just couldn't stop herself staring at him. He looked absolutely gorgeous in a dark grey, wool jacket, pale shirt and faded black jeans, carrying a soft leather overnight bag. The whale called his name, smiled and flirted and waved a package at him. He had no choice but to walk over to where they were standing to collect it. He nodded coldly in her general direction and she smelt the cool, clean, still-familiar smell of him and her stomach went plop.

'Are you OK?' Colin asked.

'I'm fine and they're gorgeous, thank you.' She spoke in a low voice even though Chris was gone in an instant, striding off into the distance without ever really looking at her.

'Lunch?'

'You really don't have to.'

'I'd like to.'

'OK, let me grab my bag.'

'I'll wait outside in the car.'

Lindsay's heart felt like lead as she joined him, even though she was really pleased to get the chance to see him again. He took her to a gorgeous little Indian restaurant and they chatted like old friends.

'I should have known there'd be a photographer somewhere. It was stupid of me. I hope it didn't cause you any problems.'

She shook her head.

'Any six-foot-four guy wanting to beat me up?'

'No.'

'He must be very understanding?'

'No, I meant there isn't anyone.' Suddenly, she found herself telling him everything, all about Paul and then Chris and he listened and she felt better. They talked about relationships and he tried to see things from Chris's side and he, too, felt she should try to talk to him and explain. 'Men are very black and white, we don't analyse things the way women do and I think sometimes we're a bit thick. We need it spelled out for us a lot of the time.'

He told her more about his wife and their relationship, about how he knew she was the one from the moment he met her and she envied him. They sat until five p.m. and became firm friends and she felt as if she'd known him for years, partly because of all the research bumph she'd read on him but mostly because he was open and honest and easy.

He dropped her back at the office and she agreed to have dinner with him on Thursday night as he was flying back home on Saturday morning and he wanted to take his parents out on Friday night. She wished she could have met him under different circumstances, but maybe her lack of interest was the reason he was so relaxed with her. Anyway, after today's outpouring he was in no doubt that she was a complete disaster where men were concerned and he certainly wasn't looking for a new relationship, not after the way he'd spoken about his wife. It all made for an easy life, which was what she needed so badly right now. Shame about the papers though, she thought as she headed for home.

On Tuesday there were a lot of funny looks directed her way and Alice laughingly asked her if she wanted to keep the file on Colin Quinn as a memento. Tom Watts wasn't as subtle.

'So, Lindsay, what's the story? What's he like in the sack?' he asked her in a crowded Tuesday morning meeting, just as Jonathan Myers entered. Everyone stared at her and she was angry with him and furious with herself for blushing.

'Fantastic, you'd better keep a tight rein on your girlfriends because one night with him and you'll be out of the picture.'

The office collapsed with laughter and Jonathan smiled at her sympathetically.

They had another strong show lined up for the coming weekend with the ex-wife of a famous rock star giving her first interview in public and expected to spill a very large tin of beans. The rest of the team were also anxious to impress Jonathan and several good ideas came to the table, including one from David who wanted to have a discussion on the subject of mistresses. He had three women willing to take part, including the former mistress of a well-known politician, a woman who had secretly been with one of the country's top businessmen for fifteen years and had recently been dumped in favour of a 'younger model', and another who claimed that wives had all the work and mistresses had all the fun and got the best presents at Christmas. Tom didn't like the idea and Lindsay got the impression he felt threatened by strong women such as these. Lindsay, though, knew it could be great with a bit of strategic planning, so she pencilled it in for later in the season, promising to talk it through with Tom as soon as she'd done some work on it with David.

On Thursday she took a taxi into town and met Colin at his hotel. They decided to eat there, where no one would bother them and once again she spent a relaxed and enjoyable evening getting to know him. They laughed a lot and he asked her for her home number and vowed to stay in touch, which she somehow doubted he'd manage, given his status and lifestyle. To her surprise he gave her his home number, asking her to keep it private and making her promise to call if she needed to talk. He even invited her to stay with him in New York for a few days, an invitation she knew she'd never take up. They'd both move on, she knew, but he was surprisingly easy to be with and he made her laugh. She felt she had found a new friend, but it was tinged with regret for another friendship that could have been so much more.

The show went very well again that week and Jonathan telephoned her immediately afterwards and said how much he'd enjoyed it. On the Sunday morning Lindsay found herself featuring in the gossip column of one of the newspapers, where it was reported that she'd spent 'several nights' in the company of Ireland's 'most eligible bachelor' after he'd 'showered her with roses' and 'whisked her away' from her busy job as producer of the country's number-one TV show. They were spotted, according to the report, 'looking lovingly into each other's eyes' in several of Dublin's hottest spots. Lindsay tore it up and unplugged her home phone in order to avoid her mother again, although she couldn't avoid the girls, who teased her gently but persistently all that day.

Next morning, as soon as she stepped out of the shower her phone rang and she answered, wondering if something was wrong for someone to be ringing her so early.

'I hear we're in love,' a warm voice greeted her and she was amazed to recognize Colin on the other end. She couldn't believe he'd taken time out to ring her and once again he made her laugh and it helped a bit.

Chapter Thirty-Five

The heavy, low skies and short, grey days of winter gave way to a watery but promising spring and life settled into a pattern for Lindsay.

She worked twelve hours a day, six days a week, ate badly and slept fitfully. For relaxation she walked Charlie or had a drink with the girls. She felt tired all the time and looked grey and drawn and even her mother was beginning to worry but she avoided all attempts to discuss anything with anybody.

The girls finally cornered her one night, turning up at her home unexpectedly with a Chinese take-away and a couple of bottles of wine.

'You've been avoiding us.' Debbie handed her the food and walked past her purposefully.

'I have not, I saw you on Sunday.'

'Yes, but we haven't really talked in ages and we're concerned about you. Besides, what are you doing in your dressing gown at eight-thirty on a lovely evening like this?' Tara wanted to know.

'I've just had a bath and besides I was in the

office at seven-thirty this morning. Anyway, I'm not feeling great.'

'No wonder. You're working too hard and playing too soft. You look awful, by the way.'

'Thanks.' They plonked the food down and Debbie poured three glasses of wine as they settled themselves on the couch and gave Charlie a few tasty morsels.

'God, that food smells awful.' Lindsay wrinkled her nose and stared at the grey mound.

'It's from your favourite takeaway, for God's sake. What's wrong with you? Maybe you're pregnant or something.' Debbie and Tara laughed at the ridiculousness of it and in a split second life changed for ever for Lindsay.

'Very funny, I'll just get us some bits 'n' pieces.' All colour drained from her face as she headed for the kitchen, anything to buy herself time.

She busied herself doing nothing and tried to concentrate and remember when she'd last had a period. She couldn't. All she could think of was the tiredness, the queasy tummy, the slightly lumpy, tender breasts – all symptoms she'd heard other women moaning about.

Stop it, she lectured herself, don't be a fucking idiot, you're on the pill. It's impossible. She sighed with relief, knowing there must be some other, logical explanation.

'Hurry up, *Sex and the City* is just starting,' Debbie called impatiently.

Lindsay returned and sat down and joined in and didn't see or hear a word or eat or drink anything.

'Lindsay, what's up? Please talk to us, we're really worried about you,' Tara pleaded later, in an attempt to get her talking.

'Honestly, I'm OK, I promise. I'm just working too hard and trying to get over things and probably not looking after myself enough, but Alan is coming back next week and I'll take a few days off and I'm going to start a health kick and go back to the gym. Just bear with me. OK?'

It must have been the performance of her life because they seemed to accept it and left around eleven, promising to join her in getting in shape.

When they'd gone Lindsay sat in the dark and tried to think clearly although her heart started beating very fast and she felt sick every time she thought of the unthinkable.

She couldn't remember when she'd last had a period, but she knew it was ages ago because she hadn't bought tampons for months. Normally, she was as regular as her Visa bill. She knew stress could affect a woman's cycle and she'd sure had her quota of that. She had been tired and a bit queasy but not sick in the mornings but, most important of all, she was taking oral contraceptives, which were virtually 100 per cent effective and she never forgot to take them. Ever. She remembered considering stopping after Paul but she'd always had problems with painful periods and decided to wait a few months because she couldn't cope with anything else, even a pain at that stage.

By midnight, she'd convinced herself that she was being ridiculous but she slept badly and found herself in the car at seven-thirty searching for a pharmacy.

Hoping the Sunday newspapers weren't following her and trying to see the irony of it all she bought a test and went home, where she sat for twenty minutes staring at the unopened box.

What was she doing? She couldn't be pregnant. It was impossible. Oh God, no, please don't let it be, she silently begged. Please, I'll accept anything else you send me but not this. Then she calmed down. This simply couldn't happen to her. Panic again. What would everyone say? She wouldn't be able to cope. Round and round it went until her head felt like a tumble dryer, and fear caused her to break out in a cold sweat and endure palpitations that could surely bring on a heart attack. What if she was? And if she was so sure that she wasn't then why did she not want to know?

Suddenly she threw the box into a drawer, deciding she was being irrational and stupid. She simply could not be pregnant so she decided to forget about it and go to work.

An hour later she couldn't stand it any longer and made some excuse and drove home again, where she sat for the same twenty-minute period staring at the same box.

It was the longest, shortest two minutes of her life and one of the toughest waiting rooms she'd ever endured and when she saw the result she didn't cry, she took the only option open to her. She went into complete denial.

* * *

If the girls thought she was behaving oddly up to this, it was nothing compared to her behaviour over the next week. She was like a mad woman. Every time they talked to her she was either in the office at the oddest hours or else she was painting her kitchen, digging the garden, or walking Charlie to within an inch of his life. Or avoiding them. Again.

Alan Morland came back to work, looking much thinner and with no definite word on his illness. All the tests had revealed nothing and he hadn't had the pain since, so he ignored advice and came back, insisting he was OK. Lindsay was glad to see him yet dreading his return, and he brought her for coffee and seemed more concerned about her than himself.

'You look awful, you've lost weight and your face is grey. I'm worried about you. What's up?'

'Nothing, honestly, I'm fine.' She was sick of people telling her how awful she looked.

'Why don't you take a few days off, get away from here? You're due the time anyway.'

'I'll think about it. Thanks.'

That evening she pulled her kitchen presses apart and was sitting on the floor with a basin of warm, soapy water, surrounded by flour and rice and spices when the phone rang.

'Hi there, stranger. What ya up to?' It was Colin Quinn. They'd been in touch by e-mail several times and she thought he was in the middle of a new movie so she was surprised and pleased to hear from him.

317

'Sitting on the kitchen floor looking like a witch cleaning manically.' There seemed no point in lying. 'How about you? How's the movie going?'

'My co-star has developed chickenpox, would you believe? So, I've ten days off and I'm just back home. They're furiously trying to reschedule so they can continue shooting. I'm glad of the break but the kids are in Chicago with my sister for a week so it's pretty lonely. Fancy coming out for a few days?'

'Yeah right.'

'You sound pretty down. Are you OK?'

'Not really.'

'Want to talk about it?'

'I don't think I can.'

'OK, look, I'm hanging up now and Shirley will ring you in a couple of hours with flight details. I'm bringing you to New York and if you don't come I'll tell the newspapers we're getting married and just think what that will do to your already complicated life.'

'Don't be ridiculous.'

'I'm going now. I'll see you soon.' And he hung up. Just like that.

Lindsay abandoned what she was doing, took a bath and went to bed, unable to cope for the first time in ages. She would have liked a drink, but was afraid to, just in case. She got into bed and jumped out again five minutes later and made a hot port, just to prove she didn't really believe what she was thinking.

At six the next morning she awoke to her phone ringing.

'Hi, Lindsay, it's Shirley. How are you?' She didn't wait for a reply. 'Sorry to call you so early but Colin was anxious that I talk to you before I went to bed. I hear you're coming to visit, so, I have you booked on a flight tomorrow at twelve noon. Is there somewhere I can e-mail you details?'

'Shirley, hi.' She sat up in bed and pulled on her dressing gown. 'Listen, I'm not sure yet—'

'I was told not to take no for an answer. It's already booked.'

'Well, I'm sorry but I cannot accept. I'll compromise though. I will come,' she said, surprising herself, 'but I'll book it myself. Give me your number and I'll call you later.'

'Lindsay, I'll be in trouble over this.'

'Tell him I'm a tough old Irish boot and I cannot be bought.'

They argued for a while longer and Lindsay hung up and jumped into the shower, feeling a bit better.

In the office she asked Alan if she could take him up on his offer and he was delighted. This week's show was a special tribute that had been planned for months and it was Alan's baby anyhow. She arranged to be back in the office the following Wednesday, giving her four nights and five full days in New York. Next she called Debbie.

'Any chance you could get me a seat on a flight to New York tomorrow, one that doesn't cost as much as a new car?'

'Does this trip involve a well-known Irish actor, by any chance?'

'Sort of.'

'Yes or no?'

'Yes.'

'Give me half an hour. Bye.'

Her phone rang five minutes later.

'You're going to New York to see Colin Quinn?' Tara, sounding shocked.

'Not really. Well, yes, I suppose so, but I need a break and he asked me and we're just friends so . . .'

'I'm delighted. Want to borrow my new Gucci bag?'

'I'd love to. Thanks.'

'I'll call round tonight. I suspect I'll have Debbie with me. Bye.'

Chapter Thirty-Six

She arrived on a typical New York day – clear blue sky, not too cold, much too busy. She'd felt better as soon as she boarded the plane. It seemed like she'd been stuck forever in the rut of her too small world of the office and the house, same faces, same routine, same problems, so it felt really good to be leaving it all behind – and being upgraded to first class, courtesy of Debbie, certainly helped. So did Tara's Gucci bag and Debbie's brand-new, long, black leather coat. She'd had her hair cut and treated herself to a facial the previous evening and she felt human for the first time in weeks. Her new Prada sunglasses combined with the cascading hair and leather made her look like a movie star herself but she felt shy and inadequate as she entered the terminal building and didn't see Colin. What the hell am I doing here, she asked herself for the tenth time. Trips to New York to meet a movie star don't get offered to girls like me. She wondered if he'd sent his driver and scanned the placards nervously but their passengers all had much more exotic sounding names and no doubt much more exciting lives.

Suddenly she saw him and he looked nothing like a movie star in his jeans, denim jacket, baseball cap and dark glasses. He looked more like a building worker. He smiled shyly and hugged her.

'You are one stubborn old broad.'

'And you're one hell of a motherfucker, thinking you could buy me off.' They laughed and slipped into easy mode immediately and she was glad she'd come.

He was driving what looked like a glamorous pick-up truck but turned out to be the trendiest 'Mammy-wagon' in town.

'All part of being a single parent with two Barbie-crazed kids,' he explained. 'Between the clothes and the cars and the houses and the horses – theirs, not mine – I need a trailer really.'

His apartment was one of the most spectacular homes she'd ever been in, about as different to her little cottage as it was possible to find, anywhere in the world. It was on two floors, the top being the living quarters, with spectacular views – a New York skyline so perfect it looked like a backdrop – and a terrace the size of a football stadium. Outside, it had a very Mediterranean feel with huge ferns, old, glazed pots, comfy chairs, wrought iron and shutters. On the upper terrace was the most amazing roof garden with a vast array of exotic plants, aromatic herbs and even vegetables and an old, much-used Victorian conservatory. There was an outdoor dining-area under a mass of greenery, fragrant even at this time of year. Huge candles nestled in antique holders; she could imagine the scene here at twilight. Inside, the pale, wood-panelled living room was filled with light and big, squashy couches, faded rugs and magnificent paintings. The kitchen had every available gadget and was cool and shiny and home to miles of stainless steel and cold, black granite.

Lindsay wasn't even sure she was staying here but he showed her to a burnt-orange room with its own terrace and ornate French doors and at least three other windows and a chaise longue and a massive four-poster bed with big, thick, old-fashioned, snow-white linen and covers.

'Wow,' was all she could manage.

'Can't take any of the credit, I'm afraid. It was all Megan's doing.'

'Did I tell you that I used to do interior design?' He shook his head. 'Well, I did and I've been in a lot of houses but this is the most amazing blend of styles I've ever seen. It feels very old, but has a modern streak – almost European, yet with an American edge.'

'Well, her grandmother was French so she loved the Mediterranean and she tried to bring a bit of that here. She was an avid collector and was always rooting in antique shops. And as you saw she devoted a lot of her spare time to the garden.'

'You must love it.'

'I do. I really look forward to coming home here.'

It felt odd to be in his home, he was famous, after all, and celebrities didn't usually invite people they met in TV studios into their lives. But he seemed relaxed as she joined him later, having unpacked and changed into a simple, long black Ghost dress and redone her make-up. 'I know you're probably tired after the flight, so I thought I'd just cook us some steaks and a salad here tonight. OK? Or would you rather go out?'

'No. That sounds great. And thanks for inviting me, making me come. I didn't realize until I got on the plane how badly I needed to get away.'

'Glass of wine?'

'Spritzer, please. Is it OK if I look at your photos?'

'Sure.' He handed her a glass and she wandered round the room. There were pictures everywhere, snapshots of an idyllic life. They looked like a very happy couple and Megan obviously adored the two girls, there were dozens of photos of the three of them and they seemed to be laughing all the time.

They had dinner tucked up on the sofa. Afterwards he made her bundle up, lit the candles in the roof garden and they took coffee there. It was magical.

'It's my favourite place. It's what keeps me going when I'm far away and under pressure. It makes me feel lucky, even at the worst times.'

'You are lucky, you've got so much, even though you've lost a lot too. I'm sorry I won't get to meet the girls.'

'Some other time. Now, tell me, what's so bad at the moment that you needed to get away?'

'I'm pregnant.' It had escaped at last and it hung out there somewhere, in the night-scented air and she knew she'd finally admitted it to herself, yet it still shocked her, but this time only for a split second.

He looked at her for a long time. 'Are you sure?'

'Yes.' Quietly. 'No.' Louder. 'Yes, I think so,' in a barely audible whisper. 'At least, I did one of those home tests, after the girls slagged me about being tired and sick looking. Imagine, I hadn't even realized. What an idiot.'

'How long?'

She gave him an odd look. 'Do you know, I never even thought of that. I've been so busy pretending I wasn't.' She thought about it for a second. 'It must have happened around Christmas. God, that makes it about two and a half months.'

'What are you going to do?'

'What do you mean?'

'Are you going to keep it?'

'I dunno.' Her voice was barely audible. 'I don't want to be pregnant. I don't want a baby. I have no maternal instincts. I hate the idea of getting fat. This will ruin my life, I'll have nothing, no social life and I won't be able to do my job properly. Besides, I'm too young to just give it all up for . . . something . . . that I'm not even sure I want.' She was shocked at her callousness. 'I know that sounds terrible and I hate myself for feeling this way but I can't help it.' She was crying now, for Chris, for herself, but mostly for the baby she didn't know what to do with.

He came and put his arms around her and his not judging her made it worse somehow.

After an age he gathered her up and put her to bed, waiting while she put on a big T-shirt and cleaned her face. He tucked her up like a child and pushed back her hair and she fell asleep immediately, exhausted yet relieved that she'd finally said it aloud.

When she awoke the next morning it was eleven o'clock and she couldn't remember where she was for a second. It was all so unreal. She lay there, remembering the time she'd been to New York with Paul, realizing with a thump of her heart that she couldn't quite remember all the details. She panicked, trying to bring his face to mind but it was another image that flooded her now and she jumped out of bed to escape him. Colin was reading a script in the kitchen when she padded in, in her bare feet with her hair tossed, desperate for some water or juice.

'Great. I thought you'd never wake up. I'm starving. Fancy some breakfast?'

'Could we go out? To a real New York diner? It's one of my favourite things to do here. That, and eating Chinese food out of cartons.'

He grinned at her. 'OK, get ready and don't be long.'

'Can I grab some juice first?'

'Help yourself.'

He took her to his favourite breakfast place and she was starving and ate a huge plate of pancakes with bacon and maple syrup and drank at least a litre of one of their famous smoothies, this one a yoghurt and mixed-berry sensation. Afterwards they went for a walk in Central Park and talked some more.

'The first thing you need to do is get yourself checked by a doctor, just to make sure.'

She nodded, knowing he was right but not at all certain she was ready. He sensed it.

'I have a friend. She's an M.D. on the other side of town. I know she'd see you. Today. How about it?'

'OK.'

'Good girl, I'll ring her now.' He took out his mobile and she knew he'd already talked to her. He made an appointment for five that afternoon. In the meantime, he seemed determined to keep her busy and when the time came he dropped her at the address and said he'd be waiting.

'You don't have to. I can catch a cab.'

'I want to. I have a script with me to read, anyway. I'll grab a coffee and see you back here.'

'I'm sorry for dumping all this on you.'

'That's what friends are for.'

'Thanks.'

'Now scoot.' So she did and the doctor was young and pretty and talked to her for ages and got her to do a urine test before feeling her tummy, asking her all sorts of questions in a soft, gentle, voice as if she were a sixteen-year-old.

'Did you take any precautions?'

'Yes, I was on the pill and as far as I know I didn't forget to take it.'

'Were you taking any other medication at the time?'

'No, at least I don't think so . . . oh, except for a course of antibiotics for a bout of flu.'

'That may have been a factor, Lindsay. You are pregnant, about eleven weeks, although it's hard to be precise at this stage.'

She nodded stupidly, as if she should have known.

'You should probably see your own doctor once you get home.'

'What are the options?'

'Well, you'll need regular check-ups and a scan, if you decide to keep the baby. Everything seems fine at the moment. You're healthy and you're still young enough.'

'And if I don't want to keep it?' She never thought she'd be even thinking this way but she wasn't sure she could go through with it.

'Your own doctor will advise you. It's a relatively simple procedure but if you are considering a termination, you should think about having it as soon as possible.'

Lindsay nodded.

'I know it must seem like a shock now, but give yourself a few days. Do you smoke?'

She shook her head, hardly able to believe she was having this conversation.

'Good. Well, eat healthily, avoid shellfish, soft cheese, pâté, raw eggs and you're advised not to drink alcohol. Here's some bedtime reading to keep you going,' she smiled calmly as she handed Lindsay a bunch of leaflets. 'Colin has my home number and, if you need to talk things through again, I'd be happy to see you.'

'Thanks.'

'Good luck, Lindsay.'

Chapter Thirty-Seven

'You OK?'

'Yep.'

'How did it go?'

'She was nice, you were right.'

'And . . . ?'

She nodded. 'Eleven weeks, and I didn't even notice.'

'You probably did but you decided to ignore it.'

'No, honestly, I never even thought about it. I was so busy trying to keep busy that I paid no attention to myself really. It only seems like about a month since Christmas anyway and because I was on the pill the thought never even crossed my mind. Swear.'

He drove in silence for a while and she felt awful, sure she was turning into the most self-pitying, wretched bore. Here she was, in New York, on the trip of a lifetime and all she could think of was that her life was over.

'OK, I want you to have a bath and get your glad

rags on. I'm taking you somewhere posh for dinner.'

'Where?'

'Never mind, just be ready at seven-thirty.'

She made a huge effort for him and they took a cab a few blocks to Dino's, a little Italian that was one of the in places to eat in New York – impossible to get a table unless you were known. It was tiny but very authentic, run by three generations of the one family and the owner greeted Colin like a son and ushered them to a secluded corner.

People glanced at them as they moved across the floor. They looked relaxed and happy and successful and she was envied, especially by those who recognized him.

Giorgio refused to show them the menu.

'I order for you, yes?'

'If that's OK with Lindsay?'

She nodded and they sipped a luscious Chianti – despite the doctor's recommendation and Colin's 'Would you like some mineral water?' They talked. Then food suddenly started arriving from all directions – pasta, meat, salad and fish and numerous dishes she didn't recognize, until they begged Giorgio to stop because they weren't able for half of it.

'I should have warned you, but isn't it delicious?' he asked, tucking into veal with porcini mushrooms.

'Yes, but even though I haven't eaten since breakfast I still can't manage another bite and I haven't tasted half the dishes.'

'No worries, I'll ask him for a doggy bag and you can try it tomorrow.'

Lindsay laughed at the thought of him leaving with the next day's lunch.

'They all feel sorry for me now because I have to cook for myself so they're always wanting me to take stuff home.'

'They must like you.'

'I only come to a few places round here. I don't go out much, to tell you the truth. Too many nights eating out when I'm on location, so when I do come out to eat I go to places where they know me well. It's much less hassle.'

After dinner they headed home because suddenly she couldn't stop yawning and he asked if she'd thought about what she was going to do. She shook her head.

'The more I think, the more I panic. The thought of telling people, what to do about my job, money – all fill me with dread. What did I do to deserve this?' She looked pathetic as she said it.

'I think you should talk to Chris.'

'I can't.'

'He has a right to know.'

'In a way, that's nearly the worst part. At best he'll think I did it deliberately. At worst, he'll doubt that it's his.' She laughed but it didn't sound real. 'He thinks I sleep around. I'd say he'll want nothing to do with this.'

'He doesn't sound like that kind of guy to me. Why do you think that?'

'I guess I'd built him up in my head. I thought we had something really special going. Then, because of what he thinks he saw, he wanted out, without giving me a chance to explain. So, what hope do you think I have with this little news headline?'

'He has a right to know.'

'Yeah, well, first things first. I need to decide what to do. Now, can we change the subject, I'm sick of me?'

The next day Colin had some meetings so Lindsay went shopping. She took a bus out to Woodbury Common and spent the day trawling through designer retail outlets, picking up two sexy DKNY tops for Tara and Debbie and some shoes for her sister. She bought lots of new things for herself, tight stretchy tops and a clingy dress and sexy underwear, in spite of her condition, all at a fraction of the original price and she even managed to pick up some funky Barbie hats for Colin's little girls. She found herself looking at baby clothes, miniature Gucci girl outfits and designer denims for boys and she was afraid to touch them, unwilling, yet, to get too involved.

When she arrived home he was already there and he laughed when he saw the number of fluorescent carrier bags.

'I can see you're really worried about money,' he teased and she was amazed that she hadn't even considered her credit card bill. As soon as she sat down the tiredness overwhelmed her and she realized she'd been on her feet for at least eight hours. He came and put his arms around her and it felt good. They had dinner in the home of some friends of Colin's that night and she knew they were wondering about her but were too polite to ask. He was a movie producer and she was a successful scriptwriter and they'd just had a baby and Lindsay wondered if that was why Colin had taken her there. If so, it didn't work. As she peered into the cot she couldn't imagine having one herself, much less being happy about it. She struggled all evening to be good company.

Suddenly it was her last evening and she insisted on ordering in Chinese food so that they could eat out of the cartons and he laughed at her face when he showed her the menu.

'It's a book. You choose, I'll pay, I couldn't possibly go through that. By the way, are you sure you don't mind staying in? I feel like the most boring visitor this town has ever seen.'

He didn't and a mound of stuff arrived. They watched a movie and he drank beer and noticed that she didn't touch hers. They ate with chopsticks and she felt like a cool American teenager for a while. Almost.

'When do the girls get back?' she asked him later.

'Day after tomorrow.' He looked at her for a long moment. 'I really miss them.' He continued to watch her. 'You know something, they're the best thing that ever happened to me, in spite of everything.'

'I wonder if I'll ever be able to say that. Right now it's the worst thing that's ever happened.'

'That will change, I promise.'

'I feel so alone in this.' She looked at him sadly and he understood. He kissed her hair, then her forehead, then her eyes, and without really knowing why she turned her mouth up to him and they kissed, and she needed it more than anything, and it went on for a long time. He slowly undressed her and kissed her all over and she touched and caressed him and they made love, and it was different to any other time she'd done it. He was gentle and exploring and unsure of himself, which amazed her, and when they climaxed it was like a massive release for her. She didn't know until he told her later that it was the first time for him since his wife's death.

'You are a very special man, Mr Quinn.'

'I'm glad it was with you.'

'So am I.' She grinned at him. 'I needed that. I think I just got rid of a bucketful of tension and stress.'

He grinned back. 'I needed it too.'

'And at least you know I can't get pregnant.'

They sat with their arms around each other in front of the fire and she found herself dozing and he asked, 'Want to sleep in my bed tonight?'

She nodded. They turned out the lights and she slept in his arms, feeling safe, and she knew she'd found someone really special – and for the first time she wished she'd never met Chris, because she suspected he was always going to be there, slap bang in the middle of any potential new relationship.

*   *   *

He took her to Greenwich Village for lunch and they strolled around, holding hands. He bought her lots of little presents and she saw a big, soft, gorgeous sweater and managed to buy it while he was browsing in a bookstore. Before she left she put it on his pillow and placed the two little hats for the girls on each side, then she wrote him a note, trying to explain how much he'd come to mean to her.

He left her at the airport and they hugged and he made her promise to call him as soon as she got home and told her not to worry and urged her to talk to Chris.

She felt like a schoolgirl leaving home as she boarded the plane and she knew that somewhere along the way she'd made a decision and it was going to be really hard.

She slept for most of the journey and her dreams were all of Chris laughing at her and her mother crying.

Lindsay arrived back in Dublin early in the morning and went home, showered, changed and left a message for the girls before she set off for work. She felt exhausted before the day had even begun. She pulled into a parking space and came face to face with Chris as they both got out of their cars at exactly the same moment. She wasn't even remotely prepared mentally, and physically she found her arms trying to protect an almost invisible bump, and she blushed and stumbled, her already fragile courage deserting her.

'Hi.'

'Hi.'

He looked really well – clean and healthy and gorgeous and out of reach. She felt old and ordinary beside him. And very frightened.

'Chris, I need to talk to you.'

'I'm sorry, I'm already late for a meeting.'

'Could we meet later?' He didn't give her an immediate no and she plunged straight in, heart crashing, just in case she never found the courage again. 'It's . . . important. There's something I need to talk to you about. Please?'

He looked at her for a long moment and she felt he was going to agree and then the mask slid slowly into place and he shook his head.

'There's honestly nothing you could say that would make any difference. It's too late. I think we've both moved on.'

And he turned and walked away, casting a very long shadow. She pretended to hunt for her keys because she felt so small and humiliated, and when finally she walked at a safe distance behind him, staring at his dark, unyielding frame, she knew she was never going to give him the chance to do that to her again. She was on her own and his coldness somehow strengthened her resolve to make something out of the mess that was her life.

Chapter Thirty-Eight

She grabbed breakfast and made her way to the office, where Alan greeted her with a shy grin.

'I didn't realize your trip was going to be so glamorous.'

'How do you mean?'

He pointed to one of the Sunday papers on his desk. It was open at the gossip column and he looked a bit embarrassed to be caught reading it as she glanced over his shoulder and saw the heading 'Lindsay leaves for love nest'. The same picture, the one of herself and Colin holding hands, was there. Her face went bright red and she immediately wondered if Chris had seen it. Could that have been the reason he was so cold towards her? She dismissed the idea, he'd told her once he never read the gossip columns.

The article told how 'sexy movie star' Colin Quinn had flown 'TV producer' Lindsay 'by Concorde' to his 'pad' in New York to 'introduce her to the two most important women in his life'. She couldn't read any more.

'Well, it was nothing like as glamorous as they're making out. I'm afraid I got myself to New York, as cheaply as possible, and his children were away for a week.'

'I see, sorry, I didn't mean to pry.'

'It's OK, I just wonder who's feeding them all this rubbish.'

'All they need is a tip-off that you went to New York – they put two and two together . . . the rest you know. Don't worry about it, how did it go, anyway?'

'It was great, very relaxing. I spent a fortune in the shops.'

'Good, you deserve it. Want to have a chat about this week's show?'

'Yes please, but I must warn you that if Tom Watts slags me today he'll have a black eye, so get ready to separate us.'

He laughed nervously, sure she was entirely serious.

Debbie and Tara and Charlie arrived that evening and Lindsay could barely keep her eyes open, so she didn't have to say too much and the presents helped their excitement, as did Colin's phone call.

'Any word from Paul?' Debbie wanted to know.

'Nope. He gave up very easily in the end, eh?'

'So, are things serious between you and Colin?'

She shook her head. 'No, I wish they could be. I've just spent a fantastic few days in New York, in the home of a movie star who also happens to be a really gorgeous guy, and my heart wasn't really in it. The last time I was there was with the man I was going to marry and do you know something, I couldn't even remember much about it, either. And the reason, a guy I've only known for a few weeks, who thinks I'm a slut and doesn't want anything to do with me and who'll never take me to New York in a million years. Sad, isn't it? No, actually, it's tragic.'

Over the next few days Lindsay made a vague plan and mulled it over before talking to anyone. On Sunday, Alan telephoned her at home and explained that he had to go back into hospital.

'More tests. I'm getting a bit sick of all this, but I've no choice. Do you think you can manage again?'

'Yes, of course, you just look after yourself. I'm fine.'

'OK, I'm just about to telephone Jonathan Myers. I expect he'll want to talk to you.'

'Fine, keep in touch if you can and don't worry.'

Lindsay arrived early in the office next morning, to a message from Jonathan's secretary, suggesting they meet at eleven. She went for coffee and came to another decision.

After they'd talked about the shows for the rest of the season, of which there were only four remaining – and Lindsay had assured him she could cope – she took a deep breath and asked if she might have a personal word with him, in confidence.

'Sure.' He smiled at her. 'What's up?'

Where to start was what was immediately up. She decided to keep it short.

'When the show finishes, I need to take a couple of months off.' He nodded encouragingly, sensing something was wrong.

'I'm pregnant and I'm afraid it wasn't planned and, well, I need to get away for a while, until after the birth. I know I've only just started work here, really, and I wouldn't ask except that I've no choice. I want to keep it as quiet as possible, I'm afraid my personal life hasn't been all that personal lately and I couldn't deal with any more publicity right now. If you could help me with this I promise I'll make it up to you as soon as I come back.' Her voice wobbled slightly and she bit hard on her lip and stared at him begging for his understanding.

'I see. Well, you've been exceptionally loyal to us so far and I think we owe you some time anyway. Let me see what I can do. Meanwhile, I think you should go and see Melanie Ingles, our staff welfare officer. You can talk to her in complete confidence, that's what she's there for. Let her tell you what she can do to help. I'll do all I can too. I don't want to lose you, I think you'll make a terrific producer some day.'

'Thanks.' She swallowed hard. 'I hope so, it's what I really want to do, I just hope I haven't screwed it up.'

'You haven't, so don't worry about it. Are you sure you're OK till the end of the season?'

'Yes, fine, I'll make sure I'm on top of things if Alan's not back.'

'OK, why don't you e-mail me directly with your plans, that way it won't have to go through the system. When is the baby due, by the way?' he asked gently.

'September and I'll come back to work within a couple of weeks. It's now I need the time off. I'm going to go away for a few months and hope no one finds me.' She grimaced. 'Being in a gossip column is no fun at all.'

'I hope you don't mind me asking, but is the father involved?' She looked at him and shook her head.

'No.' A sudden thought bounced into her head. 'And, it's got nothing to do with any of that stuff in the papers.' She was suddenly afraid he might think it was Colin's baby.

God, she thought in horror, that's all I need right now.

'Well, I won't discuss it with anyone, you have my word. I'll say we came to an arrangement about time off based on your extra commitment to the programme.'

'Thanks, this isn't the way I planned it, but you've made it possible for me to cope. I'll make it up to you.'

'You already have, without you we wouldn't have been able to cope and the show is much better as a result of your input. The next few weeks will be hard. By the time it finishes we'll be quits. OK?'

'Thanks.' They shook hands and he walked her to the door.

'I'll see you for your weekly meeting and I'll pop in and out as I did before. Meanwhile, you take care of yourself and call me if you need anything at all.'

She left feeling better than she had in ages. Only thirteen more rounds to go.

She threw herself into her work, as she had before. Tom Watts called in, annoyed about Alan and complaining of not feeling well himself. She needed him on her side so she was nice as pie, suggesting he go home and rest and promising to e-mail the running order to him that evening.

Before leaving for the day she texted Tara and Debbie, suggesting they come round for a glass of wine and some pasta the following evening. Might as well get it all over with quickly, she thought, dreading the prospect of facing her mother, which would have to be done sooner rather than later.

The following evening the three sat round her kitchen table, laughing and talking as they had so many times before.

'I've got news,' Tara announced, just as Lindsay was trying to find the words to tell them hers.

'What?' they both said together, staring at her. This was not like Tara, she looked shy all of a sudden.

'Michael has asked me to marry him.' She was red-faced and Lindsay and Debbie looked at her in amazement.

'How? When? Where?' was the best Lindsay could manage.

'At the weekend. Out of the blue.'

'What did you say?' Debbie was gulping her wine in an effort to look nonchalant.

'Yes.'

'Oh my God, this is fantastic news. I am so happy for you.'

Lindsay hugged her friend and almost burst into tears.

Debbie danced round the kitchen singing, 'I'm Getting Married in the Morning' in a completely tuneless voice and shouting, 'Champagne, we must have some. Have you any?'

'You know me, I always have champagne with you two for friends. You open it and I'll grab the glasses.'

They talked for ages, this was the best news they'd had in years. They were so excited that they didn't notice Lindsay barely touched her champagne. It turned out there were no real plans made, Michael had to get his divorce first, so they weren't announcing it for a good while yet.

'I just had to tell you two and Michael agreed, but you must keep it to yourselves.'

'Can we be bridesmaids?'

'Of course, who else would I have?'

Debbie started singing about getting to the church on time.

As they ate and drank and dissected the news, Lindsay wondered about saying anything, not wanting to spoil things for Tara. She was still doubtful until Debbie looked at her.

'You're very quiet again tonight. When are you going to tell us what's up?'

She took a deep breath and plunged in.

'I have got something to tell you but it's not like Tara's news.'

'Go on, please, you haven't been yourself for weeks. It's Chris, isn't it?'

'No. Yes. Well, not really.' Long pause, while two worried pairs of eyes tried to encourage her wordlessly.

'I'm pregnant.'

The champagne bubble burst. No one said anything. She saw confusion, elation and horror pass over their faces in a second as they continued to stare at her.

'Did you just say what I . . .'

She nodded.

Tara came and put her arms around her and looked as if she might burst into tears. Lindsay was horrified.

'I'm sorry, I shouldn't have said it tonight, I've just been keeping it to myself for so long—'

'Chris?' Debbie asked, knowing the answer already.

'Yeah.'

'Does he know?'

'I tried to tell him but he told me he wasn't interested, basically. So, I'm going to take a couple of months off as soon as the show ends in another couple of weeks. That way I'll be out of there before I'm showing. I'm going away until near the time.'

'Don't be ridiculous, you can't go away. That's like you're ashamed, or you've got something to hide . . . That's what happened in Ireland years ago. You can't.' Debbie was angry.

'It's what I want, honestly. I've spent weeks thinking about it.'

'Lindsay, you've got to tell him.'

'No. He made it clear that he doesn't want anything to do with me, so I'm doing this my way. I'm not going to risk bumping into him, if you'll pardon the pun. I've got to think about the future, so I'm going to do a three-month cookery course, which would give me a professional qualification, in case I can't manage the TV thing afterwards. It's something I've always said I'd do anyway, something I love, and something I could do from home if I had to. Then, when it's . . . all over, I can see how I'm fixed. I told my boss today and he's agreed to release me and not tell anyone the reason. I guess I'll have to forego my maternity leave but it's more important to me that no one knows. I'm only going to tell my family and you two.'

They stayed until she almost fell over with tiredness, trying to make her see sense, as Debbie put it, but she was adamant that this was what she wanted.

'I don't want anyone's sympathy, least of all his. But I can't get through this without you two and I'm really sorry if I spoiled the night.'

'Hey, we're going to be aunties, how bad can that be?' Debbie grinned and hugged her. But she didn't dance or sing.

Chapter Thirty-Nine

Telling her mother was less easy. She refused to believe it at first and then insisted that Chris would have to 'face up to it'. Lindsay began to worry that she would try and make contact with him herself, which was just the sort of thing she would do, so she had to threaten drastic action if her mother interfered. She had asked her sister to call round later and when she told her Anne was a great ally, just as Lindsay knew she would be.

It's funny how families always rally round in the end, Lindsay thought, as they cried and hugged her.

'This isn't what I'd planned for my baby sister, but if it's what you want, we'll help all we can. Won't we, Mum?'

'Yes of course, but I don't agree with it. Just because he's famous—'

'It's got nothing to do with that. The relationship was over long before I discovered this and I don't want him involved. Please, Mum, you've got to let me do this my way.'

'But he has a right to know . . .' She made one

last-ditch attempt to have a famous son-in-law, but had reckoned without Lindsay's determination.

They drank pots of tea, as the Irish always do in times of crisis, and cried lots and laughed a little but in the end Lindsay knew it was going to be OK and she went home feeling a bit better.

Colin telephoned. 'Well?'

'Well what, Mister?'

'How's my girl?'

'Bigger.' But she wasn't really. Not yet, anyway. 'I told my mother and sister tonight.'

'I'd say that was a laugh.'

'Yeah, but it was all right in the end.'

'Are you OK?'

'I'm fine, how's the movie going?'

'Slow, but I'm hoping to get home for a few days in a couple of weeks, so keep some time free for me.'

'Well, my social calendar is quite full at the moment, besides I might be too fat by then to be described in the papers as a model type, and that would really upset me.'

'Fuck them, we're going out on the town if I have to drag you by the hair.'

'I give in.'

'Lindsay, I'm glad you made the decision you did. It'll be all right, I promise.'

'It'd better be, otherwise I'll name you as the father and force you into a joint custody arrangement.'

He laughed and they talked and it brought them closer. She liked having him in her life and the worst was over, she kidded herself.

*   *   *

The following week was hectic. Tom Watts looked pale and drawn and his form was filthy. Lindsay got tired and tetchy a couple of times, but in the end the show went well and the ratings were good.

The team were ticking off the days, three more heavy weeks, three more gruelling Saturdays and then a lifetime of freedom, or at least that was how it felt. Months of working weekends, late nights and fighting for guests were beginning to take their toll. Alan was still in hospital and they seemed determined to keep him there this time, which suited Lindsay in a funny way, although she wished him well and dropped in to see him every few days, in spite of his protests. They had become friends. He was a great listener and she moaned about everyone, especially Kate, who seemed determined not to pull her weight on the show, but he made her see the funny side and she suspected he liked being involved.

Lindsay decided to treat her pregnancy – although she didn't call it that – as just another project to be got through and she was doing her best to be healthy, had started as soon as she'd made a decision to go ahead with it. She was sleeping well, going for long walks each day, eating masses of fruit and vegetables and drinking litres of water and having the very odd glass of wine in order to stay sane. It was slowly paying off and she felt better than she had in ages, with lots of energy, although she found she was getting tired in the evenings. The girls were like two mother hens and fussed over her constantly.

'Jesus, you look great, I'd almost risk it myself if I thought I'd have that glow,' Debbie teased her one evening when she called unexpectedly, as one or other of them did almost every night.

Lindsay's life took on a nondescript pattern and it suited her mood. She didn't allow herself any negative emotions and took each day as it came, rising early into the fresh spring mornings, working hard, exercising, eating well and going to bed with a book for company at nine o'clock most nights. She refused even to consider what the future had in store for her.

This week's show was looking good and everything was going according to plan until Thursday evening, when she got a message asking her if she could attend a meeting in Jonathan Myers' office immediately.

'Sure, give me ten minutes,' she told his secretary and went to redo her make-up and fix her hair, conscious that Jonathan was the only one who knew about her. She wanted to make sure he didn't think she'd gone to seed. She was glad she'd worn one of her new suits, bought in New York. The jacket was soft and unstructured and flattered her tummy. A soft, pale-grey top, with thin slotted ribbon peeped out from underneath and she felt sexy and voluptuous for the first time in ages as she made her way to his office.

Thank God I'm having a good day, she thought, remembering her last visit.

'Go straight in, they're expecting you,' his secretary smiled and she checked to make sure her jacket was closed before knocking and entering, wondering who 'they' were. She saw he was deep in conversation with someone and recognized the profile immediately, even before Chris stood and turned to face her. She stopped dead and waited for Jonathan, who was striding to meet her.

'Lindsay, sorry for the short notice but I'm afraid we have a crisis.'

He knows about us, was her first thought. She must have looked like a mad woman as she kept her eyes firmly fixed to his face. Oh my God, he's going to try and force me to tell him.

Her chest was tight and her lungs were bursting but she had a ludicrous grin pasted to her face and it didn't seem to want to go anywhere.

'I'm afraid Tom Watts has had a heart attack.'

'Sorry?' She knew she was still smiling because her cheeks were beginning to hurt.

'It happened this morning. He's in a private clinic and we have to decide what we're going to do about the show and how to break it to the media.'

'I don't understand, is he OK?' She raised her hand to her mouth in an attempt to literally wipe the smile away and stared at Chris, waiting for him to speak. She hadn't a clue what was going on and was still waiting for the bombshell that would mean the start of something, or maybe the end of everything.

'I'm sorry, sit down and I'll explain, this is Chris Keating.'

She didn't look at him. 'Yes, we've met.' Jonathan didn't seem to notice her discomfort.

'Tom collapsed at home at lunchtime. He's in intensive care but he's going to be fine. We got word immediately, so we had an emergency meeting of the editorial board to decide what to do, especially in relation to the show this week. We thought of cancelling but with the ratings so up and down we decided that the station needed the impact of a couple of strong programmes as we came to the end of the season. So, we asked Chris if he would present the show till the end of the run. He wanted a few hours to think about it but he just called in to say he'd do it so I needed to get you involved fast.'

'I see.' She didn't, but anything was OK as long as it wasn't what she thought.

'I need your opinion. It's Thursday night. How much is involved this week? What do you think? Should we consider cancelling or can we pull it off?'

Cancel, she wanted to scream, anything to buy her time. But she wouldn't give Chris the satisfaction.

'It's not a complicated show, all of the work has already been done. I agree with you that we need the continuity of a couple of strong programmes till the end of the run. If Chris is happy to take it on I propose we give it a try.'

Fuck you, I bet that's not what you expected to hear: she didn't even glance in his direction.

'I hoped you'd say that. I've already explained to Chris that you're taking over from Alan at the moment and that I'm acting as Executive Producer. He's happy to work on that basis.'

Big of him, she wanted to say. 'Great,' was what came out.

'Well, what about the three of us grabbing a bite

to eat and going through the running order?' Jonathan was smiling at them both, relieved. This ludicrously horrendous idea was more than she could handle at that very moment.

'Actually I have a lot of work still to do this evening,' she lied, with the silly grin back in place. 'Why don't I print off a couple of copies of the running order and each of the briefs, run through them quickly here and then leave the two of you to discuss it over dinner, while I work on making sure everything is up to date for Chris in the morning.' Paul once told her that she had a hundred different smiles and she had used every one of them up this evening.

'That's fine by me.' Chris spoke for the first time.

'Great, back in a mo.' She escaped and had to stop herself slithering down the back of his door, so relieved was she to be out.

By the time she returned fifteen minutes later with a file under her arm, she was much calmer, at least on the outside.

They talked through the show quickly and Chris seemed to have an immediate grasp of what it was about.

'This all looks very thorough, I'd like to spend the evening going through it and then perhaps we could discuss it.' He spoke as if he'd never met her before, but in terms of carrying off the Oscar for the coolest performance tonight, she knew that he knew she'd won hands down and it gave her a great deal of stupid satisfaction.

'Yes of course. Here are all my numbers. Please

call me if you need any clarification, otherwise I propose we meet in the morning.'

'What time suits you?'

'As early as you like.'

'Nine o'clock OK?'

'I was going to suggest eight. Is that too early for you?'

'No. That's fine.'

'Good, do you know where our office is?'

'I'll find it.'

'Great, see you then. I'm looking forward to working with you.'

'Me too.'

It wasn't sarcastic, it wasn't malicious, it was quite simply nothing and nothing was all she was able for right at this minute.

She was out of the building, nearly out of the country, in record time and she closed her front door twenty minutes later and poured herself a glass of red wine, baby or no baby.

Chapter Forty

She was in the office by seven-fifteen next morning, looking businesslike in a grey, pinstripe suit, hair tied back, minimum make-up. She even wore her glasses, which she hardly ever used, to give her something to hide behind. Just after eight Chris walked in, dressed in black jeans and a chunky dark-grey sweater, straight out of the shower. He always looked healthy, always seemed to have a tan and this morning it irritated her no end.

'Hi.' It was an uneasy greeting.

'Hi. Irene from the Press Office has just been on. We have a press conference at eleven. I said I'd check to make sure it suited you, I didn't want to give out your mobile number without your permission.'

'That's fine and thanks, I'd rather not give out my mobile number, if that's OK. As long as you have it that's all that's important.'

It was very important when you gave it to me the first time. She didn't say it but it hurt all over again and she wondered once more how he'd managed to escape so easily.

'Christ, I've just remembered, I've nothing to wear, I just threw these on because I thought we were in the office all day.'

'That's not a problem, wardrobe are already on the case. They have your measurements on file and they've arranged for a stack of clothes to be delivered here in the next hour or two. They want to meet us at ten, to decide on what you're wearing tomorrow night and I'm sure you can borrow something for the conference.'

'Great, thanks.'

'Stills want some new photos of you to release to the Sundays, so maybe you could ring them and arrange to have them taken immediately afterwards.' She wrote the contact number on a piece of paper and handed it to him.

'Would you like to talk through the show now?'

'Sure, have you had breakfast?'

'Yes, thanks.' She pulled out another of her ready-made smiles, a chilly 'I'd sooner starve' type grin.

'Oh, right, well maybe I'll just grab a coffee before we start. Can I bring you back anything?'

'No, I'm fine. I'll call the Press Office while you're gone.'

She watched him go and vowed to be the best producer he'd ever worked with, ever, ever, ever.

But you're not getting even one little bit of me personally, she thought savagely, you had your chance.

By the time he returned the phones were

hopping, news was leaking out that there was a change of presenter and everyone wanted to know what was up. Lindsay had left messages for all the team from home the previous evening, calling a meeting for nine-thirty this morning and asking people to be in as early as possible, so everyone was alerted and by eight forty-five the office was buzzing. Lindsay and Chris were working quietly at Tom's desk and as soon as everyone was in, she called a quick meeting to explain what had happened and introduce Chris. Most of them hadn't met him before, as the serious hacks in Current Affairs, where he'd done most of his work up to now, rarely came into contact with the frivolous world of Entertainment TV.

Everyone was shocked and surprised at the news about Tom and rallied round immediately, offering to work late, come in early next day, whatever was needed. A number of them were secretly chuffed that Chris Keating was taking over. He was younger and seemed to have a different attitude and appeared less arrogant, so far. There was also something nice about him, he grinned a lot and clearly had no ego whatsoever, given the number of times he put himself down. And he had grasped the show very quickly, Lindsay thought, judging by the questions he was now asking.

Tomorrow's programme was a mixed bag. The three glamorous mistresses had eventually made it on to the final running order, and Lindsay was relieved that Chris would be doing it instead of Tom, who had taken a real dislike to the item, for some reason. They had the latest American teen idol, a sixteen-year-old girl who had sold ten million albums worldwide and sang about hot sex yet claimed never to have kissed a boy. A senior government minister who had been embroiled in a complicated money scandal had finally agreed to break his silence and tell his story for the first time and they had an interview with an up-and-coming young Irish actress who had just been offered a twenty-million-dollar role in a Hollywood movie. On paper it was a very strong show.

Chris said he was completely comfortable with the government minister, happy with the actress, knew very little about the teen star but had already spent most of the night browsing the hundreds of sites devoted to her on the Internet. He was unsure about the item on mistresses, simply because he felt women would love it and most men would be uncomfortable.

'I feel they'll be threatened by it but riveted to it.' Lindsay was prepared for this. 'Statistically, men are the ones more likely to have affairs. On the other hand many women regard mistresses as traitors, claiming they degrade the female sex. But certainly one of our women will claim that mistresses keep marriages together and another will say it's a better life than being a wife. We also have an interesting mix of people planted in the audience, several women whose marriages ended when they discovered their husbands having an affair, a woman who lost everything to a mistress and a man whose wife finally left him and, once he became available, his mistress didn't want to know. All in all, I think it will make for compulsive viewing, seeing as it's Irish women openly dis-cussing this and as far as we know it's a topic that hasn't been done before on TV in this country.'

'I think you're right. I just need to get a handle on it – I feel my role is important and I don't want to blow it. Could we talk about it later?' He gave her a ghost of a smile, the first in a long while.

'Sure, but why don't you and David go through the briefs first because it's his item, then maybe the three of us can plan our approach later?'

They ran through a few final items, including the audience, and Lindsay asked Kate to work with Monica, ensuring the 'plants' were well seated and the younger invited guests got to be near their idol. She sensed the other girl didn't want to do it but she had too much on her plate to worry about it now.

The press conference was very well attended and Chris arrived looking stunning in a dark-grey, oversized Italian suit, crisp white shirt and expens-ive tie. His hair was long by comparison with the other men at the top table and he looked clean, fit, tanned and healthy as he took his seat next to Jonathan Myers. The interest was palpable. The photographers flocked around him and Lindsay could sense he was uncomfortable. There were lots of questions about whether this would become a permanent arrangement but Chris assured them he was simply filling in for Tom, which was clearly the only answer to give but not what they wanted to hear. She stayed in the background until Jonathan insisted she join them when someone asked, 'Who'll be producing the show?'

He gave her full credit and it was her turn to feel the heat of the spotlight and she liked it even less.

Afterwards, all the papers wanted a photograph of herself and Chris, partly because of her supposed involvement with Colin Quinn, she suspected, and they were forced to stand close together and look happy, which made her laugh, at least.

The day was completely mad and the office was still full at eight o'clock, with everyone anxious to make sure they played their part in what was expected to be a landmark show. Lindsay realized she hadn't eaten all day and decided reluctantly to be the first to leave at eight-thirty, feeling a bit tired and emotional.

'I'll be on the mobile if anyone needs me.' She picked up her bag and said a general good night.

Chris stood up immediately. 'Could we have a chat about things, you know, what my approach at the start should be, how I handle the whole Tom business etc.? Jonathan felt that the three of us should sit down and discuss it.'

'Yes, of course, sorry I should have mentioned earlier, his secretary rang and suggested twelve noon in his office tomorrow. I just assumed she'd rung you as well. Is that OK, or is it too early for you to come in?'

'No, I was planning to work at home in the morning but I'll be there, no problem.'

'Great, well call me if you need anything else before then. Good night.' She opened the door and almost ran to her car, needing food and air and a hug. The cool spring evening helped and she was

too tired to do anything other than grab a sandwich on the way home and the only hug available
came from an ecstatic, crazy bundle of fluff.

Her mobile rang at ten-thirty, just as she was
dozing off and she saw that it was Chris and she
diverted it, not wanting him to think she didn't have
a life, and then was sorry when he didn't leave a
message.

Chapter Forty-One

The next day went without a hitch, which was always slightly worrying. After the evening meal break they rehearsed the show from start to finish with Chris only, going through his opening for cameras, checking his seated position for make-up and lighting and reading through all his introductions. He had opted not to use autocue. They had discussed it for ages – Chris wanted his approach to be as off-the-cuff as possible and Lindsay agreed. Cards had been prepared for him as a back-up, with all the basic information he needed and they both felt his relaxed approach would come across on screen. As they finished the rehearsal she could tell he was nervous and she suddenly wished they had remained friends, at least, so that she could have assured him everything was going to be OK, instead of remaining stilted and formal with him, as she had done all day.

She insisted he take a break before the show and he headed back to his dressing room for a breather and Lindsay left instructions that he was not to be disturbed. She went to check on the audience and discovered that Kate had done nothing to help Monica so far. Lindsay, who rarely got upset over something so trivial, was furious. She found Kate swanning around the hospitality room and called her outside.

'Kate, I asked you to help Monica with the audience and I find her struggling to manage on her own. Is there a problem?'

'I'm doing things for Chris.'

'What things?'

'Just things he needs for the show.'

'I said, what things?'

'I've done them anyway.'

'Kate, I am not going to argue with you now but I want you to take responsibility for the audience this minute and if there is one problem with them tonight you will not be part of this team on Monday. Do you understand?'

'You're not the boss, you can't order me around.'

'Either do what I say or you're off the show from now.'

Kate walked off and Lindsay knew she'd won but she was too furious to care and there were already more urgent problems demanding her attention.

The baby-faced, angelic teen star and her entourage were becoming more and more demanding and refusing to come out of their dressing rooms. There were rumours of a strong smell of dope in the corridor outside, which was worrying. Also, one of the mistresses had arrived having consumed several drinks to 'steady her nerves' and the government minister was insisting that Lindsay give him a list of the questions Chris would be asking, in advance.

She sent their good-looking stage manager to try and work his charms on the teenager, despatched the hospitality hostess to fetch a pot of strong coffee for the three ladies and detoured to Chris's dressing room en route to meet the minister. She didn't particularly want to go to his room but knew these few minutes before going on air might be crucial to his performance.

She knocked gently.

'Come in.' His voice sounded slightly strained and he looked a little edgy but otherwise she thought she'd never seen him look as good. They had chosen his outfit with wardrobe the previous day and it had felt very personal, asking him to try on several suits, but the effort had paid off. He was wearing a black, fine wool suit and very dark grey shirt, open at the neck. The jacket was cut beautifully and fell from his shoulders making him look taller and broader. He'd asked her advice about his hair, wondering if he should get it cut, but she felt it worked and told him so, and make-up made his skin more even and his eyes whiter. He looked too big for the small cubby hole with his long legs and powerful frame and the overall effect was quite something.

He gave her a rueful grin. 'Christ, I'm just wondering what I've got myself into. How's it looking out there, by the way? Any problems?'

'Nope, everything's fine,' she lied. 'The audience are really lively and the warm-up artist has had them rolling in their seats for the past ten minutes.'

She didn't add that the floor manager had spent another five getting them to rehearse the opening round of applause to greet their new presenter. Hopefully he'd get a nice surprise that would carry him through.

'Has the minister arrived?'

'Yes, just on my way to say hello to him now. The mistresses are very lively and our teen idol seems in great form. You OK about it all?'

'Fine. What about notes during the show?'

'I'll talk to you at each commercial break or during a music number or recorded piece if it's urgent.'

He nodded, just as the floor manager tapped on the door.

'Chris, three minutes to air.'

'On my way.'

'I'll walk with you,' she said as he held open the door. 'I just know it's going to be a fantastic show, I really do. You're up to speed on all the stuff and I think the most important thing now is to just follow your instinct with the guests. Above all, I hope you enjoy it, it's one helluva buzz. I love it.' She grinned at him and he smiled back.

They were standing behind the set, waiting for his cue and he continued to watch her and for one moment all their animosity was forgotten. She just wanted him to do well because he was a really nice guy and she suddenly remembered why she'd fallen so hard for him.

'It's just so completely different to anything else I've ever done – and it's live. Christ, I'm nervous.' In the middle of the big black hole that was backstage they grinned at each other and her stomach lurched.

Suddenly, the music from the opening animation flooded the giant speakers and the floor manager gave him the fifteen-second cue.

'Good luck, but you don't need it. You'll be great.' It was the best she could do for him without kissing him or crying all over his expensive clothes and he glanced back at her as he walked through the arch to rapturous applause that took him completely by surprise.

'Thank you very much. Hello, good evening and welcome to the show . . .' He had to stop because the applause was still deafening and the director cut to the cheering audience and back to a smiling Chris and within twenty seconds she knew he'd be brilliant and in spite of everything she was glad for him.

The minister threatened to walk out if she didn't show him the questions and Lindsay politely informed him that the papers knew of his appearance and that she would be forced to offer an explanation for his departure. He backed down and she assured him that the format was exactly as discussed with the researcher and he insisted on going over the whole thing again.

The sixteen-year-old singer was definitely a star and Chris handled her beautifully. He treated her like an adult and she responded like a baby, giggling about her popularity with guys on the Internet and teasing Chris blatantly, as she did with all men, Lindsay suspected.

As soon as they hit the first commercial break

she slipped over to him with a broad grin on her face. 'That was as close to cradle-snatching as I've ever seen but you got away with it and the show is flying.' She was happy for him.

'I'll tell you, they didn't make sixteen-year-olds like that in my day. Whew, she was hot,' he grinned back.

'I think the entire country will have gathered that you liked her. The phones are hopping, everyone saying how great you are.'

'I don't believe that for a minute, but thanks for lying to me. I feel much better now that it's up and running.'

'The rest will be a doddle, but keep your eye on the three ladies, I think Lola has had a drink or two.'

'Thanks for the warning.'

'Twenty seconds back to us,' the floor manager announced.

'Stand by, studio, for music and applause. Chris, coming to you on camera two.'

Lindsay slipped back into the shadows and watched quietly. The millionaire Irish actress flirted outrageously with him and he got her talking about shooting sex scenes with an ageing heart-throb actor who insisted on having his bottom made up and properly lit before she even got near the bed. Her stories were hilarious as she assured him she earned every penny. The audience laughed hysterically. She was completely self-deprecating and Chris seemed to be enjoying it as much as everyone else.

The mistresses told their stories to gasps from the

women in the audience and eventually a huge row broke out, with one woman screaming abuse from the aisle. Chris immediately went down and sat beside her, which wasn't planned in rehearsals but worked a treat and made him seem even more relaxed and approachable. His manner was probing yet he seemed to understand both sides and overall it went down a storm and was completely different to the rest of the show. The interview with the government minister was one of the toughest Lindsay had seen. It was clear Chris knew his stuff and he asked all the hard questions but was polite and measured and there wasn't a peep out of the audience who'd been cheering or hollering for most of the night. They sat transfixed as Chris quietly edged the politician into a corner, from which there was no way out.

Suddenly it was over. The credits rolled, the closing music boomed out, and the audience all wanted his autograph or to have their photos taken with him. He stayed and chatted whereas Tom would have slipped away immediately.

As soon as she'd gathered her stuff together she made her way over to him and his eyes were shining.

'Jesus, I'd murder a pint. That was some buzz, you were right.' She knew he was on a real high because he reached for her and pulled her to him and gave her a bear-hug and she let him.

'Thanks for everything, you were amazing.' She avoided looking at him and she sensed he was a bit embarrassed all of a sudden.

'Pleasure, I'll ask Jan to have a very cold beer

waiting for you.' She left without looking at him and felt his eyes following her and when she arrived in the hospitality suite Jonathan hugged her again.

'Well done, congratulations, that was a splendid show. Chris was even better than I had hoped. Were you pleased?'

'I certainly was and you're right, he was terrific, I'm dying to see the ratings.' All of a sudden a wave of tiredness, unlike any other, swept over her and she could easily have slipped into a coma in a corner.

Chris appeared and everyone wanted a piece of him and he looked relaxed and happy as he sipped a beer and chatted to Jonathan. She saw him glance in her direction several times, but was too tired to care and as she walked one of the guests to the limo she used the opportunity to sneak off home, feeling a bit tired and emotional.

Of course, she couldn't sleep, her adrenalin was still pumping, so she sat up in bed and watched a tape of the show. A text arrived about an hour later.

WHERE R U? NEVR GOT A CHANCE 2 TALK PROPERLY. COULDN'T HAVE DUN IT W/OUT U.

It made her feel lonely all over again and she wished there wasn't a baby because then maybe they could go back and start afresh. But not now, she was certain of that.

Next morning Lindsay woke with a burning sensation that travelled from her navel to her throat like a hot curry. She thought she was going to throw up but nothing came. She tried to get to the bathroom but had to crawl back to bed and lie down until the dizziness passed. Frightened, she called her sister.

'Heartburn,' Anne announced. 'Are you dry retching?'

'Yes.'

'OK, you need to make sure you're not dehydrated.'

'I didn't really eat or drink anything yesterday.'

'Lindsay, this is not on. I'll be over shortly. Stay in bed.'

Like I'm going anywhere, she thought as she hung up.

Anne arrived and mothered her and made her drink lots and fed her soup later, when things had improved a little. She brought all the Sunday papers and two of them carried a photo of herself and Chris, with a short piece on Tom's illness. It was the only photo she had of them together and she tore it out and put it in her wallet and felt worse.

The girls arrived and Anne left after insisting that Lindsay go to her doctor the next day. She promised. She got up and tried to clean her teeth but the smell of the toothpaste almost made her throw up again and she caught sight of a puffy, pasty face in the mirror as she crawled back to bed. So much for her health kick.

Chapter Forty-Two

On Monday, Lindsay went to her own doctor. If Alison Crowley, who had known her for years, was surprised by her announcement, she was too experienced to show it.

'How are you feeling?'

'I was fine, too well actually, up to now, but yesterday I got the most terrible heartburn, at least that's what I think it was and I spent the day trying to get sick but not being able to. I'm also feeling a bit dizzy if I try to get up suddenly, so all in all I feel pretty grim.'

'All sounds normal, I'm afraid. How's your weight?'

'Well, surprisingly I don't seem to have put on very much anywhere except on my boobs, which are swollen and sore. But I've no real tummy and I'm over three months.'

'OK, let's take a look.' She examined her stomach gently and confirmed that all seemed OK. 'But I would like you to have a scan more or less immediately, just to be sure. Have you thought about a gynaecologist?'

'No.'

'I can refer you to Paul Boran, who's a friend of mine and he's great, really laid-back and easy to talk to. Do you want to see him privately?'

'Definitely.'

'OK, I'll arrange it and he'll send you for a scan.' She paused for a moment.

'Are you all right about all this? I gather it was something of a surprise.'

'That's an understatement, but yeah, I'm OK now I guess.'

'Have you any support?'

Why did they all ask that?

'No, well yes, at least my family and . . . I have a few good friends.'

'Well, use them because it's a very emotional time and you'll need someone to lean on. And I'm here to talk to as well, don't forget.' They hugged and Lindsay left feeling lonely.

She went straight to the office and there was a note on her desk from Chris, wondering about the ratings, which she'd completely forgotten. She was glad he wasn't there because she felt very vulnerable.

Talking about scans and specialists made her feel the baby was real and she wasn't sure how much she'd accepted that yet, which she knew was ridiculous.

The ratings were hard to believe. They were No. 1 by a mile. It seemed a huge number of people had tuned in to see how Chris would get on and, amazingly, they'd all stayed and the figure had crept even higher during the mistresses item, which made Lindsay feel vindicated. She phoned Chris on his mobile and he seemed really pleased. She couldn't resist telling him that the mistresses were the most watched item and he laughed out loud and conceded he'd been wrong.

'You disappeared early, how come?'

'I was meeting some friends after the show.' The lie came easily.

'I didn't really get a chance to talk to you.'

'Well, I made some notes on the show when I watched it again so maybe we could have a chat after the meeting tomorrow.'

'OK, fine.' He took her lead and didn't say any more and they talked through the next show and she went home early feeling a bit washed out.

The week continued with Lindsay feeling tired all the time and having to sit on the loo and hide when the heartburn got bad. She was trying to drink lots of water, to keep herself hydrated but the oddest smells sent her running to be sick even though she had very little in her stomach to get rid of.

She went to see Paul Boran, the gynaecologist recommended by her doctor and he was relaxed and easy and smiled a lot. He confirmed that all seemed OK and arranged for her to have a scan immediately, something she wasn't looking forward to.

The newspapers had given Chris and the show a resounding thumbs up, with one even going so far as to say he was the best thing to happen to the programme in years and another re-showing the photo of herself and Chris and declaring them to be a 'dynamic duo'. Lindsay was feeling anything but dynamic. Jonathan asked if she was OK when he called in during the week, and she resolved to apply even more gunge to her face and headed off to have her hair washed and dried in a vain attempt to restore some energy. She was wearing mostly black, baggy clothes these days, which didn't help her morale.

A further incident with Kate didn't help, either. Lindsay had asked her to follow up a story that had appeared in one of the Sunday papers the previous week and she still hadn't done it ten days later. Lindsay had finally had enough and she called the sullen-faced girl into the private meeting room.

'I want to place on record that I am unhappy with your performance since I've taken over. The incident with the audience should not have happened and now I find you haven't acted on another item. I need someone who is prepared to pull their weight and I'm afraid you haven't shown any commitment to the show recently. Is there a problem I should know about?'

'I don't see why I should have to report to you, you're not a producer.'

'Kate, I have been asked by the Head of Programming to act as producer in Alan's absence. If you have a problem with that I suggest you talk to him. I have tried to make this work and quite frankly I've had enough of your appalling attitude. If we weren't at the end of the season I would ask to have you taken off the show and, as things stand, I would not be eager to work with you in the future. Now, I have certain things I need done this week and I want them on my desk pronto. Understood?'

All she got was a surly nod in her direction, and the meeting left her even more frustrated. She mentioned it to Alice over coffee and immediately regretted it.

'Sorry, that was wrong of me, I normally would never discuss one team member with another. Forget I said it.'

'Actually, I was going to say something to you anyway. You see, Kate went for the job of Assistant Producer and got to the final round, then didn't make it to the Training Course. She really resents you because of that, but to be honest, I think she's unhappy anyway, she's always been difficult.' Lindsay sighed, unsure how to handle it.

'And there's something else, although I've no proof, so you must promise not to involve me. I just think you should know.'

Lindsay waited, dreading what was coming.

'I think I overheard her talking to a journalist about you, so perhaps that's how the stories are getting out. I came back to the office one evening last week to collect a file and she was deep in conversation and I heard your name mentioned. She ended the call as soon as I came in and she looked really uncomfortable.'

Lindsay felt like bursting into tears. 'Thanks for telling me.'

The younger girl nodded.

Lindsay waited for the right moment, until she

was alone in the office with Kate one evening. She walked straight up to the girl's desk, leaned over and looked her in the eye.

'One thing I forgot to mention at our meeting. If I find that you have spoken to anyone in the media about me personally, I will ensure that you never work in this business again. Understood?'

She knew from the red face that Alice had been right.

'I'm warning you, Kate, do not talk about me to anyone, or you'll regret it.' She was shaking as she picked up her bag and left the office, feeling completely drained.

The next show was even better than the previous week, Lindsay thought proudly, as she watched from the sidelines on Saturday night. She knew Chris didn't need her as much this time and she missed the awkward closeness of last week. He was more relaxed and confident and she thought how right he was for the programme as she watched him gently lead a fifteen-year-old girl through a harrowing interview, as she recalled her experiences on a bus in Kenya which had been bombed, killing three members of her family, including her mother. The girl had managed to raise the alarm as she lay injured on a lonely country road and she broke down as she remembered seeing her sister beside her but not being able to reach her.

Chris let her cry and took her hand in his own and took over when she couldn't speak and told the audience about one of his own horrific experiences while working as a journalist in the same country. It was a memorable interview and Geoff, the director, cut to several mothers crying openly in the audience and, as Chris led the young girl over to her father when she couldn't continue he unknowingly showed another, more vulnerable side to himself which she suspected would win him many more fans.

Afterwards, he was a bit more subdued and admitted to Lindsay that the interview had been tough. It was the closest they'd been after a funny week in which Lindsay had deliberately kept her distance, mostly because she felt sick and horrible and also because she'd had her scan and it had been tough.

She hadn't told anyone about it, convinced she could handle it alone but she wasn't prepared for her reaction to the sight of a little tadpole floating around in her tummy. She shook her head wordlessly when the kind woman asked if she wanted to know the sex of the baby and left clutching a pathetic picture, with no one to show it to. The loneliness finally hit and it hit hard.

Once again she slipped off home very early and she heard on Monday that he'd been in great form and that a couple of the team had gone to a club in town afterwards and she wondered if he'd been with them but didn't ask, hating herself for even wanting to know.

The following week was their last show of the season and they were all on a high, because of the soaring ratings and the prospect of a life. There was to be a big party afterwards on Saturday night with all the press and guests from throughout the season invited and a number of celebrities expected to attend. Lindsay had asked Alice to be in charge of the event and the young researcher was taking it very seriously. She asked Chris if he would be bringing anyone as his partner and he looked preoccupied and shrugged.

'I hadn't given it any thought. What's everyone else doing?' Alice explained that all of the team were bringing a guest and Lindsay felt his eyes on her. She didn't look up as she heard him ask for two tickets.

'Oh and my parents will be in Dublin for the weekend, would it be OK if they came? I was supposed to be taking them to dinner on Saturday night but obviously now I can't.'

Alice smilingly told him he could invite as many people as he wanted and he promised to confirm later in the week.

Alice approached Lindsay. 'Lindsay, how many tickets will I keep for you?'

'Four should be fine for me, thanks.' Again, she felt Chris looking at her and deliberately kept her eyes glued to her computer screen as she wondered who she could invite. She thought of Tara and Debbie but felt they might try to get into conversation with Chris to see how things were with him and she didn't want that. She was tired and irritable, and having him around all the time just reminded her of what she'd lost. She wanted to bury her head and sleep for a month and just forget about it all.

Colin phoned her that night and asked how she and Chris were getting on. He didn't agree with the way she'd handled the meeting that day in the car park and felt she should make another attempt to tell Chris, now that they were at least on speaking terms again.

'Please, don't lecture me, I can't take any more at the moment, I feel sick all the time,' she begged him between belches.

'Are you OK?'

'Yeah, sorry, I'm just a complete bore.'

He changed the subject and made her laugh with stories of the girls and he promised to call her as soon as he knew when he'd be home.

On the morning of the final show, Lindsay felt a little better and she made a last-ditch attempt to do something with her appearance, getting her hair cut and wearing a gorgeous lime-green silk ruffled shirt over a long aubergine wrap-around skirt. She had to wear a pair of 'tummy toners' underneath to hide her little bulge and a wide studded belt helped. The whole thing came courtesy of Tara and while it wasn't an outfit she'd have bought for herself it was truly beautiful and it made her feel young and summery and she hated all her own clothes anyway. She was surprised to find the colours made her skin and hair look darker and the belt pulled the whole thing together. Tara had also made her borrow some hoopy earrings and she was really pleased with how she looked, especially after she'd sneaked into make-up and begged them to do something with her dull, grey complexion.

The show was lighter than usual but she had deliberately wanted it to be meaty so they had a number of strong interviews and big names, including two of the current crop of young, foreign footballers, guaranteed to have everyone in a tizzy. As Lindsay went backwards and forwards between studio and the hospitality room she noticed a young, dark-haired Penelope Cruz lookalike and asked Alice who she was.

'She's Chris's partner, don't you just want to get sick?'

Lindsay did and not just because of her condition. She stared at the exotic young girl, heart thumping, wondering what she meant to Chris. Surprisingly, she didn't even hate him for it. Working with him had made her remember all the reasons she'd been attracted to him in the first place and now, feeling fat and old and tired, and looking at her younger, much better-looking replacement she missed him more than ever and in spite of everything that had happened she still wanted him.

Chris looked relaxed and mingled with the audience more than usual and they responded and joined in and the footballers were an instant hit, especially with the women. Lindsay watched from the corner of studio and thought again about Chris's girlfriend and wanted to run away. It had been the longest three weeks of her life, seeing him every day and thinking about him most nights and wondering if she was doing the right thing. He clearly wasn't worried at all.

Afterwards the party was in full swing by the

time she arrived in the huge marquee erected for the occasion. Alice had done a great job. There were balloons and candles everywhere, a champagne bar doing a roaring trade and a huge buffet table, full to the point of collapse. There was plenty of seating, a small dancing area and the music was relaxed. She grabbed a glass of mineral water and plunged straight in, glad that it was nearly all over.

Chapter Forty-Three

As Lindsay made her way over to a lively gang of crew members she came face to face with Chris's mother, who greeted her warmly. 'I'm glad to see you again.'

Lindsay was surprised that the older woman even remembered her.

'How's that gorgeous dog of yours?'

'Neglected, I'm afraid, but hopefully that's all about to change.'

'I hear you've had the most horrendous few months.'

'It's been pretty lively, yes,' Lindsay laughed at the irony. 'How've you been?'

'Fine, fine, Chris says you've been absolutely fantastic, by the way. It's been a big learning curve for him, this live entertainment stuff, pretty strenuous for you both, I should think.'

They chatted away and Nina was rooting in her handbag and acting as if they were best friends when, without warning, Chris appeared behind her.

'You two are looking very pally, what are you cooking up?' he smiled at them.

'Why do men always assume we're planning something nasty?' Nina Keating gave her son a friendly poke. 'Actually, Lindsay was just telling me that she's planning to take some time off over the summer months.'

'Oh, to do what?' he was looking at her intently.

'Haven't really firmed up on my plans,' Lindsay lied, not wanting him to know anything. She was sorry now she'd mentioned it at all, it had just slipped out.

'Did Chris tell you he's going to Australia on Tuesday?'

'No.' It was her turn to be surprised.

'We haven't really had a chance to talk,' Chris said pointedly to his mother before turning to Lindsay. 'I'm combining a gathering of world leaders in New Zealand, which I'm covering for News, with a trip to Oz to see my sister Lisa. It's been planned for months. I was hoping to get to talk to you before I go.'

She ignored the last part. 'Good for you, I hope it goes well, it'll be very different to what you've been doing lately and I'm sure the break will do you good.' Lindsay fixed him her brightest smile and excused herself. 'I just need to say thanks to all the crew,' she explained to Chris's mum.

'I hope we'll get to talk again,' the other woman said kindly and Lindsay fled to join her colleagues, passing the Cruz clone, who was surrounded by practically every male in the place under forty.

Suddenly, there was a buzz of activity and

flashes at the front entrance and Lindsay, along with everyone else, turned to see what was happening. To her absolute amazement, she saw Colin strolling in, on his own and glancing around. At least ten people, including Jonathan Myers, were practically killed in the rush to greet him and she saw him shake hands and stroll in the direction of the bar. He spotted her almost instantly and came towards her with a shy grin and she smiled back and then didn't know what to do. He solved that particular problem by giving her a huge hug and then kissing her on the lips while everyone pretended not to watch. He looked great, his blond hair was cropped even tighter and his eyes crinkled with laughter.

'Where did you come from? When did you arrive?' she asked, her face as hot as a toaster.

'Sure I'd get in anywhere, you know that. I arrived home last night. Did I mortify you or are you always that particularly attractive shade of plum?'

'I don't believe it, you never rang. And you came alone, I thought you big stars never went anywhere without an entourage?'

'I wanted to surprise you and the effect would have been ruined if I'd walked in with my agent, don't you think?' He was still looking very pleased with himself. 'Besides, I thought you might need some support,' he whispered in her ear and she wanted to hug him to bits. 'And, of course, the idea of a pint of Guinness was another attraction.'

They stayed at the bar chatting for ages and she was really glad and very surprised that he'd turned up. Jonathan eventually strolled in their direction accompanied by Chris whom he wanted to introduce to Colin. Lindsay knew that Colin would take an unhealthy interest in Chris and she was a little annoyed when Jonathan asked to speak to her privately, leaving the two younger men alone together.

He dragged her off to a quiet corner and thanked her again for all her hard work. 'I'm glad you went to see our Welfare Officer. She's been in touch with me directly and we've worked out a bonus package for you, which should cover most of your time off, although as I think she pointed out, you are entitled to maternity leave.'

'Let me see how I go, I really do want to keep this quiet, you and she are the only two here who know.'

'I understand but, Lindsay, people are mostly kind, you know. No one would judge you.'

'It's not that, it's just . . . complicated so I want to keep it this way.'

He kept her for ages, talking about the future, assuring her that they would facilitate her on her return and finally wishing her luck and asking her to keep in touch with him personally. When she returned to the bar Colin and Chris had disappeared and more people nabbed her and she eventually found them deep in conversation at a secluded table.

Suddenly there were speeches and Tom Watts – who was making good progress – sent them all champagne. Jonathan presented her with flowers and she was forced to say a few words, but she

384

almost ran back to Colin, who kept his arm around her for ages after.

She was coming back from the loo when Chris appeared out of nowhere. 'We need to talk.'

'I tried to talk to you weeks ago, remember, but you couldn't spare the time. Now I don't think there's anything left to say.' She was still smarting from seeing her replacement.

'Stop playing games with me, let's just—'

'Hi, I wondered where you'd got to . . .' His new girlfriend suddenly appeared at his side and Lindsay gave him the dirtiest look she could manage and made her escape, feeling sick all over again.

She stuck like glue to Colin for the next half-hour and then they sneaked away as soon as they could, narrowly avoiding Penelope and Chris's mother.

'Did you get to meet our own Penelope Cruz?'

'Yep, good-looking girl. Who is she?'

'Chris's girlfriend.'

Colin whistled. 'He certainly didn't give that impression when she stopped at our table. Anyway, she won't be around for long, I'm afraid. Girls like her are two a penny, lovely to look at but nothing to say. He'll be bored stiff in a week.'

'Liar.'

'Honest, I know these things, I'm a man. Trust me.'

He came back to her house, had a beer and she made hot chocolate, then they curled up on the couch and chatted for ages, until she felt her eyes going.

'Can I stay?'

'Are you sure you want to?'

'I think you need someone to snuggle up to and I've been lonely without you.' He kissed her then, a long, slow, gentle kiss. He borrowed her toothbrush, she cleaned her face and they snuggled down in her comfy old bed. She was asleep within seconds, despite herself.

Next morning she woke to the doorbell ringing and for a second she was startled to find someone in her bed, so she jumped up too quickly and had to lie back down again.

'Want me to get it?'

'Are you joking? It's the girls, do you want to give them a heart attack?'

She struggled to let them in, then legged it to the bathroom. When she came downstairs she found the three of them making breakfast as if it was all quite normal.

'You know each other then?' she asked, and they all stopped what they were doing.

'God you look awful, here, sit down.' Debbie was over like a flash.

'I'm OK, better now.' She cursed herself for not making any effort, assuming that Colin would have stayed in bed. He was padding around in his bare feet and looked completely at ease.

'Back in a minute.' She had to run again and this time she dressed, brushed her hair and applied a bit of stick foundation and blusher, so that she looked half human.

They sat around for hours, eating, talking and reading all the papers and watching bits of the show again, until Colin left at five to see his folks and then meet some friends. He promised to call her next morning and they arranged to spend the day together.

The girls loved him, just as she knew they would, and they wanted to hear all about the party. There was a stony silence when she mentioned 'Penelope Cruz' but otherwise they asked lots of questions, especially about Colin and Chris talking for so long.

'What was it about?' Debbie demanded.

'I don't know, I didn't ask. I don't care,' Lindsay said simply and they knew she was lying.

Next day, on her way to meet Colin at his hotel, she got a text from Chris.

WE NEED 2 TALK. R U FREE 2DAY?

She selected erase and continued on her journey, wishing she could erase him from her mind as easily.

They headed off for a walk in Stephen's Green. Colin looked relaxed in faded denim jeans and an old sweater. They took in an afternoon movie, then had an early dinner in a great new Thai place. No one bothered them at all, in fact few seemed to recognize him and they both relaxed and talked for Ireland.

'So, tell me what's next?'

'Well, I've got a couple of weeks to clear up the programme, which I can do in my own time, then I go off to the West of Ireland, to a tiny little village to learn how to cook for three months.'

'What for? You told me yourself you're a good cook.'

'This is different, it will give me a professional qualification so that, if I ever had to change my job I have something to fall back on. Besides, it's something I've always wanted to do for myself.'

'But I thought you loved TV?'

'I do, but with a baby, who knows . . . I couldn't have done this show with a child, endless late nights, all day Saturday—'

'Lindsay, I still think you need to let Chris in on this . . .'

'No.'

'Look, the other night, talking to him, well . . . he's a really nice guy – no ego, very grounded. I think he'd want to be part of this baby and it's his child too.'

'No. Look, he dumped me without even allowing me an explanation. He had another woman within a week, he couldn't even spare me ten minutes to talk to him when I told him it was important . . . and just in case I missed all that, he brought a different girl along on Saturday night. I am not giving him the chance to hurt me ever again. Why can no one understand that?'

'I do, I really do.' He could see she was upset. 'It's just that, I think somewhere you've got your wires crossed and you need to sort things out, at some point. He asked me a lot about you, about us, the other night. He didn't act like someone who didn't care, he was way too interested in where you and I were at. All this in spite of the fact that he thinks you cheated on him first.'

'I did not cheat on him. For fuck's sake, Colin, whose side are you on? Saturday night was his last opportunity to talk to me and what did he do? He brought along his latest squeeze.'

'She wasn't important.'

'He goes away tomorrow and by the time he comes back I'll be gone.' She wanted to howl at the sheer frustration of it all. 'Look, it's over as far as I'm concerned and I'm not going for a sympathy vote just because I was foolish enough to get pregnant. I don't want him under those circumstances.'

They talked for ages and he dropped her home and didn't offer to come in. She was a bit sad because she hoped they'd make love again, but felt too moany and bloated and insecure to suggest it.

They met for brunch next day but things were still a bit strained, and he left to catch his flight after promising to call and holding her tight.

She went for a walk on her own and when she arrived home at four o'clock her neighbour had taken a delivery of flowers for her – a big, fat bunch of the most amazing scented stocks, in lavender and purple and creamy white and surrounded by a mass of delicate green fronds. The card said simply 'We really do need to talk. Call me if you get this before 3 p.m. Otherwise, I'll be in touch as soon as I get back.' She tore it up.

Chapter Forty-Four

A few weeks later, on a bright Sunday afternoon, Lindsay and Charlie arrived at Inisfree Farm Cookery School, in a tiny little village in the West of Ireland. She'd left home that morning, waved off by her sister and her two best friends and it had all been a bit emotional, even though she was only going less than two hundred miles away and would probably be on the phone to each one of them every single day.

The girl at reception showed Lindsay to her home for the next three months and handed over a thick file with all the course information.

'Here we are. You're in Rose Cottage, it's tiny but it's the only one that you can have to yourself, which you asked for specifically.' She smiled. All the cottages were within a half-mile radius of the school, Lindsay was told, and all had been given the names of shrubs and flowers. 'The one closest to you is Hawthorn Cottage,' she added, pointing to a sunny yellow, higgledy-piggledy little house, 'and that's Fuschia Lodge through the trees.'

Lindsay could see a charming thatched cottage that looked like a mansion. 'It sleeps ten, so it's very big whereas you have a tiny kitchen, a living room and a bedroom and bathroom in the attic, but at least it's all yours.'

The young girl turned the key in the front door. Lindsay hoped her bump would be able to negotiate the narrow, winding staircase in the corner of the pretty, country-style living room. It was very basic but charming, with floral curtains and a big bowl of peony roses on the scrubbed pine table. It had a huge open fire with a basket of logs beside it and French doors leading to a tiny cottage garden. There was even a cosy little corner for Charlie.

'It's perfect, thank you.'

'People normally organize their own breakfast, although there'll be tea and scones each morning when you arrive at the kitchen. I've left you bread and milk and eggs and jam for tomorrow. If you need anything else just ask. Lunch is the main meal and is very substantial and you all eat together in the big dining room. When you finish there are always bits and pieces to take home, whatever you've cooked in the afternoon or some hot bread or cheese from the main kitchen. There's also an organic shop where you can buy fresh fruit and vegetables and lots of goodies and a small super-market in the village, which you probably saw on your way in. Most of the students only go to the village for a drink in the local pub. Some people go home at weekends, but I understand you'll be staying with us. Feel free to wander around the farm, the private gardens, the orchard, anywhere you like, in fact. If you go through the gate at the end of the garden it will take you down to the beach and you can walk for miles along the edge of the water. Your dog should enjoy himself, I think there are about nine dogs here altogether.' Lindsay thanked her and walked her to the door. 'They also might occasionally ask for your help in the main kitchen at weekends, in which case you'll be paid an hourly rate. It's good fun, you'll enjoy it.'

'Thanks, I'm sure I'll think of lots of questions the minute you're gone.'

'Well, call over anytime to reception, I'm Imelda, by the way, and I'm there until seven each evening.'

Lindsay thanked her and unpacked the car and went for a walk with Charlie. It was perfectly still, one of those balmy, early summer evenings and the fragrance in the gardens was almost over-powering. She sat on an old, iron seat for ages while her dog sniffed and explored to his heart's content. The sun was warm on her shoulders and she felt calm and at peace and very alone, but it wasn't unpleasant.

Next morning, Lindsay woke and couldn't remember where she was for a second. It was so noisy, but not the normal, early morning city sounds she was used to. Instead, there was a fer-ocious clatter of birds singing and cows mooing and hens clucking and they all seemed to have gathered outside her bedroom window to wel-come her to the country.

She presented herself at reception at five to nine, feeling excited and nervous and conscious of her bulging tummy, which she was still hoping to hide for a bit longer. She was ushered into the demonstration kitchen, which was already home to about twenty other people. Lindsay smiled and sat down and looked around at her classmates.

There were a lot of cute student types and they all looked like Enrique Iglesias, wearing woollen hats in summer. Judging by their accents not many were Irish and Lindsay noticed a couple of older, obviously retired people grouped together on the opposite side of the room. She couldn't see anyone even vaguely her own age and there wasn't a sign of swollen ankles or a big tummy anywhere.

The school was owned and run by a young couple, Carlo was Italian and Lucy was Irish. They introduced themselves and explained what the course was all about and it was clear within minutes that they were passionate about what they did and committed to using the finest, local ingredients in season. The room that was to be home to them for the next three months was a massive, hi-tech, stainless steel kitchen and classroom all rolled into one. It was flooded with natural light, courtesy of three sets of double doors that led across a pretty courtyard to the bakery, smoking house and organic farm shop. The yard outside was full of tubs and baskets filled with tomatoes, herbs, vegetables and fruit and there were fat cats snoozing on warm window sills, hens clucking around looking for a birthing box and dogs

– including Charlie this morning – playing kiss chase.

Each student was given an old-fashioned desk, the type that still had an inkwell and a lid for keeping books under. They also had a locker for storing their aprons, knives and other equipment that they'd been instructed to bring with them. The course was designed for students who had a basic knowledge of cooking and understood most of the terms and methods used in an everyday kitchen. It ran from nine to five, Monday to Friday, with lectures and visits to local specialists on one or two evenings each week. They were given a detailed timetable and every minute was accounted for. Mondays and Fridays were practical, hands-on days and students were expected to dress appropriately. Tuesdays were taken up with demonstrations, Wednesdays were to be spent in the classroom and Thursdays were for visiting lecturers and specialist demos, such as cheesemaking and wine tasting. There was also a strong business element to the course and a special emphasis on outside catering, which interested Lindsay. The first morning was for settling in and included a tour of the hundred-and-forty-acre farm and a visit to the family-run aromatherapy room, which housed a thriving cottage industry producing essential oils. They had morning coffee on a sunny veranda overlooking the lavender field, and everyone got a chance to meet and greet.

All the woollies wanted to know if there was a local disco and what the pubs were like, while the oldies had already organized a bridge evening for the following night in Primrose Cottage. Lindsay got chatting to Mandy, a thirty-something, passionate foodie from New York, who was planning to open her own restaurant with her business-graduate sister. They were joined by a shy forty-year-old from Scotland called Gail, who was a civil servant hoping to change career. Lindsay was in her element.

Things settled down very quickly after that and life became a not-very-complicated knitting pattern. She tried to walk on the beach each morning with Charlie, who only went along to humour her, she suspected, now that he had his own mates, Rusty and Spank. He was gone all day every day and only appeared when darkness fell. Sometimes she even went to bed before him and left the back door open – it was that type of place – and his beanbag was always empty in the morning when she struggled downstairs, wondering if he'd come home at all from the dog disco or from shagging Twinkle, the local neighbourhood tart.

About two weeks into the course Lindsay got a text message from Chris.

BACK N DUB. WUD LIKE 2 MEET. R U AROUND?

She did nothing for a day or two, nothing that is, except think about him constantly and wish things had worked out differently. But it was miles too late now.

Eventually, she sent a reply.

AWAY TIL SEPT/OCT. NOTHING LEFT 2 SAY.
HOPE THINGS GO WELL 4 U.

As soon as she'd pressed the send button she wished she hadn't. She didn't get a reply.

The days were full and Lindsay was kept busy and she relaxed and enjoyed country life, revelling in learning more about something she already loved.

In the evenings she walked around the massive gardens, got lost frequently and somehow always ended up outside Primrose Cottage, where Jack, the oldest of the course participants, invariably sat drinking his nightly brandy. They chatted for ages most evenings and he told her stories of growing up in the area, moving to London when he married and coming back to settle in the West after the death of his wife Gertie two years ago. He couldn't boil an egg when she died because she wouldn't ever let him into the kitchen but now he was a keen cook and his family had given him a present of this course for his seventieth birthday.

Later in the evenings Lindsay studied or sent e-mails on the communal computer in the library, or tucked herself up in bed with a book and a cup of cocoa. To most it would have been deadly boring but it was just what she needed at the moment and she almost got lost in her own, private little world. One evening, lying in bed, she felt the baby move for the first time and it was the weirdest feeling, confirmation that a new life was growing inside her, something she was still trying to ignore.

She needed someone to talk to and she phoned Colin and amazingly she got him. They kept in touch through e-mails and the occasional phone call. He was just finishing a movie and planning to take the girls to Florida for a holiday.

'I just felt the baby kick.'

'Wow, that's great, how did it feel?'

'Funny . . . very odd really. It made me feel sad for it, tucked away in there with its mother pretending it doesn't exist.'

'I don't think you're doing that.'

'Yes I am. I'm not normal. I don't talk to it or sing to it or play it music. When I'm not exhausted or throwing up I just pretend it's not there.'

'You're doing OK, don't worry. Next time I see you I'll recite Shakespeare to your tummy.'

As always she felt better for having talked to him and a week later an enormous parcel arrived from him, containing lots of tiny little clothes – fluffy nightwear, bobbly hats, miniature vests and fur-trimmed mittens and a pair of blue suede shoes – and she took them out and played with them sometimes as if they were doll's clothes.

She'd got to know Mandy and Gail quite well, they sat together drinking coffee in the evenings or wandered down to the local pub occasionally. Mandy was a divorcée from the Bronx, independent and tough minded, and Lindsay liked her a lot. Gail was much more refined, had nursed her elderly mother until she died the previous year, and had inherited a fortune and now felt guilty. She was kind, always trying to help or seeking approval, and the other two encouraged her as much as they could, without ever talking about it.

One evening Lindsay finally spoke about being pregnant, explaining that she hadn't planned it. Mandy said she couldn't imagine not having an abortion in Lindsay's situation, and Gail wistfully said she couldn't imagine being pregnant at all. They were an odd little threesome.

The weeks passed and Lindsay got bigger and suddenly everyone knew and they were kind to her. Lucy worried about her standing a lot but Lindsay assured her she was fine and didn't want to be treated any differently, and Carlo kissed her and put his hand on her stomach and called her *bambino*.

Tara and Debbie came over for a weekend and got a shock when they saw her in the new, stretchy black dress that showed off her swollen stomach. It was the first time she'd worn it and it felt funny to be showing off her bump, declaring to the world that she was pregnant when she hadn't really declared it to herself. She was tanned and looked healthy, although she still suffered from serious heartburn and was constantly exhausted – but had given up moaning about it.

Tara was enchanted by the place and didn't want to leave and Debbie bemoaned the lack of talent in the village. The other two grinned at her when she wondered about a Chinese takeaway or fish and chips on the way home from the pub the first night.

'Get a grip, girl. You're in the sticks, for God's sake,' Lindsay told her and the other two fell around the place laughing and Lindsay suddenly wanted not to be sober. She was fed up to the gills drinking sparkling water.

Her sister Anne came down one weekend, leaving the family behind and she had tears in her eyes when she saw her baby sister.

'Are you sure you're OK, you look very big all of a sudden?'

'I'm fine, I've checked in with the local doctor here in the village and he's keeping an eye on me and I've been to a gynae once since I got here – a colleague of my own guy in Dublin. But I had to travel sixty miles to see him, so I'm not keen to do that again. Everything's normal and I'll be back home about six weeks before the birth and I'll go back to my regular guys then.'

They talked a lot about babies and Anne offered to take him or her for as long as necessary until Lindsay organized herself.

Miriam Davidson constantly sent presents to her younger daughter but wasn't very good at talking about things.

Chapter Forty-Five

Every few weeks they had a practical or written exam. The latest was to do with baking – all about flour and yeast and methods – and Lindsay revelled in it while everyone else dreaded it. Her results so far had been excellent and this one was no exception.

They moved on to international flavours the following day and Carlo really came into his own, showing them how to cook pasta properly – 'the water for pasta should be as salty as the Mediterranean sea' – how to anoint it with a few, carefully chosen ingredients – 'coat it, don't drown it' – and blindfolding them and making them taste ten different types of cheese, until they could tell good parmesan purely from the smell and texture. They learned about the importance of seasoning, using pure flaky sea-salt crystals and freshly cracked pungent black pepper, tasted the difference in salad dressings by dipping their fingers in before they coated any leaves and bit into whole chillies to feel the heat. They gathered mushrooms at dawn and picked courgette flowers at dusk and sipped wine around the barbeque at midnight and became more obsessed with food every day.

Lindsay felt like bawling when she realized it was their final week. She didn't want to leave this haven and knew Charlie would have to be bribed to get into the car for the return journey.

On her second last morning as she walked for miles along the beach in her bare feet she suddenly felt a dull pain in her stomach. She was at least a mile from home and she headed back slowly, trying not to panic, not knowing what to do because she hadn't even attended an ante-natal class, never mind read a book. She had just arrived back at the cottage when her waters broke and so did all hell.

Afterwards she couldn't really remember the sequence of events, just knew she screamed and someone came running. Lucy called the local doctor, who was out on call in a remote part of the county and he suggested they drive her to hospital immediately.

Carlo swerved along the windy roads in true Italian style and Lucy sat in the back with Lindsay holding her hand and telling her everything would be OK. The pains were coming faster now and Lindsay couldn't ever remember feeling so frightened. Lucy wanted to ring her family but she wouldn't let her, didn't want anyone near her while she was like this.

The doctor kept in contact with them by phone

and they seemed to be travelling at lightning speed so that everything became a blur, on the outside as well as inside her head. It was a nightmare of pain and fear and dread.

The hospital had a wheelchair waiting and she was suddenly in a white room surrounded by strangers and lights that hurt her eyes, but compared with the pain that wracked her entire body it was nothing. They kept telling her not to push and she wanted to push more than she'd ever wanted to do anything else in her life. She felt she wasn't in control and that was the most scary thing. She could hear a disembodied, strangled voice screaming at the nurses to get the baby out of her body and was shocked to realize it was her own. They were all very kind but nobody told her what was happening and they kept asking if her family were on the way and she felt that must mean she was going to die and would have been relieved to do so. She didn't care about anything except that she was roaring like a mad woman and kept begging them to give her something for the pain, so that she could logically make a decision about what to do next.

'It's too late for that, but don't worry, it won't be long now.' A pair of bright green eyes held her hand and sponged her face and she felt she was going insane. Nobody had told her it would be this bad.

It got worse and went on for hours. Her throat was hoarse from trying to scream and all she could see was a big tent and her toes dangling in mid air, steel contraptions and worried faces. After what seemed like about three days they told her to push and she clawed like an animal, her eyes bulging and the sweat ran in floods down her back and suddenly it all eased and she knew the greatest feeling of relief, and someone said 'It's a boy' and she felt absolutely no emotion.

They handed her a tiny bundle. At first she was afraid to look, and when she did she saw the ugliest, pink, wrinkled prune and fell in love. Like all her love affairs it didn't last cause they took him away again almost immediately, explaining that because he was premature they needed to put him into the special baby unit where they could examine and monitor him. They promised to talk to her later.

'Is he OK?' She was suddenly terrified.

'We just need to keep an eye on him, don't worry.'

But she was worried and realized that she'd probably never stop, at least until he was about twenty.

Then they stitched her up like a chicken and cleaned her like a baby. She asked what day it was and they laughed and told her it was still Thursday. She'd been in hospital for only five hours.

Carlo and Lucy came in then and all three of them cried, and they promised to mind Charlie and bring in her things later. Lindsay phoned her mum but it rang out, her sister's answering machine was on, Debbie was out of the country and Tara was in court. Typical! She left messages asking them all to ring her and knew she had to tell someone fast, so she tried Colin and he answered on the second ring and she burst into tears and scared the hell out of him.

'Lindsay, please, just tell me what's wrong.'

But she couldn't stop crying and it was the perfect release although she didn't know it yet and all the pain of the last nine months came out in a single enormous gush.

'I'm in hospital.'

'Are you OK? Is the baby OK?'

'He's ugly.'

He clearly thought she was mad but decided to humour her.

'Don't worry, he'll be gorgeous; babies aren't ugly.' There was a slight pause. 'How do you know it's a he?'

'I saw him and he is definitely ugly but you were right. I love him.'

'Oh my God, when? Are you OK? Is he OK? Lindsay, please, you have to stop crying and tell me what happened.'

So she did and he whooped for joy and so did she.

'I'm a bit worried about him, he's in the special baby unit because he's premature, but they've promised to talk to me soon.'

'But he's going to be all right?'

'Well, I only saw him for a minute or two, but he was all there. Oh Colin, wait till you see him, he's gorgeous. I'll send you a photo.'

It seemed like ages before they came to talk to her, explaining that he would have to remain in the unit for some time.

'But he will be fine, won't he?'

Even though they were quick to reassure her, they pointed out that the first twenty-four hours were the most important, explaining that all his organs would be checked and he would be monitored for jaundice and closely watched in case of infection.

'Can I see him?'

'Yes of course, just give us another half-hour because the doctor is still with him, then you can spend as much time with him as you like.'

Then suddenly everyone seemed to phone back at the same time. Her mother cried, the girls snivelled, and she laughed and felt strong. Debbie was in Paris but her mother, Anne and Tara insisted on travelling down together that night, and they were all so happy when they saw she was OK. Her mother held her very tightly and Anne and Tara cried again. She did a great impersonation of John Wayne as she walked with them to the special unit where they were keeping her little boy under observation. They had to look at him through the window, and there were more tears but they were happy wet ones. And everyone thought he was gorgeous, especially his mother.

'What's his name?' Anne asked immediately.

She looked at him for a long moment and was about to shrug her shoulders when it came to her.

'Freddie.' She beamed and they all looked surprised, horrified even, judging by her mother's face.

It was late when they left to find a hotel and Lindsay immediately went back down to the unit to see him. The nurse on duty talked to her and warned her that he might change colour often and that his breathing or heart rate could be uneven.

'Talk to him, touch him, don't be afraid.'

'What's the tube in his mouth?'

'It's a feeding tube. Later you can express some of your own milk if you want to.'

She sat with him for ages, talking to him, telling him how much she loved him, willing him to get strong. She asked to hold him and he seemed so frail and she prayed to God not to punish her because she had been so utterly stupid in thinking she could ever not want him.

When she finally returned to her room she couldn't sleep even though she was knackered. She kept worrying about Freddie. One of the nurses brought her tea and made her comfortable and she asked for the newspapers and flicked through them for hours, trying to kill time but not really concentrating, so it took her a minute or two to take in the content of an article headed TOP TV STAR QUITS IRELAND FOR NEW LIFE AND NEW LOVE. She stared at it for a minute, saw the picture of Chris and closed her eyes quickly, afraid of what she was about to find out. When she opened them again it was all still there, and on the night her baby was born she learned that his father was leaving Ireland to take up a contract in America, which, although only for one year, was reputed to be worth a million dollars and, as if that wasn't enough, she read that one of the reasons he had decided to take up the offer was because of his stunning twenty-four-year-old actress girlfriend Lauren Berkin, whom he was expected to marry in the spring.

Chapter Forty-Six

The next night, as she sat up in bed feeling lonely for Chris and hungry for her baby, a giant bunch of lilies with legs walked into her room, with a grinning Colin behind them.

He hugged her to death and she held on to him for dear life, then he kissed her hair, eyes, nose and mouth and she cried like the big baby that she was.

'You look beautiful,' he told her in between kisses and she believed him because she needed to.

'How did you get here? You're always doing this to me,' she said with a watery smile.

'I got the first flight I could. I couldn't wait to see you, and him.'

'Come on, I'll show you,' she said, as if they were discussing a puppy.

They arrived just as the nurse was changing him and he looked tiny but not as shrivelled and he waved his arms and legs frantically and shook his fists at them.

'Isn't he absolutely beautiful?' she asked, and he gave the only reply possible to a brand-new mother.

'He's the most gorgeous baby I've ever seen.'

She put on her gown and went inside and held him up to the glass so that Colin could get a good look at him.

'Meet Freddie,' she mouthed to Colin as she held the tiny little body in her arms. He burst out laughing.

'It's absolutely right and he's beautiful,' he told her as soon as she came out.

'I'm not sure the others are as certain but I don't care. I know Freddie isn't really right for a baby but I think he's going to grow into a perfect little Freddie. Sort of like Dennis the Menace.'

They stayed for a while gazing at him, and then went back to her room, and he went out and got some decent food and they had a picnic on her bed, talking and watching TV. Much later she showed him the article about Chris and he looked troubled but didn't really say anything. She changed the subject but after a while he asked if she would consider telling him before he left the country.

'No, I couldn't do that to him now, he'd think I was trying to stand in his way.'

Colin shook his head. 'If my son was lying in a special baby unit I'd want to know before I made any major decision about my life.'

'But there's nothing wrong with the baby, it's not as if he's ill or anything, he's just small and they're keeping an eye on him.' Lindsay didn't like where the conversation was heading and Colin sensed it and backed off.

'OK, I won't mention it again.'

'Look, if he contacts me again I promise I'll try to talk to him, all right?'

He nodded, knowing he wasn't going to win.

When he left, Lindsay took the old newspaper clipping out of her purse, the one with the photo of Chris and herself together, the 'dynamic duo', then she walked down again to Freddie and showed him his dad. Lindsay stayed for hours, holding and stroking and singing to him.

Next day, Colin went shopping in Galway and spent a fortune on Freddie, buying him his first pair of jeans and a tiny, exquisite denim jacket and anything else he could lay his hands on. He also got some stuff for Lindsay – a beautiful black cashmere sweater and some sexy T-shirts and a lacy bodice and a pair of amazing black leather trousers, the softest she'd ever seen.

He had to fly back to New York that night but promised to see her again soon and was already planning Freddie's first trip to the States.

Tara and the others had taken Charlie and most of Lindsay's stuff back to Dublin from the cookery school by the time Lindsay was discharged from hospital, but Freddie had to remain in the unit. They explained that he wouldn't be discharged until somewhere between two and four weeks of his due date. His body temperature had to remain normal in an open crib, he had to be taking adequate calories and he had to be steadily gaining weight. Lindsay worried about him constantly and booked into a small hotel nearby so that she could spend all her days with him. She was able to feed him herself and he made good progress, everyone assured her.

To her surprise her mother came to stay for a few days and she looked after Lindsay while Lindsay looked after Freddie and it was an important time for all three of them.

Debbie came straight from her trip and she too was besotted by Freddie and had brought him the most gorgeous coat from Paris along with lots of smellies for his mum.

'Imagine, I'm a mother.' Lindsay smiled at Debbie. 'It feels very strange. As if I'm not really ready for it.'

'Listen, darling, I'll be auntie Debs to him. How ageing is that?'

Eventually, the hospital pronounced themselves happy with Freddie's progress and she was allowed take him home.

Tara arrived to meet them and couldn't believe how much he'd grown.

Freddie slept all the way back to Dublin, watched by an over-anxious mother and besotted aunt.

When she arrived at the house, it looked fantastic. Anne, Debbie and Tara had spent the previous day cleaning everything and the windows sparkled. There were flowers everywhere, in tubs, window boxes, on the patio and in her favourite jug on the kitchen table. It seemed like years since she'd last been here and she could never have imagined that her life would change so completely in the space of a few months.

They sat in her kitchen that evening, afraid to bring him outdoors even though the evening was mild and he was well wrapped up and the girls barbequed and they drank champagne and toasted Freddie, who was blissfully unaware of all the attention.

Anne insisted on staying the first night and kept the baby in her room so that Lindsay could rest. She expressed some milk and had her first night's sleep in months, with no tossing or turning or retching or worrying and although she felt guilty and didn't want to be without him, Anne insisted she needed the break and she fell straight asleep and didn't remember anything else until ten-thirty next morning.

Anne departed to see to her own brood and her mother arrived with a car full of groceries, nappies, baby potions, lotions and more flowers. Lindsay made a light lunch while Miriam Davidson played the doting grandmother, which, surprisingly, seemed to suit her.

Next day Lindsay sent an e-mail to Jonathan Myers asking him to call her at home and he was delighted when she told him her news and more flowers arrived. They arranged to talk again in about a month. Freddie's early arrival had given Lindsay much-needed time that she otherwise wouldn't have had.

Life with a baby meant a very ordered routine, she discovered, as summer turned to autumn and the days shortened and the nights became slightly chilly as the premiership and the schoolkids returned.

Each day was a constant round of bottles and bathing, washing and wiping, sleeping and smiling. Lindsay found it hard to believe that this was her life. It occupied her totally and kept her sane, with no time to think about herself, although she still thought about Chris at the oddest moments.

She wondered what she'd ever done with all that spare time she used to have – squandered on TV, baths, lazy glasses of wine and long phone calls, she remembered. Now she brushed her hair and cleaned her teeth if she was lucky, but Freddie made up for all the inconvenience and she loved him with an intensity that frightened her sometimes.

Colin was on the phone regularly and she had to send him photos every few weeks. The girls and Anne were constantly in and out and one or other of them stayed over at least once a week, so that sleep deprivation didn't threaten to overwhelm her, and she was able to enjoy the luxury of an uninterrupted soak. But she always missed him and found herself hurrying back to see his smile, smell him and hold him close.

In the space of a few days, it seemed, he was a month old and Debbie began to put gentle pressure on Lindsay to start going out again. She was reluctant, because she no longer considered herself single and in a funny way her life was fulfilled, if lonely. But the girls persisted and enlisted the help of Anne, who insisted on collecting Freddie one

Friday morning and offered to keep him overnight. So, in the blink of an eye, Lindsay was on her own, with no responsibilities for twenty-four hours. At first she panicked and rang Anne every ten minutes until her sister announced she was going out for the day and taking Freddie and the kids with her casually mentioning that the battery on her mobile was flat.

'OK, OK, I get the message but please, call me if he frets or anything.'

'He's fine, relax. His cousins have it sussed. Got to go. Have a good day.'

So Lindsay went into town and had her hair cut and a facial and her nails done and tried to pretend she was a happy career woman with no responsibilities, but then couldn't remember what that felt like. She met Debbie and Tara in a very trendy pub for drinks at six-thirty and felt completely out of place amongst Dublin's coolest. They went for some food to a madly expensive Moroccan restaurant and then dragged Lindsay to a nightclub where she felt even more like an alien.

'Relax, for God's sake. You've only had a baby, not joined a religious order,' Debbie teased and she tried to obey.

It was great fun in the end and she remembered that this was how it used to be all the time, but that was a million years ago before Chris and Freddie had invaded her life.

Lindsay arrived home exhausted at two-thirty and fell into bed with her make-up on. She woke next day at noon and panicked until she saw him again.

The girls were reasonably happy that she was back on the scene.

'Next stop a holiday,' Debbie and Tara vowed, but knew they'd have their work cut out.

At the end of September Lindsay returned to work and Freddie started life in a crèche, thanks to a great friend of Tara's who put her in touch with a brilliant nurse who looked after children in her own home. It was a huge wrench for Lindsay, leaving him each day, even though she knew he was safe and well cared for. Eventually, she learned to relax, although she worried about him all the time and wondered how much she was missing out on his life. He was growing fast and changing every day and she wanted him to stay a baby just in case he needed her less as he got older.

Jonathan Myers had asked Lindsay to help set up a new fashion programme aimed at sixteen- to thirty-four-year-olds. A lot of the work had already started because it was due on air immediately after Christmas. It was to be a fast-moving, lively, stylish half-hour, presented by three wild young things – a twenty-one-year-old stunning blonde with a figure to die for, a ravishing, dark-eyed Irish/Italian who was barely twenty and a fiery, completely mad redhead from Cork who was twenty-four and looked seventeen.

'That used to be us,' Debbie said with a trace of nostalgia when Lindsay showed her the stunning publicity photos.

'That was never us,' Tara said matter-of-factly, 'so let's not get depressed about it.'

'Anyway, we're not over the hill yet and you two are looking great at the moment so don't let me get fat and smell only of puke.'

The other two really were thriving. Tara had gone all soft and dreamy since she and Michael had decided to get married and she looked happy and shiny. Debbie had gone for a radical new look and her mane of curls was now straight and sleek and her body was tight thanks to a punishing gym routine. Lindsay felt very nondescript beside them. She'd lost all her weight but her body wasn't toned and she lacked energy and was eating too much junk food, all she could manage most evenings, in spite of her newly acquired culinary skills. She felt she'd lost her sparkle, which she suspected was more to do with Chris than Freddie, who had become the brightest spark in her life.

The production team on the new show were all twenty- and thirty-something females, which suited Lindsay very well. There was no studio element, which she missed, especially the live programme every week, but being on the road with a single camera was another challenge. The hours were largely nine-to-five but it was extremely busy and Lindsay decided to get organized well in advance.

She now shopped almost completely on-line and her bulky, non-perishable groceries were delivered once a month at a time that suited her. She invested in a brand-new, top-of-the-range washing machine and dryer, to cope with the unending baby clothes, blankets and towels and Anne volunteered her services for one afternoon a week to do the ironing and other bits and pieces. She found a reliable babysitter in one of her neighbours, a grandmother with plenty of experience, and roped in her mother to take Freddie for a couple of hours every weekend, so that she could do things for herself without worrying. Even with all this in place she rarely had time to do anything more than get her hair cut or have her nails done once in a blue moon. But her darling baby boy, the absolute love of her life, more than made up for it and she couldn't imagine how she'd ever lived without him.

During her first week back Lindsay called in to see the gang on *Live from Dublin*. The show was to run for only another season in its present format, Jonathan had told her, although the team had not been told. He also hinted that they were hoping Chris Keating would return, given the huge success of his shows last season, to host a new version of the programme.

Meanwhile, Tom Watts had a contract to work out, so he was back in the driving seat, fully recovered, but Alan Morland was no longer producing. His stay in hospital had made him re-evaluate his life somewhat and he had taken a year off and gone trekking through India with his girl-friend. He and Lindsay kept in touch occasionally and he had written to her and told her of his decision and she now got the odd postcard from places with unpronounceable names. The new producer was a quiet, shy, man in his mid fifties and she suspected that Tom would make mince-meat of him. Kate had been replaced and Lindsay would have loved to know why. She herself had not made any official complaint but something had obviously filtered through. There were a number of new faces and Lindsay promised to have lunch with her old colleagues as soon as she'd settled back.

Chapter Forty-Seven

Winter came early and the clocks went back much too soon, it seemed to Lindsay, who found the blanket of grey didn't help her spirits. Work was only OK. The fact that she'd come on board later than everyone else meant she'd missed out on the autumn fashion shows and major launches and therefore valuable contacts. It also meant she didn't get invited to follow-up events because no one knew her.

They were about to start shooting when she joined the team, so her role for the moment was largely administrative, setting up fashion shoots and selecting models and doing all the other vital but not very exciting jobs. Everyone wanted to be shooting and editing and as there were three producers and three assistant producers a significant back-up was needed in the office. Lindsay had eagerly offered to do it, glad of a couple of weeks to settle back and be at the other end of a phone in case Freddie needed her. The fact that she was good at it didn't help, because the senior producer came to rely on her and was therefore reluctant to move her. She hadn't made any real friends either, because everyone seemed to be out and about all the time or, if they were back at base, they were holed up in edit suites or shooting complicated computer graphic sequences, which Lindsay knew nothing about.

She was seeing less of the girls too. Debbie had been put on the New York route which meant she was missing for three or four days at a time, although she called round all the time between trips, mostly with presents for Freddie, who now had enough cool clothes to wear until he was five, provided he didn't grow more than a couple of inches. Tara was in the middle of a big court case and was burning the midnight oil in the office and seeing very little of anybody, Michael included.

Lindsay seemed to be the only one not going anywhere and she was a slave to routine. She rose at six-thirty every morning, got herself showered and dressed immediately, then played with Freddie for ages because he was always full of beans after his long sleep and wanted her attention. By the time she'd fed and organized him and dropped him off she had just about time to go to the dry cleaners, or chemist, or laundry, before hitting the office at nine-thirty. She shopped for her fresh foodstuffs at lunchtime, eating a sandwich in the car en route, and was always rushing to collect Freddie in the evenings. By the time she'd lit the fire, played with him and fed and bathed and sung him to sleep she was exhausted and found herself eating an omelette or beans on toast more than one night a week. By eleven she could barely take her make-up off, before falling into bed until Freddie woke and startled her. Then she cradled him or fed or changed him and collapsed again until morning, when it all started over again. Two things kept her going – Freddie, who was the absolute joy of her life, and the thought that Christmas, and possibly a break, were only around the corner.

It was less than three weeks away and she hadn't bought a single present and she had no real interest, which worried her.

'It's all so different to last year,' she moaned to her sister, feeling sorry for herself, as she seemed to more and more often these days. Anne sensed something was wrong and offered to call round the following evening for a chat and a glass of wine.

She hadn't seen Lindsay for a few days and noticed that her younger sister looked grey and worn out and her spirits seemed low.

'OK, let's make a plan,' she said as she poured two large glasses of a nice chilled Sancerre and curled up by the fire with Lindsay. 'How would you really like to spend the holiday?'

Lindsay closed her eyes and fantasized. 'In bed, for a fortnight, now that would be bliss.' She smiled wearily. 'You know, just not to have anything to do, not to have to make an effort, would be fab. And to be able to spend lots of time with Freddie, because he's changing so fast at the moment and I always seem to be in a hurry with him. I love him so much and I'm afraid that I'm missing out on him. I want to sit for hours just watching him, noticing every little thing he does. As it is I haven't bought one present and I've no time off until two days before Christmas and I'm completely shattered.'

Anne decided to take matters into her own hands and called Debbie and Tara next day. Between them they made a plan. Miriam Davidson was put back in charge of all the Christmas cooking and told to ignore Lindsay's offer to cook an alternative banquet – foolishly made during the heady days of summer at Inisfree.

Debbie called her and demanded a list of presents and a budget and Lindsay gave in. The only thing she bought was a gorgeous hand-made jumper for Colin and two cute dresses for both the girls and their dolls, which she couriered over to his parents, who were travelling to be with him for Christmas. It was a surprise she knew he'd love. Everything else she left to Debbie and it was a huge relief. Tara arrived the following Saturday with a Christmas tree, closely followed by Debbie and Anne, who cleaned the house from top to bottom over the weekend, after sending Lindsay home to her mother's for the night and organizing Freddie and Charlie between them.

Tara called round another evening with a collection of clothes she'd chosen for Lindsay and made her try them all on and decide on an outfit. She then returned the rest and got a refund and picked up a cute bag and shoes as a present from herself and organized Debbie to buy her some funky jewellery on her travels.

Anne gave Lindsay her present early – a complete pamper day at one of Ireland's top health and beauty resorts – and finally, the girls informed her that they'd booked a country cottage for a week for the three of them – and Freddie and Charlie, of course – starting on the twenty-seventh of December, in a tiny little village beside the sea in west Cork.

Before she knew what was happening it was Christmas Eve and Anne was collecting mother and son and family pet and depositing them in front of a roaring fire at the family home. Leaving Lindsay stretched out on the couch with a glass of champagne, Charlie comatose on the rug and Freddie in his baby chair in the kitchen watching Miriam peel sprouts, she departed to organize her own brood, feeling happy that they'd got Lindsay back on track.

'You four have honestly saved my life,' Lindsay told them emotionally after Debbie and Tara arrived to exchange presents on their way home to their families. 'I always thought post-natal depression was something to be scoffed at, wondered how anyone could feel down after having a beautiful baby, but I hadn't realized how much the tiredness gets into your bones and can wear you down, so that you barely even notice the good things in your life. And I have an awful lot to be grateful for this Christmas and I love my son more than my own life, so thanks, I couldn't have done it without you.'

All her presents were beautifully wrapped under the tree and she hadn't a clue what they were, as she handed them out. Debbie, of course, had excelled herself and chosen gorgeous stuff in New York.

In the middle of the celebrations a courier arrived with a box for Lindsay which they tore open. It contained more presents for Freddie and Lindsay from Colin – a leather biker's jacket for Freddie, which had them all in fits, and a much more sophisticated full-length soft black leather coat for Lindsay, which had them all groaning and yelling 'bitch'. In the bottom of the box they found a leather collar, studded with diamonds, for Charlie and Lindsay put their presents on and mother, adored baby and much-loved pet posed for their first official Christmas photo.

When the girls had departed for home, Miriam was busy in the kitchen and Anne and her husband were bathing the boys and organizing Santa, Lindsay dozed by the fire and thought of last year when Chris had called to see her. She'd been so happy and carefree and he'd kissed her right here on this sofa and she knew, even then, that he was going to be very important in her life. And suddenly, after months of putting him out of her mind, he crept back in and it was as if he'd never gone away. In the soft light of the candles and blue fluorescent glow of the fire she remembered it all and she could smell him and feel him and taste him. The tree lights twinkled and teased her and she was lonely for him all over again.

The girls went to midnight Mass as usual and Lindsay noticed all the carefree daughters with their mothers, smiling, shiny, fashionabie – mostly independent, well-to-do career women, she speculated, all giving up a night on the town to be with their parents and carry on the tradition of Christmas.

'I want to be like her,' she whispered to Anne as a tall, dark-haired, slim young woman sat nearby with her parents. She had long legs and high heels, a Prada bag and a short skirt and her jewellery was expensive. 'I bet she has a boyfriend who's a stock-broker, who'll buy her a diamond necklace as a trinket. And they're probably heading off to a really cool party after this.'

'I think you've been reading too many fairy stories,' Anne grinned. 'Anyway, who cares? I'd say she doesn't have a Freddie in her life, and I bet you wouldn't swap him for a million Prada bags or diamond rings.'

She's right, Lindsay thought, and realized once again how important her little boy was to her and she gave thanks for his life and promised God to try harder and remember to count her blessings.

Christmas Day was warm and peaceful and Lindsay slept till twelve. Miriam had kept Freddie in her room and Anne had warned the boys not to wake Lindsay and so another tradition was broken and she was sorry to have missed the Santa routine, but knew she'd have a new one with Freddie in a couple of years and resolved never to miss a single moment of it. Charlie had spent the night under the Christmas tree, close to an untidy-looking parcel with his name on it that smelt suspiciously like meat. As it was from Debbie, Lindsay suspected that it was indeed meat and when the boys came down to check if Santa had arrived they found a tell-tale trail of paper and there was no prising the remains away from Charlie who gnawed at it for hours on the rug, much to Miriam's disgust.

Colin phoned in the afternoon and they laughed and chatted. He sounded happy and she was glad, because she knew Christmas would always be difficult for him and the girls.

Lindsay, Debbie, Tara, Freddie and Charlie headed south on the twenty-seventh to a stone cottage by the sea. It was freezing but the heat was on and a big fire was burning when they arrived, thanks to a kind owner who knew they had a small baby with them. They unpacked a mountain of food and drink in gale-force winds and torrential rain and they just about managed to see the funny side of it as Freddie – 'typical man', according to Debbie – snored throughout the adventure.

'God, suddenly I've acquired quite a bit of baggage,' Lindsay remarked ruefully as she hauled in a mountain of baby stuff and a beanbag for Charlie, who refused to sleep on anything else no matter where he was.

That night Lindsay cooked a proper dinner for the first time in months and the girls were seriously impressed with her confit of duck leg with honey and spices and roast pheasant with red cabbage and real potato crisps. Afterwards they listened to music and the sound of rain lashing and drank hot whiskies and fought over the armchair nearest the fire.

Each day they walked for miles and took turns to carry Freddie in a very clever and practical sling that Debbie had picked up in New York, which gave him a great view as they trundled along. They stopped to buy fresh fish and home-made bread from the locals and the baby was unconscious most of the time, thanks to an abundance of fresh air. Charlie revelled in the attention and Lindsay gave him loads, sorry that he'd been a bit neglected in the past few months.

On New Year's Eve they'd planned to go out, but everywhere was miles away and no one wanted to drive, so they dressed up, Debbie cooked and they drank bottles of ice-cold pink champagne, toasting themselves over and over again and making their resolutions.

Tara went first cause she was the easiest. 'I'm going to be Mrs Michael Russell and I'm going to have the nicest wedding and hopefully live happily ever after.' They hugged her and desperately wished for it all to come true for her. Lindsay knew she missed Michael but she had insisted on being with her two friends on this special New Year's Eve and Lindsay knew it was largely because of her.

'This time last year I never thought I'd be so lucky,' she grinned. 'You deserve it.' They smiled and toasted 'Tara and Michael'.

Debbie's resolution was succinct. 'I'm going to date someone for more than a week,' she announced and they both knew what she meant. 'I'm going to stop looking for great sex and try for a great laugh. I figure that's where I'm going wrong.'

'Good sex sometimes happens when you get to know someone,' Tara smiled.

'But don't you dare settle for a relationship

without stupendously good sex,' Lindsay warned, knowing there was no chance of that happening.

'Also, I'm going to think about changing my job,' Debbie surprised them by saying. 'I've had enough of being a trolley dolly.'

'Good for you.' Tara looked at Lindsay and neither of them could picture her doing anything else, but somehow knew she'd find something.

'OK, madam, what about you?' Both girls looked at Lindsay.

'Well, this time last year I was already pregnant, can you believe that?' They couldn't.

'The night before New Year's Eve was the last time I was with Chris.'

They all went quiet for a moment. 'So I've decided to go back to how I used to be.' They were confused.

'I've spent so much time looking backwards and being scared all the time and worried about the future, that I want to be a bit more like the old Lindsay. I've become a bit of a moan and a wimp. I want to be gutsy and courageous again.'

They all had tears in their eyes, a bit emotional from too much heat and far too much champagne, as they hugged and kissed and wished. It was a special moment and each knew exactly what the other two meant.

Chapter Forty-Eight

Lindsay put her resolutions into practice as soon as she went back to work. She spoke to Barbara Laing, the senior producer on the show, and explained how she felt. Before she'd stumbled over the first three sentences, the other girl stopped her.

'You're absolutely right and I'm to blame. You've just been so good at organizing things that I've let you do it all, and it's meant you've had all of the slog and none of the glamour. So, from the end of the month you're on the road and I want you to go to the two main fashion shows this week and meet all the stylists. Also there's a major Cosmetic Hall opening in town on Thursday and they have a special night for invited guests and celebrities on Wednesday. Go and say hello to all the make-up artists and hairdressers.'

'Are you sure?'

'Certain, and sorry for not doing something sooner. You've been great for the show.'

'Well, in a way it suited me, you see, I have a

young baby and I'm on my own.' It was the first time she'd said it to a stranger.

'I didn't know that, you never said anything. Well, look, I know how rough that can be, my sister's in the same boat, so please shout if the schedule gets too tough or you need time off or anything, OK?'

Lindsay was really happy and her working life took off again after that and it was everything she wanted it to be. She went to all the press shows and fashion extravaganzas, which were usually held in the mornings anyway, and she got into all the latest trends in clothes and hair and make-up and started to blossom again. She was constantly advising the girls to 'buy a wide belt to go with that' or 'bigger earrings would be great' and they teased her and borrowed all her new make-up colours.

Freddie got bigger and longer and started to crawl and make sounds and he was an absolute treasure and everyone spoiled him rotten.

Lindsay loved him more than she had ever believed possible and adored being his mother. He had Chris's intense blue eyes and sallow skin, and he looked nothing like her until he smiled.

And Lindsay no longer fantasized about the three of them being a happy family. She knew she'd been somehow hoping to hear from Chris over the Christmas period, but that hadn't happened and she'd finally accepted that this was her lot in life and was content. She knew she was heading for another crisis if she read about his wedding to the American actress, but she no longer thought about him all the time and anyway, she had a big chunk of him and no one could take that away. And when she looked at Freddie and saw Chris she was glad, deep down, that he was his father and she had great hopes for her son's future.

Meanwhile, the threesome was back in business, planning Tara's wedding and helping Debbie find a man by invading all the local hot spots and enjoying themselves immensely. Lindsay was back in contact with her friend Carrie from the Training Course, who was in a serious relationship with Dan Pearson, the floor manager. Lindsay had told her about the baby but hadn't said who the father was, mainly because she knew Chris and Dan were friendly and she just wasn't sure. As far as Carrie was concerned Chris and Lindsay had never really been an item and she didn't know him at all. Lindsay liked her and knew she'd tell her the whole story someday, but meanwhile she asked her not to tell anyone, even Dan, although Chris was far away and unlikely to come back in the foreseeable future.

In March, Lindsay took a long weekend off and brought Freddie to the States to meet his cousins, as Colin called them. Once again they flew first class thanks to Debbie, and Freddie was no trouble, to Lindsay's amazement.

Colin collected them again in his pick-up truck and she finally got to meet the girls, who were absolutely adorable and terribly excited about having a real baby to play with.

'You look terrific.' Colin hugged her as they left the airport. 'Better than I've ever seen you look.'

'I decided to stop feeling sorry for myself,' she grinned at him. 'Anyway, I had to tone up because I'm a bridesmaid in a couple of months and I'm damned if I'm letting the bride steal all the limelight.'

'Well, your efforts have been worthwhile, you look wonderful.'

'All that water and fruit had to pay off sometime. So for the next couple of days it's pancakes, beer and Chinese.'

They went out on day trips and ate together in small restaurants and they were a lively, noisy bunch and Lindsay loved it all.

On her second evening there they sat on the roof terrace when the kids were all settled and Lindsay marvelled at how far she'd come since her visit last year.

Colin put his arms around her and kissed her.

'What about you and me?' he asked, not taking his eyes off her face.

She'd known that this moment would come but she still wasn't prepared for it.

'Is there a you and me?' he asked gently.

'You've been one of the best things that's ever happened to me, you know that . . .'

'But?'

She was silent for a long time.

'But I don't think I've let go of Chris,' she said in a whisper.

'That's OK, I think I've known that all along. I think we just met at the wrong time and I'm sorry, because I think I really wanted you to be the one.'

They sat for ages, not talking, holding on to each other.

'I've banished him from my thoughts and I don't dream about him any more, but the bastard just won't shift his ass out of my heart. Can you understand that?'

'Sure and I'll get over it, so don't worry. I think I always knew. But it didn't stop me hoping.'

'Maybe it's because of Freddie. Sometimes I look at him and it's like a miniature Chris smiling back at me and I feel so lonely for him. But deep down now I think we were never meant to be.'

'I still think you should have talked to him.'

'I will someday, but he's probably married to someone else by now and I don't think talking to him would change anything. Too much time has passed.'

They chatted for hours and agreed to go on the way they were for the moment.

'I don't want to lose you from my life. I couldn't bear it, I've lost too many people already.'

'You won't, don't worry.'

'Will you come to Tara's wedding with me?'

'Yes, if I'm not filming, I'll be your sweetheart for the day,' he bowed and grinned at her.

'And what about you, where are you at?'

He sort of smiled at her.

'You know, I think I'm ready to get out there again. In a way, you were just what I needed too.'

She hugged him and was happy and sad at the same time and she wished that he could have been the one, because if there was a second-best father out there for Freddie, it was surely the man sitting in front of her tonight.

It was a great trip. Lindsay was sorry to be leaving him again but the girls were devastated and he promised to bring them to Dublin in the summer when Lindsay swore they could spend as much time as they liked with Freddie.

The girls spent long nights and lazy Sundays helping Tara with her wedding plans. She and Michael had decided on a small wedding, only about thirty people at the ceremony, then lunch in one of Dublin's most exclusive restaurants, followed by a big party for all their friends that night. Thanks to Lindsay's new contacts they'd found a hip young designer who was making all the dresses, and they pored over books and magazines searching for ideas. Tara decided quickly that she wanted something simple, in cream silk with a detailed bodice and a long veil. The girls were much more fussy and spent days going around the shops looking for inspiration, and had great fun trying on meringues. It was now less than three months away and they were all on a serious health kick, so many evenings were spent in the gym, with Freddie laughing up at them from his chair.

Spring turned to summer and her 'baby' became a little boy and started to walk and talk. He was almost one year old and got cuter every day. His skin was toasted from days in the sunshine in the garden, despite his hat and masses of sun block. It was simply Chris's skin all over again and his eyes looked even bluer against the sky and he was tall

434

with a mop of dark curls that Lindsay couldn't bring herself to tame. She thought he was absolutely gorgeous and was always kissing him and telling him so.

One day she was in her tiny front garden, weeding and moving around plants. Freddie was having a ball with a bucket and spade nearby. He was wearing his first real pair of jeans with a denim shirt and he looked all grown up as he grinned at her and tried to talk. A tall hedge hid them from the outside world and she hummed to herself while working, glad to be outside, feeling the sun warm on her arms and neck and shoulders in her little pale blue, strappy, floral dress, with her hair caught back in a ribbon. One of her neighbours passed and told her she was a sight for sore eyes and she laughed. When she looked up at the gate again Chris stood there. She blinked and took off her sunglasses and squinted, convinced her mind was playing tricks once more. But when she looked again he was still there.

Chapter Forty-Nine

'Hi.'

She stared at him.

'Hi.' She couldn't move so she remained on her knees, looking up, trowel in hand.

'Da Da,' or something similar, said a small voice but he didn't hear it cause a car was passing and she knew no one would believe her anyway, when she told them later.

'I rang the office and they said you'd taken a few days off and I wasn't sure you'd return my call so I took a chance and came here. How've you been?'

'Fine.' What else could be said in one sentence, in a small front garden on a hot Tuesday afternoon, with the traffic drowning them out and their son playing nearby?

'Can I come in?'

'Erm, I was actually just going . . .' But he was in already and he saw Freddie and she went cold and was frightened.

He bent down. 'Hello, are you digging the garden too?' he asked the little boy and Lindsay saw father and son together for the first time, both in blue jeans with piercing eyes and different smiles, yet with the same sallow skin and hair and legs that were too long, and she knew she was completely unprepared for this moment. He held out his hand and Freddie grabbed it, almost toppling over yet determined to hold on to his independence.

'I'm sorry, I didn't realize you were babysitting. Shall I call back later?'

She wanted to say yes, come back later, when I'll be more able to cope, but was afraid that the temptation to send Freddie away in advance would be too strong and for the first time she knew with certainty that too much time had already passed. Now that she'd seen them together she wondered if she had been right to keep them apart. He was watching her closely and she knew at that moment what she had to do.

'No, come in, I was just going to stop for a cup of tea or maybe even a glass of wine. It's almost six.' She kept talking, rubbish, anything to make him stay. He stood up and so did she and Freddie grabbed his leg and he laughed.

'He's just started walking and I'm afraid he won't be picked up easily.'

'You are one gorgeous little guy, do you know that?' Chris held out his hand, Freddie grabbed it, and father and son walked slowly after her into the house and neither knew it. She led the way into the kitchen, washed her hands and poured some wine to buy time. Charlie came to sniff Chris and he bent down and rubbed the animal, then Charlie rolled over and Freddie laughed.

'Woof,' or something vaguely similar, he shouted, pointing to Charlie and Chris smiled and nodded.

'Silly dog, always wants his tummy rubbed. Don't you, Charlie? Do you ever want your tummy rubbed?' he asked and the child smiled. Chris pulled up Freddie's shirt and rubbed his tummy and the little boy lay on his back and put his hands and legs in the air and laughed, the way he did with Lindsay when they played with Charlie. And she watched, mesmerized, as both her dog and her baby rolled over and became putty in his hands and she wondered how long it would be before she did the same.

He caught her looking at him and stood up quickly, as if remembering why he was there. 'Sorry, I got carried away. He's very cute. What's his name?'

'Freddie.'

He laughed and nodded agreement. 'Great name for a little boy. I'll bet he's definitely a Freddie.'

She changed the subject quickly, not remotely ready to go there just yet.

'Want to sit out in the garden? It's cooler. I'm afraid the kitchen is stifling with the heat of the Aga.'

'Sure.' He followed her and kept an eye on Freddie, who tottered along holding on to Charlie.

She sat down at her little garden table and Freddie started digging again nearby.

'How've you been?'

'Good, thanks. When did you get back from the States?'

'Yesterday.'

'Did it go well?'

'Yes, I think it did.'

'How long are you staying?'

'I dunno, I've told them I'm not renewing my contract.'

'Oh, why?' What about his fiancée, or maybe his wife, she wondered but hadn't the courage to ask.

'I'm not sure I want to live there, too many things I miss.' He hadn't said 'we', she noticed.

She said nothing and after a moment he stood up and walked away from her, as if to put some distance between them. He turned slowly to face her, ran his fingers through his hair and looked down at her and spoke quietly.

'You broke my heart, do you know that?'

She shook her head and he searched her face and looked as if he was going to say more then changed his mind. She wanted to tell him how she felt, but too much had happened and she was afraid to trust him again after all this time.

'I didn't mean to dump all this on you, but I think we need to talk. Maybe you could call me when you're ready. It's been doing my head in for a long time now and I want to sort it out, one way or the other. I think you owe me that, at least.' He looked at her, waiting, and her heart was thumping. When nothing happened he picked up his glass and walked back into the house and she grabbed Freddie and ran after him, not sure what to say but afraid to let him get away again.

'Call me, please?' he said and turned to pick up his keys on the little table by the door and suddenly he stopped dead and stared, then turned sharply to look at her, then turned back again to the table.

He picked up the little framed photo and stared at it, then turned back once more to look at her.

'Why have you got this picture of me as a baby? Where did you get it?' He looked puzzled.

She said nothing because her voice had deserted her and her legs were just about to do the same.

'It's almost the same as one my mother has at home. Did she give it to you that night, after the last show, when I caught the two of you looking very pally?' He looked confused and stared at it and then at her and back at the picture again. Still she said nothing.

He tried again. 'But, what I don't understand is, why would you want it and why would you keep it . . . ?' He came a bit closer. 'Unless . . .' He paused for a long moment. 'Unless you still care too.'

He didn't move but continued to look at her.

'Do you care about me, Lindsay?'

'Yes.' It was a whisper. He smiled at her slowly.

'I still don't understand why you'd keep this, or why she'd give it to you, although she always carries around baby photos of the three of us.' He grinned at her. 'Hell, even our Press Office could have given you a slightly more up-to-date one. But then again, only just. They're still churning out pictures of me taken five years ago.'

He was grinning at her, and looking at her in a funny way. 'Anyway, I'm very glad you care.' It was their first really close moment in nearly two years and she was just about to spoil it for him.

'That's not you.'

He looked at it again.

'Listen, you can't get away that easily.' That grin again. 'I've seen thousands of these and been humiliated by them often enough down through the years.'

'It's not you,' she repeated stupidly.

He was still smiling at her, indulging her.

'OK, who is it then?'

She'd always known this moment would come. 'It's Freddie.'

'Freddie? Freddie who?' He looked from her face to the little boy with his arms wrapped around her neck. 'This Freddie? I don't understand.'

She didn't know how to tell him so she drip fed it to him, waiting all the while for some terrible reaction that would shatter her world.

'Freddie is my son.'

'Yours?'

She nodded, just as a skinny little tear made its escape. This wasn't the way it happened in the movies. She was supposed to be glamorous and he was meant to run to her with his arms outstretched, not stand there looking dumbstruck.

She wasn't supposed to be in her gardening clothes with dirty knees and a tear-streaked face and a grubby little boy clinging to her neck and practically strangling her.

'How do you mean, yours?'

'He's mine.' She looked away before delivering the final blow. 'He was born a year ago.'

'A year ago?' He moved closer to her and looked at her and then at Freddie, who grinned shyly but continued to strangle his mother. He stared at the little boy for ages and touched his face with his finger, as if checking he was real.

'He's your son?'

She barely nodded.

'Who's his father?' She bit her lip and tightened her grip on Freddie and still couldn't bring herself to say the words.

'He's mine?' His eyes were boring into hers.

She barely nodded, desperate to soften the impact.

He closed his eyes and she saw the colour drain away. He bit his lip and she knew he was struggling too.

'No.'

She knew exactly how he felt. She'd felt the same when she'd first discovered it. 'I'm sorry—'

'Why didn't you tell me?'

'I tried to . . . that day in the car park . . .'

He clearly couldn't remember and then did.

'Oh my God,' he said slowly.

'I'm sorry.' She kept repeating herself and it sounded more and more inadequate.

'And you went through all this by yourself . . . Why didn't you grab me and make me listen?'

'I was afraid you wouldn't believe me.'

'But how could you . . . you were on the pill.'

'I was, but I was taking antibiotics at the same time and sometimes—'

'Christ, what am I saying? I'm sorry, none of this matters . . . nothing matters except you telling me that this is my son.' He couldn't take his eyes off the little boy's face. 'Now it all makes sense.'

'What does?'

'I ran into Colin Quinn last week at a movie premiere. We talked for ages. I kept bringing the subject round to you. He said you two weren't an item. He asked me to come and see you as soon as I could, but he kept insisting that I didn't phone you in advance, or meet you at the office. He said I had to call to see you at home.'

'He's wanted me to tell you for a long time.'

'Oh Lindsay, I wish you had. I really wish you had.' He had the saddest eyes she'd ever seen. 'Was I such a monster?'

She smiled at him forlornly. 'On the day he was born I read about you going to New York and also about you getting married and I knew I couldn't tell you then.' He looked confused. 'But I always knew I'd tell you someday and I knew it would be sooner rather than later.' She looked at him and knew she had to know. 'Are you married?'

He stared at her as if she was bonkers.

'I've just told you that you broke my heart. How could I marry someone else, for Christ's sake? I'm in love with you, have been for ever.'

'What about the American actress?'

'Who?'

'The papers said . . .'

'I don't give a fuck what the papers said . . .'

'Me neither.'

'I'm not married.'

'Me neither,' she laughed.

'I want to know everything.' He still didn't move. 'When did you find out?'

'Not until I was about eleven weeks' gone and

the girls were slagging me because I looked so awful. Debbie laughingly asked if I was pregnant and I realized I hadn't had a period since before Christmas. It must have happened that night I stayed over at your house.'

'The bathroom.' He remembered.

'Probably.' She smiled shyly at him.

'That day in the car park, I was so angry with you. I'd just seen the thing in the papers about you going to New York with Colin Quinn. I wanted to kill you both.'

'He begged me to tell you and I tried to, but when you just walked off like that, it really hurt me and I vowed not to let you do that to me again.'

'So, all through the time we worked together you were . . . ?'

She nodded.

'But, we were close once or twice. Could you not have given me a second chance?'

'I thought we might talk on the last night of the show, but then I saw Penelope Cruz . . .'

'Who?'

'Your girlfriend, everyone thought she looked like Pen—'

'For God's sake, she wasn't my girlfriend, I barely knew her. She's a friend of my sister's. I only asked her along because the researcher said you were all bringing partners. I don't think I spent more than two minutes with her all night. I really tried to talk to you several times . . .'

'I was too angry with you. I was also very jealous . . .'

'You had no need to be.'

'I was pregnant, remember, hormones all over the place.'

'Then I sent you flowers, texts . . . I was desperate to talk to you . . .'

'I guess you didn't try hard enough. I was convinced you didn't care and I wasn't going to trap you into anything.'

'Didn't I have a right to know?'

'I know, I know that now. I am so sorry. It was just that after I saw you that day with the girl in your apartment, so soon, I just fell apart and I guess I never really trusted you after that . . .'

Now it was his turn to be sorry.

'I'm not proud of that day. I went out and got very drunk the previous night and she somehow ended up back in my house. I'd never normally do that, you know how paranoid I am about my privacy. I woke up the next morning and she was asleep on my couch. I don't have to tell you that nothing happened, I was way too far gone. I'm sorry for what it did to you but I was so pissed off with you because of Paul.'

'Nothing happened with Paul.'

'I saw him get out of his car, I was right behind him, about to call in and try and persuade you to come out for an hour. As soon as he turned into your house I just sort of knew who he was. I don't know how but I did. I went back to my car, then I saw you upstairs in the bedroom and then you pulled down the blind . . . I still didn't believe it. Then the light went out and I stayed outside for ages. Several times I tried ringing the house. Then I went back to the party. I was the last to leave at nearly six o'clock. I walked by your house again and saw his car still there.'

'Nothing happened, I swear. We talked for an hour or so. He'd been drinking before he arrived, so he had to abandon his car. He said he wanted me back, I told him it was over. I don't know why, I just realized at that moment that I didn't love him any more.' She looked straight at him. 'I think it may have had something to do with you.'

She sat Freddie slowly on the floor and went to him then, needing to be near him.

'I love you.' She looked up at him. 'I have done for a long time.' He grabbed her and held her as tight as he was able.

'Oh God, I badly needed to hear that.'

They stayed as they were for a while, until Chris gently broke away. He looked down at the little boy clutching his leg, trying to stand up, then picked him up, swung him in the air between them, kissed him and smiled.

'Hi, Freddie, I'm your dad.'

THE END

A SELECTED LIST OF FINE NOVELS
FROM BANTAM BOOKS

81305 5	VIRTUAL STRANGERS	*Lynne Barrett-Lee*	£5.99
81304 8	JULIA GETS A LIFE	*Lynne Barrett-Lee*	£5.99
50631 5	DESTINY	*Sally Beauman*	£6.99
50326 X	SEXTET	*Sally Beauman*	£6.99
81277 7	THE CHESTNUT TREE	*Charlotte Bingham*	£5.99
81398 6	THE WIND OFF THE SEA	*Charlotte Bingham*	£5.99
40373 7	THE SWEETEST THING	*Emma Blair*	£5.99
40372 9	THE WATER MEADOWS	*Emma Blair*	£5.99
81331 5	THE PROMISED LAND	*Marita Conlon-McKenna*	£5.99
81394 3	MIRACLE WOMAN	*Marita Conlon-McKenna*	£5.99
81333 1	FAR FROM THE TREE	*Deberry Grant*	£5.99
50556 4	TRYIN' TO SLEEP IN THE BED YOU MADE	*Deberry Grant*	£5.99
81219 X	ON MYSTIC LAKE	*Kristin Hannah*	£5.99
81396 X	SUMMER ISLAND	*Kristin Hannah*	£5.99
50486 X	MIRAGE	*Soheir Khashoggi*	£6.99
81186 X	NADIA'S SONG	*Soheir Khashoggi*	£6.99
40730 9	LOVERS	*Judith Krantz*	£5.99
40732 5	THE JEWELS OF TESSA KENT	*Judith Krantz*	£6.99
81337 4	THE ICE CHILD	*Elizabeth McGregor*	£5.99
40943 3	CITY GIRL	*Patricia Scanlan*	£6.99
81292 0	FRANCESCA'S PARTY	*Patricia Scanlan*	£5.99
81355 2	THE RESCUE	*Nicholas Sparks*	£5.99
81393 5	A BEND IN THE ROAD	*Nicholas Sparks*	£5.99
81299 8	GOING DOWN	*Kate Thompson*	£5.99
81298 X	THE BLUE HOUR	*Kate Thompson*	£5.99
81372 2	RAISING THE ROOF	*Jane Wenham-Jones*	£6.99